FIELDS OF FIRE

J.N. CHANEY
TERRY MAGGERT

VARIANT
PUBLICATIONS

LAS VEGAS, NV · PORTLAND, TN

CONNECT WITH J.N. CHANEY

Don't miss out on these exclusive perks:

- Instant access to free short stories from series like *The Messenger*, *Starcaster*, and more.
- Receive email updates for new releases and other news.
- Get notified when we run special deals on books and audiobooks.

So, what are you waiting for? Enter your email address at the link below to stay in the loop.

https://www.jnchaney.com/backyard-starship-subscribe

CONNECT WITH TERRY MAGGERT

Check out his website
http://terrymaggert.com/

Connect on Facebook
https://www.facebook.com/terrymaggertbooks/

Follow him on Amazon
https://www.amazon.com/Terry-Maggert/e/B00EKN8RHG/

JOIN THE CONVERSATION

Join the conversation and get updates on new and upcoming releases in the awesomely active **Facebook group**, "JN Chaney's Renegade Readers."

This is a hotspot where readers come together and share their lives and interests, discuss the series, and speak directly to J.N. Chaney and his co-authors.

facebook.com/groups/jnchaneyreaders

CONTENTS

1

"You know, since coming out here, I've noticed that everyone is a refugee. More or less, anyway," I said, feathering the controls to send four missiles streaking off downrange.

Perry turned to me, his amber eyes glowing. He was a machine, an AI construct crafted like an oversized raptor, but his gestures and body language had evolved since I'd first met him. In the angle of his head, I saw what I took to be understanding.

Of course, seeing all that in the angle of his head might say more about me than it did him.

"As an aside, I've noticed that since coming out here, you're way more casual about delivering fearsome destructive energy at the bad guys—like that, in fact."

He pointed a wing out of the *Fafnir*'s canopy, just as three pulses of light announced detonating warheads. The armored class 8 raider that had been their target simply ceased to exist, the shattered debris starting their long plunge toward the wind-torn, ruddy-orange clouds of the gas giant looming beneath us.

I lifted one shoulder, but barely. "They were slavers, the scum of the scum. If there's one thing that truly pisses me off, it's the imposition of will by force, and we see it out here to a degree that makes me see red." I sat back with a satisfied nod. These slavers, part of a cartel that worked out of Dregs, had been guilty of crimes that made even the normally unflappable Zenophir pause and curse softly when she'd read them.

I turned back to Perry. "But even they were probably refugees."

"Color me intrigued. How do you figure?"

I held up a finger. "Torina, have you got him?"

She'd been watching her instruments closely. Our fourth missile had been loaded with a tracker warhead, intended to tag anything that might have escaped the destruction with a device we could use to follow it. And, sure enough, a class 3 workboat had been kicked free just before the slavers' ship had been destroyed.

She nodded. "Yup, got 'em. The tag's signal is loud and clear. They're not going anywhere without us being able to find them again. Our hound is on the trail."

The workboat's small engine lit, struggling to deliver enough thrust to lift the ship out of the gas giant's prodigious gravity well. For a moment, it looked like it wasn't going to make it, and all our tag would show us was the thing's trajectory into the howling oblivion under the racing clouds. But it slowly gained velocity until it was clear it would inevitably break free—at least as long as its engine kept firing. Of course, that freedom was an illusion since we just wanted to track the bastard to the next link in the slavers' evil chain of misery.

Torina turned to me, her face hinting at no qualms or remorse about the kill, either. She'd read the same list of crimes Zeno had.

"So I guess whoever's on that workboat are refugees now, too, and what makes you bring it up in the middle of a space battle anyway?" she asked.

I stared at the retreating workboat.

"Boss?" Perry asked.

I blinked. "Huh?"

"Wow, you're a study in introspective distraction today, aren't you? How do you figure? Everyone being a refugee?"

I realized my whole crew—Torina in the copilot's seat to my right, Zeno behind me, Icky behind Torina, and Perry perched in the middle—were watching me.

I sighed, and even to me it sounded bitter. "We're all running from something, aren't we?"

Icky frowned. "I'm not. Well, except maybe for the weird social convention of wearing pants."

I smiled at her. "Kinda think you're running from your mother's memory as well, aren't you?"

"I—" she began, then stopped. Her frown deepened, and she shrugged. "I guess I kinda am, yeah."

Netty, the *Fafnir*'s AI, cut in. "Van, I hate to interrupt this deeply philosophical moment, but did you want to actually pursue the bad guys we just tagged? Once they're clear of the gas giant's immediate gravitation, they'll be moving fast—and we have to assume that that workboat is twist capable."

I turned back to the instruments and nodded. "Yes. By all means, Netty my dear. Keep us gaining on them but slowly enough that we won't catch them before they twist. Hopefully, they'll head for whatever they consider their nearest safe house to lick their wounds."

Ordinarily, when a ship twisted away, it was gone. There was no way to tell if it had spatially distorted itself just a few light-years, or hundreds, or even in which direction. But Icky, Zeno, and Netty had perfected a tracker that could effectively do the math as the ship to which it was attached started to twist, then squirted the data back to us via burst transmission. We could now discern the twist destination of a ship we'd tagged nearly ninety percent of the time.

"What about you, Van?" Perry suddenly asked.

"What about me what?"

"What are *you* running from?"

I frowned. I guess it was inevitable that my refugees remark would circle back on me like this. I mean, the others were pretty clear—Icky ran to put distance between her and her mother's criminal legacy, Zeno ran from her daughter's untimely death, Torina ran from the stodgy, privileged life back on Helso that everyone assumed she'd quietly inherit—

As for me?

"That's a really good question, Perry. And when I actually have an answer to it, I'll let you know," I said.

I waited for more conversation, smart-assed or otherwise, but no one spoke. Instead, we all just flew along with our thoughts, running from things that were as inescapable as our own shadows.

NETTY INTERRUPTED OUR BROODING REVERIE.

"That's strange."

I sat up. "Netty, when a spaceship tells her crew that something is *strange*, I think it's customary to go into specifics."

"Sorry, Van, but I'm not sure if this is even significant. That workboat's drive is behaving strangely."

"How so?" I asked, hoping Netty wasn't about to say it was going to explode, turning our only decent lead in the slaver case to an ionized cloud of... *well, shit.*

"It's... pulsing. It's very slight, only a miniscule fraction of a percentage change in power output."

"Yeah, now that Netty's pointed it out, I see it too," Icky said. "Just a teeny tiny bit of variation, but it's regular."

"Some sort of harmonic?" Zeno asked. I expected that would be the answer—fusion drives were notorious for developing harmonic resonances while they operated, sometimes so severe they needed specific systems to dampen them out. But Icky shook her head.

"Don't think so. It's repeating in some—yeah, a pattern," Icky said.

I sat up a little more. "What sort of pattern?"

Netty answered. "There are two pulses. Then a pause, then three. A pause, then five. Pause, then seven, then eleven, then it starts at two again. It's the first five prime numbers."

Now I was sitting up as straight as I could. "Okay, that *is* strange. What could cause it?"

"Realistically, the drive's power setting would have to be deliberately manipulated to result in repeated fluctuations that correspond to the first five prime numbers," Netty replied.

"Yeah, whether it's a computer or an AI doing it or a person, it would have to be on purpose," Icky agreed.

"Gotta agree. It's really, really, *really* unlikely to be random," Perry added.

I gave him a quick glance. "Really?"

"Really."

I glanced at Torina, who shrugged. "Somebody's trying to get our attention maybe?"

"Well, they succeeded," I replied, then paused a moment, biting my lip. The whole point had been to let the workboat escape and lead us to a slaver safehouse. But such a subtle and deliberate manipulation of the boat's drive just smacked of being a signal of some sort.

Like maybe… a call for help.

"Netty, change of plans. Let's overtake that boat. Icky, Perry, you're coming with me. Torina, you and Zeno watch our backs," I said, unstrapping and heading aft.

Icky grinned as I passed her. "Sweet. Maybe we'll get to bust some heads."

I rolled my eyes at her. "Hold that thought. I have a sneaking suspicion this isn't going to be a boarding action."

Icky huffed. "Then what is it?"

I grabbed my blade and began arming up. "A rescue mission."

I WAS RIGHT. We boarded the workboat ready for a fight but found it had been launched, and was being controlled, by its onboard AI. Unfortunately, its preset destination was Dregs, which wasn't of any value to us since that's where we'd picked up this lead in the first place.

But while it wasn't crewed, it wasn't unmanned, either. Bound in the cargo bay we found two people. One was a lone man—human, powerfully built, and three inches short of six feet. He had lively hazel eyes, dark skin, and black hair shaved down to his scalp except for a busy topknot. His boots lay nearby, as did one of his socks, leaving him with one bare foot.

The other was an alien of a species I'd never met or even *seen* before. Five feet tall and bipedal, it reminded me of a sloth, with a short tail and a thin coat of fine hair in tones of rust and gray. He had prominent, white-tufted ears like a caracal and bushy white eyebrows that somehow gave it a weary, resigned, and slightly puzzled look.

I moved to the human and pulled the gag from his mouth. He'd been bound at wrists and ankles but had both feet near an open access panel filled with cabling. Icky assisted the alien.

"Oh—I thank you," the man gasped. "Was starting to get a touch despondent, thinking we'd escaped whatever happened to those bastards and their ship just to end up—" He frowned. "Where were we headed, anyway?"

"Dregs," I said.

He blinked up at me, then sat up and grinned so big that it somehow made me want to grin right back. "Wait, you're a Peacemaker," he stated.

"I am. Peacemaker Van—"

"Tudor, right. You're making a name. A good one, I might add. I like the targets you're selecting."

I narrowed my eyes at him. He gave Icky a grateful nod for untying him, then sat up and rubbed his wrists. "Please, no need to look so suspicious, my friend. I'm Peacemaker Blessing Mbana, though everyone calls me Essie." He gestured at his companion, who'd also sat up. "And this is Cheerful Enthusiast, but I call him Funboy. He's another inmate of our charming little Guild."

In utter contrast to the grinning man called Essie, Cheerful Enthusiast—a name I had difficulty using—gave me a look like a man who'd just seen the Internal Revenue Service appear on his front porch. "Yes. Thank you for postponing our deaths. I guess."

"Uh... you're welcome?" I said, blinking at the alien's dreary monotone. He reminded me of Eeyore from Winnie the Pooh, except not quite as upbeat or chatty.

I turned to Perry, who dipped his beak. "Yup, they both match those identities—voice print, facial recognition, the whole ball of uniquely characteristic wax. And since I know you're going to ask, Cheerful Enthusiast is a Surtsi, a race from outside known space and galactically down relative to the ecliptic. His name is the closest approximation our translators can manage."

"Which is why I call him Funboy," Essie said, turning to the little alien. "Isn't that right?"

"Those bonds did some serious chafing. I hope it doesn't lead to infection. Or worse."

Essie laughed and reached out a hand to me. I accepted it and he shook it like a paint mixer. Still, I gave him a wary look. "Okay, so you know me, but—don't take this the wrong way, I've never heard your name before, nor any cases involving a Peacemaker with your description." Sometimes, Peacemakers used field names for sensitive work that usually led to their deaths—or losing cover. Badly.

Not that that really meant much. In four years, I'd probably either met or at least heard of the vast majority of Peacemakers, but there were still some loners who prowled the fringes of known space society. They did their jobs, but they did them in isolation, a few of them rarely even coming close to Anvil Dark. They hunted bad guys, caught them, then hauled them back to the Guild's prison barge, *The Hole*. Lather, rinse, and repeat. I'm sure there were as many motivations for a solitary life of law enforcement as there were Peacemakers who pursued it, and Essie must be one of them.

As for Funboy—

I had no idea what to make of him, aside from his unrelenting grimness being *so* unlike Essie's equally boundless good cheer that I was almost afraid to let them touch in case they annihilated each other in a colossal blast of pent-up karmic opposition.

"You not ever hearing of us is a good thing," Essie said. "It means we're doing our jobs. Well."

I'd removed my helmet and now cocked my head quizzically at him. "Sorry, I don't get it."

"Our specialty is undercover work, mostly gathering criminal intelligence. You know when you get a briefing or read a report about some bad guys and it says *sources report* this or that? Well, say hello to *sources*."

I glanced back at Perry. "Two for two, boss," he said. "Netty just checked, and both Peacemaker Blessing and Cheerful Enthusiast here had open Guild records until about five years ago, and then they both went dark under a Master's Security Seal. That's pretty much a giveaway."

"Well, okay then. If Netty and Perry are good with you guys, so am I."

As I helped Essie to his feet, Icky peered into the open access port. "That line, right there, it's gotta be one of the data cables from the cockpit to the drive, right?"

"It is," Essie replied with a firm nod.

"And you somehow used that to affect the drive?"

He nodded. "Credit for that goes to Cheerful Enthusiast. He managed to get his gag out and talk me through it."

I turned to the little alien, who gave a languid shrug. "This model of workboat went out of production at least ninety years ago. There's no evidence it's ever been upgraded, so I presumed it still had its original metallic conductor cables. By pressing it against that power conduit beside it, I assumed it would induce enough variable impedance to make the drive controller think the flight controls were varying the thrust demand from the drive."

"Wow. That's... brilliant," Icky said.

Cheerful Enthusiast gave another slow shrug. "I suppose. There were many reasons it might not have worked, though."

"But it did."

"But it might not have."

"But... it did—"

I'd been tennis-balling my attention between Icky and Funboy, and I shook my head, then interrupted them. "Okay, wait. So you're saying you figured out how to make the drive pump out prime numbers—" I turned from Funboy to Essie and pointed down. "And you actually did it with your *feet?*"

Essie retrieved his boot and sock and shrugged. "I couldn't get my hands free."

"That was—" I shook my head. "How the hell did you guys even think of doing that?"

"Well, for one, Funboy here is a skilled engineer. For another, when you work undercover, you learn to be resourceful. You must. That's why I only wear boots that are easy to take off. In fact, the hardest part was getting that damned sock off so that I could get the access port clasps open and grab the cable with my toes. You ever try to take a sock off without using your hands?"

"Does having my girlfriend do it for me count?"

Perry gave a distinct tongue click of disapproval. Icky snorted and shook her head. Essie, though, laughed a great, booming laugh that filled the cargo bay.

"If I'd had your girlfriend here to help me, it would have been much easier, yes!"

I started to grin back but stopped. "Wait, *my* girlfriend—"

Essie laughed another booming laugh and clapped me on the shoulder, almost knocking me off my feet.

AFTER MARKING the workboat with a salvage beacon, we took Essie and Cheerful Enthusiast back aboard the *Fafnir*. There, Essie was able to check in with their handler—an unnamed party back on Anvil Dark identified on the comm only as an alphanumeric code—and finalize confirming his identity.

"So how did you end up in the hands of those slavers anyway?" I asked Essie as they both settled gratefully into the *Fafnir*'s galley.

"They grabbed us nearly two weeks ago on Plenty. Not sure why, since they were supposedly negotiating a ransom for me with The Quiet Room."

Torina frowned. "The Quiet Room? Not the Guild?"

He shrugged. "They really had no reason to connect us with the

Guild. Although why they thought we had anything to do with The Quiet Room, I don't know. Maybe they thought we were someone else."

"It was probably my fault," Funboy said.

"How so?" I asked.

Essie chuckled. "Funboy assumes everything's his fault."

"I do not. I'm well aware that the universe is a cold and lonely place, and that some unfortunate events are just dispassionate, empty expressions of random chance."

"In case you're interested, he's available for parties," Essie said.

"Excellent. I'll remember that at the next wake. Okay. Anyway, your captors were talking to The Quiet Room about a ransom? That suggests they thought you were someone specific," I said.

"Well, they might have thought that, but The Quiet Room apparently didn't, since they never paid the ransom."

"Kind of surprised they didn't just space you, or—well, they were slavers, so—" I left it at that, since we all knew what slavers—particularly these ones—were all about.

Essie shrugged. "Not sure what to tell you, Van. They got the drop on us, then grabbed us, and we've been pretty much in the dark aboard their ship ever since."

"How did you end up in the workboat, though, when the rest of the slavers apparently died aboard their ship?" Zeno asked. She still had a distinctly wary edge to her, seemingly not quite ready to trust these two, even if their credentials checked out.

"We were originally stuck in cells aboard their ship. A couple of days ago, they suddenly moved us into that workboat."

"They were making room for some more *cargo*, as they put it," Funboy said, then looked up at me with dark, soulful eyes. "I have very good hearing, which means I can overhear things, whether I want to or not."

I nodded. "*Cargo.* For slavers. Yeah, the euphemism is obvious."

"Being stuck on that workboat saved your life, though," Torina said, pouring coffee and offering some to Essie.

"So it would seem, yes," he said, accepting the steaming mug with an appreciative smile. "You must be the lovely girlfriend who removes Van's socks."

She blinked. "What?"

I held up a hand. "Anyway, Cheerful Enthusiast—uh, do you mind if I call you Funboy?"

The little alien shrugged. "It's as good a name as any, and you're less likely to damage your teeth while saying it."

"Right. Anyway, Funboy here worked out a scheme by which Essie could manipulate the workboat's drive with his foot, and that's where the whole sock conversation came from. I will tell you about it later."

Torina nodded. "Yes, you will."

"Va-an's in shi-it," Icky muttered in a sing-song.

Torina nodded again, smiling incandescently. "Yes, he is."

Zeno, though, was clearly still not convinced Essie and Funboy were entirely on the up-and-up. "That was very clever. But how did you even know to signal us in the first place?"

"I heard the slavers go to whatever passed for them as battle stations, then a few minutes later the workboat got kicked free. I heard something strike its hull, figured it was debris, and reasoned that someone had just blown up their ship," Essie said.

"We could have just been more slavers."

"Or something even worse," Funboy put in.

Essie gave another offhanded shrug. "What did we have to lose?"

We talked a while longer, probing for more information—or any inconsistencies or mistakes that might hint at them actually being something other than what they seemed. Yes, he was a credentialed Peacemaker, and Funboy an auxiliary. It was by no means uncommon, though, for undercover intelligence types—law enforcement and military—to get a little too deeply immersed in their roles and start becoming the bad guys they were only supposed to be emulating.

But we found none of that. There was nothing at all to even hint at either Essie or Funboy being anything other than undercover Peacemaker intelligence operatives who, for some reason, had been kidnapped and then kept pretty much in the dark until we'd bumbled into rescuing them.

"So where can we take you guys?' I asked.

"Well, speaking for myself, to your shower," Essie said. "I'm sure you're all politely ignoring the fact I probably stink after two weeks without one."

Icky wrinkled her nose. "*Thank* you. Yeah, you smell like an armpit." She gestured at her own, under her big right arm. "And an upper one at that." She smirked at me. "They stink more than the lower ones."

"I could have happily gone my whole life without knowing that, Icky, thanks."

Essie barked out his effusive laugh. "I do so love the Wu'tzur. What you see is what you get, am I right?"

Icky bared her teeth in her own version of a grin. "Finally, someone who gets me!"

"Okay, a shower, and then—?" I asked.

"And then back to Anvil Dark, if we can. I need to inform my handler about what happened, then get debriefed. After that, I probably need to see Gerhardt. He's the one who owned the op I was involved in when I got taken."

"Huh. Gerhardt was the one who put us onto the slavers," Zeno said.

"Could just be a coincidence. Of course, Gerhardt works in mysterious ways," I offered. Which was true—for everything I'd come to learn about Master Gerhardt, there always seemed to be more. For instance, he was deeply enmeshed in the shadowy cabalistic origin of the Guild, called the Galactic Knights Uniformed. I'd learned about them separately, from Petyr Groshenko and the cryptic B, so I hadn't known if Gerhardt was even aware of them, at least until he turned out to be one of their senior members.

Along with my mother.

I pulled my thoughts firmly off that track before they could drift any further. The subject of my mother was still both complicated and intimately painful. It was… familial.

Still, Gerhardt sending us after the slavers on some opaque and fluky mission to rescue Essie and Funboy might be a stretch, but I couldn't entirely rule it out either.

"Are you hungry?" Torina asked Essie and Funboy.

Funboy just shrugged. Essie nodded. "Oh, I could definitely eat. Have you ever heard of stavosia?"

"Why, as a matter of fact, we have—"

Netty cut her off. "Van, we just got a distress call from Luyten's Star, the Saetsu. They're reporting a theft of cultural antiquities."

"Huh, one of our specialties. Have they sent any details?"

"I'm getting the nav data now. The thieves are still outbound, which, taken with our estimated transit time, should give us a window of about one hour to deal with them before they can twist away. Oh, and the Saetsu are offering a payout of one hundred and fifty thousand bonds.

"Sorry, Essie, looks like you're going to have to settle for a sandwich," I said, turning for the cockpit.

"Hell, for that kind of money, I'd sure be willing to forgo lunch," Zeno said, following me.

I glanced back at her. "Thought you were more of a breakfast girl?"

She sniffed. "I'm many things, Van, and one of them is too old to be called a *girl*. Now, as the kids say, kick the drive and let's go get that bag."

Icky frowned. "Seriously? The kids say that? Does *anyone* say that?"

"What's that, Icky? I was distracted by being such a respected elder."

Icky grinned. "Nothing, ma'am. I'm just here to help out you old folks."

Their banter followed me into the cockpit. So did Torina.

"So, Van, about your conversation with Essie, the one that had something to do with socks and implied you talk about our personal life with strangers—?"

"I really am in shit, aren't I?"

"Yes. Yes you are."

2

We'd only been to Luyten's Star once before, to visit the planet called Dustfall. It had been left irradiated by an ancient thermonuclear war but had subsequently been colonized by Zenophir's people, the radiation-hardy P'nosk. Saetsu was another planet in the system, home to its namesake race, an ancient and insular people with little interest in starfaring. Unfortunately, that meant they also had a limited ability to defend themselves from the predations of scumbag antiquities thieves. In fact, their greatest defense was their reputation as an inoffensively gentle race noted for its artists and musicians, whose popularity was cross-cultural. A sort of unspoken agreement to leave the Saetsu alone, out of respect for their antiquity—some of their music was written while my own ancestors were still learning to walk upright—and their rich cultural achievements.

Which was why stealing things from that same ancient culture seemed particularly vile. The Saetsu shared many, and maybe even most of their artistic achievements with essentially anyone who wanted them. They'd more than earned the right to keep some aspects of their civilization uniquely to themselves.

The thieves' ship was an up-armored class 10, making her one hull class smaller than the *Fafnir*. Our ship had taken a beating in the final confrontation between the GKU and the Seven Stars League, the latter under the insidious control of the parasitic race known as the Tenants. We'd actually had to cable Perry into her fusion reactor as an ad hoc controller, then we eventually had to have the reactor shut down and the *Fafnir* towed back to Anvil Dark for repairs.

Those repairs had led to upgrades. She'd gained two hull classes and now mounted four petawatt laser batteries, two mass-drivers, a pair of rotary missile launchers, and four point-defense batteries. We'd also retrieved a particle cannon from the sinkhole back on the farm in Iowa in a stealthy nighttime operation and had mounted it. Unfortunately, though, it still needed some refurbishment before we could use it.

The *Fafnir*'s power plant and drive and weapons were upgraded, and she had the internal space and resources to support a crew twice the size of our current one. We'd also upgraded the workboat snuggled up into the underside of her hull, its rounded hull nearly scanner invisible for anyone taking a look.

The end result was that we could now call the *Fafnir* a corvette, and just another couple of upgrades away from a frigate, if we wanted to use military parlance. The best part was that we ended up not having to pay for the vast majority of it. Between funds allocated from the Guild's treasury by Gerhardt and generous contributions from the Schegith, we'd managed nearly a million bonds worth of upgrades and ended up about fifty thousand out of pocket.

So the oncoming, up-armored class 10 didn't unduly worry me, from a strict space-battle point of view. The *Fafnir* had a definite edge in both performance and firepower, so if we'd wanted to just blast the thieves into bits of loose debris, we probably could. Unfortunately, that would also entail blowing up whatever cultural artifacts they'd stolen from the Saetsu. That left us with only one choice —a boarding action—and those were always dirty and dangerous.

Without taking my eyes off the screens, I issued my first order. "Icky."

"Yes boss?"

"Hammer."

"Excellent."

She unlimbered her weapon, then seated it again, but at a loose hold, like a sheriff getting ready for an old west shootout.

"Data pouring in. I want everyone's opinions, okay? Nothing is too small."

"That's not what—" Perry started, but Zeno hissed in a sound that was pure maternal guilt.

Zeno turned to Perry, her whiskers twitching. "I'm not angry—"

"Just disappointed. Thanks, despite being a created person, I now understand what it's like to have a boomer mom," Perry said.

Torina snickered. "Can confirm… it's *any* mom."

"My moms left me," Funboy said over the comms.

In the silence, I chose the simplest response to such an uplifting confession. "Thank you for sharing, Funboy. That was… unexpected."

"So was waking up with my moms gone. Are there snacks on board, by the way?"

"Um… yes, actually—"

Netty saved me, highlighting a data point on the main screen. "They're in motion, Van."

"Thanks for the nudge."

Since the thieves were outbound from Luyten's Star, and we were inbound, we'd have a single pass to disable their ship, knocking out their drive so they wouldn't reach a twist point before we could come about and board them. And they were burning their drive furiously, resigning themselves to the fact they were moving too fast to outmaneuver us. Instead, they wisely tried to minimize our window of opportunity to threaten them. We responded by spinning the *Fafnir* about and decelerating relative to the other ship, trying to do the opposite—increase our engagement time.

"How long do we have, Netty?" I asked, watching the tactical overlay where her mark still glowed.

"From maximum effective range to closest approach, about forty-five seconds, and then that again back out to maximum effective range."

"So ninety seconds total to disable their ship, and at some ungodly closing velocity."

"That about sums it up."

I turned to Torina. She'd proven herself the best gunner among us, so I tended to leave complicated firing solutions to her. "Think you can knock out their drive in ninety seconds of shooting?"

"Sure, no problem. It's going to be like hitting a mass-driver slug with another mass-driver slug a bazillion klicks away, but what the hell, I've got this."

"I'll take that as a definite maybe."

She shrugged. "Honestly, without that spiffy, high-end fire-control system Gerhardt gave us, it wouldn't even be that. I mean, I'm sure I can hit them, but put a shot somewhere where it's going to knock out their drive without blowing them to bits?" She shook her head. "Yeah, that's a *very* definite maybe."

"Why don't we make it a team effort?"

I turned to the voice. It was Essie, who was sitting in the back of the *Fafnir*'s expanded cockpit on a jump seat, next to the radiant personality that was Funboy. We'd outfitted both with spare b-suits and helmets since our standard operating procedure was now to depressurize the *Fafnir* before battle. Evacuating her atmosphere meant no explosive decompression, which could multiply the damage of a mass driver hit many times over.

"You're a gunner?" I asked him.

He nodded. "Started out as an Auxiliary for Gerhardt, in fact, back before he became a Master. He made me his gunner since I seemed to have a knack for hitting things."

I nodded but couldn't help thinking that here was *another* link between Essie and Gerhardt. I felt Zeno look at me, meaning she'd noted it too.

"Don't ask me to shoot anything. I couldn't hit a gas giant from orbit," Funboy intoned.

"No, but you could strip and reassemble a laser battery with your eyes closed," Essie said. "I keep telling you, stop selling yourself short."

Funboy shrugged. "I find it better to keep everyone's expectations low. That way, it's less likely I'll disappoint them."

"Okay then. Essie, if you'd like to use Zeno's station and coordinate with Torina, that'd be great."

While Zeno and Essie switched places, I focused on the overlay. We were about two minutes from maximum range. Notwithstanding Torina's analogy, the fact was that the *only* useful weapon would be the lasers. Even at the speed of light, they'd have nearly a full second of transit time between emitter and target. Missiles were too blunt an instrument, while the mass drivers would be entirely useless.

I sighed. "You know what we need? A more reliable way to disable a ship that doesn't involve just shooting holes in them and hoping not to hit anything explodey."

"Charge pulse," Funboy said.

We all turned to look at him. He immediately hung his head. "I'm sorry, I shouldn't have spoken out—"

"No, it's fine. There are no bad ideas on the *Fafnir*," I said.

Perry gave me an amber stare. "Really? Remember that time you told Icky she could pick out the décor for the new crew-hab module?"

"What do you mean? That shag carpet would've looked great!" Icky snapped.

"Oh, it would not. It would have looked like some wannabe playboy's pad from 1975—which, if memory serves, was the very image that inspired you. I mean, you wanted to put purple shag on the bulkheads."

"It was Mojave, not purple, and—"

"Mauve, you barbarian, and—"

I held up a hand to interrupt. "Sorry, Funboy—there are *almost* no bad ideas on the *Fafnir*. So what do you mean by charge pulse?"

"Well, drive plasma consists of positively charged atomic nuclei and negatively charged free electrons. Most of its reaction mass comes from the positive nuclei, so if you generate a strong enough pulse of positive charge in the drive plume, you'll effectively push a disruptive wave of reverse flow into the—I'm sorry, am I boring you?"

I shook my head. "Not at all. Our silence is rapt attention. What you're saying is that this would shut down a fusion drive?"

Funboy nodded. "The fusion reaction would destabilize and the drive's safeties would shut it down, at least until it could be restarted. And if the pulse was strong enough, it might knock the containment system out of alignment, which would keep it shut down for—well, until the drive was completely overhauled."

"To do that, you'd need to generate a super-strong pulse right in the fusion plume. How the hell would you engineer that?" Icky asked. Her tone suggested she was intrigued but maybe also a little put out by the sudden appearance of a skilled engineer on her ship.

I stepped in. "Guys, this is really good stuff, but we're close to engagement range here. How about we save this for later?"

Funboy sank back into his seat, while Icky just gave a grumpy nod.

I turned my attention back to the overlay. Funboy's idea was intriguing. If we could rig up something along the lines of what he'd suggested, it would make taking down the bad guys without taking them out far easier. Of course, a brilliant idea was one thing, but engineering it into something that actually worked was something else altogether.

"One minute to engagement range," Netty said.

We strapped on our helmets and depressurized the *Fafnir*. Torina and Essie both glued their attention to their weapons controls. The artifact thieves were still furiously thrusting away, trying to reduce their exposure time to our weapons as much as they could.

The instant the fire control system registered positive firing solutions, Torina and Essie cut loose. The thieves did likewise, and for the next minute or so petawatt beams of laser energy lanced back and forth between the two ships.

It was dangerous. And lethal.

And it was beautiful.

We took a couple of solid hits, but the reactive-ablative, or REAB armor, absorbed the damage. More importantly, Torina and Essie landed hits on the other ship in turn—precision shots that tore into its drive section.

I braced myself. We'd either knock the thieves' drive offline, or we'd cause them to lose fusion containment, and that would be that —they, and the artifacts they'd stolen, would vanish in a blinding flash.

Fortune smiled on us, and the thieves' drive died, its searing plume of fusion plasma abruptly going dark. It left them coasting at a constant velocity, which would still get them to their twist point. It would just take far longer now. The question was how long, and that was simple math. For Netty, that is.

"Netty, your verdict?" I asked.

"Assuming they don't get their drive online, by the time we manage to reverse course and match velocity with them, we should have a solid hour window for a boarding action."

"That should be more than enough." I turned to Torina and Essie. "Good shooting, guys."

Essie grinned and gave a thumbs-up. Torina shrugged.

"It didn't get all explodey, as you so eloquently put it, so I guess that's a win," she said.

I nodded. "Not explodey is good. Now, let's go retrieve some stolen cultural heritage. Essie, Funboy, care to join us?"

Essie's grin shone behind his visor. "I'm always up for cracking some bad guys upside the head."

"Now *this* is a man after my own heart," Icky announced.

Funboy stewed in his emo silence.

Perry spoke in my earbud. *I think we just adopted a surly teen.*

Great. That makes two on one ship.

THE THIEVES WERE DETERMINED to put up a fight. As we approached, they fired whatever they could at us, including missiles and point-defenses. Torina had to scrub anything resembling a weapon off their hull with some dead-eye shooting so we could finally close in. Before we crossed, though, I broadcast a warning.

"If you resist in any fashion, I have authorized my crew to use lethal force at their own discretion."

Perry cut in on our internal comm channel. "How is that different from any other time, Van?"

"It's not. Sounds good and ominous, though, dontcha think?"

I was hoping that, as antiquities thieves, these assholes weren't hardened criminals who'd fight to the bitter end. In fact, I was convinced of it.

I crossed the fifty meter gap between the *Fafnir* and their ship, drew the Moonsword, and cheerfully began cutting away. In seconds, the blade opened a brand new hatch, the section of hull tumbling away after I tapped it with the pommel. We entered the hull in a rush—Essie and Funboy cleared aft and found the damaged engineering section unoccupied. Icky and I, with Perry in tow, went forward.

"Are you shitting me?" I asked the locked blast door. My answer was silence because the crew had petulantly locked themselves in the cockpit.

I sighed and turned back to the comm. "Okay, we know you're in there," I said, my tone flat with disgust.

"Go away."

"You know we're not going to do that."

"Go away, or—"

"Or what? You'll taunt me a second time?"

Perry snickered. "Good one, boss. Now say *ni!*"

"Oh, I'm saving that for a last resort," I replied, then switched back to the broadcast channel.

"Look, bad guys, we know how this is going to end. The only thing that's still up in the air is whether anyone gets hurt or not. Now, I know you're not bloodthirsty killers... right? You're not bloodthirsty killers, are you?"

"Maybe."

Icky had reached the end of her patience. She groaned and wound up to slam the hatch with her hammer. "Van, let me crack this sumbitch open."

I opened my mouth to tell her to restrain herself but thought better of it. "What the hell. Go ahead, you honorary redneck you."

Icky grinned, then swung her hammer hard enough that I felt the shock of its impact through the soles of my boots. Remarkably, her blow left a slight dent in an alloy hatch intended to hold back exploding ordnance.

She swung again. Again. From her feral grin, I suspected she had a bunch of full-powered swings in her yet. It would take her hours to make any appreciable headway at all, but that was okay. I had no intention of slowly beating our way into the cockpit.

I drew the Moonsword. "Here, Icky, let me give you a hand," I said, slamming the blade into the door and cutting. I made a slice about a half-meter long, then the door abruptly slid open. It yanked the Moonsword out of my grip. I yelped and grabbed for it, but the sword slammed against the hatch coaming… and stopped the door dead.

While I cursed and tried to King Arthur my sword from the door, Icky barreled into the cockpit with a shout. Essie and Funboy both showed up and stopped to stare as I pried at my blade, swearing richly under my breath.

"What the hell happened?" Essie asked.

"You're witnessing the result of unexpected success," Perry replied, then followed Icky.

Perry told me to stand clear, then closed the door again. I yanked out the blade and examined it, surprised it hadn't shattered but certain it must have been damaged when the door's motor pulled it against the coaming. But it didn't show even a hint of a chip, bend, or scratch.

"Linulla, you do damned good work," I said, sheathing the blade as Perry opened the door again. I stepped into the cockpit, pulling as much of my remaining dignity as I could along with me.

The crew turned out to be a Yonnox and a pair of Skels—so a criminal, and two more criminals. They offered some meek resistance but quickly folded under Icky's bared-teeth glare and started babbling things about crimes and their perpetrators before we'd even asked them. I actually had to interrupt the string of nasty revelations to work in the standard Guild disclaimer about arrest rights.

"We found the stuff they stole back in the midships hold," Essie said. "Quite a haul. Looks like they cleaned out a whole museum."

"At least they didn't blow up the ship," Funboy said. "Then we'd have all died, although one of us had a nine percent chance of living, albeit in screaming pain for a few hours. Tops."

I stared at him. I tried to imagine him laughing and gave up after a few seconds. It wasn't in his makeup, and I didn't want to waste time.

"Bit unnecessary to add the *then we'd have all died* part," Perry said. "Kind of figured that was understood."

"It never hurts to spell these things out," Funboy replied. "Details save lives. Unless you're in hard vacuum."

"Of course," Perry said, tapping Funboy on the back with one wing like they were chums.

"Let's split up and begin sweeping. Eyes open, and if you have a question, ask before you grab something," I stated.

We processed the ship in minutes because it was small and well-organized, as criminal vessels went, gleaning all the intelligence we could from it while transferring the crew into the *Fafnir*'s cells and assessing the damage. Either Torina or Essie had neatly bisected the main power tap from the reactor with a through-and-through laser shot, a true golden BB. A meter left or right and it probably would have triggered a containment failure in either the powerplant or the drive.

"That was me," Essie said, and I could hear the smile in his tone. "Right where I was aiming."

"My Gramps used to say 'if you can do it, it ain't braggin.' And, well, you did it," I told Essie, because it was true. It had been a perfect shot, and somehow I didn't think Funboy would heap praise on Essie.

Or anyone else, for that matter.

3

"THE PREEMINENCE WISHES to extend her thanks to you," the voice of the Saetsu gravely intoned. I glanced at the screen concealing their Preeminence, upon whom no non-Saetsu was allowed to look. My best understanding of the Preeminence was that she combined holy figure, divine ruler, and CEO into one person. Perry confided that it was all probably more theater than anything else, a way of maintaining an aura of mystique around the race.

"Their main export is culture. You know, music, writing, poetry, drama, that sort of thing. Think Hollywood as a planet—well, without everything being a derivative sequel or prequel or gritty reboot of some profitable franchise," he said.

"So... nothing like Hollywood at all."

"Except for the money-making part, yeah, I guess not."

The cultural artifacts the Yonnox and his Skel cronies had heisted were a suite of clay tablets said to contain some of the oldest known Saetsu poetry, in a precursor language their scholars were still struggling to translate. It made them fantastically valuable and underscored an important point. While the Saetsu may not be above profiting from their cultural exports, it was all still based on a genuinely rich and ancient cultural heritage.

Which was why we'd brought them straight here, to an orbital maintained by the Saetsu for visitors to their home planet. Apparently, an invitation to the surface was a great honor for any non-Saetsu. Still, the orbital itself was a stunning display of artistry rendered in exotic plant materials, metals, and crystals, sort of an orbiting Louvre with fewer gift shops.

And exactly *zero* places hawking overpriced coffee. I was instantly charmed.

I kept my attention on the Voice, who supposedly *knew the mind* of the Preeminence. Whether he did or not, Perry's protocol instructions had been explicit—speak only to the Voice and pay no attention to the Saetsu behind the curtain.

"I am gratified to be able to return your artifacts to you, and I assure you that the thieves will be dealt with accordingly," I said. That last bit was important. The Saetsu had a deep distaste for things like crime and punishment and contracted most of it out, exporting their problems along with their artful music and poetry. The Voice seemed satisfied.

"We trust you to ensure that. And, as promised, your reward is now being transferred to your designated representative."

I glanced at Torina, who nodded.

"Very well, then," I said, finishing our farewells before returning with Torina and Perry to the *Fafnir*.

"Did we get the prisoners off-loaded?" I asked as we padded along a luxuriously carpeted corridor toward the airlock.

Torina nodded. "Peacemaker Batis swung by and took them off our hands on their way to Anvil Dark. Seemingly just in time, too."

"What do you mean?"

"Netty didn't want to interrupt you in the midst of your diplomatic niceties, but we received a message from Anvil Dark just a few minutes ago," she said.

I raised an eyebrow. "Oh? Gerhardt?"

"No. It was from Bester, actually."

That prompted a surprised glance. Bester was the famously reclusive and eccentric head of the Guild's archives who took items of personal significance as payment for some of his services. No one knew what he did with them, aside from presumably hoarding them somewhere. It was more than unusual for him to get on the comm to anyone beyond Anvil Dark for any reason, unless he was called first.

She shrugged. "I know, right? Anyway, Bester says that Gerhardt wants us to proceed to the Fren-Okun homeworld with all due haste, as he put it."

I stopped, echoes of the word *moist* ringing in my ears. "Really??"

"Really."

"Um—and this, I might regret—why?"

She shrugged. "Not sure. Netty, over to you," she said as we resumed walking.

"Gerhardt's instructions were explicit—we are to proceed to the Fren homeworld and report to a Magisterial named Weskinut for, and I quote, *required participation in legal proceedings*," Netty said.

"Why wouldn't Gerhardt just tell us that himself? Why route it through Bester, of all people?"

"Once more, unclear. It may have something to do with the fact that we are going to receive an order from Master Kharsweil, apparently directing us to—and again, I quote—*engage in a glorified babysitting operation*. Gerhardt wants us to travel and participate in these legal proceedings with the Fren first."

I glanced at Torina as we reached the *Fafnir*'s airlock. "Sounds like some internecine warfare between Masters."

She nodded. "The kind you don't get in between. More of those shitty internal Guild politics that stop us from doing our jobs."

I put an arm around her shoulders, and she leaned into me. "Different verse, same tune. Perry, what do I do in the case of contradictory orders from two Masters? Because I have a sneaking suspicion Kharsweil is going to expect his job to take priority."

"You're Gerhardt's Justiciar, so his directives take priority. And if Kharsweil doesn't like that, just refer him back to Gerhardt and let them fight it out."

"That's probably *why* he made you his Justiciar, the wily old bugger, to head off situations like this one," Torina noted.

"Wheels in wheels," I groused, then we stepped aboard the *Fafnir*.

I was beginning to realize that Gerhardt, who I'd originally taken to be a hidebound martinet, had far greater depths. Aside from his one major failure regarding the security of data belonging to the Seven Stars League—from which he'd clearly learned a lesson—he knew the laws and procedures, processes and protocols, with such intimate familiarity. He was also smart enough to know how to exploit, manipulate, and otherwise work around them. It was probably *why* he knew the chapter and verse of everything so well, so he knew exactly what he could get away with.

I *almost* completely trusted him. Unfortunately, my experience with Guild Masters had involved whole graveyards of skeletons in their closets, and I hadn't yet really had a chance to peek into Gerhardt's.

Bones have a way of appearing at the worst times, and I might be a touch cynical, but I was alive.

And away from the Masters.

As a kid devouring science fiction books and movies, I'd imagined aliens would generally fall into one of two categories. They'd either be nightmarish monsters that hunted humans for sport or, for biological reasons unknown, required them to horribly gestate their young—not exactly a winning evolutionary strategy, in hindsight—or mysterious, inscrutable beings of vast intellect and either utterly amoral or slightly on the beneficent side.

What I hadn't expected was that they'd just be annoying.

And yet so many of them were. Yonnox were rank opportunists, Nesit were inveterate manipulators, Skels were parasitic assholes, and the Fren-Okun—

They were just *annoying*. They were obsequious to the point of being toadies, had a greedy streak, and, when their females became sufficiently elderly, wanted to slather everything in sticky mucus. The last was apparently a biological imperative left over from the race's younger days and, as we'd discovered, was sometimes played up by wily old females to take advantage of their own people. More often, though, they genuinely wanted to scream *Moist!* and fling mucus around, which can be… *awkward.*

And damp.

Anyway, I'd braced myself for the worst. But when we arrived at the squat, authoritarian building just outside the spaceport's gate and were shown inside, we were taken to a spartan meeting room already occupied by two pleasantly mannered Fren-Okun. One introduced himself as Magisterial Weskinut, and the other as his clerk.

"Now, before we can proceed, I need confirmation of your identity as the Peacemaker known as Clive Van Abel Tudor," he said.

"The third."

"I'm sorry."

"Clive Van Abel Tudor the Third. It's my full legal name."

Weskinut returned the Fren equivalent of a grin. "That certainly helps, but I still need proof of identity."

I showed him my credentials, then we all sat. I had Torina and Perry with me, and also Icky. We'd brought her as part of an effort pioneered by Zenophir to give Icky something resembling even rudimentary social graces. She'd grown up essentially alone with no one but her father, both of them obsessed with tracking down her miscreant mother, so she'd had effectively zero socialization.

"She needs to develop some interpersonal skills beyond smashing things with that damned hammer of hers," Zeno said. "Emotionally, she's still an adolescent, and I think she needs an opportunity to grow… and get used to pants."

I agreed. Zeno had taken on a motherly role for Icky, which I wholeheartedly supported so was happy to help—even if it had meant cajoling Icky into attending this meeting and sitting quietly and attentively while fully clothed.

"I hate these damned things," she said, gesturing down at herself and her fabric-clad legs. "They look stupid and they *itch*."

"Might I point out you're covered in fur?"

"I condition it weekly. It's very soft. Here, touch—"

"I'm good, and… I did not need that information, but thank you. And as to social conventions, which you need to observe, one such item is not, you know, putting it all out there, if you know what I mean. Like, how do you think it would look if I walked around without pants?" I asked her.

She sniffed. "I've seen what a naked human male looks like. What's up with that, anyway?"

I almost made the mistake of answering.

Instead, I just took her by the arm and led her toward the airlock, then to the office, and then through an awkward series of introductions to the Fren-Okun while Icky pulled and tugged at her pants like they had electric current running through them.

Icky sat down across the table from me, looking like a giant, hairy version of a kid who'd been jammed into their Sunday best and was listening to a sermon on a summer morning. I gave her an encouraging wink, and in response she stifled a belch.

It was progress.

The Fren-Okun began to bustle, and we were off.

"I am hereby convening this Circle of Law," Weskinut said, nodding to his clerk, who made an entry in a data slate. "Now, I suppose you're wondering why you've been brought here, Peacemaker Tudor."

"Uh… yes? I know it's some legal matter, but I'm a Peacemaker.

Legal matters are pretty much all I do, so that doesn't narrow it down very much."

"Understood. Well, Peacemaker Tudor, I am happy to inform you that you are to be the recipient of a significant bequeathal."

"I—what?"

"A bequeathal. It's an inheritance—"

"Yes, I know what it means." I frowned and shook my head. "What sort of inheritance? And from whom?"

"To answer your first question, you are being bequeathed a Holding, a Fren-Okun legal term for a package of property, assets, and interests. In this case, they comprise a parcel of land here on our homeworld, which includes a permanent dwelling, as well as controlling interest in a shipping business that operates terminals here and in the Tau Ceti system."

"I—what?"

"We seem to have circled back to this point again."

"I—" I shook my head again. "I'm sorry, but you've just informed me that someone has left me property, a home, and a shipping business on an alien world—sorry, alien from my perspective."

"I understand."

Torina leaned forward. "Who named Van their beneficiary to receive this Holding?"

Weskinut glanced at his clerk, who handed me a document. He spoke as I read it. "As you can see, the party—or parties—in question are identified only by an eight-digit number. Unfortunately, that's all that I know. I was retained by their Magisterial to contact you and was only provided with that number as an identifier."

"Which implies that whoever it is, they want their identity kept a secret," Perry put in.

"But why?" Torina asked.

Weskinut just shook his head. Clearly, whatever reasons my unexpected benefactor had to remain anonymous, anonymous they would remain, at least for now.

"Van, I just scanned the Fren-Okun media. To the extent that they note obituaries, I can't find any reference to anyone who would logically want you to inherit their estate," Perry said.

I just shook my head. "What Fren-Okun could possibly want me to inherit their estate? We haven't had that many dealings with them." I thought about the cunning old Fren woman we'd been hired to escort to The Quiet Room, but she'd made it clear that her intact faculties were a secret. Besides, she'd been a passenger, albeit an interesting one, and she paid us, so that was that. I couldn't imagine such an ordinary transaction convincing her to make me her heir.

"In any case, Peacemaker Tudor, there it is. My clerk has prepared the necessary documents for you to execute, in order to finalize the—"

The door abruptly opened, and in burst a doddering old female Fren. I winced, knowing what was coming.

"Moist!"

Torina and I both braced ourselves to evacuate the moist line of fire, but neither of us could resist grinning as we did. Weskinut was not amused, giving us all the stink eye.

"Excuse me, but these august proceedings are not a matter for amusement." He spun on the two Fren who'd accompanied the old crone into the room. They were clearly mortified as they struggled to get her under control and back out of the room. Icky, though, turned to the old woman and pointed at her own legs.

"Icky, what the hell are you doing?" I asked.

She abruptly stopped pointing and gave a sheepish shrug. "Hey, if she spits or drools or does whatever moist stuff she does on me, I'm taking my pants off."

Weskinut's expression turned appalled. "What? Why?"

"For comfort."

"For comfort? What?"

"For, uh, comfort, your *honor*?"

"No, I mean—oh, never mind!" Weskinut addressed the other Fren in a voice that cracked with authority. "Would you get her—"

"Moist!"

"—out of here, please?"

The two Fren crone-handlers finally got their charge under control and ushered her out of the room, trailing a moist litany that receded as the door closed. I'd probably have wondered why she was here in some building adjacent to a spaceport to begin with, why she'd busted into our meeting, and if it might be just an act, she really wasn't addled and simply wanted to see who was here and what was going on. It struck me that the moist routine was a great way to barge into all kinds of things without really being held accountable for it.

As the sounds faded, I was still stuck on the fact that I apparently now owned property, a house, and a shipping company—none of them on Earth.

I reached toward Weskinut's clerk, giving Icky a sharp glance as I did. "Icky, keep your pants on no matter what, and that's an order." I turned back to the clerk and Weskinut. "Let's get this done and get back to the ship before we end up in jail ourselves."

When we returned to the *Fafnir* and recounted for Zeno, Essie, and Funboy what had happened, the first two laughed at the absurdity.

Funboy, though, had an observation about possibly being thrown in a Fren jail.

"Statistically, almost all of us would survive incarceration in a Fren prison."

Icky just scowled and interrupted. "Okay, we're back on the *Fafnir*. Can I take these damned things off now?"

Essie laughed again, made a wide-eyed face, and shouted, "Moist!"

I turned to Torina.

"This is going to be a long flight."

I'D ASSUMED that the transaction giving me ownership of an alien house and property had been concluded, and that details would follow thereafter. Once they did, I'd—

Do something about it. I had no idea what. My education in the Iowa school system had left me woefully unprepared for the realities of owning property and shipping companies fifteen light-years from Earth.

I gave Torina a bemused headshake. "I wonder if I owe taxes to the IRS on this."

"What's an IRS?"

"Oh, there are *so* many things I could say to answer that question."

Perry cut in. "Actually, Van, the IRS doesn't impose taxes on foreign inheritance or gifts if the recipient is a US citizen or resident alien. However, you may need to pay taxes on your inheritance, depending on your state's tax laws."

I stared at him.

"However, if you receive an inheritance from a foreign estate or non-resident alien, or gifts from non-resident aliens exceeding one hundred thousand dollars, then it must be reported to the IRS," he went on.

"You took the time to learn US tax law?"

"It was three of the most boring milliseconds of my life. Oh, by the way—non-resident alien? Get it?"

I couldn't resist a smile. "Leave it to you, Perry, to inject humor into the tax code."

"I'm here all week."

"Van, we have company. A Fren-Okun named Nulic is requesting permission to board the *Fafnir*. She says it's related to your recent inheritance," Netty said.

"She's not old, is she?"

"Van, there are some constants in the universe—the Planck Constant, the value of pi, the density of water at standard pressure and temperature. The list also includes, *don't ask women how old they are.*"

Another smile. Netty tended to be more serious about things than Perry, but she had her moments. "Well, as long as she's not going to start spattering mucus all over the *Fafnir*, she can come aboard, sure."

"Is that what you want me to tell her?"

"Just the *she can come aboard* part, thanks."

Despite the fact that she wasn't human, Nulic's clipped efficiency and mechanized charm immediately marked her as someone in the legal profession. She'd brought actual hardcopies of the documents regarding my new status as an interstellar shipping tycoon and landowner. They were printed on thin, flexible sheets of what felt like smooth rubber.

"I'm not used to actual—I was going to say paper"—I rubbed the material between my fingers—"but whatever this is will work. I figured it would be electronic."

"Fren-Okun law requires you to receive durable copies of all pertinent documents. If you're ever involved in a legal dispute over any of these assets you just inherited, you'll need to present these to officiants," she replied.

I handed the documents to Torina, who'd already helpfully offered to talk to her parents about having them oversee my new business interests on my behalf. "Don't suppose you know anything more about this? Like, even a *hint* regarding who bequeathed this to me?" I asked Nulic.

"Actually, I don't. And before you ask, it's not that I'm not allowed to tell, it's that I honestly can't. The bequeathing party's representative just said that you were the only person of character who could be entrusted to hold the Okun-Basti Concern."

"That's the name of the company I now own, right?"

"It, and the property. Okun-Basti started as an agri-food exporter nearly two hundred years ago. The farm is still operating, but the shipping arm has grown into several ships carrying general cargo."

"A farm." I grinned, then laughed.

"I'm sorry, that sound you're making—that signifies humor, right? I don't deal with humans often," Nulic said.

"Humor, yeah. Sorry, but it just struck me as funny that, for the *second* time in my life, I've inherited a farm."

"And that's humorous?"

"Well, yes. Because if you'd asked me just a few years ago how likely I thought it would be that I'd inherit two different farms, I'd probably have said something like, *about as likely as me becoming a spaceman.*"

"I see," Nulic said with the desiccated humor of a tax attorney.

Whatever. It was funny to *me*. "Anyway, don't you think it's odd that someone would bequeath to me a shipping company and property out of the blue?"

"It must have been some Fren-Okun you dealt with in the past," Zeno said.

But Nulic shook her head. "Not necessarily. We opened our economy to external investment and ownership nearly fifty years ago. The owner—actually, the previous owner—may have been almost anyone."

Torina, who'd been listening with pursed lips, spoke up. "I'm curious. Would this Okun-Basti Concern be a worthwhile target for some sort of hostile takeover?"

Nulic blinked. "I... suppose, yes. It's profitable but relatively small."

Torina turned to me. "Who might be interested in a small, low-key shipping company with a reputation for transporting fruits and vegetables?"

I nodded. "Smugglers. Not that that narrows down the list much."

"Exactly. Whoever left this Concern to you might have thought that transferring ownership to a Peacemaker was a good way of ensuring it didn't end up in the wrong hands. I mean, can you imagine the Arc of Vengeance, say, coming to you with a purchase offer and finding themselves negotiating with a member of the Guild?"

"Good point," I said, whereupon the conversation ended and Nulic departed. But I found myself chewing on Torina's words like they were a piece of gristle. It might taste like food, but it really wasn't. In the same way, while I could see her being right about that being part of the previous owner's motivation, I couldn't help thinking there was more to it.

Because, if there was one takeaway from my new life in outer space, it was that there was *always* more to it.

WE'D ACTUALLY RECEIVED the order from Kharsweil to meet with the subject of what Gerhardt had called a *babysitting operation* while we were grounded on the Fren homeworld. Instead of specifying a hard time for it, though, it simply said that we were to transmit a confirmation code to a numbered twist-comm address when we were on our way.

"Kharsweil must have talked to Gerhardt," Zeno noted.

Icky sniffed. "You mean Kharsweil must have bowed and submitted to Gerhardt."

"I wouldn't read too much into that. Kharsweil probably just didn't want to give you an order that you weren't going to obey because Gerhardt takes precedent. It would have lost him some face," Perry replied.

I glanced at Perry as we climbed through the last dregs of the

Fren-Okun homeworld's atmosphere to orbit. "What makes you say that?"

"I've been marinating in Guild politics for a long time, Van. Trust me, nothing a Master does is without at least a little self-interest—and usually a *lot* of self-interest. That goes double for someone like Kharsweil. His default setting is to climb the ladder at any cost, and damn the circumstances."

I nodded, taking Perry's word for it. Kharsweil was something of a blank, a Master who'd mostly stayed on the sidelines, never *quite* taking sides as the Guild had gone through its various upheavals. Unlike Gerhardt, though, he hadn't established himself as truly neutral. Instead, he leaned this way and that as threats and opportunities arose, like a tree bending in response to changing winds.

I didn't trust him. Not one bit.

"Van, we're ready to break orbit," Netty said.

"Okay, then. Let's head for—where the hell are we going again?"

"SCR 1845-6357."

I glanced at Torina. "Now that's romantic."

She batted her eyes at me. "Van, kiss me when we get to SCR 1845-6357 to preserve the moment forever."

Funboy grimaced. "I can provide a list of potentially lethal biological agents transferred by kissing, if you'd like. I don't recommend it."

"Kissing, or giving me that list? Because one is fun, and the other will irritate me," I told Funboy, trying not to laugh as Torina rolled her eyes.

"I'm not surprised. Irritation is a sure sign of bacterial—"

Icky's pants hit Funboy in the face, and he stopped speaking.

"Icky, was that necessary?" Zeno asked after a moment of stunned silence.

"Not really. Funboy, are you irritated?" Icky asked.

He thought for a moment, sniffed, then said with some dignity, "Yes, but only because your pants smell like cheese."

Icky paused, then grinned in real pleasure. "Thank you!"

4

WE'D INTENDED to take Essie and Funboy back to Anvil Dark, but they were content to come along with us for a ride in the meantime. With the *Fafnir* as upgraded as she now was, it wasn't like we didn't have the room. Funboy spent time with Icky and Zeno, discussing the various elements of the *Fafnir*'s engineering, while Essie spent his time working on a report he had to file regarding his undercover work. Every few moments, he would mumble in disgust, proving that no matter where you were in the galaxy, paperwork would find you.

I hated to admit it, but since neither of them seemed in any particular hurry to get back to their regular duties, I found myself with a glimmer of distrust of them, too. Again, they were clearly legitimate members of the Guild, but they'd been embroiled in undercover work as their daily assignments. As we made our way to our destination, I went to my cabin, closed the door, and asked

Netty to ensure that all of the *Fafnir*'s critical systems were locked out to anyone not a permanent member of the crew.

"Actually, Van, I already have. And Perry made the same suggestion."

"So you guys have your doubts too, eh?"

Perry, who Netty had looped into the conversation, replied. "Let's just say that not being able to see into their recent records is a little concerning. It's not unusual for undercover operatives, but let's face it, we've got enough targets painted on the *Fafnir* to make her look like a carnival shooting gallery."

"That's an interesting turn of phrase for an AI bird."

"Hey, I get around."

"To carnivals?"

"Sure. I've been to the Iowa State Fair a bunch of times."

"Really?"

"As long as I don't let anyone get too close, they write me off as just another predatory bird, albeit an unusually large example. One year I had a kid throwing me popcorn. Some asshole raven beat me to it, though."

I chuckled. "Okay, so the obvious question is why the hell are you going to the Iowa State Fair?"

"Honestly, I think it's tacky and overpriced, but Netty likes it. I share the experience with her in real time."

"Netty, you have hidden depths," I said.

"I do. But, to be blunt, it's also pretty boring sitting in a barn, sometimes days at a time. Perry acts as my eyes and ears on the extra-barn world."

I laughed and shook my head. There was nothing *artificial* about these two beings at all.

"Anyway, guys, keep an eye on Essie and Funboy. Especially Funboy. He's obviously a skilled engineer, which means he probably knows the *Fafnir*'s systems pretty well."

"He's also a doctor," Perry said.

I stared at the speaker on the terminal. "A doctor. As in, a medical doctor?"

"Yup. Fully accredited on Tau Ceti and in the Eridani Federation, and recognized by the Guild."

"So he's an engineer *and* a doctor?" I found it hard to reconcile the dour, glass-is-half-empty little alien with someone who could be an expert in two entirely different fields.

"It's not uncommon among the Surtsi. They live a long time— as much as two hundred years—so they customarily change their vocation periodically," Perry replied.

"Huh. Yeah, I guess that doing the same job for a hundred and eighty years could get you into a rut."

THE ROMANTICALLY NAMED SCR 1845-6357 was a binary system—a dim brown dwarf orbiting an only slightly brighter red dwarf about thirteen light years from Earth. It was utterly unremarkable in almost every way, used only as a navigational waypoint. In other words, it was the equivalent of a rest stop alongside the interstate but with less of a stale urine smell.

And I would have leaned over and kissed Torina when we got there, but the contact alert sounded and the tactical overlay lit up with a bogie.

I cursed. "Really? Can't we go anywhere without it turning into a space battle?"

"It's a class 8," Netty said, painting the relevant data onto the overlay. "Standard armament, including the two missiles it just launched at us. It's also damaged. I'm detecting a plume of water, ice, and other gases. It's probably leaking atmosphere."

"Fine. Netty, go hot with the point-defense batteries. Torina, send them light speed dissuasion from further hostilities."

"You mean shoot them with the lasers?"

"Pardon me for trying to be erudite."

Torina grinned, then she activated the fire control system, got a firing solution, and triggered the lasers.

A second later, the class 8 blew apart in a spectacular fireball.

"Torina, what the hell?"

She sat back from the weapons controls. "Sorry, Van. I'm not used to one-shotting things like that."

"It's the universe restoring order," a new voice said. It was Funboy, who'd slipped silently into the back of the cockpit.

"Restoring order? How so?" I asked.

He gave that languid shrug. "We disabled those culture thieves with a fortuitous shot to their main power coupling." He gestured at the fading fireball. "That's the universe's way of making up for it. It's like the law of entropy, except instead of energy, it applies to goodness."

Icky gave him a puzzled scowl. "How do you figure that?"

"One law says the total amount of disorder in the universe must decrease over time until everything is perfectly uniform and ordered everywhere. The same thing applies to goodness. It must diminish over time."

A long and sullen silence hung in the cockpit. Perry finally broke it.

"You'd make one hell of a morale officer, you know that?"

ASIDE FROM THE cooling remains of the class 8, there was nothing else here. No sign of any ship. No sign of anything at all.

"Looks like we lost our mark," Perry said.

I studied the data on the overlay. "I'm not sure they were even ever here."

"Why would Kharsweil send us to the equivalent of a stellar road sign, only to find there's nothing here?" Torina asked.

"Well, there was the class 8 that you vaporized."

"I said I was sorry."

"Actually, Van, it wasn't entirely vaporized. Much of its forward section is still intact and on its way toward the galactic core. If there are still intact data stores in it, it might shed some light on what this is all about," Netty suggested.

"Huh. That's a damned fine idea. Netty, follow that piece of debris. Dead men tell no tales, but dead ships might."

I WATCHED ANXIOUSLY as the chunk of what had once been a spaceship tumbled and corkscrewed about a hundred meters away from the *Fafnir*. It brought back uncomfortable memories of the debris field where we'd lost Rolis. More to the immediate point, though, its gyrations meant it was probably too dangerous for us to try and board. Netty had calculated the likely g-forces it would exert on anyone trying and found them well beyond any reasonable limits. We'd either be squashed against it or flung away from it.

We finally settled on having Perry approach as close as he could to see if he could scavenge any data remotely. If he couldn't, then he was the one best able to analyze the various rotational forces in real time and determine if he could realistically board it. He'd attached himself to one of our EVA maneuvering units, since it gave him far more thruster fuel than the tiny amount he could store internally.

"Perry, what do you think?" I asked him as he crept to within a few meters of the gyrating wreck and puffed himself to a stop. I'd halted myself about ten meters further back. We were both tethered to the *Fafnir*.

"Well, related to our discussion about carnivals, this would make one hell of a ride."

"Which means—?"

"Which means I think I can do this as long as I stay within a very small area close to the point it's rotating all crazy-like around."

"Is that going to be useful, though?"

"Only one way to find out. But I'm going to have to release my tether, or it's going to be like the *Fafnir* lassoed a merry-go-round."

"Not excited about you being untethered, Perry."

"I'm not excited either, but here we are."

He disconnected his tether, activated the thrusters, and nudged himself closer. At the same time, he applied thrust to account for the rotation of the wreck, making a multitude of fine adjustments that would only be possible for someone able to do complex vector math with constantly changing variables in their head.

"Okay, here we go," he said, then moved into contact with the wreck.

"Perry, talk to me."

"This isn't bad. Kinda fun, in a yawning chasm of time and space sort of way. Nietzsche would *love* it."

"Perry—"

"Yeah, yeah, I'm working on it. There's a maintenance port about two meters away. If I can access it, I should at least be able to tell if there's any hope of finding anything at all."

I waited, gritting my teeth. I found that I had to keep looking away from the wreck as I did. My eyes wanted to follow it, which created a weird sense of motion that wasn't real, which, in turn, started down the path toward vertigo. I had to avoid looking down between my feet, too, at the dull, red spark of SCR 1845-6357-A, the system's primary. Every time I did, I was slammed with a sudden, wrenching sense of scale of being far above something with nothing underneath me. "Heraclitus," I said. "Being, becoming, stuff like that out there."

"Yeah, him too. But the German is a bit more accurate about all this nothingness," Perry clarified.

I smiled but had other things to worry about. For instance, if this was the worst-case scenario, a trap into which Kharsweil had led us—unwittingly or otherwise—we were far enough from the red dwarf and its brown dwarf companion that a ship could twist in right on top of us. And I'd hate to find myself in the middle of a space battle, on the end of a seventy-meter tether.

"Okay, I've got access," Perry said.

"You still okay?" I asked him. The sheer scale of things was unsettling, despite how many times we'd been out between the stars.

"It's not like I get dizzy, Van. Mind you, I am burning through a lot of thruster fuel here, so I need to make this quick."

I resumed waiting. This was taking too long. As much as I wanted to unravel the mystery of what was going on here, I was seriously starting to second-guess myself, wondering if the risk was worth it—

"Aha. Okay, I've managed to access some data. It's mostly junk, but I'm downloading it all anyway—and I'm done," Perry said.

"Okay, Perry, let's get the hell out of here."

"You don't need to tell me twice—oops."

"Oops?"

"Yeah, oops. See that small object hurtling toward the Andromeda galaxy? That would be me."

I could see him, a small dot trailing a faint tail of gas. "What happened? Are you okay?'

"One of the thrusters on this damned maneuvering unit is stuck in the *on* position. When was the last time we had these things serviced, anyway?"

I opened my mouth, about to say something urgent and panicky, but closed it again. Perry was accelerating away at about one-half g, and on a limited supply of fuel. At that rate, it would take him hours to travel even a few klicks.

I laughed in relief at Perry being okay and the general absurdity of the situation.

"You find my current predicament funny, Van?"

Thanks to the magnification function of my visor, I could watch him crawling toward deep space. "Actually... kinda, yeah. Sorry."

"That's it, you're off my Christmas card list."

"You stare into the void—"

"And the void gives you a stocking full of coal."

WE RECOVERED Perry and examined the data he'd retrieved. As he'd said, most of it was junk. After he and Netty scoured it, they found a few useful nuggets, including nav data that recorded repeated trips to 40 Eridani, the system that hosted the refueling orbital called Plenty.

That was… troubling. Plenty was an unusual place, hugging the edge of a gas giant called Good as it orbited, scooping and refining deuterium and helium for fusion fuel. It was also home to a terrifying but admittedly badass form of tourism that involved diving down into Good's cloud tops using elaborate wingsuits. To add to the fun, the planet hosted enormous delta-shaped creatures loosely known as whales that happily assumed wing suited thrill seekers were just another part of the ecosystem—and therefore eligible to be eaten.

No thanks.

But the tourism thing was really just a sideshow. Plenty was actually a non-sovereign holding used by organized crime, similar to an old offshore oil-drilling platform on Earth being used to host nefarious activities in international waters. All of the major players in known space put up with it, partly because it kept a lot of criminality in one place, but mainly because of huge kickbacks to keep putting up with it.

I drummed my fingers on the chair, staring at the vivid image of a wingsuit diver being torn in half by something that looked like a transparent flounder with wings. And fangs. And, just for good measure, a few tentacles.

"Please tell me that's not an advertisement?" I asked Netty, who'd put the image up of her own accord.

"Oh, it is, boss. Most popular one according to metadata."

"A few people actually just fall into the gravity well and get pulped. Or shredded by the tornadic winds," Funboy reported. "They have gift cards, you know."

"For—for that? Diving?" Torina asked, incredulous.

Funboy lifted one fuzzy brow. "You save twenty percent. Thirty if you agree to sign a hold harmless clause. You also get a keychain, if you come back alive."

"Well, at least I know what I'm getting Icky for Christmas," I remarked.

She thought it over. "Thirty percent off?"

Funboy gave a vigorous nod. "It's substantial."

I feathered a command, and Netty began the twist. "Or maybe we'll just stick to—"

"As long as it ain't pants, I don't care," Icky said, and Netty flashed a ready sign for the workboat. "Am I taking Zeno, Essie, and Funboy?"

"Please do. Load up, kids. Your chariot awaits," I said. The four of them buckled in the workboat, and Netty twisted us to 40 Eridani in a smooth process.

"Separate now, Icky. Meet you there," I said, feeling the slight *thump* as the workboat pushed away, its drive firing seconds later.

They'd make their own way to Plenty, arriving separately from us as just another unremarkable boat on unspecified business— which put it into company with most of the traffic here. It gave us the flexibility to put some people on the station anonymously, which made us that much more free to move about unnoticed.

It also gave us the opportunity to test Essie and Funboy a little, a fact that I had discreetly discussed with Icky and Zeno some hours earlier, prepping them to watch Essie and Funboy with the intent of removing *any* doubt as to their allegiances.

We arrived at Plenty, and as soon as the *Fafnir* hit her berth, I called our contact, Fonsecur. A retired Peacemaker, he ran a "whale"-watching business that sounded only slightly less dangerous than the wingsuit nonsense. He answered the call immediately.

"Van! You in town?"

"I am, just pulling in to dock now."

"Come to try your hand at some windrunning?"

"Yes, because I've decided this is how I want my life to end, plunging into a hellscape of toxic, supersonic winds while being chased by a drooling monster that wants to eat me."

He laughed. "Hey, you ain't gonna live forever, so might as well make it memorable, right?"

"Agreed, but I was thinking more along the lines of, in the midst of an especially pleasurable moment when I'm a hundred or so."

Torina, who'd been unbuckling from her seat, gave me a cool stare. "Really."

I shrugged. "I haven't shown you my entire bucket list yet, sorry."

She grinned, then muttered, "Make it a hundred and forty. Got plans for you, killer."

I fought a blush and turned back to Fonsecur, sketching our purpose in as few words as I could, which was easy because—

I didn't have much to go on.

Fonsecur summarized the molecular thinness of our lead quite well. "So you found the remains of a ship that traveled to and from Plenty, at a place where you were supposedly meeting... someone."

"That's about it, yeah."

"Good luck with that."

"I'm actually hoping that our presence here incites somebody to do something, particularly if we put word out about exactly what we're looking for."

Fonsecur laughed. "That you're a Peacemaker looking for somebody? This is Plenty, Van. I can say with confidence that the only person you're *not* looking for here is me."

WHILE THE OTHERS did an initial inspection of Plenty, Perry and I had lunch with Fonsecur in a tidy little restaurant with a breathtaking view across the swirling bands of cloud that striated Good. We spent the first part of the meal—remarkably good—mainly getting caught up on Plenty gossip and street lore. Fonsecur offered up enough leads to fill my remaining career as a Peacemaker, but none of them really jumped out as something relevant to our case. However, he did have a suggestion as to how he could help us.

"If your plan—" He paused, grinning. "Plan. You're gonna walk around and look for some unspecified person. Sure, let's call that a *plan*. Anyway, to the extent it can work at all, you'd probably end up with someone watching you. I can provide you with some cover to watch out for *them*."

"Who are these *someones* going to be?"

"Sorry, I can't tell you that. The whole point of these folks is that no one knows who they are. That way, they could be anybody."

I made a face. "That makes sense. But how are we going to know if your *someones* spot a person of interest if we can't communicate with them directly?"

Fonsecur frowned in turn. "Yeah, normally they'd just route it through me. But I'm taking a tour group down to do some whale watching on Good in about two hours, so—" He glanced at Perry. "How about we use your AI, and you just give him a memory-lock directive not to reveal who he talked to?"

"Perry, would that work?" I asked.

"Sure. The moment you pressed that button on the doohickey you found in your old desk back in Iowa, I became subject to your directives."

"It's this level of technical explanation that really solidifies our relationship."

"It's a doohickey. I stand by that nomenclature," Perry asserted.

"Fair enough. And… I didn't know that. About your relative adherence to my directives, that is." I rubbed my chin, then shook my head. "Ah, the missed opportunities."

"Which is why I didn't tell you I was subject to your directives at the time—so you didn't order me to do vapid stuff."

"But I could order you to do vapid stuff now."

"You *do* order me to do stupid stuff now."

"What? When have I *ever*—"

Fonsecur cut in, laughing. "Now this is how I know you've got a good partnership going here, Van. Some Peacemakers treat their combat AIs like glorified drudge bots and miss out on all the witty banter."

Perry gave me a stare. "Yeah, Van. *Banter*."

I rolled my eyes, but I didn't mean it and he knew it. I addressed Fonsecur, working through some of what we faced. "Okay. Get Perry hooked up with your people. Perry, you are not to divulge to anyone, ever, the identities of whoever Fonsecur is about to connect you with." I narrowed my eyes at him though. "Wait, this isn't one of those situations where the wording has to be exact so it can't be twisted in some way, is it?"

"I'm a sophisticated AI capable of high levels of reasoning and judgment, Van, not some role-playing game genie granting wishes," Perry shot back.

Okay, *that* made me curious. "What do you know about role-playing games?"

"The best individual to answer that would be Peritus the Magnificent, eighteenth level sorcerer, but we don't have time for that right now."

"Huh. You seem like the kinda guy who would spam *fireball* no matter what," I said slyly.

Perry flicked his wings back with great dignity. "My preferred spell is *magic missile*, you... you *casual*."

5

WE SAID GOODBYE TO FONSECUR, then rendezvoused with Torina. She'd been scoping out the orbital, a fact that made me a little uneasy, her being on her own. Of course, she was smart, switched-on, a master of Innsu knife-fighting and a ruthlessly crack shot. Still, my senses were on high alert simply due to the environment.

Under the dirt and trash, Plenty had a lot more to offer than simple crime. It also had despair. And that made me nervous, regardless of Torina's considerable abilities.

We met her near a tech vendor from whom, on our last visit here, Zeno and Icky had purchased some nifty flexible tools that had repeatedly come in handy. That included the time Icky had brandished one as a probe at Tony Burgess, our UFO-ologist back on Earth. The look on his face still made me snicker with glee.

"See anything interesting?" I asked Torina as we started ambling. Perry flew overhead from vantage point to vantage point, an additional layer of cover.

"Well, let's see. An attempted murder, more incidents of petty thievery that I can count, two cases of outright fraud—oh, and a half-dozen propositions that pretty much span the whole spectrum of disgusting. By the way, if someone complains about me breaking their wrist, ask them where that hand was trying to go when I broke it."

"That's my girl," I said, grinning. "Did you leave them their digits?"

"Most of them."

I smiled warmly. "Your generosity is an inspiration."

She fluttered her lashes. "Thanks. I try."

We ambled on, pausing occasionally to check out kiosks and market stalls, peer into shops, and even take in a surprisingly entertaining virtual fighting game set up in an empty compartment similar to those containing the various stores we passed. Each person actually fought the other's life-sized digital avatar, trading kicks and punches that were scored by the game, with severe penalties if you let any part of your body extend beyond a zone marked out on the floor. You could fight as yourself or as any number of weird and wonderful pre-built avatars.

Torina took a go at it—wearing the skin of a green and gold beast that had rippling scales—and won three times in quick succession. At that point, the crowd was taking definite notice and laying wagers with increasing fervor as she won more bouts, the last two in spectacular fashion with stunning knockouts. Out of nowhere she finally lost one, making much of the crowd erupt in delight and leaving the rest cursing and sullen.

When she rejoined me, I muttered to her, "You threw that last one. Rookie mistake to drop your guard arm there, dear."

She grinned and shrugged. "Pissing off a bunch of criminals who gave long odds on me losing? That never gets old."

I'd noticed Funboy and Icky in the crowd and hadn't paid any attention to them, but they joined us shortly after leaving the fighting rig.

I glanced at Icky. "Uh, hello. Is there a reason you guys just blew your cover?"

"Yeah. You're being tailed."

I opened my mouth, but Perry spoke in our ear bugs, cutting me off.

She's right, Van. Fonsecur's people just told me the same thing. At your current four o'clock, a Skel. He's doing what Skels do best, skulking behind a kiosk.

I glanced at Icky, and she nodded. "That's the one, yeah. Funboy here noticed him."

"There are threats everywhere," Funboy said, then peered at a countertop smeared with food residue. "Some of them are even visible."

"Of course there are. Why didn't you guys just relay it to us via Perry, like we'd planned?" I asked.

Icky shrugged. "Funboy here might be a little, uh, alarmist, but I don't know—I've got a bad feeling about this, Van. Essie and Zeno are staying clear, but we decided to join you in case things got hammer-worthy, if you know what I mean."

I nodded. I wanted my crew to exercise their judgment and not slavishly adhere to a plan, so if Icky thought this was the right way to go, I'd give her the benefit of the doubt.

And, sure enough, the four of us had gone maybe another

couple of dozen meandering paces when a chubby Yonnox stepped in front of Torina.

We stopped, Icky moving to one side to give herself some room. Even so, if she started swinging her sledgehammer here on the orbital's crowded main concourse, she'd have to be careful to not crack some collateral heads.

Torina smiled sweetly. "Excuse me," she said and made to move around the Yonnox.

"Not so fast, my dear. We have an issue to settle here, you and me."

"Oh really? And what issue would that be?"

"I just lost a lot of money to some scumbag Nesit who bet against you in that last bout at… good odds for him, bad for me."

She shrugged. "Easy come, easy go," she said and tried to step the other way around him. Again, he moved to block her. I started splitting my attention between Torina and the crowd. This Yonnox would be nowhere near this brazen if he didn't have muscle nearby. He clearly thought he could get away with trying to intimidate an obvious member of a Peacemaker's crew.

"Yeah, see, it's the *easy go* part that concerns me. I think you threw that last match, probably part of some scam. So, I'll tell you what. I'll get over the sting of defeat for a suitable recompense in bonds."

Torina, still smiling, shifted her body slightly. I recognized the Innsu Fourth Stance, one of three that was intended to lead to a killing blow.

"Let's try another cliché. A fool and his money are soon parted," she said, and again made to step around the Yonnox but using the Fourth Stance's first move to do it, keeping herself ready.

I braced myself, my hand near the hilt of the Moonsword. Icky had spread her legs apart and flexed all four of her arms.

Funboy—

He looked petrified. And he was an undercover operative? Really? Maybe the problem wasn't that he was untrustworthy but more that he was just shitty at his job.

"I've got all kinds of friends around us right now who can help me... you know, *insist* on some compensation," the Yonnox said in a sibilant hiss. The Yonnox really did villainy well, right down to the voices and phrasing.

Van, Fonsecur's people tell me that this is a thing here on Plenty. Our boy down there makes a big deal of defying a Peacemaker, and it gains him all kinds of street cred. Or corridor cred, I guess. Anyway, he's not going to back down, Perry said.

Torina would have heard Perry, too, but she didn't budge. Instead, she spoke simply and quietly.

"You are really going to want to give me some space, my friend."

"Or what? You gonna use your little hands on me, gorgeous? This isn't no fighting game."

Perry clicked his tongue. *What a moron. He literally* just *watched her beat the shit out of a succession of people. Yonnox, am I right?*

But his flat, uncompromising defiance made me bristle. He would not be this brave unless he genuinely thought he could win this.

Torina glanced at her hands, then at me. "How do my hands look?"

"Elegant. Let's keep them that way," I replied, to put as much warning tone into my voice as I could. I really wanted to find some way to de-escalate this, because a crowd had assembled, no more than a meter or two away from what might be a fight involving a massive sledgehammer and a preternaturally sharp sword.

"Last chance, sweetie, then me and my colleagues are going to have to switch from *requesting* to *assisting*."

"Oh, I suspect my colleagues have more arms than you and yours, you—" She glanced at me. "Can I call them shitheads, Van?"

"Feel free."

"Sweet. Than you shitheads."

"And hammers," Icky growled, unlimbering hers with a gleam of light off the menacing head. It really *was* impressive, and in her capable grasp, it moved as if made of air.

I started to draw the Moonsword, but Funboy chose that moment to step forward, right alongside Torina. He reached out and poked the Yonnox with his thumb just below and to the left of where a human's breastbone would be.

Whereupon the Yonnox dropped to the deck like a wet sack of grain.

Silence reigned as we all looked at Funboy. Then, I shook off my surprise and prepared for the Yonnox's promised colleagues to attack.

They didn't move.

Funboy's casual disabling of their leader dissuaded them from pursuing this any further. If anything, I suspected that the ones abruptly beating a hasty retreat were the Yonnox's muscle.

I let go of the Moonsword as the tension that had been thrumming through the crowd dissipated into whispers and chatter. "Um, Funboy? You wanna tell me your strategy there?"

"Statistics indicate that the longer we engage them, the greater our chance of dismemberment."

"Dismemberment?"

Funboy gave his slow shrug. "Worst-case scenario, but still. I saw a limb regrown once. It took weeks, and it was expensive. Not to mention the cost for adjusting tunics while the arm continued to—"

"What the hell did you do to him?" Torina asked.

"I applied pressure to a neural node typical of Yonnox physiology. They normally keep it protected in some way, but this one didn't." He said it as though he felt sorry for having done it.

He then looked up at me. "Also, I'm hungry."

Torina grinned. "And I'm buying. They've got noodles, right?"

"Sure, but—"

Funboy, if you mention a choking hazard, I'm going to be pissed, and I don't even eat, Perry told me.

"Never mind them. Can we get extra sauce?"

"All the extra sauce you want, sure," I said as we started for a noodle stand. The crowd parted to let us through, many of those moving aside giving Funboy nervous looks. It was almost funny, considering they were scared of *him* when Icky was right behind him.

We bought what amounted to ice cream cones of noodles— apparently a universal staple—with some sort of crispy fried veggies. Funboy slathered his with extra sauce and dripped it on the deck as we ambled off.

After a few steps, something caught my eye. "Perry, are we still being tailed?"

Yup. That Skel is right on your six, about ten meters back.

"Interesting," I said.

Icky, who had a noodle cone in each of her four hands, glanced at me. "Wath inthrething?" she asked, noodles and sauce dripping down her chin.

"Well, first, the way you eat, and the volume of noodles now spattered on the deck because of it. But second, that drone over there rolling along on a balloon tire, the one that looks like a standard maintenance rig. It's been keeping us in view since we left the fighting game."

Torina looked at me sidelong. "How do you know it's the same one?"

"It's got a scratch on it shaped like the letter J."

"Funny that Fonsecur's people didn't pick up on it," she said.

And that you did, Perry added.

"Remember how you said you've been marinating in Guild politics, Perry? For me, it's been a long soak in a warm bath of paranoia. I'm getting pretty good at spotting things that want to, as Funboy put it, *dismember* me."

We walked along for a while, and sure enough, the drone followed us. So did the Skel, but Perry had intercepted a comm link between him and some bad guy doing something nefarious elsewhere on Plenty. So we ignored him, and focused on the bot.

At some point, it must have realized the gig was up and suddenly wheeled away.

"Shit. Perry, can you track it?"

I'm trying.

A new voice cut over the comm. "Van, Zeno here. Essie and I are following the bot."

I smiled, warmly content that my trust in my crew was well-placed—and also feeling a little more easy about Essie and Funboy.

We started after the bot ourselves, until Essie and Zeno reported that it was heading for the docks.

"Bugging out," I said.

"Probably."

Van, I got a lock on the thing and could track it right until I couldn't. It just vanished, as though it never existed, Perry said.

"Yeah, Van, Essie and I can see why. The bot just rolled into an airlock, number fourteen-alpha-two. I caught a glimpse of one of the crew aboard the ship that's docked here. It's a Trinduk."

Anger flushed my face. The Sorcerers were here.

THE THREAT POSED by the Sorcerers was an order of magnitude greater than any Yonnox trying to shake us down or some miscellaneous criminal worried we were going to crash his illicit little party. The game just got a whole lot more sinister and dangerous.

"That explains why Perry lost tracking. The Sorcerers suppressed it," Torina said.

"Yeah, that'd be my guess." I thought about our options for a moment. "Okay, folks, back to the *Fafnir*. I want to take those Sorcerer bastards in one piece, and I want to do it well away from these crowded warrens. Netty, what have you got on the ship docked at fourteen-alpha-two?"

"Class 10, typical armament for a fast freighter, otherwise unremarkable. But it has requested priority clearance to undock and enter the departure pattern."

"I'll bet. Okay, my dear, preflight us and get ready to depart as soon as the inner door is closed."

We hurried back to the *Fafnir* and arrived at almost the same time as Zeno. Essie had rushed to our workboat and cast it off so we could recover it on the way out. Sure enough, Netty was ready to cast us off as soon as the airlock sealed and had already backed us a hundred meters away from Plenty by the time we were in our seats. Torina and I were already in our b-suits, and the others scrambled to suit up so we could depressurize the ship if and when it came time for the shooting to start.

Netty rotated the *Fafnir* and used the thrusters to move us away from Plenty until we had enough clearance to light the fusion drive. Our quarry, the class 10, was doing the same. As we coasted away, Essie caught up with the workboat and snuggled it up into its dock with a series of thumps.

Based on the tactical overlay, we had the Sorcerers outgunned by a considerable margin, but we couldn't very well start shooting in midst of all the active traffic around Plenty. That was unfortunate because we currently were close enough that Torina probably could pick off their engines and weapons. But if something went wrong and the Trinduk ship exploded instead, we could kill hundreds, maybe thousands of people on Plenty and other ships. That wouldn't exactly cover the Guild in glory.

So I resigned myself to a tedious stern chase that, if nothing went wrong, should give us a good chance to disable the other ship.

Of course, something went wrong.

First, the collision alarm sounded. I glanced at the overlay but didn't see any icons painted with a crash-alert icon—until I did. Two of them, flickering in and out of existence.

"Netty, talk to me."

"Two heavily stealthed objects heading our way. Based on their trajectories, they were released by the fast freighter we're chasing."

"Fast freighter my ass," Torina muttered.

"Hey, I just call them like I see them," Netty replied. "And if I had to guess, I'd say those two objects are mines, heavily stealthed. What little emissions they're giving off match the signature of that stealthed satellite we encountered over Ajax, the home planet of the Daren-thal."

"Our hunter friends with the rangy hounds," I said.

"That's right."

I muttered a curse. The satellite in question had used horrifying tech that was a fusion of electronic and biological, typical of Sorcerer R&D. That satellite had led us first to Zenophir, and then to *Ponte Alus Kyr*, which meant we'd effectively closed a big circle that brought us right back face-to-face with our Trinduk nemeses.

More immediately, though, I didn't even have to ask how the mines were triggered. If we followed the Sorcerers, they'd detonate and inflict untold damage on Plenty and the ships clustered around it. But they'd eventually explode anyway because the Sorcerers were just assholes like that.

"We've got to take those two mines out," I said.

"Van, if we destroy one, the other's bound to go off," Zenophir replied.

I nodded. "I know. So we have to destroy both at the same time."

"Easiest way would be to just detonate a missile between them. The speed of the blast would make their destruction virtually instantaneous," Zeno said.

"Yeah, unfortunately that means detonating a missile among about a dozen ships. We need a plan B."

"We pretty much have to use the lasers," Torina said. "They're the only zero time-of-flight weapons we've got."

"It's going to be difficult to generate reliable targeting solutions because of the stealth effects," Netty pointed out.

I almost ground my teeth in frustration, glaring at the tactical overlay as if demanding it to give me an answer.

So it did.

I sat up. "Netty, what if we had scanner data from a bunch of different directions and combined it?"

"Targeting resolution would increase dramatically. I see where you're going with this, and what a great idea."

"What? What's your idea?" Torina asked.

"We get every ship here to scan the hell out of those mines and transmit the data back to us so Netty can combine it all. That should give us a detailed, 3D picture that's way more accurate than us scanning alone. Netty, general comm broadcast please, across the Plenty traffic control channel. Everyone should be monitoring that."

As soon as the indicator flicked to ready, I spoke. "All ships in Plenty traffic control space, this is Peacemaker Van Tudor. There are"—I caught myself. If I said there are two freakin' mines amongst you all, I risked starting a panicked flight of ships in all directions that could lead to collisions—"there is a navigation hazard currently located about five klicks away at my current twelve o'clock. We are having difficulty registering it, so we're requesting that you scan that approximate space and send your scanner data to my ship, the *Fafnir*, in continuous real-time. My ship's AI is ready to receive the data."

I repeated the same message, then sat back and waited.

"All of these ships are civilian cargo and passenger vessels. It's likely that their scanners can barely even detect the mines as anything more than slight scanner ghosts," Netty said.

"Is anyone responding?"

"Not yet."

"Well, hell."

"They probably all think, yeah, a Peacemaker wants a comm link to my ship? I don't think so," Perry noted.

"Netty, open the comm channel again—"

"All ships, this is Fonsecur aboard Plenty. Do what the Peacemaker says or… you know what'll happen."

I blinked at Fonsecur's voice. I was about to ask him what he meant, but Netty cut me off.

"Van, we're receiving data—holy shit, we're receiving data, including from Plenty itself."

Torina gave a slow nod as the screens flooded. "Our firing solution just went from less than forty percent to seventy—oh. Make that over ninety—and make that as close to one hundred percent as I've ever seen."

I stared at her. "What are you waiting for?"

Smiling, she triggered the lasers. At five klicks, they hit with no range attenuation, so at full power. Both mines puffed into vapor before they could even start triggering.

I hit the comm. "Fonsecur, thank you. Gotta ask, though, what would have happened if these ships, you know, hadn't helped us?"

"Oh, they know, Van. They know," he said, then he laughed and signed off.

"Now I want to know what would happen even more," Essie said.

Funboy shook his head.

"I don't."

6

WITH THE MINES DESTROYED, we could get on with our pursuit. The Sorcerers' ship had broken the traffic pattern and lit its fusion drive, then burned furiously away from us. Still, it wasn't much of a head start, maybe twenty minutes or so. We lit our own drive as soon as nothing was going to be roasted in our wake and followed. We both still faced an arduous climb out of Good's formidable gravity well, so our quarry's lead would increase given that they were higher up it than we were. But I was confident we could catch up to them—

I blinked.

I was sitting in darkness. A distant part of me was vaguely aware of my surroundings: the cockpit of the *Fafnir*, albeit lightless and silent.

What—?

I raised my head. It felt like I had a weight tied to my forehead. I tried to speak, but my throat, mouth, and tongue seemed to have forgotten how to work.

"Van!"

Okay, that was—

Perry. Right. It was Perry.

I fought to get my voice working again.

"Per—" I managed, then my mouth and throat disconnected again.

"Van, can you hear me?"

I blinked into two amber points of light.

"Per—" I coughed. "Perry?"

"Yeah, it's me. Okay, so you're still alive. Netty's gone into safe mode, but she's trying to get things back online. I'll check on the others."

The next moments passed in a blur of disconnected sounds, sudden flashes of lights as instruments came back to life, and someone saying "Ow—!"

I blinked furiously before I finally remembered I had hands and scrubbed at my face.

"Perry? What the hell happened?"

He reappeared. "The Sorcerers twisted away."

"Oh." I stared. "Wait. Okay. They twisted. And?"

"And they twisted, as in, deep inside Good's gravity well."

I nodded. "Oh."

It took a few seconds, then I frowned. "Oh. Wait. They can't do that."

"Apparently they can. And it generated a gravitational wave when they did, distorting space-time like the ripples from a rock thrown into a pond. All matter in its area of effect got alternately squeezed, pulled apart, and squeezed again until the effect damp- ened out."

I sat up. More systems came online. The soft, pervasive hum and whisper of the life-support system restarted. The tactical overlay reappeared and, with it, Netty.

"I've got all critical systems back online. The rest should be up momentarily," she said.

I looked around. My crew were all blinking and staring stupidly, pretty much as I was.

I turned back to the panel, my eyes flickering over a story of failure and recovery. "Netty, what's the damage?"

"Technically didn't suffer any actual damage. The safeties interpreted the gravitational distortion as a failure of the inertial dampers and scrammed everything, put it all into safe mode. Otherwise, though, we're fine."

"Speak for yourself," Torina said, shaking her head groggily.

I slumped back, a thin whine like a dentist's drill shrilling behind my eyes. "Netty, ships can't twist when they're inside a strong gravity well."

"That's right."

"So... uh, what happened?"

"I don't know what to tell you, Van, sorry. The mathematics of it are incontrovertible. Until the value of the gravity variable falls below a certain threshold value, based on things like the type, size, and efficiency of the drive, it simply isn't possible to do the space-folding thing."

"But the Sorcerers did."

"They did."

"So they must have one hell of a powerful drive," Zeno said.

"If they do, it's an entirely novel design. The physical size of the drive is a factor. The *Iowa's* twist drive is much too large to put into a class 10 hull, and even it wouldn't have been able to twist this close to Good."

"Van, do you remember that short-range teleporter thing we found on Dregs?" Perry asked.

I nodded, regretting the flare of pain it caused. "Yeah, I do. You think that's related somehow?"

"It was a twist effect inside a gravity well. Of course, it was limited to a couple of hundred meters range. But if the Sorcerers have figured out how to scale that up—"

"Shiiiiiiit. It's a game changer," Icky said.

But I sighed.

"It's more than that. It's a weapon."

⁂

Weaponized space-time. The thought was abhorrent.

And just when I didn't think the Sorcerers could get any worse.

We had ample opportunity to see the effects that such a weapon could have. Since the waves that propagated through reality affected literally everything, down to individual atoms, in the same way at the same time, it meant that they didn't really inflict damage. They certainly had effects, though, disrupting the neurochemical processes in our brains and convincing the safety systems built into ships that inertial dampening was off-kilter, which automatically shut everything down.

And that was where the damage came in. There had been a half-dozen collisions around Plenty, as suddenly dark ships coasted into one another, or, in the case of a small workboat and a larger class 4, straight into the orbital itself. Damage was serious but fortunately not catastrophic. And there had been a multitude of injuries but thankfully no deaths.

"Guess the Sorcerers burned their bridges here, huh?" Torina said.

I nodded as we swung back to Plenty to help with the rescue efforts. "Yeah. And now I want to burn them—*really* bad."

"You mean revenge?" Funboy said.

Icky gave a fierce nod. "Damned right."

"Preferably the sort of revenge where we don't all die in the process." He sighed, then unbuckled and headed aft. "In the meantime, I'm going to finish those leftover noodles. Having my atoms distorted has made me hungry. Let me know when you need me, and please, no sudden ship movements. I don't want to spill the sauce."

Torina rolled her eyes. "He's the kind of guy who'd be miserable about winning a prize because everyone's expectations would be higher."

Essie chuckled. "He has literally done that. The Guild awarded him the Star Streak Medal, Third Class, for bravery. He was depressed for a week."

Zeno looked at him. "Really. Just exactly how does Funboy act when he's *depressed*? And how can you tell?"

Essie just laughed.

———

DEPRESSED OR NOT, Funboy proved invaluable for his medical skills in the aftermath of the gravitational waves that had walloped Plenty. We spent almost a full day operating the *Fafnir* as a sort of ambulance, shuttling injured crew members from damaged ships to the orbital, which actually had pretty good medical facilities. Funboy quickly assessed their injuries, rendered aid with the rest of us helping, and prescribed treatments.

He examined Icky last, checking her neural reactions for any sign of degradation.

Funboy tapped one of her elbows. "Do you feel that?"

"Yes."

He did it again. "And that."

She narrowed her eyes at him. "Yes."

"And what about—"

"If you tap my elbow again, I'm gonna turn you into a throw rug, Funboy."

Funboy gave a helpless shrug. "Unfortunately—"

"Yes?" I asked, my nerves jangling.

"She's completely fine," Funboy finished.

I felt myself deflate. Torina snorted. Zeno sighed.

"Funboy, would you care to continue assessing injuries on other ships?" I asked him with as much patience as I could muster.

"Sure. At least one of this rabble has to have an infectious disease or three. I'll wash my hands carefully."

Torina waved grandly to the airlock. "Your opportunity awaits, sunshine."

Icky glared at him, then slid her pants back on with a defiant curse. "I'll go with him to the other ships. He might get punched. Because of his tabletop manners."

"Bedside manner," Zeno offered.

"Whatever."

Our collective efforts at helping actually had an unintended benefit. By throwing ourselves and the *Fafnir* into the rescue effort, we gained enormous goodwill on both the orbital and the ships around it. We received genuine thanks from people who might have otherwise scuttled for cover when we appeared, or even tried—like the unfortunate Yonnox Funboy had so deftly taken out—to take us on.

"Can't ask for better marketing for the Guild than that," Torina said as the last injured from our final run were offloaded into Plenty.

I nodded. "Yeah, silver linings and all that. I'd rather have not had to experience that damned Sorcerers' souped-up twist drive to find this *particular* silver lining, though."

As we departed Plenty for Anvil Dark, Netty had more ominous news.

"Van, I've been analyzing the data we managed to collect before the gravitational distortion knocked everything offline. We were fortunate, insofar as the wavelength was something on the order of a kilometer. It means that anything smaller than that, like the *Fafnir*, was affected more or less uniformly along the propagation axis of the wave. But if you look at this—"

She flicked an image of Good onto the central display. Its characteristic bands of color had become diffuse, swirling and blending into one another instead of forming typically uniform bands.

"—you can see the effect on larger objects. In the case of Good, it just messed up the clouds in the upper atmosphere. It probably affected the interior as well, but its nature and density likely allowed it to absorb the effect without any permanent distortion. If a powerful enough version of that was activated close to a rocky planet, with a rigid crust—"

She left it at that.

"Great. So not just a weapon, but a potential planet-killer weapon," I said.

"Let's just hope they don't figure out how to shorten the wavelength of the distortion effect. If it was, say, only a few hundred meters instead of more than a kilometer, the gravitational gradient could be enough to rip a ship like the *Fafnir* to pieces," Perry put in.

I sighed. "Any more good news?"

"Well, I came through it pretty much unscathed," Perry said.

"Yay."

"Hey, I'm the one who got started on a long journey to nowhere retrieving the data from that wrecked ship. I deserved an *attabird* for that."

We made our gloomy way back to Anvil Dark. I badly needed to bring Gerhardt up to date on what happened and its terrifying implications. It only underscored that we needed to deal with the Sorcerers, and fast, before they smashed a planet to fragments with their new and evil take on a twist drive.

Like Earth.

I didn't even let my thoughts start down that path because nothing good waited along it.

By the time we got to Anvil Dark, word that something unusual had happened at Plenty, something that caused mass damage and casualties, had already arrived. Rumors were rampant, everything from Plenty having been completely destroyed to an especially bizarre story that someone had deliberately crashed the orbital into Good. The crash was—allegedly—a religious statement by a cult that hated themselves so much they insisted on not reproducing.

The trouble was, they hated everyone *else*, too.

"Make a note of that cult, Netty. What's their full name?" I asked.

"It's a phrase. Let me translate. Oh, you'll love this one, boss. Their name means *More Pure Than All Others*," Netty responded, her voice rich with disgust.

I sighed. "Naturally."

We berthed the *Fafnir* in a maintenance hangar so that Icky and Perry could work with Netty to go over her with a fine-toothed comb, just to make sure we hadn't suffered any lingering damage—hairline cracks, for instance, in structural members, or loosened electrical connections. Essie, in the meantime, came to me with an outstretched hand.

"It's been fun, Van. Thanks for the rescue."

I shook his hand. "Don't mention it. So what's next for you and Funboy? Going back undercover?"

He shrugged. "When it comes to me, I'm not sure. I'm going to report to my handler, probably spend the next five days debriefing, and then I'll do whatever comes next."

I smiled. "Well, don't be a stranger, okay?"

He met my gaze and smiled. "Don't worry, I won't." He then leaned in and lowered his voice. "Truth be told, Van, I wasn't sure how much I could trust you. I mean, I know we're both Peacemakers, but, well, there are Peacemakers, and then there are Peacemakers, if you know what I mean."

I returned an earnest look. "I know exactly what you mean. Oh, and I was the same about you, as far as the trust thing goes."

He grinned. "Of course you were. I sure as hell would have been!"

He clapped me on the shoulder and started to leave the bay, but Torina intercepted him.

"I have a present for you," she said, handing him a package. "Stavosia. I'm a fellow addict."

He bellowed his big laugh, hugged Torina, and thanked her. But he turned quickly serious. "I love baking, but these ingredients are going to be harder to come by."

Torina and I both gave him a quizzical look. "Why?" she asked.

"I'll give you guys a preview of what I learned before I got nabbed. Piracy is on the upswing. Someone out there is getting them a lot more organized and aggressive. They're already cracking more and more shiploads open, which is bad, but it's what they're after that's worse."

I frowned. "This doesn't sound good. What are they after?"

"Staples. Basic foodstuffs. Not the small, high-value cargoes they can easily flip for quick cash."

"Why?"

Essie narrowed his eyes. "Now that's the question, isn't it?"

He waved and walked away.

I turned to Torina, but she just shrugged. "Ominous warning is ominous."

"Yeah, because we didn't have enough to worry about——"

Something caught my eye. It was Funboy, standing and talking to Icky by a tool cart. I hurried over to him.

"Funboy, Essie's leaving."

He gave a slow blink. "Okay."

"Aren't you going with him?"

"I've got to go see my own handler, but Essie and I aren't permanent partners. We just did the one operation together." He sighed. "The one where we both got kidnapped and taken prisoner, of course."

I glanced from Funboy to the *Fafnir*, then back.

"You know, with our upgrades, we've got lots more room on our ship. We could really use a skilled medical officer, and it never hurts to have another engineer aboard. If I run a background check and it comes back *relatively* clean, how'd you like a job, Funboy?"

"Me?"

"I don't see any other Funboys around here."

He looked at me with his sad puppy-dog eyes for a moment, then shrugged. "I suppose that a final and fatal end aboard your ship is as good as it happening anywhere else."

Icky grimaced. "That's the spirit."

I told Funboy that I'd talk to Gerhardt and make the necessary arrangements. There might be some pushback from his current superiors, but tough. My crew and I had earned enormous cred in the Guild and very rarely traded on it.

It was time to tap the account. A little, anyway.

GERHARDT FINISHED READING my summary report, then puffed out a breath and sat back in his chair.

"Yikes."

"That's putting it mildly," I said.

He nodded. "Alright. Have your AI send all the data she managed to collect to me. I'm going to forward it on to our intelligence and technical people, as well as a few others."

I nodded. A few others meant the GKU—which brought up a

point that had been hanging, Sword of Damocles-like, over me since our battle against the Tenant-infested Seven Stars League fleet.

"Did you know about my mother?"

"That you had one? I assumed as much. That she was Peacemaker Wallis? No, I had no idea."

"Does she still even count as a Peacemaker? Isn't she off doing her own thing as part of the GKU?"

Gerhardt shrugged. "She's still on the Guild's roll. But she is, as you allude to, her own boss. She clearly has her own agenda, and she appears to answer to no one but herself."

I leaned back in my seat. "As if the universe wasn't complicated enough."

Gerhardt toyed with a data slate on his desk. "Let me ask you something, Tudor. What difference does it make?"

"Uh... she's my mother?"

"I realize that. But I also realize that she exited your life while you were too young to even understand it. She's had no contact with you since, so she's clearly not interested in making an effort to rejoin your life. So, aside from the fact that you happen to share some genetic material with her, what difference does it make that Peacemaker Wallis is your mother and not just another Peacemaker?"

"I don't know, and that's the problem. I mean, intellectually, I totally get what you're saying. But—" I shook my head. "I know it's stupid, but I can't let go of the fact that my mother is still alive."

Gerhardt leaned forward. "Well, if you intend to pursue this, Tudor, let me warn you—she may be your mother, but she is not *at all* maternal. She is dangerous and unpredictable, almost to the point of being feral. Even the GKU, to the extent there is a single thing called the GKU, is wary of her. I would *not* presume too much just because she gave birth to you."

"You're telling me to not trust her."

"No, I'm telling you that you *can* trust her—to do whatever is best for her, or for her agenda, and nothing else."

"I appreciate the candor."

Gerhardt gave that thin, cold smile. "You should know by now that candor… is what I do."

WE ENDED up spending almost three days on Anvil Dark. Sure enough, Icky found a cracked longitudinal spar that had to be replaced, a laborious job requiring removal and replacement of multiple hull plates. Funboy proved his value as an engineer, dealing with a slight instability in the fusion power plant that reduced its efficiency—another byproduct of the gravitational wave.

I also ended up in hours of debriefing sessions, mainly about the Sorcerers and their apparent new twist drive. The Guild's engineering people were all in a tizzy about it, excited by the prospect of a new breakthrough in twist technology. I'd have joined in their enthusiasm if the ones who possessed it weren't *the Sorcerers*. The Guild's intelligence shop was enthralled by my news, to put it lightly.

"This is potentially a very serious problem," the human intelligence officer I'd been speaking with said.

I stared in mild derision. "You think? The ability to destroy a planet fits in the *very serious problem* category, I'd say, and blows right past it. Ma'am, this is catastrophic. This is a shift in power."

"I—yes, I see your point. I'm of the mindset that keeping things calm is, in and of itself, part of my mission. So if I seem blasé about this, I can assure you, I am *not*. Inside, my guts have gone to water, and I can smell the ashes of burned worlds if we let these monsters off the leash. Does that match your current mood, Peacemaker?"

I inclined my head with a tight grin. "Perfectly, ma'am."

"Then go eat. Shave. Get fresh uniforms. We'll be here," she said in a gentle tone that brooked no disagreement.

On the third day, we received a new set of orders from Kharsweil, and this time, Gerhardt made no effort to intervene. So I sat in Kharsweil's office, which was somehow even more spartan and unwelcoming than Gerhardt's, and received the mission briefing. It didn't amount to much.

"You will conduct an escort of an important scientific personage. The navigational data will be uploaded to your ship's AI," the pale, slender Master said. His expression was a mild one, but I wasn't sure his alien face was even capable of anything else.

"Escort of?" I asked.

"As I said, an important scientific personage."

"You can't be more specific?"

"I could."

I sighed. "Alright. We'll get right on it."

"See that you do. This is a mission of the utmost importance. To that end, I'm assigning another Peacemaker to accompany you," Kharsweil said.

I braced myself. Great. Kharsweil was going to send along one of his cronies, who was going to have me constantly looking over my shoulder, while probably also getting in the way to boot. I was surprised at their identity, though.

"May I ask who, or is that somehow something I don't need to know either?"

Kharsweil's expression again didn't change. I could have been speaking to a doll.

"It is a Blessing Mbana."

That caught me by surprise. Blessing? Essie? Really? Did this mean that Essie was one of Kharsweil's cronies and I'd gotten him wrong? And did that also mean that, by inviting Funboy to become a member of the *Fafnir*'s crew, I'd just recruited a spy?

I decided to stay quiet—for the moment. My gut told me that Essie and Funboy were legit assets with not inconsequential skills, and that if Essie *was* a pawn, he was an unwitting one at worst. Second, and more pragmatically, if I was wrong, then it was better to find out sooner rather than later. And the best way to do that would be an op with Essie—one that seemed relatively innocuous, rather than heading into battle with him.

And it didn't seem that this would likely be a battle situation. The job was a straightforward escort mission, picking up this *important scientific personage* at a location called Rolling Fields, a farming orbital at Teegarden's Star, and taking them to Tau Ceti. That made me a little suspicious—why was such a routine job being tasked to two Peacemakers, and personally by a Master, at that?

Essie, who we met before the job, suggested why. "Remember how I told you that pirates are targeting shipments of staple foodstuffs? Well, this scientist we're escorting is probably involved in food production—"

"Hence the farming orbital," I added, and Essie gave a friendly nod.

Without fanfare, Essie headed for his ship. He had his own

Dragon-class, about one upgrade behind the *Fafnir*, so a class 9 equivalent. She was called the *Ngwenya*, Zulu for crocodile, an homage to his ethnic heritage. Essie had told me during our trip back to Anvil Dark that one of his biggest regrets was that he'd never managed to make the journey to Earth to visit his ancestral homeland.

"Have you ever been to southern Africa, Van?" he'd asked me.

"Once, for a tech conference in Johannesburg. And before you ask me if I had a chance to travel while I was there, I did, yes—from the airport to a hotel conference center, and back to the airport."

He'd been genuinely disappointed I wasn't able to give him first-hand accounts of southern Africa, or at least what I hadn't managed to see out the window of an airport limo.

We backed the *Fafnir*, which had been inspected from prow to drive bells and declared sound, out of the maintenance bay. Then, in company with Essie's *Ngwenya*, we set course for Teegarden's Star.

7

Teegarden's Star was one of the lower-key systems in known space, and also one of contrast. It was the location of Gajur Prime, the race's homeworld, a smoggy, overcrowded shithole of a planet with a wealth disparity so wide you could barely see across it. But it also hosted Faalax, a frozen world on the outer edge of the star's habitable zone. It had a small population that lived in a series of palatial subterranean colonies whose artful tapestries and embroideries were in as much demand as the music and poetry of the Saetsu. Or, as Perry put it, the Faalaxi economy was essentially based on knickknacks.

"Take an upscale curio shop in some hotspot like Paris or Florence, expand it to a subterranean paradise, and you've got Faalax," he said.

"Complete with arrogant shopkeepers determined to turn your hard-earned money into high-end trash you don't need and will barely even acknowledge once you get home?" I asked.

"Oh, so you've been to Faalax then."

Our destination wasn't Faalax or Gajur Prime, though. Rolling Fields was a massive farming orbital that revolved around a rocky planet called Faalax Opposing. The name referred to the fact that it was a celestial oddity, a planet that shared both an orbital path and period with Faalax, except on the opposite side of the system's primary star, a dim red dwarf. It was a weird but stable arrangement of planets that Netty noted no one could really explain.

"It's possible they formed that way, but most researchers have come to think it's artificial," she said as we coasted in toward Faalax Opposing.

"Artificial? Why the hell would someone—what, move a planet there? Or make one?" Icky asked.

"That would be the no-one-can-explain-it part. It served a purpose for someone. It might have been a failed effort to make more living space, or even a test run for a similar project somewhere else."

"Well, whatever the reason, it works out well for this Rolling Fields place, right? It gives them a planet on the edge of the Goldilocks zone to work with," I said.

"It does. It gives them enough sunlight for their purposes, at least. And it's beneficial both for Falaax, which frankly needs the economic diversity, and Gajur Prime, which needs the food," Perry said.

I pointed to the screens, which were free of incoming comms. "Well, let's make contact with them to confirm that they know we're—"

"Van, scans are showing that the orbital is damaged," Netty cut in.

We all sat up. "Damaged how?"

"We're too far away for details. All I can say is that we're detecting some debris and a tenuous plume of what seems to be atmospheric gases."

"Oh, not now—I, hey, Essie, you seeing that?"

"Yeah, I am," came his reply. "That's not good."

"No, it is not. Netty, are they broadcasting a distress call? Or… well, a distress anything?"

"No."

"That's even worse," Torina said, bringing our weapons and fire control system to standby mode.

"Van, do you want us to suit up and depressurize?" Icky asked.

I considered it, looking at the tactical overlay as I did. There was no other traffic in anything even resembling a threatening position, just routine-looking stuff heading toward and away from Faalax and Gajur Prime.

On the other hand, I was mindful of the two heavily stealthed mines we'd had to contend with at Plenty. "Let's suit up. We won't depressurize—not yet."

Line abreast with Essie, we continued our approach to Rolling Fields. About an hour away, we finally received a distress call. It was weak and distorted, probably being broadcast from a comm intended for local use. That implied that the orbital's primary comm system was down. We tried responding to it, but it was an automated loop, simply repeating a call for all ships, that the orbital needed immediate assistance.

"Who would attack a bunch of farmers?" Icky asked.

"If you want to undermine an entire society, strike at its food supply. We're all just a few meals from complete anarchy anyway," Funboy replied.

"Grim but true, Funboy," Torina said.

He managed a sigh. "Put that on my tomb."

ROLLING FIELDS WAS a series of concentric rings about three klicks across. The central hub contained the essential systems, power plant, comms, crew habitat, and other ancillary spaces, while each successive ring had a flat earth configuration, as Perry put it. Imagine a flat ring, set on edge so that one of its sides pointed directly at the sun—in this case, Teegarden's Star—then enclose that side in glass. Now imagine a bigger, concentric one and another, even bigger concentric one. That was the essential design of Rolling Fields.

Except the outermost of those rings was damaged along about a quarter of its diameter. Most of the damage was concentrated into a section about two hundred meters long. I'd thought the rest of it was unharmed, until Netty pointed out a smashed comm and scanner array on the hub.

"That explains their lack of comms," Perry said. We'd already informed the Guild, as well as Faalax and Gajur Prime, what had happened. Both the latter were surprised and assured us they were dispatching ships to help posthaste.

"Yeah. Whoever attacked them did it to leave them blind, deaf, and mute," Zeno put in.

"The location of that damage is very specific. It looks like whoever did this wasn't out to destroy the orbital, just that part of it," Essie said over the comm.

"Yeah, but what was there that they wanted so badly to destroy? It looks like just more crops," Torina added as we did a flyby about ten klicks away.

Torina sniffed. "Maybe somebody really, really hates their veggies."

But I shook my head as I eyed a zoomed-in view of the damage on the main display. "I suspect it's not what they were after, but who."

"What makes you say that?" Torina asked.

"Well, we've been sent here to escort some scientist, right? Escorting implies the need for an escort—"

"Which implies that they were under some sort of threat," Zeno finished, nodding.

When we were satisfied there was no immediate threat, we moved in to dock at an open and undamaged port. Essie kept the *Ngwenya* about a thousand klicks away, providing top cover against anyone showing up unexpectedly.

As soon as the airlock slid open, we were hit with a stew of smells—damp foliage, humid air, fertilizer, and an acrid tang of burning. We were greeted by a pair of tired and harassed-looking techs in overalls, a human woman, and a Nesit.

"It's about damn time you got here," the woman, whose name tag said *Wheeler*, snapped.

I gave what I hoped was a reassuring smile. "Sorry, we were en route here anyway and only just arrived. Have you called for help from Faalax or Gajur Prime?"

"We can't reach them. We can't reach anyone."

"Our comm system was shot to hell," the Nesit, whose tag said *Kelir-Nof*, added.

"Please tell me you called for more ships," Wheeler said.

I nodded and explained that we'd put out the call, and that ships were on the way. "In the meantime—what's your status? Is this orbital, like, sound? Or should we be looking at an evacuation?"

"Our engineers have said that structurally, we're okay. And the damaged sections have been isolated by airtight blast doors, which seem to be holding fine. We do have casualties, though—more than we were equipped to handle. So if you've got any medical supplies or expertise—"

I turned to Funboy.

He nodded. "Let me gather up what I can from the *Fafnir*, then you can take me to your infirmary." His morose, Eeyore-like tone didn't change—he might have been telling us he'd just found out he was being divorced. But he moved with purpose, speaking to a brisk professionalism underlying his gloomy exterior.

I turned back to Wheeler. "So what happened?"

"It was three ships. They claimed they were a research delegation from Tau Ceti. We told them we hadn't been informed about any delegations coming to visit, and they kept us strung along with some convincing bureaucratic bafflegab about mixed-up research communiques and lost briefing notes and the like. Whoever they were, they knew all the right buzzwords and how to use them."

"It kept us convinced long enough for them to get close and then start shooting," Kelir-nof added. "Their first attack took out our comms and scanners. One of them started hammering Outer Ring with lasers and stuff, then moved in and boarded through the openings they'd made. While that was happening, a second ship moved in and broke into the Hub. The third one stayed back, not getting involved.

"Probably top cover, just like Essie's doing for us right now," Torina said.

Without delay, I sent Icky and Zeno with Kelir-nof to go check with the orbital's engineering team to see if they could help. Torina, Perry, and I followed Wheeler toward the Hub, where she mentioned that the attackers had ransacked several labs and compartments, apparently looking for something.

"Any idea what?" I asked, touching both The Drop and Moonsword, then unsnapping their holster and scabbard respectively, making sure they were ready for use. Torina did the same with her sidearm and a big-assed Innsu knife she'd taken to carrying since our run-in with the fat Yonnox on Plenty.

Wheeler noticed and frowned. "Are you expecting trouble?"

"Are you one hundred percent certain the bad guys who attacked you didn't leave anyone on board?" I asked.

She missed a step, then shook her head. "No, I… I hadn't even thought of that. Do you think they did? We have people in the Hub."

"Do I think they *did*? No, probably not. Am I willing to bet my life on it? No, I am not," I said.

As we made our way along one of the spokes that connected the rings to one another and to the Hub, I quizzed Wheeler for as much detail as possible about what the bad guys did while they were here. When Torina asked her if all of the crew of the Rolling Fields was accounted for, she again seemed surprised.

"You mean you haven't checked?" I asked her, a little incredulous.

She waved her hands helplessly. "I'm a plant biologist. This isn't what I normally do!"

"What do you mean, what you normally do?"

"I'm standing in for the Station Director. He's away on other duties."

I exchanged a glance with Torina. "Is he now."

The fact that it took Wheeler a moment to even get what I was hinting at told me, as much as anything, that she was what she appeared to be—a guileless scientist suddenly thrust into a situation she'd never been trained for or expected to face. After all, who would attack a farming orbital?

She stopped. "Wait. You're not saying the Director was involved in this somehow, are you?"

I shook my head. "No, I'm not saying that, because I have no evidence that that's the case. But we can't rule it out either."

"But he's a *good* person. He'd never be involved in something like… like this."

I raised a hand to placate her, and because I sensed she was genuinely alarmed at the specter of betrayal. "Again, I'm not making any accusations here. It's my job to keep an open mind and examine all the possibilities."

"Kind of like a scientist," Perry added.

I gave him a look. "And he could be a good person and still be involved. Even good people can rack up gambling debts or do things to get themselves blackmailed—or, for that matter, can be coerced into doing things they don't want to do. I once worked with someone whose family was threatened by the bad guys to force him to do what they wanted."

Wheeler slumped a little. The harsh and ugly world of *realpolitik*, of bribery and extortion and intimidation, had intruded into her neat and tidy world of science. It was like walking into your own home, your safe haven from the world, and finding it had been tossed and robbed.

We resumed walking and reached the orbital's Hub to find evidence of the boarding action. Decks and bulkheads were marred by slug hits and laser scars. I saw some blood, but not as much as I'd feared.

Torina noticed the same thing. "They did a lot of shooting but didn't seem to hit much," she said, brushing her finger along a scorch mark.

"What, now we're fighting the Empire?" Perry asked, sounding alarmed. Torina gave him a puzzled look.

"The Empire? Who the hell are they?"

I shook my head. "Pay no attention to pop-culture bird. It is a good point, though. Assuming these were the Sorcerers, they sure didn't seem to be trying very hard to actually kill anyone. Seems a little out of character for them."

"If pop-culture bird could venture a guess, it's probably because they scared the ever-loving shit out of every one of these techs and scientists who aren't exactly, you know, the firefight sort of people. And every one of them is going to go and tell the story to others, probably embellishing how awful it was because that's what people who tell stories do," Perry said.

I nodded. "Yeah, that I can believe—not the Sorcerers suddenly becoming crappy shots. Sometimes, there's value in sheer terror."

We spent the next couple of hours working our way through the Hub with Wheeler and her people, trying to determine just what the Sorcerers had been after. It turned out to have mostly been a large quantity of high-end, research-related tech—chunky, mainframe computation systems that were cumbersome but still useful. By then, Wheeler's people had also worked up a list of everyone remaining on the station.

She slumped some more when she read it. "There are fourteen people missing."

I stepped away a few paces and lowered my voice into the comm. "Essie, have you scanned any bodies near the station?"

"One. We've already recovered it. Poor bastard was apparently blown out when that damaged ring decompressed."

I turned back to Wheeler. "We can account for one of them, unfortunately deceased. The others must have been taken by the Sorcerers—the ones who attacked you."

She shook her head, her face dull with a shell-shocked glaze. "Thirteen people, just... gone."

"Look at the list of those missing, please. What do they have in common? Anything? Are they all from one department, or one field of expertise, or—well, anything at all? If they are, that might help us understand what happened here," I said.

She skimmed the list. "These two are plant biologists. And this one is a systems tech. This is a hydroponics specialist, and she's in information management—"

She shook her head again. "I'm sorry. These people don't seem to have anything in common at all."

"Van, Essie, can you send me the list of those missing?"

I nodded to Torina, who'd uploaded the list to her data slate. She nodded back and tapped at it. A moment later, Essie replied.

"Yeah, I thought so. I think I know what—or who—they were after."

An image appeared on the data slate, that of a female humanoid vaguely reminiscent of Kharsweil's race, although distinctly different—tall, rangy, and tomboyish, with dark eyes and dark hair. She had metallic black circles inset around each eye, giving her a permanently startled appearance.

"Meet Adayluh Creel, the woman who might feed the stars," Essie said. Icky and Zeno arrived with Kelir-nof as he spoke.

Wheeler looked up. "Creel? She's a plant biologist with a specialty in productivity—getting the maximum caloric yield out of a unit of growth medium."

"Essie, what makes you think she was the target?" I asked.

"Because she was a key component of the undercover op I was just involved in—the one involving piracy of staple foodstuffs."

"Another piece of a nasty puzzle. It's like someone is angling toward using food shortages and starvation as a weapon," Torina said.

Zeno sighed. "As if weaponizing space-time wasn't enough."

Icky peered at the image on Torina's data slate. "Boss, we've gotta get her back."

I glanced up at her. "Icky, are you looking for justice or just hungry?"

"Both."

8

Essie loaded up with six of the most severe casualties to take them to somewhere with advanced medical care suited to a range of alien physiologies. Unfortunately, both Gajur Prime and Faalax were each mostly inhabited by single races, meaning their xenomedical capabilities were limited. It ultimately made the most sense to send them back to Anvil Dark. At the same time, Essie would take back a full report on what had happened here—and also try to get approval to get us read-in to the undercover op he'd been running, or at least get the files cracked open a little wider for us. In the absence of that, neither he nor Funboy had the authority to give us more than cursory information about it.

"Not that I knew much," Funboy said. "I was along mostly as a technical expert."

"Sure, but they must have wanted your specific expertise for something," Torina said.

He shrugged. "Maybe. I just do what I'm told."

I bit back a reply. I'd come to realize that Funboy wasn't just a gloomy and pessimistic sort of guy, but that it was baked right into his genes. Or, as Icky put it to him—

"Parties on your homeworld must be a real riot, huh?"

"We rarely have parties," Funboy replied.

"Color me unsurprised."

While Essie returned to Anvil Dark, we hung around Rolling Fields, continuing our investigation. Perry led our effort to determine why the computer equipment had been stolen from the Hub, Zeno and Icky combed over the battle damage to see what they could learn from it, and Funboy continued offering his medical expertise to help with the remaining wounded. Torina and I focused on the people who'd been taken. Adayluh Creel seemed like a pretty good bet, but we couldn't just assume it was all about her and leave it at that.

"You think the Sorcerers grabbed one person they were interested in and then a bunch more as a smokescreen?" Torina asked.

I shrugged. "That's how I'd do it if I was going to kidnap someone and delay any effort to come looking for them." I sighed at the list. "But, for all we know, they might have been after someone else entirely, so we have to check."

She nodded, and we split up the remaining list into six each, pulled their personnel files, and dug into the twelve missing individuals. In the midst of it, Netty interrupted with an urgent call from Essie.

The twist-comm message was weak and distorted. Netty had to filter and clean it up before we could even make out more than the fact Essie was talking to us. She finally ran the reconstructed message over a flickering, grainy image on the *Fafnir's* main display.

"Van, we were just attacked at Wolf 424, where we'd twisted for a nav fix. Some asshole popped... put some sort of super-luminal projectile right through us... knocked most of our systems offline and nearly breached the *Ngwenya*'s reactor... dead in space for now but got lucky... two other Peacemakers here chased off the bad guy... no ID on who attacked us. My AI thinks it... military grade, a twist-enhanced mass driver... a Powerfist... keep you posted."

The message ended, the display flicking back to its default display of time and essential ship data.

"Netty, is he receiving?" I asked.

"I've tried. There's no response. If I had to guess, I'd say he only ran his reactor long enough to transmit, then took it offline again," she replied.

"Shit."

"Netty, what's a Powerfist?" Torina asked.

"It's a code name for an Eridani military weapon, a twist-enhanced mass driver that can reduce the time-of-flight of a slug to nearly zero. The offset is that it's expensive, burns antimatter fuel, and has a phenomenally slow rate of fire. It's also prone to breaking down. And did I mention it's expensive? Public sources claim as much as ninety to a hundred thousand bonds per shot."

"Doesn't sound very practical."

"It isn't. The Eridani are still fiddling with it, trying to turn it into something more usable, but right now it would be considered experimental at best. It's a potential ship killer, but right now, it mostly kills bank accounts."

"So either the Eridani Federation just got themselves involved for some reason, or that tech has managed to leak out into the wider world," Torina said.

I nodded, still staring at the display. "I can't see it being the Eridani. They've got no obvious dog in this fight. I mean, we can't rule it out, but——" I shrugged and looked at Torina. "I think we have to assume that somebody somehow got their hands on one of these things. And since the attack targeted Essie's ship in particular, we further have to assume it's our bad guys."

Torina leaned back and sighed. "So now we've got a twist drive that can work inside a gravity well and potentially rip apart a planet and a mass driver that can shoot slugs that transcend the speed of light. And that's on top of all that other spiffy Sorcerer tech, like those funky cuffs they wear and, oh yeah, their identity theft capabilities and the horror show of their Cusp machines." She gave a thin, hard smile. "Have to admit, I'm kind of feeling outclassed."

I flashed her a grin. "But you've got me."

"Well, maybe we'll win anyway."

"I am mildly annoyed, woman."

"You adore me," Torina shot back, sitting up. "Anyway, what's our next move?"

I frowned at the blank display again. "That's a good question. I was kind of hoping a deep dive into the people who got kidnapped would tell us something, but"—I picked up a data slate from the *Fafnir*'s galley table, then dropped it again dismissively—"I think that's going to be a dead end. Your point about them being a smokescreen is probably bang on."

We sat in brooding silence for a moment, then Torina stood and stuck her hands in her pockets. "Maybe we're overthinking this. Why don't we do what we always do and follow the bonds? I mean, where do *they* lead us?"

"Well, let's assume that this really is about Adayluh Creel, and that we want to find her. Netty, feel like a chase?"

"Always, boss. It's what I'm for, after all. Where to?"

"Let's start by looking around where Adayluh was grabbed— that is, here. Is there anything like a… I don't know. Something like a pawn shop, a place you can buy and sell pretty much anything, no questions asked, anywhere nearby?"

"Gajur Prime is an obvious candidate."

"Hmm. No, not in this system. After all, from the available data, the bastards who attacked Rolling Fields were from outside the Teegarden's Star system and came straight here, right?"

"So outside of this system? That's everywhere, Van."

I smiled. "Okay, let's try somewhere between *right here* and *everywhere else*. Our Sorcerers might be vile, evil assholes, but even they're going to want to save money on gas, not to mention avoid losing weeks or months of objective time twisting here from some distant place like Spindrift. So let's say candidates within a nice and easy twist distance of Teegarden's Star—one that wouldn't burn too much fuel or cost them more than a few days."

"There really aren't any locations in known space that qualify. There is a place just outside the spinward boundary of known space, but we don't know much about it."

I studied the star chart Netty put on the display, with one system highlighted in red.

"Hold On. That's what it's called?"

"It is now. It was established as a unique type of mining operation around a Jupiter-like gas giant. Instead of skimming the upper atmosphere like Plenty, though, this was designed to take advantage of plumes of material ejected from the gas giant and channeled by its magnetic field into a torus of vapor surrounding the planet. The idea was that the station would orbit right in the middle of the torus and scoop up the ejected material as it did."

"I notice this is all past-tense—*was* established, *was* designed to, the idea *was*. I gather it didn't work," I said.

"Unfortunately, no. It simply couldn't collect enough material fast enough to pay for itself. The company that built it finally went under about thirty years ago, leaving the place in a sort of owner-ship limbo. Nobody wanted it, so it kind of just came into possession of the people living there."

"So they got abandoned aboard a defunct industrial project? That's not very nice," Torina said.

"It is not. Anyway, it's still inhabited, more or less. It doesn't have much of a profile otherwise. Guild intelligence notes sporadic criminal activity there, but it mostly seems that the people living on Hold On are doing just that, holding on, at least for as long as they can."

"Sounds like a desperate place."

"Yeah, it does." I tapped the red icon on the display. "And desperation means everything is potentially for sale, for the right price. That usually includes information. Shall we?"

IT ALWAYS BOTHERS me when people say things like, *if you don't like where you live, why don't you just move? If you don't like the politics, or the crime, or the corruption or whatever, why don't you just get out?*

That's easy to *say*. The trouble is that uprooting yourself, and your family if you have one, and moving to another place doesn't happen for free. It costs money to leave, it costs money to make the move, and it costs money to set yourself back up at the other end— if you can find a place to live and a job and manage all the other necessities in the first place. Sometimes, you end up stuck where you are, whether you like it or not.

That was very much the case for the decrepit shithole called Hold On.

Spindrift, Dregs, Crossroads, and Plenty had an element of shit- holery to them, too. But they were at least thriving, even if a lot of the thriving came from criminality. An underground economy was still an economy. Even a slum was usually part of a city, giving it a reason to exist. But none of that was true for Hold On. This place was more like one of those old ghost towns that had once been pros- perous, but from which the prosperity had long since moved on. A cluster of shacks around an old, played-out mine site in the Australian Outback, the American Southwest, or the northern wilderness of Canada was just that, a cluster of shacks. People could still live there, but they were so far removed from everything else that even criminals couldn't be bothered with them. There was just no good reason for anyone to be there.

And yet, here at Hold On, there were people. They were the descendants of those stranded here by uncaring corporate greed thirty years before—the ones who'd gone to operate the place in good faith but were abandoned and forgotten when the place didn't prove profitable. What remained was a pathetic huddle of desperate people doing their best to just hold on and live up to their ramshackle home's name.

I shook my head at the sprawling structure filling the forward view. It had once been a spherical station about a klick in diameter, sprouting towering, gantry-like structures from its opposite poles. According to Netty, these were the emitters for the magnetic scoops that had been intended to slurp up the gaseous effluent from the gas giant looming nearby. They'd long since been built up with a mismatched collection of cargo pods, disused spaceship hulls, old fuel tanks, girders, cables, and all manner of sundry bits and pieces. The smooth curves of the spherical hull were likewise covered with a bolted-on sprawl of even less reputable flotsam, making the whole thing look like a jumble of scrap that had slowly accreted into a single massive agglomeration of junk. In short, a disaster waiting to happen.

"Is that rust?" Torina asked. "How the hell do things rust in space?"

"Oh, I suspect they were rusty long before they were ever brought into space," Zeno said.

I curled my lip at the dreary mega-mess. Atmospheric gas must have vented from some of the corroded remains.

"Worst timeshare ever," I said.

"Actually, that's in Bayonne, New Jersey, and it overlooks a landfill. You can't really appreciate it until the full heat of summer," Perry said.

"And how would you know that?"

"Your grandfather was looking for an out-of-the-way place to take Valint for a few days off. He asked me to check some places out for him."

"Van, if you ever take me some place like that, it's over," Torina said.

I pulled out a data slate from the pocket beside my seat and mimed tapping on it. "Scratch timeshare in Bayonne, New Jersey, check. Now then, who's going to——"

"We've got a local asking for a landing fee," Netty cut in.

Icky scowled. "*Bah*, they should be paying *us* to come to their shithole station."

"Now, Icky, be nice. I doubt that many of these people are living here because they want to. Netty, tell them we'll be happy to pay, in person, just as soon as they direct us to a working airlock."

"That isn't going to break free of the station as soon as we dock at it would be nice," Funboy put in.

I nodded. "Yeah. Not breaking off would be nice."

———————

Torina touched a grimy bulkhead, pulled her gloved finger back, and grimaced. "What I don't get is why somebody doesn't... I don't know, *do* something about this place. Tau Ceti, the Eridani Federation, somebody. It's an embarrassment, frankly, that a place like this is even allowed to exist."

We decided to wear our full suits, with helmets slung, just in case the whole damned place depressurized—that's how bad the orbiting tenement called Hold On was. I didn't even want to touch the decks with my booted feet, much less the bulkheads. I lifted a foot with a soft, wet, crackling sound.

"Yeah, this is sticky with an extra 'ick.'"

"So stick-icky? Sticky-icky?" Perry said.

"I see where you're heading with this bird, and it's gonna be *kicky*-icky, if you don't watch out," Icky snapped back.

"Van, she's threatening me without any provocation whatsoever. I'm clearly the aggrieved party here, and—"

"Oh for—would you two just belt up, please? And Icky, would you take your place as we discussed while we wait for our official reception party to show up?"

After Icky crammed herself into a tool locker just outside the airlock where we'd docked the *Fafnir*'s workboat and closed the door as much as she could, Zeno spoke up. "To answer your question, Torina, no one does anything about this place because no one wants to assume responsibility for it. Responsibility leads to liability, and no one wants that."

Torina sighed. "Yeah, I get that, but still—how can we have the ability to fold space, but we can't give a few people a decent place to live?"

It was an excellent question but also one we all knew was rhetorical, hanging asked and unanswered over every advanced society since time immemorial. In any case, we were interrupted by the arrival of a gang of several thuggish types, clearly intent on misbehaving. There were five humanoids, a pair of Gajur, and a hairy, chimp-like alien I didn't recognize, all in grubby vac suits. They were draped with an array of slug throwers and vicious-looking melee weapons. I smiled as they approached.

"I assume you gentlemen are the official reception party."

Their leader, a man with a face like creased leather, returned an evil grin. "Yeah. Sure. Official. So you can hand over that landing fee. Oh, and there's a surcharge."

I kept smiling. "How much?"

"However much you've got. And if it turns out to not be

enough, well, I'm willing to bet your Guild will cough up the balance to get one of their precious Peacemakers back."

I sighed. "Now is this any way to greet visitors to your lovely station?"

"Yes, if word gets out that you shake down new arrivals, it's going to really undermine your appeal as a tourism destination," Zeno said.

"Might even prompt us to leave a bad review—you know, one star, would not recommend," I added.

The thugs closed menacingly closer. "You're funny. That's good. They say laughter's the best medicine, and you're gonna need lots of medicine."

I sighed again. "Icky?"

She swung open the locker and stepped out, unlimbering her hammer as she did. "I learned something in there, boss. I kinda stink," she said.

Torina wrinkled her nose. "How can you tell, Icky, when the air smells like"—she narrowed her eyes at your reception party—"well, them."

Icky lumbered forward until she stood alongside me.

"When it comes to how you smell, Icky, I prefer the term *natural*. But you do you, big girl. Oh, this is—actually, he never gave his name, but I don't think it matters. Anyway, he's trying to extort money out of us so we can begin questioning this den of criminals about our stolen ally," I said.

She leaned menacingly toward the man. "Really? Extort, as in intimidate?"

"Pretty much."

"Are you intimidated, Van?"

I shrugged. "Not particularly."

She grinned, a nightmare of teeth poised above the man's face. "Neither am I."

The man took in the new odds—eight against six, but we had Icky—were brandishing our own arsenal of weapons, and, most importantly, weren't backing down from him and his gang, not even a centimeter. The truth was my gut was tightened toward the inevitability of a fight. Not because I wanted one, but because these guys really had nothing to lose. They were desperate in a way that actually made them more dangerous than their counterparts on Spindrift or Plenty.

I could even see the gang's ringleader sizing up the odds. Before he could decide *screw it* and take his chances against us, I spoke up.

"How about we split the difference here? I'll give you five hundred bonds in *landing fees*, and you'll be our tour guide?"

The man glared from Icky, to me, then shrugged. "What the hell. I think five hundred will cover it, don't you guys?" he said over his shoulder.

His gang muttered and nodded, a mixed air of anger and relief among them. I handed over the bonds and waited while they split it up, then the gang dispersed until only their leader remained. He turned back to us.

"Seriously, what could you possibly want aboard our little shithole anyway?"

"Well, first, how about your name?"

He narrowed his eyes at me. "Let's go with Garen. I don't think that name'll show up on any warrants."

"Perry, we have any outstanding warrants for Garen? Serious ones, murder or anything like that?"

"Garen? Like, just Garen, nothing else? No, we don't."

"Good enough for me. Okay, Garen, I'd like you to take us to the shittiest, scummiest bar in the place."

He grinned. "Oh, hell, that's easy. I own it."

We fell in behind him as he led the way. I glanced back and noticed Funboy, who'd been lurking at the back of our group until now, was fully suited up with his helmet in place.

"Funboy, what the hell are you doing keeping yourself sealed up like that?"

"Someone's got to avoid breathing the stew of toxins and pathogens that passes for air in this place—to, you know, deal with everyone else's inevitable debilitating illness."

Zeno curled her lip at him. "Leave it to you to make a shitty place suddenly seem even shittier."

9

THE TOOLSHED ENCAPSULATED Hold On in a single, ramshackle compartment. It was a dim, smoky space enclosed in rusty, grimy bulkheads, one of which was in the process of buckling under the weight of the structure above it. The artificial gravity wobbled, varying in slow rolls I felt in my stomach like a roller-coaster ride that would never end. We had to pick our way around patrons who studiously ignored us, including a couple slumped over entirely who might have been dead.

"They'd better not be. They both have open tabs," Garen said when I enquired about them. Near the bar, a bot banged into a bulkhead, again and again, apparently determined to pass through an opening that didn't exist.

I opened my mouth to speak, but the ceaseless *whirr-THUNK-whirr-THUNK* of the bot kept cutting me off. I glanced at two scruffy aliens sitting nearby.

"How long has that been going on?" I asked, raising my voice and pointing at the bot.

Whirr-THUNK.

One of them shrugged. "About a week."

Whirr-THUNK.

"And no one—"

THUNK-whirr.

"—has thought to stop it?"

Whirr—

Icky unlimbered and swung her hammer in an arc, slamming it into the bot and halting it amid a shower of sparks and more acrid smoke.

The alien facing me shrugged. "Not my bot, not my problem."

I glanced at Torina, who just said, "Wow."

I turned to Garen, who'd gone behind the bar. He nodded at a sallow human in a filthy apron. "Berk, we have customers. Get off your ass and do your job."

Berk leaned on the bar and leered at Torina. "Believe it or not, I'm single."

"You may be surprised to learn that I *do* believe it. Quite readily, in fact," she replied.

The man grinned, displaying the gaps of several missing teeth, then turned to Zeno. "How about you? You're kinda cute."

"Despite the fact that it's the best offer I've had in a while, I'll pass, thanks. I prefer my consorts a little less—well, *you.*"

Icky leaned on the bar. "How about me?"

Berk looked her up and down, then shrugged. "Works for me."

She blinked. "Really?"

I intervened. "Icky, go smash another bot or something. Look, we're here for someone specific," I said, then described Adayluh Creel to Garen and Berk but didn't use her name. They both gave me blank looks that I believed.

"Oh, I'd have remembered someone like that, believe me," Berk said, his leer firmly in place.

Okay, it had been a longshot. I went on to ask about any Trinduk visiting Hold On—and got a hit.

"Trinduk? Those creepy assholes? Yeah, we had a cadre of them here about… oh, a week ago. Maybe two," Garen said.

I reached into a pouch on my harness, extracted another five hundred bonds, and offered it over. Garen snatched it up before anyone but Berk could see it. Berk immediately spoke up.

"Hey, Garen, what's with that—"

Garen slammed a hand over Berk's mouth. I thought about putting my own flesh anywhere near that snaggle-toothed maw and shuddered a bit.

"Yeah, yeah, you'll get your cut, you miserable piece of shit," he snapped.

Berk spoke, his mouth muffled. "Ah uv oo oo, ah-ren."

He pulled his hand away. "What do you want to know?" he asked me.

"Everything you can tell me about the Trinduk that were here—who they talked to, what they talked about, all of it."

"Not much to tell. They spent some time with Gygarus, talked to him for a while all secret-like, then left."

"Okay, and who, or what, is Gygarus?"

"Yonnox. A smuggler. Specializes in weapons and getting high on Windup."

"What the hell's Windup?"

Perry answered. "A powerful narcotic that's administered through the eyes."

"Through the *eyes*?"

Torina sniffed. "Yuck. And ouch."

"Yeah. Users wipe it right into their eyes," Perry said. "It's highly addictive and super illegal, which isn't much of a problem because it's also super unpopular."

"Go figure, sticking the stuff into your eyes," I said.

"It's not unpopular around here," Garen said.

I grimaced. "Okay, so this Gygarus—is he around right now?"

"I saw him yesterday. Not sure if he's still around or not, though. He comes and goes."

"Van, Netty says a ship registered indirectly to a Yonnox named Gygarus is docked here," Perry said.

Garen shrugged. "There you go. He's probably wasted on Windup, though, so not sure you'll get much out of him besides belligerence and drool."

"Charming." I passed Garen another two hundred and fifty bonds. "There might be more, if I need your services again."

"I'll be here. Hell, I'll even give you folks a free round of drinks."

I looked at the glasses—stained, cloudy, and chipped. Garen brandished a bottle that looked remarkably like mucous but with an insouciant hint of glitter mixed in. Wisely, I shook my head. This was where Funboy and I had a meeting of the minds.

Funboy let out a dolorous sigh—as if he knew any other kind. "One time, when I was young, my eldest matron thought I was lacking in Manners of Way. She arranged for me to be transported for instruction and cleansing, all at a Purification Tent in the

Moxuvar Swamp of Wailing. This may surprise you, but it had very little tourism."

"But of course." I drummed my fingers on the filthy bar, then waved. In for a penny, in for a pound. "Continue."

Funboy lifted a frizzy brow. "I know. It's gripping. So, in the middle of this swamp, being lashed with water reeds and forced to recite songs about the heart of a loving mother, I was asked to consume a *fultica*—that's like a kilogram, or thereabouts—of semi-sentient bivalves that had purple eyes and fangs. When you pried their shells apart, they screamed, and then they bit you as you tried to eat them."

"For the love of—why?" Torina asked.

"They're mildly hallucinogenic, and they build character."

"Of course," I said. "And you are sharing this heartwarming tale of youth because?"

Funboy lifted the bottle of boogers, as I had come to think of it, and swirled the foul liquid in a sedate ooze. "I would do that again before I drank this shit, Garen."

I mimed wiping a tear. "Funboy, you tell the *best* stories."

Icky looked at the bottle, then took it in a massive hand and shook the hell out of it. She looked... curious. "Garen?"

"Yes?"

"Does this scream when you drink it?"

He shook his head. "No. But you might."

———

WE PULLED BACK to the workboat for a strategy session but had barely gotten started before Garen called me over the comm channel I'd given him.

"Ask and you'll receive, Peacemaker. Gygarus just popped into *The Toolshed*, looking for more Windup."

"We'll be right there."

"Bring more money."

"We'll see how this turns out." I cut the comm and turned to the others, sending Torina, Zeno, and Funboy to stake out Gygarus's ship, while I took Icky and Perry back to *The Toolshed*. A pair of lowlife assholes tried to accost us on the way, but Icky slammed one in the bulkhead with bone-cracking force and the other beat a hasty retreat. I glanced down at our would-be assailant, who was moaning on the deck, and shrugged as I went by.

"Play stupid games, win stupid prizes."

Perry paused as well. "What part of seven-foot-tall, four-armed primate with massive hammer did you not get, anyway?"

We left him there and pushed on to the bar. We arrived in time to see a sinewy Yonnox wiping what must be Windup into his eyes at a table against one wall. I didn't really need Garen's nod to know this was our guy.

"Gygarus?"

He blinked up at me, his eyes red and bleary. I opened my mouth to go on, but he suddenly exploded out of his chair, flung out his arm, and jabbed me with a wicked stiletto-like blade that had suddenly appeared in his hand. It thumped harmlessly against my b-suit, but it made me flinch enough that he had time to dodge past Icky and vanish from the bar with surprising speed.

I sighed. "After him, boys." I started jogging along in Gygarus's wake. I wasn't especially worried about catching up with him, assuming he was heading for his ship and his intended escape. And, sure enough, after a half-assed chase, Gygarus ended up crashing right into the waiting arms of Torina and Zeno, who we'd already alerted.

He stumbled back, brandishing his knife and shouting. Another Yonnox appeared in the airlock, a slug pistol half-raised, whereupon Zeno jammed her own gun into his face.

"Your call, my friend," she said. The Yonnox looked cross-eyed at the gaping muzzle almost touching his nose, then dropped his weapon with a clatter.

"Get away from me! Get back!" Gygarus snapped, swinging his blade from me, to Icky, and back to me.

"So Windup makes you paranoid, too. Great," I said, holding up a hand. "Look, Gygarus, I just want some information."

"No you don't! You wanna kill me, just like the rest!"

"Dude, seriously, if I wanted to kill you I'd just pull this massive gun I got bouncing on my hip and blow you away."

He blinked back at me. Surprisingly, that seemed to cut through the narcotic fog a little. "What... do you want then?"

"A list of your recent arms sales."

"Does he look like a Virgo?" Perry asked.

I glared at Perry. "Can we skip the astrology and just keep acting like hardasses for now?"

"What's a Virgo?" Funboy asked.

Torina answered. "Oh, I know this. According to Earthly humans, who for some reason base it on the relative positions of stars in their sky, it's a person who's methodical, a quick thinker, loves lists, but is also self-effacing and humble——"

"Since when are you into *astrology?*" Perry asked.

She shrugged. "I'm trying to learn about Earth so I can better understand Van."

I glanced at her. "So you decided to learn about *astrology* to better understand me?"

"I guess I'm a Virgo then," Funboy said. "I like lists."

"Yeah, of potential causes of death," Icky said.

"I'm just being prudent—"

"Folks, can we stay focused on the matter at hand, please? Our Yonnox friend here?" I said.

Funboy stepped forward. "Do you want me to debilitate this one like I did the last one? I know how to make it particularly painful, if that would be helpful."

Gygarus shook his head. "I can hear you, you know."

Funboy blinked up at Gygarus through his helmet. "I know. That was the point. To be threatening. Did it work?"

Gygarus turned his wild, red eyes to me. "What do you *want?*"

"You sell weapons, right?"

"Uh—no, that's illegal—"

Funboy reached for him. The sight of the smaller alien reaching for him must have triggered his paranoia because he yelped and shrank back. "Okay, fine, yes, I sell weapons sometimes! Call off your muscle!"

I glanced down at Funboy, essentially a slow loris in a spacesuit.

Muscle? Really? That Windup must be potent stuff.

"There's an Eridani weapon called a Powerfist—a twist-enabled mass driver. Have you sold any lately?"

Gygarus blinked back at me fast. "*Sold?* No."

"But?"

"But, I had two stolen from me. And I want them back." He blinked some more. "Can I put in a complaint, get you investigating this? It is a crime, right?"

"You want me to investigate the theft of experimental military-grade weapons that you undoubtedly stole yourself?"

"Ah—well, when you put it that way, no. Forget it."

I leaned in. "Who stole them from you? And where?"

"System called Bugout, down in The Deeps. Bastards down there have a stranglehold on everything," Gygarus replied, licking his lips. He blinked even faster. I sensed that I had to move quickly, before the Windup took him too far off into La-La Land and he lost his grip on lucidity entirely.

"Who? *Who* has a stranglehold on everything?" I asked him.

He opened his mouth—

And his head exploded, spattering the bulkhead beside him with sloppy gore.

Commotion erupted around me, Icky shouting, Torina pulling me back, and Zeno shooting at someone, her gunshot clapping against the surrounding structure like a church bell that made my head ring. I glanced at the direction Gygarus's head had been splashed, then I turned and looked the opposite way, up an intersecting corridor, one of three that converged just outside this airlock. It billowed with pale yellowish vapor.

"Shit, suit up!" I shouted, grabbing my helmet and snapping it into place. Funboy extracted an instrument from his harness as the vapor wafted around us and consulted it.

"Neurotoxin, military grade. See, this is why I keep my helmet on all the time. Death is always just a breath away," he said over the comm.

Perry had taken off after the assassin but had to give up the chase when he detected an explosive charge planted on a bulkhead just ahead. By the time we were able to clear it, the shooter was long gone, vanished into the labyrinthine bowels of Hold On.

"We could spend days looking for him in here," Torina muttered.

I nodded. "Yeah. And we'd be risking our lives doing it. That was a well-planned hit."

"Who the hell keeps that sort of expertise just hanging around a place like this?" Zeno asked.

"Someone who can afford it," Perry replied.

We returned to the remains of Gygarus. "Well, it wasn't a total bust, at least. We got a location, Bugout, somewhere down in The Deeps, at least," I offered, sighing down at his body. "Just when I thought we were making a connection, too. It's so hard to make friends as an adult."

NETTY WAS unsure as to the exact location of Bugout—it could have been one of several systems, based on the scant intelligence available to the Guild.

"We haven't had much to do with The Deeps, so our knowledge is pretty limited," she said as we settled back into the *Fafnir*. It was nice to put the grit and grime of Hold On behind us and be somewhere I didn't mind touching stuff with my bare flesh.

"Seems like a pretty gaping hole in the Guild's intel," Torina said, taking a grateful sip of coffee she'd just poured for herself.

"To be fair, there's way more space out there than there's Guild capability to monitor it, especially outside of known space. We don't even have jurisdiction in The Deeps," Perry replied.

I nodded at that, but we had another angle. "The Guild might not know much about The Deeps, but I suspect I know who would."

Perry looked at me. "The GKU?"

"Bingo. A lot of them spend their time lurking outside known space, so some of them must have spent time in The Deeps."

Torina looked at me over the rim of her mug. "So who are you going to ask?"

I stared back at her. "If you mean my dear old mom, I'm not ready for that yet. I was thinking more along the lines of Gerhardt, or maybe Groshenko."

I glanced around. I still felt a little self-conscious talking about the GKU so openly in front of the crew but had decided to hell with it after our battle with the Tenants and the Seven Stars League. They had a right to know about this mysterious force and its inscrutable agenda that had inserted itself into our lives. But they also all seemed to know that the specific subject of my mother was a particularly sensitive one, so I got nods in return and that was it.

"Van, before you make any long-term plans, we've received a message from Master Kharsweil. He's ordering us back to Anvil Dark," Netty said

"Is he now?"

"He's pretty explicit. We are to report back to Anvil Dark—and I'm quoting here—forthwith, for a new assignment."

"Sounds like more tug-of-war going on among the Masters," Torina said.

I gave a curt nod. "Yeah, and we're the rope." I frowned down at my feet for a moment, then made up my mind.

"Perry, what can Kharsweil realistically do to us if we don't immediately obey his orders?"

"He could get mad."

"Oh, I'm kind of counting on that. I mean, what substantive things can he do to us?"

"As long as Gerhardt's willing to support you as his Justiciar, not much. The Guild Charter is clear that a Justiciar is primarily answerable to their Patron Master in all ways. That takes precedence over any other Master's demands."

"I'll say it again—that's probably why Gerhardt made you his Justiciar," Torina said.

"Yeah, almost like he knew there might be trouble coming. Netty, send a message back to Anvil Dark—to Gerhardt. Tell him we're following a lead in our Crimes Against Order case and heading to Helso."

Torina stopped with her mug to her lips. "Helso? What sort of lead are we following there?"

"The kind that I just made up out of thin air. Frankly, I just want to make a point to Kharsweil that we're not going to instantly jump when he expects it."

"So why are we really going to Helso?"

"Two reasons. One, the prick used the term *forthwith*."

"And the second, dear?" Torina asked, her eyes dancing with glee.

"The same reason we usually go. I think we've earned a couple days off."

"The veranda. Wine. A couple of sunsets. You sure do read my mind," Torina said, her lips curving upward in a bow.

I leaned down to kiss her, earning a stare from Perry. "I'm a team player."

She narrowed her eyes in mock anger. "As long as that team only has two players."

Icky sighed in disgust. "And you say me not wearing pants is gross. Romance is *way* worse."

———

To say Kharsweil was unimpressed was an understatement. We received two more messages from him, each more heated than the last. We also received a transmission from Gerhardt, which I took in my cabin.

"Why are you antagonizing Kharsweil?" he asked.

"Actually, I'd argue it's the other way around. Why is Kharsweil suddenly singling us out for attention? I mean, there are a whole lot of Peacemakers out there that can run his errands."

Gerhardt gave me a hard look. "Kharsweil is still a Master, Tudor, and is entitled to the respect owed him."

"Oh, I'm giving him all the respect I believe he's entitled to. And while we're on the subject, the last job he gave us, escorting an unspecified scientific person who turned out to be this Adayluh Creel, went completely sideways. She's gone missing, but he just so happens to have *another* new job for us? Doesn't that strike you as a touch convenient?"

"It's not my place to presume the intentions of a fellow Master," Gerhardt said, but his voice lacked its usual conviction. I smiled at his silent admission.

"Even if you have doubts about them?"

"I never said that."

"You didn't have to."

Gerhardt stared back at me for a moment. "Tudor, you're playing an increasingly dangerous game here. I can back you up only so much. Kharsweil is well-connected, both inside the Guild and outside of it."

"You mean with the GKU."

"Again, I didn't say that."

"Again, you didn't have to."

"You've got three days to follow up on this so-called lead, Tudor, and then you'll have to respond to Kharsweil. There are certain bridges I'm not prepared to burn on your behalf—at least, not without a much better reason than this."

"Understood. And thank you."

Gerhardt signed off, and I leaned back in my seat. Three days on Helso was more than I'd expected. But that was good. I could use two of them to genuinely relax. As for the third one, though, we had work to do. We had about a dozen different ways we could proceed from here but could only pick one of them.

I braced myself to stand but didn't and just kept staring at the terminal. Torina's hinting at my mother had stuck with me, like gum on my shoe. Eventually, I was going to have to talk to her. She'd given me the comm channel to do just that.

I sat a while longer, staring at the terminal, then stood and headed back for the *Fafnir*'s cockpit. I'd told Torina I wasn't ready to talk to my mother, and I meant it. Eventually, though, I'd have to *make* myself ready for it. At some point, I needed to hear from this woman what story she'd told herself when she left, how she'd given herself permission to give birth to me, then walk out of my life.

But not today.

WE ARRIVED to find the Helso Self-Defense Force, a small but capable fleet of ships, engaged in a training exercise. The planetary leaders had bulked up the force to eight class 8 corvettes and two class 9 frigates, a respectable amount of firepower for a single planet with a relatively small population. More critically, it was a lot of expense, suggesting that the leading families—including Torina's, the Milons—had gone all-in in seeing to their own defense.

"Actually, we had help from the Schegith," her father told me when we landed at the Milon Estate. He was a Commander in the Self-Defense Force but had taken leave to deal with some business matters and had stayed groundside during the current exercise. He now lounged on the terrace overlooking the estate, fussing with something on a data pad.

"The Schegith? So your relationship with them is working out, I gather," I said, accepting a glass of wine from Torina's mother and taking a seat. The combination of placid, pastoral view, warm light from Van Maanen's Star, and a cool breeze rendered the moment a nearly perfect one. I leaned back in the chair gratefully and sipped at the wine as the first star pulsed into view, a bright point low on the smudged horizon.

Her father nodded carefully. "They take a little getting used to, but yes, they're damned good people. They speak very highly of you, by the way." He looked up and smiled as Torina sat nearby. "And you too, my dear. But you're my daughter, so I'd expect you to be eminently lovable."

The rest of the crew filtered onto the terrace. Zeno and Icky had been here several times before, and Torina's parents greeted them warmly. Funboy moved right to the railing around the terrace and stood, blinking at the view.

Torina's father sat up. "This must be the new crewmember Torina mentioned to me while you guys were inbound." He stood and offered Funboy his hand.

Funboy looked at it, then blinked up at Torina's father. "Please don't take this the wrong way, but physical contact is one of the primary means of pathogenic transmission."

"Funboy, right?"

"That's what they call me, yes."

Her father smiled and withdrew his offered hand. "I'm sure they do."

I grinned and sipped some more wine. Torina's mother gave me an expectant smile. "What do you think?"

"About the wine? It's very nice."

"It's our first batch."

"Oh, you're making wine now?"

She nodded. "Thanks to the Synergists and the work they did to restore our land, it's become almost shockingly fertile. We decided to try our hand at a bit of a vineyard. The grapes were imported from Tuscany."

"Tuscany, as in Earth?"

She nodded.

I took another sip. It was good, and I wasn't much of a wine drinker. Bourbon was more my thing—it had a rambunctious, kick-ass-and-take-names character to it that I always found more interesting than the refined nature of wine.

Still, I held up the glass. "Well, if this first batch is any indication, you've got a winner here."

Zeno and Icky were both eager to try it. Funboy, to no one's surprise, declined.

"Ethanol is a metabolic toxin," he said.

I'd never heard six people manage to sigh in perfect unison before.

10

WE SPENT the next couple of days just lounging around the Milon estate, eating our body weight in cheese, and achieving very little. I spent a few hours with the Innsu Master, Cataric, in his dojo, fighting bouts with him and Torina. Zeno, Funboy, and Icky knocked off some minor maintenance tasks on the *Fafnir*, and we all perfected a new napping skill in which we fell asleep on the veranda —as a crew—then awoke just in time for cocktails and dinner.

It was a true feat of dissolute relaxation, and I saluted our newfound ability by draining a glass of excellent wine just as a plate of fried cheese was passed around.

"Pregaming on the veranda is the single greatest achievement of my career," I announced, taking three more triangles of cheese.

Icky agreed, with enthusiasm. "Way better than, um—"

"Work?" Torina offered.

Icky pointed with her glass. "Yeah. That."

I'd intended to make full use of the three days Gerhardt had given us, but at the end of the second, Netty put through a call from someone who asked to speak to me in private.

I sighed and headed back for the *Fafnir*, which was on the landing pad a few hundred meters from the estate. When I arrived and settled into the pilot's seat, I found myself facing the image of someone who could have been the male version of my grandmother, Valint. He was pale, slender, and strikingly handsome—similar, it struck me, to the way I'd envisioned the fantasy notion of an elf—elegant, but aloof.

"Van Tudor here," I said.

"Yes. I am Ausburk, a fellow Knight Errant."

I nodded. By introducing himself as a Knight Errant rather than a Peacemaker, he was declaring his primary allegiance to the Galactic Knights Uniformed. Technically, I held the same title in the GKU, but I didn't use it. I still had greatly mixed feelings about the GKU, a mishmash of suspicion about their true motives, worry about their apparent belief that they existed at least partly outside the laws they ostensibly enforced—and, of course, resentment about my mother, who seemingly wielded enormous influence in the secretive organization, or at least one of its splintered parts.

I put on a smile. "Nice to meet you. What can I do for you?"

"Assist me with a problem, I'm hoping. You're currently at Van Maanen's Star, correct?"

"I am, yes."

"Then you are considerably closer than I am to Tau Ceti, specifically the planet Fulcrum. There's an auction occurring there involving several ships, and I'm hoping you can attend."

"An auction." I shook my head. "I'm sorry, but why do you need me to attend a ship auction?"

"Because one of the ships involved is stolen."

"Ah, okay. So you want me to go there and impound it?"

Ausburk frowned. "I'm afraid it's a little more complicated than that."

I smiled with maximum patience. "It always is."

"One of the ships being put up for auction is a class 5 planetary defense cutter. It was purchased from an aging Fren-Okun matron, who happens to be my engineer's beloved great aunt."

I shook my head again. "Wait—did you just say it was *purchased?* Because I thought you said it was *stolen.*"

"It was purchased under false pretenses by a Yonnox—" The next word didn't translate, which typically happened when someone used a profanity so race-specific that the translator couldn't find anything even close to matching.

"I'm sorry, it would appear that your language lacks a word sufficient to describe someone so foul and contemptible as to deserve being tossed out an airlock," Ausburk said.

I grinned. "Oh, no it doesn't, believe me. I can offer a few suggestions, but how about *asshole.*"

He mouthed the word, asshole, taking a few tries to get it right. "Asshole," he finally said, then brightened. "Yes, asshole. It's suitably acerbic, if a bit undergunned for the moment. It will do."

"I'm glad I could share my culture with you."

"As am I. So, this Yonnox asshole convinced the elderly Fren that he was an *adoptive spirit,* or some such bullshit."

I smirked, noting that his language had an analog for *bullshit.*

Asshole was anatomical and accordingly limited, but *bullshit*, it seemed, was universal.

"And he convinced her to sell him the ship," I said.

"That's correct."

"Well, okay—the trouble is, though, that if the sale was made in accordance with applicable laws, then I'm not sure what we can do. I mean, that's more of a civil matter, right? Not a criminal one?"

"I consider it criminal."

"Alright, but if I show up and claim the ship was stolen, and this Yonnox *asshole* just produces a duly executed bill of sale and—well, then what?"

"Then you use your best judgment as to how to seize the ship and return it to its rightful owner. I would consider this a personal favor. I'm sending you the details now," Auburk said.

I sat back. And there it was. I'd just mused a moment ago that the GKU had an arrogant, above-the-law streak running through it, and Ausburk had put it on full display. If the old Fren got conned out of her ship, well, that sucked, but cons could be tough to prove. I'd have to show not only criminal intent—the good old *mens rea*, or guilty mind—but also a criminal act. And that would depend on just how infirm the old Fren was, which all added up to a complicated case with an uncertain outcome.

But as I skimmed the summary that Ausburk sent, I sat up. The Yonnox—and we seemed to be dealing with a lot of nefarious Yonnox lately—was identified as one Parlix Tarik, a true miscreant with a long rap sheet. It listed extortion, blackmail, making threats, theft, smuggling—

And weapons trafficking. A *lot* of weapons trafficking, notably including several indictments for running weapons into and out of known space.

"Ausburk, I'll make you a deal. I'll go interrupt this auction and seize that ship under some pretense. At that point, though, I'm handing the case over to you to dispose of."

"I see. That's unfortunately inconvenient for me—"

"Hold on. You won't owe me anything going forward. We'll just call it a wash."

Ausburk narrowed his almond eyes at me. "Really."

I sat back and nodded. "Really."

A moment of silence hung between us. He was obviously waiting for me to go on, to explain why I was willing to do this for free.

But I didn't. It wasn't much of a victory, but it gave me more than a little satisfaction to put the GKU on the receiving end of a secret for a change.

He finally nodded. "Very well—"

"Van, I hate to interrupt, but we just received another message from Kharsweil. To say that he is annoyed would be an understatement," Netty said.

I sighed. "Oh. Right. Master Kharsweil is after me to—I don't know, go hand out parking tickets or something—"

"I'll take care of Kharsweil," Ausburk said with an airily dismissive wave. "You may rest assured that his vitriol—at least in this matter—will end with a word from me. Of course, it may cause further issues for you in the future, but I can't really do much about that."

"Oh, that's okay. I don't know how he can be *more* of an asshole."

Ausburk's lip twitched. "That word again. It is such a good one. Anyway, trust me, Kharsweil will certainly find a way to be even more of an *asshole*."

"He really seems to like that new word you taught him," Netty said.

I smiled and leaned my head back against the seat.

"What can I say? I take my role as Earth's ambassador to the stars very seriously."

———

WE BID a regretful farewell to Helso and launched ourselves toward Tau Ceti. Helso had become a home away from home for all of us —well, except Torina, of course, because it was her actual home— and leaving it was always bittersweet. It did my heart good to see the Helso Self-Defense Force continuing their exercises, though. Torina's homeworld had twice been ravaged by outsiders, and I frankly had some constant worry about the place simmering away in the back of my mind. It was nice to know that between their own defense force and the Schegith, Helso was now in pretty good hands.

Which left Earth.

My own homeworld had none of those sorts of protection. All that stood between it and chaos descending from the stars were the laws protecting pre-spaceflight societies and people's willingness to obey them. The fact was that Earth was horribly vulnerable, its eight billion people blissfully unaware of the hideous dangers lurking in the sky. It meant that *I* was just as vulnerable. So far, none of my growing number of enemies had tried to leverage Earth's effective helplessness against me, but a grim part of me knew that could, and probably would change in an instant.

I had to do something about that. I just wasn't sure what.

In the meantime, we twisted to Tau Ceti and made our way to Fulcrum, the fourth planet outward from the star. Tau Ceti was the busiest and most populated system in known space, home to tens of billions of people from every race imaginable living across a half a dozen planets. Fulcrum was the commercial trading hub, a metropolis of megacities planet-side, connected to sprawling orbitals by space elevators and continuous streams of shuttle traffic rising to and falling from orbit in a never-ending flow.

It was everything I thought the galactic society would be. And more.

"We don't seem to end up coming here much," I noted, watching a massive freighter festooned with cargo modules slide by on our port side. "Our work always takes us to the out of the way shitholes."

"The Ceteans have some pretty sophisticated law enforcement machinery of their own. The fact is, they really don't need us very often," Perry said.

"For that matter, they don't really want us involved in their affairs, either. The Ceteans kind of consider themselves the hub of known space. Everyone else are the yokels, and we're the yokels' cops," Netty added.

I thought about the attitudes of New Yorkers toward the rest of the States, Londoners to the rest of the UK, or Paris to the rest of France, and nodded. Yeah, that attitude wasn't unique to Tau Ceti by any means.

"I got called a peasant by a waiter in Quebec once," I said.

Torina snorted. "What did you do?"

"I pointed out—reasonably, I might add—that it was better to be a peasant than to be one who serves peasants."

Torina threw her head back, laughing in silvery notes. "I'm guessing you didn't order anything else?"

I made a face. "What, and let Jean-Claude VonDouche put his own touch on my food? Momma didn't raise no fool, dear."

"I wouldn't have ordered at all," Funboy said. "Safer that way."

"I would have—" Icky started, but Perry interrupted.

"... not made it in the restaurant. No pants, no French food," Perry informed her.

"Canadian," I corrected.

"*French* Canadian," Zeno chimed in. "Read it in a travel guide."

I gave her a wink of approval. "Very cosmopolitan of you.'

Zeno shrugged her thick shoulders. "I like to be fancy now and then."

"As fancy as the Ceteans?" I asked.

"We're about to find out," Torina said.

The auction was being conducted in a designated volume of orbital space near Fulcrum's largest moon, Kelthin's Locus. About the same size as Saturn's moon Titan back in the Solar System, Kelthin's Locus was an embodiment of that old song lyric about covering paradise with a parking lot—or, in this case, taking a moon that had apparently started with the pastoral charm of Helso and turning it into a blighted sprawl of mines, smelters, refiners, and supporting infrastructure. As we dropped into orbit, I looked down on a barren surface pocked with the gaping wounds of pit mines and their detritus, rambling industrial infrastructure, and a myriad of connecting pipes and conduits, roads, and tramways.

It was a Dickens novel married to a dystopian nightmare, and that was at a distance.

"Netty, what's with this huge volume of forbidden space all around the moon's equator?" Torina asked, pointing at the tactical overlay. Sure enough, a broad torus of no-go surrounded the moon.

"Loads of refined metal are periodically launched toward Fulcrum using big ol' mass drivers. They fall into orbit there and are recovered by robotic ships for further processing."

"So they fire loads of metal right at the planet, the way we shoot at targets with the *Fafnir*'s mass drivers."

"They do. It's an incredibly efficient way of moving masses from one body to the other."

I shook my head at the thought of a kilometers-long mass driver launching tons of metal ingots into space, aimed at a narrow orbital slot. "What happens if they miss?"

"Well, either the load of refined metal starts a long journey to the stars, or it slams into the surface of Fulcrum."

"Does that ever happen?"

"Not often."

"I can't help but notice that *not often* isn't *never*."

"There are no certainties in space, Van."

"I've noticed that, too."

We slid into the spot assigned to us by the traffic control AI overseeing the auction. There were two ships here, arrayed around a presentation space into which those up for auction would be flown and paraded around. We settled back to enjoy the show.

"So we know which ship is the one we're after?" Torina asked.

I nodded. "It's the fourth one in the auction catalog, named the *Rampant Rhapsody*."

"Hell of a name for a ship," Icky said.

Zeno shrugged. "I'm sure it means something to someone."

"So, Van, what's the plan here? When the *Rampant Rhapsody* comes out for bids, do you intend to, what, seize it?" Perry asked.

"Something like that."

"On what grounds? All we've got is a third-party complaint, without any paperwork to back it up—no warrant or anything."

"That's not our problem. We're just acting as Ausburk's deputized agent, pursuant to Interstellar Commerce Agreement Article Nine, Chapter Four, Paragraphs Six through Eight. We'll execute the seizure, put a cease-and-desist order in place, and then leave it up to Ausburk."

Perry whistled. "Van, I'm impressed. You're really learning how to abuse the law, paragraph by paragraph."

I smiled at him. "It's nice to be appreciated. Anyway, what I really want to do is get my hands on Parlix Tarik. Like I told you, he's an inveterate gunrunner who seems to specialize in moving weapons in and out of known space. I'm hoping we can lean on him enough to cough up some useful information about weapons smuggling in The Deeps—"

"Van, they're bringing out the first ship," Netty chimed in.

We watched as a colossal, cylindrical ship was nudged into view by a small armada of drone tugs and YardBoats. She was easily one of the biggest ships I'd ever seen, probably well in excess of class 20. She was also, not to put too fine a point on it, a corroded pile of scrap.

I glanced at the auction roster. The first ship, Lot 1, was listed as "unnamed bulk water carrier," with a registry number and her operational pedigree. It seemed she'd spent most of her life hauling cometary water to outposts and orbitals in the Eridani Federation—not a very glamorous job but an essential one. No reclamation system was one hundred percent efficient, so every ship and station had to be occasionally topped up to offset small but constant losses. It actually made the colossal ship, more than two klicks long, an unsung hero of life in space. It almost seemed sad to see her end up like this, but at least she wasn't bound for the ship breakers.

Assuming anyone wanted to buy her.

As she slid into full view, though, something else about her became clear. Zeno noticed it first, of course, but the rest of us quickly followed. Mutters and snickers followed that. Only Icky sat staring in silence.

"That graffiti she's got all over her—are they what I think they are?" Torina asked.

Zeno giggled. "Depends. What do you think they are, Torina?"

"Yeah, what are they, Torina?" Icky asked.

Torina turned to her, and then to Zeno. "Haven't you had the talk with her yet?"

"What? No. Why is that my responsibility?"

"The talk about what?" Icky persisted.

Perry turned. "Dicks, Icky! Winkies! Thingies! Genitals, lots and lots of genitals!"

Icky stared for a moment, then shrugged. "Oh," she said, then her eyes widened. "Oh. Wait. You mean those are—"

"Reproductive organs, or crude representations of them, anyway. It's hard to tell for sure, but I'd say at least five different species are represented," Funboy said matter-of-factly.

"Why the hell would someone decorate their ship with *that*?" Icky asked in bewilderment.

"Good question. It's definitely going to diminish the resale value," Funboy replied.

Torina was tilting her head to one side. "Oh, I don't know. A few of them are fairly realistic. Like that one, about two-thirds of the way back along the hull. Whoever did it managed an almost 3D effect."

I nodded. "Which is really something, when you consider it has to be, like, a hundred meters long."

Zeno clicked her tongue. "Seventy-five at most, Van. Typical man."

The big ship slid to a halt. The AI running the auction gave a summary, then opened the bidding.

A ponderous silence followed.

"No one wants to be the first to bid on the *SS Dicks Everywhere*," Perry said.

Torina sniffed. "Can you blame them? I'd sure as hell want to repaint the damned thing before I admitted buying it."

The silence persisted.

Perry turned to me. "Hey, Van, we could—"

"No."

"But if we—"

"No, Perry, I do not want to buy that ship. I mean, what they hell would we do with a bulk water carrier?"

"It'd be one hell of a conversation starter."

"Yeah, not of any conversation I want to have—"

The comm suddenly came to life. One of the attendees finally put in a bid, immediately meeting the opening of one hundred thousand bonds.

That started a timer, which ticked relentlessly down to zero.

"Sold, to bidder number seven, for one hundred thousand bonds," the AI auctioneer said.

"Yes yes! We win! For almost nothing, we now own the Free Commerce Vessel *Big and Long!*" a new voice crowed over the comm. There was no mistaking the tone of a Fren-Okun.

Torina sighed and crossed her arms. "The FCV *Big and Long*? Come on, they're not even trying."

"We shall dominate the water transfer and resupply market for decades to come!" the voice crowed.

"Van, one of the other bidders just asked how much the *Big and Long* will charge per load," Netty said.

Torina rolled her head back and groaned. "Of course they did."

The display lit up a general comm broadcast. It showed several Fren-Okun, obviously aboard their ship—wearing party hats?

"We will let you know, loser-bidder person!" a Fren shouted into the image, spraying spittle with unalloyed glee.

I had to shake my head. In a life that had, in many ways, left surreal dwindling in the rearview mirror, this had to be one of the most surreal of all. I was watching aliens wearing party hats and tossing around glitter because they had won an auction for a giant spaceship festooned with crude images of phalluses—or their equivalent—from half a dozen other alien species. And they'd just bragged about it all in a way that had only one possible answer.

"I fart in your general direction, you empty-headed animal-food-trough wiper," I shot back, sporting a toothy grin that wouldn't go away.

I felt everyone look at me. Perry clicked his tongue.

"Actually, Van, the correct quote is—"

I turned on him and he bobbed his head.

"Close enough."

I turned back to the screen. "Now all we're missing is—"

A face filled the screen, which suddenly went blurry.

"Moist!"

"Okay, there it is."

11

THE NEXT COUPLE of auctions had none of the insane drama of the first. They were relatively sedate affairs focused on relatively unremarkable ships. I called everyone to alert when the fourth ship slid into view, this time under its own power.

"Netty, is that our target?"

"Hull configuration and registry information match those sent to us by Ausburk," she confirmed.

"Okay, then. Netty, take us in. General broadcast, please."

The class five came to a halt, but before the auction AI could launch into its spiel, I cut in.

"This is Peacemaker Van Tudor. I am seizing the subject of this auction pursuant to Article Nine, Chapter Four, Paragraphs Six through Eight of the Interstellar Commerce Agreement. Effective immediately, I am placing a cease-and-desist order onto any sale of the subject vessel, and a seize-and-hold order onto the vessel itself pending the resolution of this matter."

Okay, I was reading from a script that Petty had prepared for me. And while I read it, Perry transmitted my credentials and the two orders to the auctioneers, as well as the current owners of the ship. The result was a curt acknowledgement from the auction AI, which immediately removed the ship from the bidding list, and a predictable howl of outrage from the Yonnox master of the ship.

"What the hell is this about? You have no authority!"

"Sorry, my friend, the Interstellar Commerce Agreement, which is fully applicable here, says that I do. Now, prepare to be boarded."

"On what grounds?"

"You have been accused of acquiring that ship from its previous Fren-Okun owner under false pretenses."

"That sale was legitimate—!"

"In which case this matter will be speedily resolved in your favor. In any case, we don't want to keep the folks who came here in good faith from their auction, so please pull your ship out of the bidding area and prepare to be boarded."

"Go to hell!"

"That wasn't very nice," Zeno said.

"Van, he's going to make a run for it. Are we going to pursue?" Netty asked.

I hesitated. Trying to flee had been a risk, certainly. But pursuing him through the crowded space and bustling traffic around Fulcrum could be a serious issue. It would be the cops trying to pursue a fleeing suspect the wrong way down a Los Angeles freeway, with the cars admittedly much farther apart but also traveling *much* faster. The seize-and-hold orders would follow the ship no matter where it went in known space but wouldn't carry any weight outside of it, so there was that.

In truth, I wasn't really interested in the ship itself—that was Ausburk's problem. I'd done my part for him. What I wanted was the Yonnox, and whatever he knew about arms deals in The Deeps. If we lost him now, we might never find him again.

I was about to make the hard decision to pursue and get Netty to warn off Fulcrum traffic control, but we received help from an unexpected source. Even our Yonnox friend knew that lighting his fusion drive in such crowded space would be a death sentence—the Cetean military would blast him to vapor well before he got close to a twist point. So he powered up his thrusters instead and tried to break away into clear space. Before he could, though, the ponderous bulk of the newly minted FCV *Big and Long* abruptly wallowed right into his path. It forced him to thrust hard to avoid a collision, which gave us ample time to catch up and stick the muzzle of a point-defense battery straight into the class 5's cockpit.

"I was asked to minimize the damage to this vessel, not avoid it completely," I said over the comm.

The reply was a surrender, albeit one delivered in terms that made even Perry perk up.

"I have not heard those profanities arranged in that particular order before. Have to remember that," he said.

While we docked with the class 5, I called up the new owners of the *Big and Long*.

"Thanks for your help."

The screen lit up with a Fren in a party hat who was obviously a little inebriated on whatever got Fren inebriated. "You said this ship had been scammed from its Fren owners, right?"

"I did, and it was."

"Then screw 'em. Oh—"

I waited patiently.

"Oh—right. Remember we did you this favor, huh?"

I smiled. "What's your name?"

"Mavis—er, Renko. Yeah. Mavis Renko."

"Well, Mavis Renko, you're definitely on my *owe-you-one* list."

Mavis nodded but a distant "Moist!" cut him off. He scowled.

"I have to go. She's drunk and—ah, things can get messy."

He signed off. We all sat in silence for a moment. Icky finally broke it.

"Anyone else as grossed out as I am?"

Everyone nodded.

"We all are, Icky," Netty said. "We all are."

I'd ACTUALLY WORRIED that our Yonnox mark, Parlix Tarik, might not even be on board the seized ship and just had some minions overseeing the sale. But he was, along with three of the said minions, a human, and two Nesit. All of them were the usual surly, thuggish sorts, except for the human. She was a petite, beautiful woman with a buzz cut and eyes that twinkled with mischief.

"So… you're the infamous Van Tudor," she said to me, offering a sly grin.

"I'm sorry, do we know one another?"

"I know you. Well, by reputation, anyway. You've made quite a name for yourself among the riffraff. A bit of a superstar, actually."

I made myself meet her startling green eyes. Her whole attitude was both off-putting and intriguing at once. Torina must have sensed my sudden uneasy fascination because she moved in beside me.

"Who's your new friend?" Torina asked me.

"I'm not sure. She hasn't yet introduced herself. Instead, she's been telling me how famous I am among the lowlifes of known space."

"Not just known space," the woman said.

Torina held up her data slate to take an image and run a facial recognition scan, but the woman laughed. "Don't bother. My name is Alannis Myer, I'm five feet six inches, have a noticeable scar on the right side of my neck, and I'm wanted on four outstanding warrants."

Torina eyed her slate. "Five, actually."

"Oh, yeah—that Eridani thing. To be fair, though, I really *am* innocent of that one."

I narrowed my eyes on her. "What about the others?"

"Oh, guilty as hell."

The woman's easy dismissal of the fact that she'd just notified us she was wanted, and that we'd now be taking her into custody, set off all sorts of alarm bells. Perry and Zeno were questioning Parlix Tarik, Icky was glowering at the two Nesit, and Funboy was checking over the ship's systems.

Funboy opened a panel, his eyes staring at the circuitry like it was an unexploded bomb. "If it's rigged to blow, at least we'll be vaporized before our nervous systems can transmit the horrific miasma of pain."

Icky raised one of her hands like a student.

"Yes, Icky?"

She pointed at Funboy. "I don't want him at my birthday parties. Ever."

He sighed again. "Why would I attend marking the inexorable march toward your inevitable death, even if there was cake?"

Icky stomped her boot. "See?"

Now it was my turn to sigh. "Torina, you and Icky escort Alannis here to the *Fafnir* and stick her in a cell. We'll take her back to Anvil Dark to have her case—*cases*—disposed," I said.

Torina nodded crisply and cuffed Myer, who wore an enigmatic smile and watched me the whole time. As Torina and Icky started to lead her back to the airlock, though, she spoke up.

"There are things I know that you want to know, Peacemaker Van Tudor," she said.

I turned. Myer looked like she was thoroughly enjoying herself. Torina shot me a look of warning.

"Everyone does, Ms. Myer," I said and turned away.

I could feel her eyes on me like an itch between my shoulder blades as she was escorted away. It only faded when she was gone.

Zeno gave me a wary look. "What the hell was that all about?"

"Good question, Zeno. I don't know. Now, what does our Yonnox friend have to say about—"

We were walking past the two Nesit as we talked, and one of them—apparently emboldened by no longer being pinned in the watchful glare of Icky—produced a short spike-like weapon and lunged at me.

For the first time in my life, I faced a potential life-and-death situation without one knee that I had to work around. Instincts hammered into me by repeated drubbings at the hands of both Master Cataric and Torina on the sandy floor of the Innsu dojo instantly kicked in, my healthy knee saving me critical reaction time. I deflected the blow, grabbed the Nesit's arm, and slammed a foot against his leg, then yanked him forward. Before he could pitch down and slam his face into the deck plates, though, I levered his arm back up behind him and left him hanging that way under his own weight. He wailed in pain.

"How long to heal a broken limb for your race?"

"I—what?"

"How long?"

Funboy turned and gave me a mild look. "For a Nesit, a major bone, when broken, requires eight to nine weeks to fully heal. That can vary with age, physical condition, and diet, of course—"

"You're *hurting me*," the Nesit wailed.

The Yonnox, Parlix Tarik, shot me a glare. "Aren't you supposed to be on the side of the law?" he sneered.

I grabbed the Nesit and lifted him, sending a burst of pain through his arm but relieving some of the weight on it. "Setting aside the fact that this asshole just tried to kill me, I am on the side of the law, because I *am* the law. See, I'm giving you an out. Zeno, Perry, that would have constituted resisting arrest, don't you think?"

Zeno nodded. "Definitely."

"Actually, you could throw in assault on a Peacemaker during the performance of their duties, for good measure," Perry added.

Icky returned just then, took in the sight of me grappling the Nesit, and groaned.

"Aww, why does the good stuff always happen when I'm not around?"

"Oh, it may not be over yet, Icky," I said. "That depends on these gentlemen. I mean, they can end up being injured while resisting arrest and assaulting Peacemakers, or they can settle for a hit to their pride. And that will, I think, heal a lot faster."

Parlix gave me a hard stare. "What do you mean?"

I slammed the Nesit against the bulkhead and stuck a finger in his face. "Try anything else and we'll see how right Funboy is about the Nesit capacity to heal broken bones—which I suspect Icky here will be more than happy to break."

She hefted her hammer. "Just say when, boss."

Funboy blinked up at me. "What do you mean, how *right* I am? I'm basing that on—"

Zeno touched his shoulder. "Funboy. *Shh.*"

I turned to Parlix. "Frankly, none of this"—I gestured around at the ship—"really interests me. You're going to relinquish your ownership of this ship, I'm going to return it to the poor old Fren you scammed it from, then I'm going to drop you off at Fulcrum and let you be on your sleazy way."

"You—really?"

"Yes, really, but on one condition."

Parlix's eyes narrowed another notch. "What condition?"

"I want information. I want to know who's selling arms in The Deeps, and where."

The Yonnox scoffed, and even the two Nesit snorted. "That's easy. Everyone's selling, and everyone's buying. Ever since tensions started amping up between the Seven Stars League, the Eridani Federation, and the Tau Ceteans, Rodantic's World has turned into an arms bazaar."

"Rodantic's World. That's in The Deeps?"

"Yeah. Used to be a hub for all sorts of, uh, *commerce.* Lately, it's been all about weapons. Private traders want to protect themselves, mercenaries want to make themselves more marketable, and even the big players are always hunting for deals."

"Have you heard of this place?" I asked Perry, who lifted his wings in a shrug.

"Sorry, boss. You want info about stuff in known space, I can hook you up. Outside, though, not so much."

Funboy nodded. "I have heard of it. Wayyyy down the ecliptic."

"How far is *wayyyy down?*" I asked.

"One hundred and thirty-nine light-years, give or take."

"One hundred and thirty-nine light-years through The Deeps. A whole lot of empty and not many nav fixes," Zeno said.

Parlix nodded. "It ain't for the faint of heart. More than a few would-be gunrunners have ended up adrift with nothing but nothing for a few light-years all around because they didn't take along enough fuel. Bad way to go."

"That's a long run just on the say-so of this asshole, Van," Zeno said.

Parlix bristled. "Hey—!"

"Shut your cakehole," I snapped back at him. "If this works out, you've got your deal."

"What do you mean, if this works out—?"

"Relax, I'm going to let you go. But if this Rodantic's World bears fruit, then we can enjoy a profitable future together."

Parlix grinned. "Oh, that's how it is, huh? A little of that *squid pro go?*"

"It's quid pro quo, you mouth breather. And no, that's not what I mean. What I mean is that I'm going to provide you with a secure comm channel and an authentication code, then you're going to provide me with useful information as you come into it, and I'm going to pay you for it."

"You want me to become a filthy, backstabbing informant?"

"You have an objection to that?"

"No, not at all. Just trying to understand the terms of our arrangement."

Zeno leaned toward me. "Van, you're not going to trust this sleazebag, are you?"

"Not even to take out my trash. But if he proves useful down the road, then, well, maybe he'll end up on my Christmas card list," I replied.

"I'll pretend I understand what that means."

Parlix grudgingly signed over ownership of the ship to me for the consideration of a whopping one bond, whereupon we loaded him and his crew into the *Fafnir*. Zeno and Funboy piloted the class 5 back to Fulcrum and put it into a parking orbit where Ausburk could reclaim it at his leisure—and after full payment of the exorbitant parking fees. We summoned a shuttle to deplane Parlix Tarik and his two goons.

As he stepped into the airlock, I handed him a data chip Perry had prepared. "This is how you contact me. I want to know anything, and I mean *anything* you learn about the Trinduk in particular. I don't care if you learn a new Trinduk joke, I want to hear it."

Parlix frowned. "The Trinduk. Those bastards are—hell, they're bad news. Even us careerists give them a wide miss. Doing otherwise is a way to end up very dead very fast."

"Which is why I will make it worth your while," I said.

Parlix returned my stare, then shrugged. "What the hell. If you want to tangle with those maniacs, enjoy."

When he and his cronies were gone, I glanced aft. "How about our friend Alannis? Is she secure back there?" I asked.

Torina nodded with satisfaction. "Locked up nice and tight. That was after I thoroughly searched her and Netty scanned her for... everything." She curled her lip. "She's dangerous, Van. I'm not sure how, exactly, but she's dangerous. We need to offload her as soon as we can."

I caught the meaning in Torina's look. She meant that Alannis was dangerous because she was a criminal. But she meant something more, too.

I nodded. "Yeah, agreed. We'll drop her at Crossroads before we head into The Deeps. Gus can send her back to Anvil Dark."

Torina nodded. "Good."

"So, now we just have to figure out how to traverse a hundred and forty or so light-years without running out of gas," I said.

"No problem going one way. The real issue is whether we'll be able to refuel at Rodantic's World," Netty said.

"Yeah, I'd rather not have to stake our well-being on the availability of fuel at a world full of criminals. Netty, find a tanker and see if they can fuel us up and provide us with a full fuel pod. And see if they take Guild credit. If they do, go ahead and commit to it. I've found it's always easier to apologize than to ask permission."

Torina smirked. "Someone might be annoyed. Gerhardt, or even Dayna Jasskin, depending on which account we use."

I shrugged. "He's a Guild Master, and she's a banker. *Annoyed* is their default state. But speaking of Masters, how do we avoid Kharsweil?"

In answer, a loud snap erupted from the twist-comm panel, accompanied by a puff of acrid smoke.

"Oops. Sorry, Van, I accidentally let a power surge from the main bus pass through the twist-comm interface. I'm afraid we're restricted to local comms until we get it fixed," Netty said.

I grinned. "Oh, Netty, that was *very* careless of you. How long will it take to fix?"

Funboy spoke up. "We have a spare interface. I could swap it out in about ten minutes."

I sighed at him. "Let me ask this again. *How long will it take to fix?*"

Icky put a meaty hand on Funboy's shoulder, then peered at her tool harness as though the concept of a screwdriver suddenly eluded her.

"As long as you need, boss."

Funboy looked from her, to me, then blinked, and understanding dawned.

"Ah. A ruse. I get it."

I patted Funboy's other shoulder.

"We'll make you part of the crew yet, you joyous little varmint."

12

EVEN WITH A FUEL pod slung beneath her, the *Fafnir*'s performance was degraded only a little. She was big and powerful enough to pretty much shrug off the extra mass, her upgraded drive more than capable of offsetting the slight thrust asymmetry introduced by her changed center of mass.

Netty gave her final blessing before we departed Crossroads, where we'd rented the pod. "We have enough fuel to travel to Rodantic's World and back again, then return there again."

"So, lots," I said.

"Yes. Lots."

"I love the scientific specificity of it all. We also have the latitude to do some jaunting around in The Deeps, if so needed," Zeno noted. "And speaking of jaunting around, I've finished my little pet project. Here, let me show you."

I followed her to the *Fafnir*'s workboat, nestled into its docking adapter just aft of amidships. Only her upper hull was visible, the hatch open to reveal her interior. It wasn't much, just a cockpit and a small living space behind it, reminiscent of those boxy sleeper cabs mounted on big-rig trucks where the driver could rest and catch some sleep. It was a little bigger than that, though not much, but it did have a broom-closet lavatory that would have been at home on an Airbus.

Zeno pointed down into the cockpit, at a new panel at the pilot's left side. "That's the weapons panel. Right now, she can mount two missiles, and I've rigged up a hardpoint for something else—a small laser rig, or a point-defense battery. Fire control is rudimentary, but we can slave it into the *Fafnir*'s if we want and basically use her as an auxiliary weapons platform."

"But she can fly and fight on her own, if needed."

Zeno nodded. "Like I said, it's not much—she's got teeth, but they're not very sharp."

"Doesn't matter. That's good work, Zeno," I said, smiling and nodding enthusiastic appreciation. It was a pet project Zeno had been working on in her spare time, mainly using components she was able to scavenge. Overall, she'd kept the direct cost of the workboat's upgrade to about ten thousand bonds, which was a steal.

We had one last bit of business before we left Crossroads—a prisoner to hand over to Gus, the Peacemaker Guild's chief on the station.

I'd deliberately stayed away from Alannis Myer while we had her in our holding cell, leaving her care and feeding to Icky and Torina. I wasn't entirely sure why. There was just something about her—a coy smugness that went deeper than the bravado of an accomplished liar and scoundrel. A fugitive cunning lurked deep in her green eyes, hinting at hidden depths both as dark and dangerous as the Undersea sprawling far beneath the surface of Schegith's Null World. I somehow found myself both uncomfortable and, at the same time, a little *too* comfortable around her.

Her physical beauty was an issue, too, though I was doing my level best to ignore it. And failing.

Torina and Icky both kept a watchful eye on her as she exited the *Fafnir* and stepped into Crossroads and Gus's custody. They both seemed on edge around the enigmatic woman, too. Torina made no secret of the fact she despised Alannis, although I was worldly enough to know that part of that was triggered by the familiar ease —wholly unearned—she demonstrated with me. As for Icky, well, Alannis just rubbed her the wrong way.

I signed off the transfer paperwork on Gus's data slate, a little relieved to be free of the woman. Alannis watched it all with that unceasing, slightly contemptuous amusement.

"Aw, and here I thought you'd be the one taking me to prison, Van," she said, having the excellent sense not to pout her lip. It wasn't her style, and I knew it.

"It's Peacemaker Tudor."

"So formal. Well, I'm okay with you calling me Alannis."

I turned to Gus. "She's all yours, my friend. Enjoy."

"Van—sorry, *Peacemaker Tudor* certainly did," Alannis purred, grinning. "I could tell."

"Gus, would you just get her the hell out of here, please?" Torina snapped.

Gus resembled an octopus merged with a slug, but despite his utterly alien demeanor, he still managed to convey emotion with ease. In this case, it was weary resignation.

"With pleasure—and by pleasure, I mean entirely without any pleasure at all," he said.

I frowned at him. "You know Ms. Myer here?"

"Oh, yes. I had her in my cells once, and I've run her off Crossroads a few times."

"I didn't see any arrest reports here in her file."

"Of course not. If she was a windshield, squashed bugs would slide right off her."

I blinked a couple of times. "Where did you hear that?"

"What, you think humans are the only ones to figure out that something that blocks the wind, but not your view from a speeding vehicle, is just a damned good idea?"

"Okay, you got me there." I laughed, at least partly because I had a sudden image of Gus in a speeding convertible, one tentacle resting on the door.

But the burst of humor lasted only a moment, and my laughter died. Who the hell was this woman, whose Guild file—supposedly among the most secure documents in known space—was now suspect?

"See you around, Peacemaker Tudor," she said, giving me a wink and another grin as Gus and his people led her away.

"I don't like her," Icky said.

Torina turned to me. I shook my head.

"I don't like her either."

She gave me a *good* nod and returned to the *Fafnir*, Icky following. I glanced once up the corridor leading from the *Fafnir*'s berth to the Crossroad's docking concourse, to find Alannis looking back at me, smiling.

I HEAVED a grateful sigh as we cast off from Crossroads, glad to be rid of Alannis Myer. I couldn't help thinking, though, that she'd live up to her word, and would eventually fall back into my life, like a stone skipping across water—striking briefly, bouncing away, only to inevitably return again.

But not today. We'd packed the *Fafnir* to the gunwales with provisions and had enough fuel to twist over four hundred light-years, so we started on our way to the ominous part of space known as The Deeps.

We'd actually poked a toe into The Deeps once before, right after visiting the rambling, lawless outpost known as the Torus. Then, we'd been on the hunt for the Puloquir, the unwitting progenitors of the Tenants, the insidious parasitic race that had nearly brought all-out war to known space. We hadn't gone far, though, before realizing we were in over our heads and returning to Null World and the long wisdom of the Schegith. We decided to stop in at the Torus again and start our trek into The Deeps from there.

It gave us a chance to gain a little intel while replenishing the fuel we'd burned getting here. While Icky, Zeno, and Funboy took care of the ship, Torina, Perry, and I headed for the bar colorfully named *The One-Eyed Yak* and its aging hippy of a proprietor, Skrilla.

"Well, if it ain't the man," he said, grinning broadly. "Come to do a little oppressing on behalf of the state?"

I glanced at his t-shirt—bright red, with that famous image of Che Guevara, Cuban revolutionary and counterculture icon. I curled my lip at it. "Little on the nose, don't you think, Skrilla?"

He looked down at himself. "What, my comrade Che here? He's my guiding spirit, the Clarence to my George Bailey."

"Old movie references for the win," Perry said.

"Don't you be dissing the great George Bailey, my shiny-feathered friend. He's as much a hero of the revolution as old Che here."

"He was a banker."

"Yeah, but a subversive banker, forever sticking it to Mister Potter, the establishment, making sure everyone had a decent place to live, giving away his own money so the working class had enough—you don't get any more proletariat than that."

Perry turned to me. "You know, I'd never thought of *It's a Wonderful Life* as a Marxist treatise before."

I held up a hand. "As interesting as this all is, we're actually here for some information."

"And a drink," Skrilla said. "This proud member of the proletariat still has bills to pay."

We ordered a round, for which I handed over a more than generous tip, then told Skrilla I wanted to know about Rodantic's World.

He scowled. "Why? That place is nothing but capitalism at its worst, man. I mean, money for guns? Nothing like making death and destruction profitable."

"I don't disagree that there are more than a few Undershafts soiling that area of space."

"Undershaft? Is that a—"

"George Bernard Shaw character, a war profiteer playing both sides. You really are a collegiate revolutionary, aren't you?"

Skrilla's face fell. "I think you just called me poorly read."

I waggled a finger. "Not at all. I'm merely implying you're narrowly read."

Skrilla brightened. "I accept your apology. Still, man, that place is—"

"We've got reason to go there. We're looking for someone in particular and have evidence she's connected to weapons trafficking," I said.

"Oh, well, in that case, Rodantic's World is your go-to. And while you're there, why don't you clean up the place, too? Take some of the evil wind out of those corporate sales?"

Torina frowned. "Corporate sales?"

"Well, duh. Yeah. Rodantic's World is nothing but a front for big corporations, anyone in the business of making money from weapons. You don't think they're happy with just selling their death wares to *legitimate*"—he made air quotes—"customers, do you? Not when there's money to be made selling them to mercenaries and revolutionaries. Hell, anyone with a grudge and some bonds in their pockets."

I glanced at Torina and Perry. Perry bobbed his head in a nod. "Actually, it makes sense. If the big corporations want to sell stuff on the gray market, they'd do it somewhere outside known space, probably through a string of holding companies."

Torina nodded. "Which means there's probably some big players involved. Big players with lots of money—"

"And lots more money riding on this place, yeah. We're going to have to watch our step," I finished, nodding.

Back on Earth, I'd only brushed up against the arms trade a few times, and peripherally at that—most noticeably while hacking some transactions involving a Russian oligarch who'd made more than a few payments to suppliers in places like Mogadishu, in Somalia. A couple of those suppliers had been linked, in turn, to some surprisingly big names in the global arms market, makers of advanced weapons used by the world's largest militaries. I'd never chased any of it any further, though, because it wasn't what I was being paid for. But it had stuck with me, well-known companies that employed thousands of middle-class westerners peddling machine guns and anti-tank weapons to Third World warlords through a shadowy string of shell corporations. It was money of the dirtiest sort.

And it seemed that Rodantic's World filled the same role as Mogadishu, a place where big companies could sell their wares to shady buyers. If I'd thought the place was dangerous before, it was far more so now. There were few things more perilous than getting between a faceless corporation and its bottom line. Getting between a mama bear and her cubs, or between a black hole and its event horizon, maybe.

Maybe.

WE MADE our first twist into The Deeps, to a waypoint defined by a rogue planet, a silent, frozen world about the size of Neptune. We could only see it as a black disk occulting the stars beyond it, although in thermal it was a little move vibrant, some residual interior heat bubbling up through thin spots in its crust. Needless to say, it was utterly lifeless.

"I shiver just looking at it," Torina said, and I nodded.

"Yeah, not exactly very welcoming, is it?"

There was nothing else around us, aside from a few stray motes of dust and gas molecules. The Deeps was aptly named, a void in the Milky Way caused by the random vagaries of gravitation. From its center, it was virtually empty for nearly three hundred light-years in all directions, aside from a scattered handful of stars. As Netty put it, it was the negative image of a nebula, a region packed with unusual amounts of matter.

We planned to make four twists to Rodantic's World. A series of smaller twists would cost us less subjective time displacement than one long one, while also allowing us to navigate more accurately. We hadn't expected to find much else along the way, which is why a contact alert on the tactical overlay caught me completely off-guard.

"Uh, Netty, is that another ship I see?"

"It is. Class 8, a cargo cutter configuration. It's currently racing along at a whopping eight meters per second, which will have it fall onto the surface of that rogue planet in about two years. Oh, and they're broadcasting a distress call."

"Put it on, please."

The center display lit up with the image of three wild-eyed aliens against the backdrop of a grimy bulkhead, the air fumed with pale mist. One was a Nesit, one a Skel, and the third a lumpy, bluish humanoid whose species I didn't recognize.

"Any ship, we need help, please! They took our fuel and left us to die! They deliberately put the brakes on us, just to be true assholes! Please, help us!"

The message started to loop. I cut it off.

"Well, looks like they need a Good Samaritan," I said, sighed at the blank looks I got from the others, and shook my head. "They need help, is what I mean."

Torina shrugged. "Okay, so let's give it to them."

"Just like that? There are so many reasons to be wary, starting with the state of their ship. Who knows how many toxins, or pathogens, or radionuclides are filling their air. They could be contagious. We might try to help them, only to die a miserable death out here ourselves," Funboy said.

Zeno raised an eyebrow at him but nodded. "Maybe it's not as dire as all that, but I'm with Funboy, Van. I suggest we be cautious."

I nodded. "Yeah, I hear you." I glanced at the overlay, at the position of the class 8, and of the nearby rogue planet, then tapped my chin.

"Zeno, I think we need to test your upgrades to our workboat before we, you know, have to count on them. This seems like a good opportunity."

"What did you have in mind?"

"Remember that ship-killing missile B gave us, the Deconstructor? Can the upgraded workboat handle firing it?"

"Shouldn't be a problem. It might have a fancy warhead, but as far as basic tech goes, it's meant to be plug-and-play with a standard launcher."

"Good. Let's pull it out of the *Fafnir*'s magazine and load it onto the workboat. And then, I've got a specific job in mind for you, Zeno."

"Does it involve blowing something up?"

"Potentially."

She grinned. "Well, then, I'm all ears."

I watched the overlay as we approached the stricken ship. I'd told the crew that we were here to be saviors—but that we'd also assume the worst and be ready.

Funboy was somewhat mollified. "I'm glad to see that you're finally assessing the dangers we face. But I have to raise the issue of their hygienic state again. That ship is a biohazard. I didn't see a disinfectant dispenser anywhere."

Icky pulled a face. "That crap you brought on board on Earth— what did you call it, Van? Hand sanitizer? Anyway, it stings my nose."

"You get used to the smell," I said.

"No, I mean it stings my actual nose."

"You—what? Why would you put it—?"

Perry extended a wing. "Do you really need, or even want to know, boss?"

I thought about it, then shook my head. "No. No, I don't. Okay, Zeno's in position, so everyone else, put on expressions of care and concern. I know, Funboy, that's not your natural setting. Please do your best to pretend. Let's sell this and get as close as we can."

"You really think these are pirates?" Torina asked.

I shrugged. "Crippled ship, located at a known nav waypoint out in the literal middle of nowhere, not too far from a rogue planet that could be hiding all sorts of mischief—I don't know, call me suspicious, but I'm suspicious."

"Suspicious is my middle name. If my people had such things, that is," Funboy droned.

Torina snorted and kept her fingers near the weapons panel. We hadn't powered up the fire control scanners and kept the weapons offline, so that if anyone was watching it would seem that we were suspecting nothing and were just here to help.

Netty deftly matched the class 8's velocity, which had required a hard burn from our fusion drive to bleed off our own delta V. She'd also had to maneuver in a very particular way, if this was going to work the way we wanted it to. In fact, she was the only one with the ability to juggle all of the variables simultaneously. With a puff of thrusters, she eased the *Fafnir* toward the other ship.

"Okay, places, kids. Operation Rube to the Rescue commences... now," I said.

As we moved in to dock with the class 8, I kept my attention riveted on the tactical overlay—particularly on the rogue planet. This might all be on the up-and-up, a ship genuinely in distress, and our Good Samaritan act not an act at all—

The contact alert triggered, and a new icon appeared, racing out from behind the rogue planet straight toward us.

I sighed. "Ah, my lack of faith in people is rewarded yet again. Okay, Netty—"

Without warning, everything went pitch black.

13

A MOMENT PASSED IN SILENCE, then lights began to flick back on as systems started to reboot.

"What the hell happened?" I shouted at the cockpit generally.

As I did, something flopped against my right arm. It was Perry. He'd gone stiff and quiet. I cursed and nudged him aside. Whatever had happened to him would have to wait.

"The ship we were about to rescue just hit us with a hell of an EMP. It's taken all our systems offline," Icky snapped with the annoyance of a true engineer.

"We're looking at a complete reboot from a cold state, at least five minutes. That's more than enough time for us to die," Funboy said, his voice flat and resigned—so no different than it ever was.

I glanced at Perry. He'd become a statue of a bird.

"Perry!"

Nothing.

"Shit. Netty, are you with us?"

Nothing.

"Damn it. Icky, I need comms, now!"

"They should be back up in about two—"

"Now."

I heard her tapping controls. "Moving the comms up in the reboot list."

The next minute seemed to drag out forever. Without scanners, we had no way of telling how close the oncoming ship was. It was pretty clear how this was meant to work, though. The supposedly crippled class 8 would lure in a potential rescuer and then disable them with a powerful EMP. This gave their co-conspirators lurking behind the rogue planet time to move into position, placing their would-be saviors into a position where their only options were surrender or destruction. It was clever, cold, and calculated. I wondered how many ships had already fallen prey to the cunning, evil scam.

"Van, I've got comms back," Icky said.

I reached for the panel, just as an incoming transmission erupted from the speaker.

"By now you've figured out that this ain't exactly going the way you thought it would. Unless you want to be heroes and just die, you'll stand down and wait to be boarded. Do that, and we'll make sure you get back to something resembling civilization in one piece. Your call. Message repeats in ten seconds."

I glanced at Torina. "Sitting here, in the dark, still desperately trying to get our systems online, that voice blaring out of the speaker as soon as comms come back up, not knowing what's going on out there—it's actually pretty terrifying."

She nodded. "It is."

I switched to another comm channel, one that we used for local comms when we were suited up. "Zeno, please tell me you're out there and good to go."

The reply started out faint and distorted but immediately cleared when Zeno powered the lifeless workboat back up.

"Van... hear you... online, yeah. With everything shut down, that EMP didn't affect me. Anyway, I'm ready."

"Go for it."

I would have loved to have seen the reaction of the bad guys when Zeno's scanners abruptly lit them up. For the past three hours, she'd been coasting along in a dark, silent workboat, sitting in her suit, trusting Netty to maneuver the *Fafnir* to keep her and its incandescent fusion plume front and center in our opponents' scanners. The workboat, a small target to begin with, had quickly cooled as it drifted along utterly without power. Unless the bad guys were actually looking for it, it simply wouldn't have stood out against the noisy background still provided by the star-scape back toward known space. At least, that had been our hope.

Zeno interrupted the repeating broadcast on the other comm channel.

"By now you've figured out that this ain't exactly going the way you thought it would—"

"Right back at you, assholes," she said and fired the Deconstructor at the oncoming ship. We could see a desperate eruption of point-defense fire, but in celestial terms, it was nearly point-blank range. The Deconstructor raced through the reaching fingers of tracers and detonated with a spectacular blast. When it faded, all that remained was glowing plasma and a few superheated bits of debris.

A few seconds later, Netty came back online.

"I'm baaa-aack."

"Netty, we're not out of the woods yet. We need fire control and weapons—"

"You've got them," she said as Torina's panel came to life. She didn't hesitate in targeting the class 8 that was hanging just a few klicks away. The downside of the EMP was that it had taken down the ship that generated it as well, so by the time their own fire control scanners came back online, they found themselves staring down the barrels of the *Fafnir*'s far greater firepower.

I activated the comm.

"By now you've figured out that this ain't exactly going the way you thought it would. Unless you want to be morons and die, you'll stand down and wait to be boarded. Don't worry, we'll make sure you get back to something resembling civilization in one piece—and by civilization, I mean jail," I said.

"You don't have jurisdiction out here," a voice snapped back.

I sighed. "You're right, I don't. We'll just destroy you then and be on our way—"

"Wait!"

I handed the situation over to Torina to resolve, then turned to Perry, who was still flopped lifeless against the back of my seat.

"Perry?"

Nothing.

"Shit. Netty, can you contact him? Is he still in there?" He was hardened against EMP, but only to a point. I hoped he hadn't been irreparably damaged. In theory, we could restore him from a backup kept on Anvil Dark, but that hadn't been synchronized since the last time we were there. It meant he'd lose everything that had happened since, but, more critically, it meant we wouldn't be able to bring him back to life until we returned there—

"Van?"

Perry's eyes had finally lit up with their amber glow.

"Perry?"

"Van… tell my wife… I love her," he gasped, then coughed weakly.

I scowled at him. "Very funny, bird. Are you in one piece?"

He whirred back to life and flexed his wings. "What'd I miss?"

"Us winning."

"Sweet. And you even managed to do it without me."

"I was sure you were irrevocably dead," Funboy intoned.

"Sorry to disappoint you. Or is that your way of telling me you're glad I'm okay?"

"Yes."

"Yes, you're disappointed, or yes you're glad—"

Torina cut in. "Van, the bad guys have stood down their weapons and agreed to be boarded. It seems they really are out of fuel, and failing stealing ours, that other ship was their ride out of here."

"Oh, so they're completely at our mercy then?"

Torina gave an evil grin. "Yes, they are. And I made them admit it."

I paused, thinking. "Okay, tell them we'll give them some fuel. But it's going to cost them."

"Cost them what?" she asked.

I smiled. "Netty, send the all-clear to Zeno to come on home to the *Fafnir*. Then, I've got a little job for you to do."

OVER THEIR UNRELENTING PROTESTS, we relieved the pirates of their EMP generator. "You guys won't be needing this where you're going," I said.

"Do you know how much that cost us?" one of them howled.

I jammed my face into his—my helmeted face. We'd boarded them fully suited up, both in case they decided to fight and because the disgusting state of their ship wasn't entirely an act. Funboy might see everything in the worst possible light, but these guys were actually pigs when it came to hygiene.

"Do you know how much I don't give a shit?" I blasted back at the pirate from my suit's speaker. "Just count yourselves lucky that I'm arranging for you guys to be rescued and not just turned to vapor like your friends."

The pirate's mouth moved a few times, then went still.

"Okay, Netty, we're done over here. How's the refueling going?" I asked.

"Icky's just disconnecting now. Zeno tells me that she's finished transferring the provisions and water."

"Awesome. How about you? Have you finished programming their nav system?"

"I have. The program is entered, locked, and ready to run."

"Thank you, my dear." I returned my attention to the pirate. "So here's what's going to happen. We've given you enough food and water to last you for sixty days if you ration it well. I mean, feel free to pig out and eat it all now—I don't really care. We've also given you enough antimatter fuel to twist as close to the Torus as we're comfortable doing, without draining our own supply unduly.

It's going to leave you about fifty-eight days short, so you'll have to travel the rest of the way in normal space. We've locked you out of your nav system and helm controls, so all you have to do is relax and enjoy the ride. Once you arrive at the Torus, you'll be taken into custody by another Peacemaker, who'll take you back to Anvil Dark for arraignment, a trial, and some well-deserved time in our prison barge, The Hole."

The pirate opened his mouth, but I raised a finger and cut him off. "Before you object in any way, shape, or form to this plan, your alternative is for us to remove the food, water, and fuel we gave you and leave you here."

"We'd die!"

"Yes, I imagine you would, and in an especially drawn-out, horrible way. So your third option is that we just destroy your ship and give you a quick end instead."

"But… why don't you take us with you?"

"Yeah, I've got more important things to do than lug you assholes all over The Deeps. So, choose now. Do you want the slow boat back to Torus, or would you like to take what's behind doors two or three?"

Unsurprisingly, the pirates decided to take the long, drawn-out return to the Torus. It didn't stop them from howling and bitching right up to the moment we sealed the airlock in their faces. I had Netty decompress the *Fafnir*'s airlock entirely to blow the stink and whatever else might have slithered into it from the pirates' ship into space.

"You think that ship's bad now, imagine what it's going to be like in two months when they arrive at the Torus," Torina said.

"I don't have to imagine it. It smells like communicable diseases and a violation of personal space," Funboy said as we settled in and prepared to get underway.

"Uh, those aren't actually smells"

"They are to me."

"All I know is that poor Dugrop'che is going to have to deal with it when those idiots arrive at the Torus. I think I'm going to owe him a drink or two next time we're on Anvil Dark," I said.

"You're splitting the prize fee for that ship with him. That should make up for the stink," Torina said.

I shrugged. "I'm not sure about that. Anyway, Netty, go ahead and start them on their way."

"Will do."

Netty transmitted the twist command to the pirates' locked-down nav system. An instant later, their ship vanished.

"Okay, now that that bit of unpleasantness is out of the way, we can get on with what we actually came out here to do. Netty, onward to Rodantic's World, if you please."

OUR NEXT TWIST destination was another arbitrary point further into The Deeps, this time a wandering star, a white dwarf whose trajectory suggested it had been kicked out of the galactic core by some ancient cataclysm. This time, we fired the scanners up to full power when we completed our twist, more interested in locating any threats early than trying to hide from them.

"Netty, I'm seeing a ship here on the overlay—a few light-hours away and heading away from us? Where the hell is he going?" I asked. It made little sense because there was literally nothing for light-years ahead of him. Netty examined the data, then pronounced her verdict.

"That ship is a class 5 of an antiquated design. It's coasting without power, as are two small objects following it. They appear to be missiles."

I frowned at the display. A powerless ship coasting along, being chased by two powerless missiles?

Torina was thinking the same thing I was. "How long has that little chase been going on?"

"I can see if I can access any of its systems, but it's going to take a while."

I glanced at Torina, who shrugged. "We're not really on a schedule here. Go for it, Netty."

It ended up taking her nearly three hours of painstaking work, trying to access the mostly dormant systems of a ship several light-hours away. We took the time to have dinner and catch some downtime, a much more pleasant affair now that the *Fafnir* had so much more interior space. She finally had some answers while I was lounging in my bunk, rereading Tolkien's *The Lord of the Rings* for the umpteenth time. I made a point of reading it every couple of years, partly because it was the book that had ignited my lifelong passion for speculative fiction when I was twelve or so, and partly because it was just so damned good.

"Van, I was able to retrieve a distress log from that ship. It stopped broadcasting it about thirty years ago, but the log itself is still accessible," Netty said.

I sat up. "Thirty *years*?"

"That's right. It seems that the crew abandoned it ninety-two years ago. It's been on the same trajectory ever since, still being chased by the missiles they were trying to avoid."

"Ninety years. Holy shit. So it's… a ghost ship."

"I suppose you could say it is, yes."

I returned to the cockpit to find the rest of the crew staring at the image Netty had put on the center display. It was pretty much at the limit of her ability to collect such a distant image with any detail, the dead vessel a vaguely ship-shaped blur.

"That's—wow," Icky said softly.

We all nodded.

"It's a perfect metaphor for life—a long, pointless journey into an inevitable and endless night," Funboy added. We all turned to look at him. He blinked back at us.

"What?"

Perry turned to me. "Van, I'd hereby like to nominate Funboy as the *Fafnir*'s morale officer."

Funboy shook his head. "I don't think I'd be a good fit."

Zeno glanced at him sidelong. "No shit."

I turned back to the forlorn image. "You know, it's hard to fathom just… just how much is *out* here."

We all watched the derelict speeding away for a moment longer, forever chased by the cold, dark missiles. Then I flicked the image off.

"Netty, save whatever you retrieved from our ghost ship. Maybe we can use it to figure out a port of call for her, so to speak. There might be people who'd like to know about her—did you get her name, by the way?"

Perry answered. "She was, or still is, I guess, the *Yeshika-stul*. It's an old trade-language phrase that roughly translates to *a crown made of music*."

"What a romantic name," Zeno said.

"I agree. Elegant, noble even," Perry replied.

"Since we know her current position and her velocity, anyone should be able to use that to find her—ah, a long way into the future, I'd imagine," Torina said.

"Barring her encountering some external force in the meantime, we can predict her exact position to about eleven million years in the future when she'll finally enter the gravitational influence of a celestial body. Of course, there might not be much left of her by then, owing to simple abrasion with dust and gas," Netty said.

I smiled and shook my head. "Only eleven million years, huh? Well, I guess we'd better work fast to get that information to whoever owns her now."

OUR NEXT ENCOUNTER was two twists later, one short of our final arrival at Rondantic's World. If our last, with the *Yeshika-stul*, had been eerie and bittersweet, this one was the exact opposite.

"Van, I'm receiving a transmission," Netty announced as soon as we'd twisted. This was another rogue system, a red dwarf slashing its way through the galaxy from bottom to top, its origins unclear. Unlike the last star, though, this one had brought a gaggle of planets along with it—five gas giants, one nearly twice the size of Jupiter and approaching brown dwarf territory, the others all about Saturn-sized. One even had a spiffy set of rings about twice the width of Saturn's, making it look like an old 45 rpm phonograph record with a marble-sized planet centered in the hole in the middle.

"What sort of transmission?" I asked, bracing myself for another distress call or more threats. What I hadn't expected at all is what Netty put through the comm.

"—low prices for preferred customers! Apply now and receive ten percent off your first purchase—plus, start receiving Cosmic Club loyalty reward points right away!"

I stared at the comm. "Advertising? Really?"

"Yup. The source of the broadcast is a gas refinery and refueling station orbiting the largest of the gas giants. It's operated by a corporation called BeneStar."

"BeneStar?" Funboy said, then shook his head.

"You know something about these guys, Funboy?" I asked.

"It was inevitable that we'd encounter them out here. BeneStar is a megacorporation based outside known space, with dozens of subsidiaries and affiliates. That includes several *inside* known space, one of which kept coming up in Essie's undercover work. It's called Group 41."

We all turned to him. "Group 41? We encountered them ourselves," I said.

"Guess we know who their sole shareholder is now," Perry put in.

I nodded. We'd encountered Group 41 as the owner of the Bulwark, a mercenary outfit that stood out as sketchy even among the sketchiest of guns for hire. They'd styled themselves after an ancient clan of Japanese *samurai* but in reality had just been exploiting some desperate Eykinao, turning them into what amounted to cannon fodder. Since Group 41 had been privately owned by a single shareholder, there'd been no requirement for any meaningful disclosure of any type, leaving the company completely opaque. We then moved on to other things, but I'd been keeping Group 41 and the Bulwark parked in the back of my mind.

And here they were—or, rather, here their apparent owners were, the megacorp called BeneStar.

"What does this BeneStar do, anyway?" Icky asked.

"A better question is what *don't* they do. Heavy industry, high-end electronics, bioscience, mining, shipping, consumer goods, lots more—all of it done through a web of subsidiaries, affiliates, partnerships, joint ventures, and just about any other corporate relationship you can imagine," Funboy replied.

"And fuel, apparently," I said, turning back to the tactical overlay. The presence of the gas refinery here, at the last navigational waypoint before Rodantic's World, on the only realistic route from known space, was telling. It was a choke point, with essentially all traffic heading up toward or down from the galactic ecliptic having to pass through here. Not only did it offer a profitable business opportunity for fuel sales—and I was willing to bet that if we looked into it, we'd find that BeneStar had a monopoly here for that—but it also let them keep tabs on who was passing through The Deeps.

And it let them broadcast an incessant barrage of advertising. We listened to it for a while, Torina taking note of the number of free products and services being offered.

"If someone is offering you something for free, then you're not their customer, you're their product," she said.

I nodded. That was the conventional wisdom back on Earth, certainly amongst us tech types. Free email and social media wasn't free at all—you were just a product, being marketed to people who wanted to market not-so-free stuff right back at you.

"I *already* hate these guys," Zeno said.

"Oh, well, then you'll love this," I said, gesturing at a new ad on the center display. "Check out these fuel costs. They're, what, at least twenty percent above typical costs back in known space?"

"More like thirty," Perry said.

"Yeah. But look here—if we open a BeneCast account, those fuel prices drop by fifty percent. All we have to do is sign up at a low introductory interest rate of five percent, and then there's a ton of fine print I'd have trouble reading with an electron microscope."

"What it boils down to, Van, is that you'll agree to that introductory interest rate increasing to thirty-five percent after three standard months, while also accepting a lien on your ship and all of its 'fixtures, chattels, upgrades, and additions,'" Netty said.

Torina scowled. "That's just evil."

"Predatory," Perry said.

"Kinda want to fly these guys right into that gas giant," Icky added.

Zeno sniffed and shook her head. "Did I mention I hate these guys?"

Funboy just sighed. "Such is the nature of existence. The strong prevail at the expense of the weak."

I nodded. "So we're not going to be weak. Netty, let's politely refuse the amazing offer of the BeneCast and just fill up our tanks at full price."

"You sure, Van? If you sign up for a BeneCast account in the next thirty minutes, you'll qualify for a free gift—a lovely tote bag."

I glanced at Torina, who rolled her eyes.

"As tempting as that is, I'll pass."

Icky considered the image. "Kinda matches my fur."

Torina took one of Icky's hands in hers, staring earnestly into her eyes. "We don't wear color on color, big girl. Contrast is what makes you stand out."

Funboy sniffed derisively. "Maybe last year. I see fashion *and* hygiene are challenges in this part of space."

Torina gave me a look. "If he critiques my clothing, I'm spacing him."

Zeno grunted in laughter. "I'll get the airlock."

14

WE REFUELED WITHOUT INCIDENT, albeit at a grossly inflated cost. The big orbital gas refinery was mostly automated, but it did have a small crew, one of whom—a humanoid alien with shiny skin, like a polished marble statue—greeted us when we pulled into our assigned berth. The station also offered crew amenities and provisions, mostly of the sort you'd find in an airport duty-free shop— niche and luxury items, all as bloated in price as the fuel. It was the BeneStar employee's job, it seemed, to try to get us to buy some of the offered crap.

What immediately struck me was how strained the alien's demeanor was. He had what I'd come to think of as *call-center cheerfulness*, a reluctantly put-on good humor that was mostly read from a script. I declined each of his offers for sundry goods and services, all of my refusals seeming to trigger the next line in the sales pitch. I finally cut him off.

"If that doesn't suit your needs, sir, we've got—"

"No—as in, I don't want this, or anything else you're selling, thanks."

The alien deflated a bit, genuinely disappointed. I cocked my head at him. "You're under some sort of pressure to sell me something, aren't you?"

"Why, no, sir. I'm just here to cater to your—"

I held up a hand. "You've got some sort of quota to fill, don't you?"

"I—" He stopped, blinking. "I mean—"

Zeno, who'd been listening, spoke up. "What happens if you don't meet it, this quota you obviously have?"

"I—I'm sorry. I'm not supposed to discuss—"

"Anything that isn't in the proforma script, right," I said, nodding. I turned and selected something claiming to be *The Ultimate in Confections, Delicious to a Wide Range of Tastes and Species!* "Here, I'll take this."

The alien's relief was palpable. His enthusiasm sparked back to life, and he immediately went on. "If you'd like to open a BeneCast account, sir, that item is reduced by twenty-five percent—"

"No, no, just this, thanks."

We concluded the sale—the damned box of candy cost me at least four times what I'd expect to pay for it on, say, Tau Ceti—and the alien seemed much more at ease. He bid us farewell when we returned to the *Fafnir*, and I waved back at him. As soon as the airlock closed, I turned to Zeno.

"That was weird," I said, then looked at Icky, who was picking her teeth with a combat knife. "Relatively speaking, of course."

She gave me a small grin. "He was quite sour that you weren't going to jump at any of his overpriced trash."

"I know. I think your point about a quota is bang on. And that makes him seem more like an indentured servant than an employee."

"Maybe he's both," Torina put in as we entered the galley. "While you guys were off shopping, I was curious and actually went through the fine print on that BeneCast agreement. It's more insidious than we thought. Technically, if you ever end up in a position where you can't make two payments in a row, you are—how did they put it, Netty?"

"Liable for provision of services on behalf of BeneStar and its subsidiaries, at the sole discretion of and under conditions solely determined by BeneStar," she said.

I stared for a moment, then cursed softly. "That's debt slavery. There used to be prisons and workhouses where debtors would be locked away, working off what they owed to their creditors."

"At thirty percent or more interest, that could take a long time," Torina said.

Zeno crossed her arms. "Have I mentioned just how much I hate these guys?"

"Van, in case you're interested, we had a tracker attached to the *Fafnir* while we were refueling. It was tagged onto the hull by a discrete little arm that extended itself from the fuel boom."

"Good work, Netty. How'd you happen to notice it?"

"I'm an AI steeped in criminality. I trust no one."

"Words to live by," Funboy said.

Torina glared. "That's a crime no matter where it happens."

Icky blinked at her. "We've tagged a bunch of ships."

"That's different. We're the law." Torina turned to me. "Should we get Evan to remove it and lodge a formal complaint?"

I pondered it a moment. Evan, our external maintenance bot, was certainly more than capable, and it would be satisfying to rub their clunky attempt to tag us in BeneStar's face. But I shook my head.

"Nah, let's leave it, at least for now. We'll raise the issue with them at the appropriate time."

"And when will that be, boss?" Icky asked.

"Oh, about the time our tanks are running low and I feel like *requisitioning* some fuel. You know, in the name of justice and all that."

WE FINALLY MADE planetfall at Rodantic's World to find the place was somehow both more and less of a shithole than it had been made out to us.

At about twice the size of Earth, Rodantic's World had a considerably lower density, some vagary of its internal composition having more abundant lighter minerals than my homeworld. The result was a much larger planet, but with a surface gravity only about fifteen percent higher than Earth's. It was also an incredibly busy world, reminiscent of Fulcrum in the Tau Ceti system, which was all the more remarkable given the nearest star system was eighteen light-years away, with only a dozen or so within fifty light-years. That made Rodantic's World a bustling oasis amid a bleak expanse of nothing, kind of like plunking New York City down in the middle of Antarctica.

That didn't mean it was nice, though. The planet was broadly divided into three types of demographic zones. The most distinct was a blue belt following the equator, where the weather was consistently nice, population density was low, and wealth density was high. The rest of the planet, short of the frozen poles, was a patchwork of the other two types of zone—drab, cheerless suburbs sprawled around grimy, overpopulated industrial blights full of factories, power plants, and packed, ramshackle tenements crisscrossed by polluted, trash-laden canals. Where the latter two blurred into one another in a dreary cycle repeated across the planet's temperate zones, the blue belt might have been partitioned off from the rest by a wall.

And in some places, it was.

Torina was perusing an upload euphemistically called *Getting to Know Rodantic's World*. She'd read a few passages aloud. It managed to mostly gloss over the industrial hellscapes and cookie-cutter corporate suburbs and focus on all the wonderful things the planet had to offer.

"Says here that there are several dozen resorts called Vacation Sanctuaries scattered through the blue zone, where hard-working employees and their families can go to—and I quote—*Rest, Revive, and Recommit*," she said.

"Yeah, that doesn't sound at all like an authoritarian slogan," I said, shaking my head.

"The beatings will continue until morale improves," Funboy chimed in.

But Torina shook her own head. "Oh, I think it's more insidious than that. Guess who owns all of these Vacation Sanctuaries?"

"Does it begin with a B and sound like BeneStar?" I asked.

"Correct. Workers can either pay exorbitant fees out of their pocket for the privilege of spending a few days being able to, you know, actually see the sun totally unfiltered by smog, or they earn—"

I glanced up from the tactical overlay, which was a furball of traffic. "They can earn what?"

"You're going to love this. If they put in extra time at their job, they can earn Relaxation Credits that they can cash in for a stay at one of these Vacation Sanctuaries."

"Great. So they blow their hard-earned savings on a few days away from the salt mine, or they can put in some extra back-breaking hours at said salt mine for a break. Hurray for choice?"

"In case you're interested, a number of the Vacation Sanctuaries are open to off-worlders, Van," Netty said. "Think really expensive resorts and theme parks."

"Yeah, I spent a few days at a mega-resort at Nassau in the Bahamas once. It was basically bars and casinos with a hotel bolted on and a sandy beach I could share with about a million other tourists. Oh, and I could parasail—for three hundred bucks—behind a boat that probably served during the Spanish-American War. No thanks."

"Did you get your hair braided?" Perry asked.

"I chose to stay natural that trip, thank you."

"Great choice, boss. *American Finance Bro Meets News Anchor* is really the sweet spot for your hairstyle."

I touched my head. "Thanks. It is."

"The real question for us is, where to begin?" Zeno said. "If we're going to try to get even a toe in the arms-smuggling door, we're going to have to find an in."

"That *in* might actually be right in front of us. Check out the icon I just highlighted," Perry said.

I looked at the red-outlined icon on the tactical overlay. I tapped it and brought up an image. It was a bulky freighter emblazoned with a logo I was sure I was going to come to know and hate, that of BeneStar. Several hatches gaped open along its flank, into which cargo pods were being nudged by what were probably robotic tugs.

"Okay, what am I looking at, besides a ship being loaded with things and stuff?"

"Watch the cargo pods," Perry said, zooming in the image.

I did. It was about as exciting as it sounded. Imagine standing on a dock and watching containers being stacked on a ship. It was that, just more three-dimensional.

I frowned. "Perry, what the hell—?"

One of the cargo pods abruptly disappeared. It didn't just move out of sight. It literally winked out of existence.

I sat back. "Okay, let me rephrase that. What the hell?"

"Van, Netty's going to apply a filter to the scanners. For it to work, it's going to require us to focus the emissions from the scanner array in a way that might attract attention to us. I don't want to do that without your permission," Perry said.

Torina turned a hard look on him. "Cryptic bird is cryptic. How about just telling us what's going on?"

"Because I'd be speculating. This would determine it one way or the other."

I sat up again and looked at the overlay. We were one icon amid many, a single ship surrounded by a bustle of traffic inbound to and outbound from Rodantic's World. Of course, we were also a pretty distinct type of ship among a multitude that all seemed to be based on a similar hull design I assumed to belong—like everything else around here seemed to—to BeneStar Corporation. We'd put our transponder into location-only mode, not broadcasting my Peace-maker credentials, but if anyone took a close enough look at us, they'd probably figure out who we were.

Still, we'd come here looking for answers, so we couldn't really pass up an opportunity to investigate vanishing cargo pods. I nodded. "Netty, Perry, go ahead."

A few seconds passed, then a new icon appeared on the overlay, flickering inconstantly. At the same time, a ghostly outline appeared on the center display, depicting a sleek ship, about class 11, of a type I'd seen before—most recently, in the immediate aftermath of our conflict against the Seven Stars Leagues and their Tenant puppet masters. It was a hull design favored by the Galactic Knights Uniformed, and it hung about a klick away from the cargo ship.

"They're GKU," I said.

"They are. Netty noticed a slight scanner ghost, so I was curious. Your grandfather, bless his thorough soul, uploaded a filter and asso-ciated instructions that could defeat the Phantom stealth system used by GKU ships. And, sure enough, that's a GKU ship using the Phantom stealth system," Perry said.

"Mark must have known that would come in handy," Zeno said.

I nodded. "Yeah. And he was right—" A warning chime cut me off.

"That ship just lit us up with its fire control scanners," Torina said, reaching for her weapons panel.

"Aw, hell—Netty, open a comm channel please—" I started, but this time she cut me off.

"They beat you to it. I've got an incoming transmission. It's not coming from the ship we've revealed but from what's probably another stealthed ship nearby."

"They've got a friend out there," Icky said.

"So it would seem. Netty, put it on, please."

"Peacemaker, stand down. You too, Amazing. Don't get twitchy."

Amazing? Somebody on the first GKU ship was named *Amazing*? I shoved the thought aside for the moment. I was more worried about missiles and laser shots and things starting to fly.

"I'll second that. Can we talk about this, before someone gets hurt?" I said.

An image appeared on the center display, that of a striking alien, reminiscent of my grandmother, Valint, but with golden skin and an even more arrogant curl to their lip. A companion species to Valint's, maybe? A genetic offshoot?

"Peacemaker, you're interfering with an ongoing operation. Every moment we spend communicating risks compromising it," the alien—a female, I was pretty sure—said.

"I'd apologize, but I'm not really that sorry. We came here looking for answers to some burning questions that are damned important to the well-being of pretty much all of known space, and your operation seems like a hell of a good place to start. By the way, your name is Amazing?"

"Amazing 22, actually. I am the latest in a clone lineage descended from a progenitor who was given the name by someone on your homeworld."

"Earth? Someone on Earth named you Amazing?" Perry asked.

"Actually, they named my progenitor Ahura Mazda, but the more popular title of Amazing was more appealing, so it stuck."

"Ahura Mazda. Really. Also known as Oromasdes, Ohrmazd, Ahuramazda, Hourmazd, Hormazd, Hormaz, and Hurmuz, the creator deity of Zoroastrianism, who first appears in the Achaemenid period of Persian history in the Behistun Inscription of Darius the Great," Perry said.

I blinked a few times at that. "Wait—Persia? As in Earth? Your progenitor was an—and I can't believe I'm saying this—an ancient Persian *god?*"

"That's correct."

"Well, if someone asks you if you're a god, you say *yes,*" Perry muttered.

I shook my head. "Okay. Putting aside the massive moral and ethical implications of an alien pretending to be a god, Amazing 22—"

"I hasten to add that I've never claimed to be a divine entity. That was my progenitor," Amazing said.

"Okay, sure, fine. Anyway, putting all that aside, what the hell are you doing here? What's this operation of yours all about?" I asked.

"That's classified. And again, this ongoing communication risks compromising that operation—"

"Fine. So put me in touch with whoever's in charge—"

I stopped, a sudden, uncomfortable gnawing starting in my gut. "Let me try this a different way. I'm Van Tudor, a member of the GKU myself. So someone better read me into this operation of yours really quickly, because I'm not going anywhere." I took a breath. "And as for that '*whoever's in charge,*' would it happen to be—?"

"Tudor? You're the son of Jocelyn—"

"Wallis, yeah. She's on that other stealthed ship, isn't she?"

"I... can neither confirm nor deny that. But—" Amazing looked offscreen for a moment, then turned back. "Suffice it to say that she will be along in due course," she said, then raised an eyebrow. "And, based on what I've heard, I suspect the two of you have some catching up to do."

I stared right back.

"You have no idea."

———

WE WITHDREW TO A DISTANT, arbitrary point in space where Amazing unstealthed her ship, the *Daggerthrust*. She offered to let us dock, but I declined. We were in what was, as far as I was concerned, hostile space. I didn't want to dock and limit our ability to react to anything unforeseen.

"So where's my mother?" I asked.

"As I said, she'll be along in due course."

"That is *such* a non-answer."

"Nevertheless. Knight Wallis doesn't answer to me. It's quite the other way around, in fact."

I sighed. "Fine. Then let's move on to the next burning subject, that of arms sales." I went on to explain what had brought us out here, and what we hoped to learn. I emphasized we were especially looking for a connection between the Sorcerers, who'd somehow gotten their hands on the twist-enhanced mass driver known as a Powerfist and the case of the missing bioscientist, Adayluh Creel. And bonus points if we could link any or all of that to our long-running identity theft case.

Amazing listened, then shook her head. "I'm sorry, I can't provide you with any information about any such links."

"Can't, or won't?"

That earned a thin smile. "Can't, actually. I know all about the Sorcerers, but I am only vaguely aware of your identify theft case, and I have never heard the name Adayluh Creel before."

"Okay, fine. Tell me about the Sorcerers."

"Well, they're the law out here, filling essentially the same role as the Peacemakers do in known space."

That made all of us sit up.

I just stared, something I'd been doing a lot of since meeting Amazing. "What?"

"To the extent there are laws out here, they are enforced by the Sorcerers."

"The Sorcerers. The Trinduk. They're what passes for *the law* out here in The Deeps. You're… kidding."

Amazing shrugged. "I am not. However, while they're Sorcerers, they're not Trinduk."

"What does *that* mean?"

"The Sorcerers are more of an ideology than a particular group. The most obvious version of them in known space is associated with the Trinduk, but they aren't the only species that puts themselves under the Sorcerers' mantle."

Well, this was a *holy shit* moment. But Amazing doubled down on it.

"BeneStar isn't particular about who acts as their enforcers."

I raised a hand, conceding her point. "Okay. BeneStar uses the Sorcerers as their enforcers. That's what you're telling me here."

"Just when you thought they couldn't get any more cuddly," Zeno muttered.

Amazing nodded. "In case it isn't apparent by now, BeneStar is evil embodied. But it's actually worse than that. Evil usually implies at least some intent. It generally has some sort of personal component to it, some immoral or wicked desire to inflict harm. BeneStar has none of that. It has no intent beyond enriching itself. All other motives are utterly irrelevant."

She smiled thinly again. "Evil hates you. It wants to hurt you. BeneStar simply doesn't care. It has no regard for you at all."

"You talk about BeneStar as though it's a living thing," Torina said.

"That's because it is. It is darkly synergistic, more than the sum of the parts, the people that make it up. It has an identity all its own. Call with a complaint, and you'll speak to some faceless drone or menial AI with no authority. Try to find someone who has authority, and you won't. Even those supposedly in charge of it, its Board, its shareholders and management, they all submit to its money-making processes and shrug. It is an entity unto itself, an emergent intelligence, and it has grown out of *anyone's* control."

"And here I thought rogue AIs were going to be the boogeymen of the future," I said.

Perry glared at me. "Hey, I'm right here."

"Hear, hear," Netty said.

"Present company excepted," I added, then frowned as our contact alarm sounded. Another ship was inbound, burning hard and fast.

"Ah, has my mother finally deigned to put in an appearance?"

But Amazing shook her head. "No. You had wondered about the Sorcerers—well, here they are. No doubt they've noticed our presence out here and have come to *investigate*, although it's more likely we'll be shaken down for bribes." She sighed. "And that's damned inconvenient. Now that they know we're here in the Rodantic's World system, they'll know to look for us. I *told* you we risked compromising our operation."

"I apologize for inconveniencing you," I said in a tone that made it absolutely clear I was not, in fact, apologizing. "What was your operation, anyway, aside from stealing from BeneStar?"

"Isn't that enough?"

"No argument here to that, but you must have had some sort of—"

"First, that remains classified, even to the son of Knight Wallis himself. Second, we have more pressing issues to deal with, and they are rapidly closing."

"I agree with the issue of time," I grumbled. "Once this is taken care of, I expect some answers."

I spoke with finality, which was truncated by the sudden explosion of the approaching Sorcerers' ship. A moment later, another ship unstealthed and accelerated toward us.

"Class 12 attack cruiser, as heavily armed as the *Iowa*," Netty said.

I nodded. "Ladies and gentlemen, you are about to meet retired Peacemaker and current Knight of the GKU, Jocelyn Wallis. But I prefer to call her *mom*."

Guitar music filled the cabin, followed by a nasal, twanging voice that was pure Appalachia.

"What the hell is this, bird?" I asked.

He held up a wing. "Listen to the lyrics, boss."

I did. The singer—a man, presumably, or a woman who gargled asbestos—began to wail like a strangled cat.

"I miss momma's pie, but I don't miss her switch, she done hit me too much with that son of a—"

"Perry."

"Yes, ah, Van?"

I made a cutting motion at my neck. "Kill the tune."

"Sorry, boss. I was just trying to lighten the mood."

"By playing—"

"That's Stank Jenny, the pride of Ringgold, Georgia. Her family was killed in a—"

"At the hands of a vengeful GKU agent who'd been pushed too far by a smarmy avian?" I asked.

The music died abruptly, and everyone was relieved. Except Icky, who'd been tapping her toes. She shrugged when I looked at her, and she managed a sheepish glance.

Icky spread all four arms. "What can I say? I've got rhythm."

Funboy regarded her with an expression of perfect neutrality. "That is debatable."

I TOOK a moment to just study the woman framed in the center display.

I had her chin, I decided. And maybe her cheekbones. The rest of me was my father, but there was enough of this woman in me that you couldn't fail to see it if you looked for it.

"Well, Mom, I guess I should thank you for killing the local law enforcement," I finally said. "Of course, it paints a target on us, and probably means we'll never be able to get anywhere near Rodantic's

World now, but what the hell, right? You don't strike me as being a fan of subtlety."

"Are you finished?"

"Not even close. But I'm not excited about having this little reunion out here on the edge of the Rodantic's World system, and there aren't that many places nearby to—well, this is The Deeps, so there just aren't that many places nearby. With that in mind, where do we go next?"

"Van, those Sorcerers were planning to board a ship I have an interest in seeing kept free of encumbrances. Not that I need to explain myself to you." I opened my mouth, but she went on. "As for where we go now, we don't need to leave this system. We'll find sanctuary in the one place on Rodantic's World BeneStar will never look."

"Sanctuary? So, what, a church?" Perry said, his tone rich with derision.

"Yes."

"Wait, what? Really? In a church? They have churches down there on that soulless hellhole of a planet?"

"That's right. A church rarely used and almost always available. Amazing signed a one hundred year lease with BeneStar, and as long as the payments keep rolling in, they have no further interest." She curled her lip. "It's BeneStar's one vulnerability. It's easy to predict what they'll do because it will always be whatever maximizes their profit. And that, in turn, makes them easy to manipulate."

"So we're just going to fly back to Rodantic's World, slip down to the surface, and have a strategic meeting that masquerades as an old timey revival? How am I doing so far?" I asked.

"Something like that. Amazing and I will stealth our ship and use some other measures. As for you, I'm sending you a new transponder code. Have your AI install it over your existing one. It will declare you as just another BeneStar ship on some mundane and menial corporate business. Oh, and avoid drawing any attention to yourself otherwise. Your death would be a considerable inconvenience for me, Van."

Her image flicked off as the comm link was severed. An uncomfortable silence hung over the *Fafnir*'s cockpit.

Icky leaned forward and patted me on the shoulder. "Welcome to the club, Van," she said.

"What club is that?"

"The club for kids whose moms are absolute *bitches*."

Funboy sighed. "You think that's bad, wait until I tell you about *my* mother. She—"

I cut him off with a gesture. "I don't doubt your mother is a harridan of—"

"Great word, boss," Perry interjected.

"Thanks. Been saving it. Funboy, as much as I'd love to hear about your mother and her shortcomings, I've had enough of familial disappointment for one day. Save it for now, and we'll get to it on a day when I'm in a good mood and need to feel bleak."

Funboy shrugged. "Okay. When you're ready, just use the code word *emo*."

"I—sure. And bird?"

"Yes?"

"If you play *any* music from 1997 to 2009, it's straight into a gas giant for you."

Perry saluted with one wing. "Copy that, boss. And I'm

genuinely sorry about your mom. No one deserves to be an orphan."

"I'm not an orphan, Perry."

He paused, his eyes glowing from within. "Sorta feels like it from over here."

15

"I DON'T LIKE BEING HERE," my mother said.

I crossed my arms and gave her a steady look. "A church? Why? Because you're afraid you might burst into flames or something?"

She looked around. "No. Among people I don't know. Among strangers."

About a dozen possible replies whipped through my mind, most of them variations on outrage. I finally settled on one that didn't seem too hotheaded. I didn't want to give this woman the satisfaction.

"Whose fault is that, Mom?"

She actually winced at that, but she didn't answer right away and headed for one of the dusty pews. I used the moment to regain my equilibrium and take in my surroundings.

The church was just that, a place of worship, albeit one dedicated to a religion I didn't know. The religion hadn't survived, or if it had, it had moved on from this particular place, leaving a sorry, desolate shell, empty of belief and anything except dust and time. There were pews arrayed in an arc around an altar, but whatever had once resided there was gone, leaving a cold slab of gray stone. The altar's bulk was shot through with pink crystals that caught the light in a cheerful counterpoint to the gloom of our setting, and a strange double-sun device was inscribed on the wall behind it. A few bookcases remained, with some lonely books, forgotten by time and people. I picked one up and leafed through it, but my translator could only decipher some of it. The rest was a smear of the unknown.

It struck me as both sad and sinister that a place presumably once devoted to trying to answer the big questions had become nothing but a derelict question all its own.

"It's the DNA," my mother said, sitting in a pew, her eyes closed.

I put the book down and turned to her. "The DNA. Is that supposed to be an explanation?"

I was surprised to see her open her eyes and reveal an expression of—loss? Regret, even? "As much as there is one, I suppose. My family before me was never very good at keeping relationships together. They were also prone to... not dealing well with things, so maybe I inherited some of that, too."

Now pain joined the loss and regret. I made myself push past it.

"What *things* are you talking about?"

"My grandfather fought at Gettysburg. Three days of hell, and he never even took a scratch. But just because he walked away from it doesn't mean he survived it. And his son, my father, was one of four survivors of his freighter being torpedoed somewhere near Ireland in the Great War. Again, his body recovered and lived on another few decades, but the fragments of his mind are still out there somewhere in the Atlantic."

She shrugged. "And then there's me, and the *things* I've seen and done. I'm… not lucid every day. Amazing knows. So do a few others. They look after me when I have an, ah… an episode. A collapse. It's a weakness, and I hate it, and it's also a constant threat. A companion I can't outrun."

She sighed, leaning forward in the exact same way I did when I was thinking. "I try not to hurt people. I never even really wanted to, but it's the only thing I've ever been good at. That, and running away."

I crossed my arms. As much as I wanted to hate this woman as the shitty mother who'd abandoned me, I knew I would not. Her reasons for leaving didn't matter, at least not in the moment, and people, I'd come to learn, were rarely one-dimensional. And, sure enough, now that she was drawing back the curtain on herself, I was starting to see some of the messy complexity behind it. She was deeply flawed, and I could glean that much just from watching the fugitive emotions parade across her features. She couldn't hide them, and she *certainly* couldn't keep them from her own flesh and blood.

I put my hands on the pew and saw dust motes rise from that simple contact.

"You left to do what, exactly? Protect me?"

She looked past me at the double suns behind the altar that were muted with dust and age. "Not the first time, no. But the second time, yes."

That left me staring for a moment. "I didn't know you—"

"Left more than once? I had to. Your father was so good. He

could be all of the things he had to be to succeed in what he did. He was a warrior, Van. He flew machines of war. He could be cold, calculating, and ruthless. Vicious, even."

"But?"

"But, he could… recalibrate. He could become human again. He put aside the gift of killing and became a father. A friend." She held herself rigid now, her eyes still on the double suns, carefully avoiding me.

"I am *barely* civilized, Van," she said. "None of us are. It's a flaw that we carry coded right in us, and nothing has ever changed it." She finally let her gaze flick to me. "You're your father's son. A good man. Yes, a Peacemaker. And yes, GKU. I can tell in the way you wear your authority. You can do the hard things you need to. But like your father, you can recalibrate. You can leave it behind, if only for a day."

Perry cut in, his voice humming in my ear bug. *Still all quiet out here, Van. Dare I ask how it's going?*

Perry kept watch outside. He was the only member of my crew I'd brought here, the rest staying in the *Fafnir*, grounded amid scrubby trees filling a shallow ravine a few hundred meters away. Part of it was that I didn't want to risk any more than necessary coming to this disused church. Another part, though, was that I genuinely felt this was something I had to do alone.

Things are going, Perry.

Ah. Well, I'll leave you to it then.

I turned back to my mother. "It's been almost five years. I'm still learning. How good I am at recalibrating, as you put it, though—" I shrugged. "I'm not so sure."

"You've seen new and terrible things out here, Van. You will never *stop* seeing new and terrible things out here, ever." She gave a faint smile and an equally faint shrug. "And yet, there you stand, clearly still that good man I mentioned a moment ago."

I turned and spent a moment looking at that enigmatic double sun myself, consolidating my thoughts. I was still looking at it when more words finally came to me.

"What about the first time?"

"That I left?"

"Yeah."

"That was out of necessity. There were things happening out here that I had to deal with. Urgent things that couldn't wait." She offered a faint chuckle. "You have no idea how close you came to being born somewhere between Crossroads and Spindrift instead of Cedar Rapids, Iowa."

"Considering how my life has evolved, that might have made it easier, at least in some ways," I said.

"Do you really believe that?"

I turned back to her. "I don't know. Maybe? I mean, I recently acquired a grandmother who I thought was deceased but turned out to be a starfaring alien warrior of considerable ability. And now I've picked up a mother, too, who I'd thought had just walked out of my life, but now turns out to be"—I shook my head—"*another* starfaring warrior—oh, and so is my grandfather, the man who effectively raised me. I said I'd been doing this for five years, but that's not really very long. This is all still new to me, Mom, so yeah—maybe just skipping the twenty-odd years I grew up on Earth and going straight to the starfaring warrior part would have been simpler."

My mother twitched as if stung but said nothing.

I had more to say. "So what do I do, Mom? Do you know how

many mornings I looked for you when I was little, sure I'd wake up to find you'd come back? How much it absolutely killed me to walk into school, always believing that if my mother didn't care, then no one really did? Wondering if I was really wanted or just a burden my father and Gramps were forced to carry? I was alone, Mom. Sure, Dad did what he could, and Gramps filled in, but——"

"They were men, not your mother," she said.

"Yeah. They were actual, real, living men. And damned good examples of it, too."

"I know. I married one and respected the other."

"But they weren't my mother. They weren't you."

I could see the effort it took her to meet my eyes, and I cursed inwardly. What the hell was she doing, being genuinely regretful, full of doubts and second-guesses and sorrow? She was supposed to be cold and uncaring, a detached and distant bitch I could just hate. That would be so much easier.

"What are you asking me here, Van?" she said.

"Good question. Maybe I'm asking if I should make the effort to care and open myself to all the… the good things, and the possible bad ones, that could come from that. Should I? Should I do that, Mom?"

She waited a long moment, staring toward the double suns but clearly not actually seeing them anymore. "Well, for what it's worth, I'd like to try. I don't know how, but I would like to try."

I moved to the pew and sat down beside her. I actually thought about taking her hand, but—no. I wasn't ready for that. Maybe I would be, but right now, I wasn't. Still, sitting beside her was something. It was a shift in my reality, and it was enough. Or maybe it was all I could tolerate for the time being.

So we sat for a while, side by side, saying nothing as the building settled and creaked around us. Night was coming, the air outside was cooling, and the air inside was turning wan and gray.

When she finally spoke into the growing gloom, I caught a hint of ease in her voice that hadn't been there before. Again, it was something.

"What case brought you here, anyway?"

"All of them," I said, then shrugged. "Everything seems to come back to the stolen identities we've been working on for years now. But most immediately, I guess it would be finding Adayluh Creel. She's a bioscientist with a specialization in food production. She can feed people. Maybe *all* of the people. And someone stole her because of it. I suspect they want whatever she's discovered or invented, and—"

"And the money." She nodded. "They want *all* the money. The money and the power that comes with it. It's a constant out here. Although I suspect you already know that, Van—" She paused and looked at me. "Son."

She tried on the word like a new shirt and seemed to find it was a close fit, at least, but might need some time, and maybe some alterations. I knew it would for me.

"Anyway, BeneStar rules everything out here. And if they don't, they'll make it their purpose to subsume it, so they do. Vid stars, news talkers, actors, all of them are willing and complicit because it gives them fame and money. So they flood the channels with propaganda and use it to shape public opinion. In fact, they've got the latest and number one star on their payroll. Calls himself Perfect Three—I think he's a Synth, some humanoid. Huw'arde, maybe even a touch of Vesilax, those arrogant bastards. Anyway, he's beautiful and articulate and charming, and he knows it, and the camera loves him for it. So do a billion fans, maybe two billion, across and beyond The Deeps. He's hypnotic, and he's bought and paid for."

She glanced at me. "Anyway, it's through things like him that they manipulate the people, which means they own politics and public policy, which means they ultimately own the people, too."

I thought about the Earthly analogs to BeneStar. "Sounds familiar."

She nodded. "Same recipe, just a different bowl. And now there's an angle to their perpetual grabbing for power and control, one I must admit I didn't see coming. None of us did." She sniffed. "Food. Huh. I thought they'd stick with transport and energy, at least for now." She pursed her lips for a moment. "Where was she taken from? This scientist?"

"Rolling Fields."

My mother nodded, slowly, her eyes now bright with thought. "What brought you out here, to this area? Specifically?"

I summarized the chain of events and logic that had brought us to Rodantic's World and she nodded again.

"Well, if she's out here, it can *only* be BeneStar. But that doesn't help us. The real question is *who*, in Benestar? Because it isn't just a corporation. Not any longer. It's become something more than the sum of its parts. As long as it's making money, it doesn't care."

"Amazing said much the same thing."

"She's right. To say *it's BeneStar* is useless. It's like saying *it's the bad guys*. So it's a part of BeneStar, someone or something within it who sees an opportunity to feed the beast, as it were. To please its corporate overlord. To find this Adayluh Creel, that's the question you need to answer."

"Great. So all we have to do is tunnel our way into a massive megacorporation and find out who among… thousands of executives, and middle-managers, and employees? Tens of thousands?"

"Millions, probably."

"Even better. Sift through *millions* of these parts that make up BeneStar, without attracting undue attention, and find Adayluh Creel."

"Oh, it's more difficult than that. About five years ago, my GKU cadre fought a BeneStar fleet. They have a subsidiary, Group 41, that's Navy and ground force, with a full and sophisticated command and logistics structure."

"Yeah, we've encountered Group 41 before."

"Wait, there's more. If BeneStar really wants you dead, they'll manipulate entire worlds into mobilizing against you, turning their armed forces into extensions of their own. BeneStar can entertain you, charm you, give you everything you want, convince you to owe them money until you die, and even kill you—"

Ground vehicle just pulled up and stopped about two hundred meters away. I count six guys dismounted, armed and armored up, Perry informed me.

I turned to my mother. "Well, shit. It's as though you summoned them. We've got company."

She nodded and drew her weapon, a chunky gun that resembled The Drop but came with a folding stock that basically turned it into a long arm.

"Looks like Amazing's lease has just been canceled," she said, standing and heading for the door.

I unholstered The Drop and followed her.

"SIX OF THEM. This is just a fishing expedition, some local commander catching wind of something happening at this old church," my mother said, her voice low and quiet over the comm. Torina and Zeno were on their way, but these BeneStar agents— probably just local muscle, according to my mother—were a lot closer. And while they might be thugs, they weren't dumb. They'd deployed in a wide horseshoe, essentially trapping us between them and the old church while maintaining decent mutual support.

The closest one is about fifteen meters in front of you, slightly right, Van. Mom, yours is just over ten meters, slightly left, Perry said.

"Got it. And don't call me Mom unless I actually gave birth to you."

Well that's pretty arbitrary.

I was hoping we could avoid a fight with these guys. Both my mother and I wore b-suits, and we'd both brought our helmets, so we were hardened. Our suits also had a limited ability to store body heat, mitigating the effectiveness of our opponents' thermal imaging, at least for a short time. But we had to do something here, and quickly, or they'd stumble right into us.

My mother was apparently thinking the same way, but instead of suggesting we try to withdraw, she simply opened fire. Her gun boomed, and the round slammed through the BeneStar man closest to her, blasting most of his chest organs behind him in a spectacular shower of gore.

"Subtle," I mumbled.

No warning, no preamble, no attempt to get away. The first card she played was *violence.*

I thought of her admission—*I try not to hurt people. I never even really wanted to, but it's the only thing I've ever been good at.*

218

Yeah, I'd say she was good at it.

A fusillade of automatic weapons fire truncated any further introspection, though, ripping apart the deepening night with muzzle flashes. They'd all laid their fire into my mother's approximate location, rounds shaking and chewing up the foliage, smacking into the church and splintering off chips of it. The air was filled with whining rounds as stone spalled away with each. I cursed and raised The Drop.

The man dead ahead of me, now less than ten meters away, kept snapping bursts in the direction of my mother. I had an easy shot, but my finger hesitated on the trigger. If I squeezed it, I'd just kill the shooter, no questions asked. By my mother's own words, he was a tiny cog in the vast machine of BeneStar, whose corporate dominion wouldn't even notice his loss.

It just didn't seem *right*.

I thumbed The Drop's fire selector, switching to the stun beam, and fired it instead. With a flash and a snap, the man dropped like a sack of stones.

Unfortunately, that just made me a second target. Two of them swung their fire and started hammering the foliage around me, every round chewing into the church wall with a vicious crack. A slug punched me in the right arm. Another smacked into my left shoulder. They stung but didn't penetrate my suit.

They did, however, tap into my primal anger. I was *pissed*.

I dodged aside and tried to line up another shot. But one of them kept up a rapid fire, while the other abruptly charged straight at me, determined to blitz me into submission. Two more rounds smacked into me, and I cursed again, thumbing the selector back to the slug thrower.

"Of all the days to come under my sights," I said, taking aim, "you picked the one filled with family angst." I snapped off the shot, then chased it with another.

My round slammed into the onrushing man's chest, and he pitched forward with a cry of sheer agony.

But the other shooter had my range, and I was hit three more times in rapid succession—shoulder, chest, and a round that clacked off my helmet in a dizzying flash. Without my b-suit, I'd have been dead. I banged two shots back and changed position again, but whoever this guy was, he was good. His slugs followed me relentlessly, hitting me two more times.

I had to end this before he got lucky—or switched to armor-piercing ammo.

I boomed out another shot and got another burst in return. I lined up another, but something swept in from above and struck my target, driving him to the ground.

I charged.

Perry flapped and raked at the man's face, while the man swung his gun like a club and landed a heavy blow on his wing. Perry staggered back but immediately lunged in again. I stopped, took careful aim, and double-tapped two rounds into the man, dropping him.

"I had this all under control, you know," Perry said.

I grunted an acknowledgement and turned back toward my mother, only to find her walking my way.

"I think that's all of them," she said.

I flicked The Drop back to *safe* and holstered it. As I did, I glanced toward the one I'd stunned. I considered mentioning him to her but didn't.

"For the next few minutes. Then another wave's going to show up, and I doubt it'll just be six guys," I said.

"All the more reason to make ourselves scarce. Get back to your ship, get to orbit, and then run. I'll find you, don't worry," she said, then reached out her hand.

I looked at it, then took it. Despite us both wearing gloves, it struck me that this was the first time I'd made any sort of physical contact with my mother since... since being born.

Torina and Zeno arrived, ready for battle, but I waved them off. "Run to where?"

She smiled, squeezed my hand once, then released it.

"Home."

16

I LEANED on the porch railing, and it creaked in exactly the way I knew it would. Beyond, in the yard between the farmhouse and the barn, grass glowed golden in the low rays of the autumn sun.

I took a deep breath. The *Fafnir*'s air purifiers were top-notch, but there was no replacing the fresh air of an Iowa fall. It tasted of soil and the vestiges of harvested corn, of air starting the long slide toward winter's deep chill and a faint tang of woodsmoke from some distant bonfire or stove. It was that perfect scent I call the *glory season*, a time of change and, in its own way, renewal, even among the browns and yellows of deep autumn.

Icky appeared in the door of the barn and waved at me. We had a standing rule that none of the aliens were to reveal themselves on the farm by daylight, despite Perry's assurances he could find no surveillance devices around the place.

"I flew a pattern, scanned, and took two more laps. The only thing I found of note was a pair of asshole ravens who apparently thought I was trying to muscle in on their territory," he said.

"Corvids can be dicks. Agreed," I said.

Perry gave me an appreciative nod. "Thanks, boss."

"I'm on your side. Always."

Still, it didn't hurt to be careful. It was the same reason I kept Tony Burgess and his people at arm's length from the farm. I wouldn't put it past any number of parties to be keeping an eye on them, from the Defense Department to other UFOlogists to even more sinister types from beyond the sky. I still wanted to believe the farm was a safe space, a refuge, even if a growing part of me was coming to suspect it wasn't.

I headed for the barn. Inside, Icky and Zeno gestured at the *Fafnir*, which gleamed in the bright overhead lights. We kept her cloak, proof against mundane detection, engaged as a matter of course.

"Got the particle cannon tuned up and ready to go. All we need to do is give it a few test shots," Zeno said, pointing at the chunky barrel protruding from the turret atop her hull, just aft of amidships.

"Yeah, I think we'll hold off on that until we're spaceborne again. It might get tough to explain particle beam furrows plowed into the neighbors' fields," I replied.

I did a walkaround of the *Fafnir*, just for the hell of it, taking in the fact that the expanded barn was already getting cramped. If we lengthened the ship by more than a couple of meters, we'd have trouble getting her to fit again. And doing another expansion on the barn might attract attention we didn't want. Miryam had fielded a casual inquiry from a neighbor she'd met in town about why we'd brought in contractors to lengthen the barn in the first place. She'd provided our bullshit cover story that I was considering getting into horse breeding and felt the barn needed to be bigger, but I'd probably have to, you know, buy some horses before trying that one a second time.

Don't get me wrong. I like horses. I just don't ride them very often because they strike me as being a half ton of *strong opinion*.

"Van?"

I'd been examining the starboard main landing strut, trying to determine if a slight discoloration on the gleaming metal was something leaking, some corrosion, or just a trick of the light. It seemed to be the latter, so I turned to the voice. It was Torina.

"Something wrong?" she asked, crouching beside me.

"I was just looking at this strut. Thought I saw something—" I stopped at her expression. "You're not talking about the landing gear, are you?"

"Well, I am—"

"It's fine."

She nodded. "But not *just* the landing gear. When do you expect your mother to arrive?"

I shrugged. "No idea. She said she'd meet us here. But—" I shrugged again. "Who knows, right? She might have got embroiled in something else. And even if she didn't, well, it wouldn't be the first time she's let me down."

Torina said nothing.

I sighed. "She's a complicated person, Torina. There's a lot more going on there than I'd have ever imagined."

"Van, I have to ask—do you even want her in your life?"

I glanced at her as I straightened, ducking my head to avoid smacking it on one of the muzzles of the starboard point-defense battery. "She's my mother."

"That doesn't answer the question."

"Are you suggesting I shouldn't want my mother in my life?" I deflected.

"No, I'm suggesting that you're not *obligated* to if you don't want to. Just sharing some DNA with her isn't much of a basis for a relationship. I think you have to *want* her in your life, Van."

Now it was my turn to say nothing.

"So, back to my original question. Do you *want* her in your life?"

I thought back to the church on Rodantic's World, how I'd entered it intending to hate the woman who was my mother and instead finding out she was complicated and damaged. How I'd left the church feeling much more ambivalent. And how, when confronted by the BeneStar security troopers, her first instinct had been to open fire and kill them.

How I hadn't wanted to mention that I'd only stunned one of them because I had no trouble imagining her simply executing him, tying up a loose end.

I shook my head. "I don't know."

"Honesty is good, especially now," Torina said, then brushed my neck with her fingers. It was a momentary touch, but it had the desired effect. I smiled at her, both in thanks and admiration. She understood me.

"Van, there's an incoming transmission for you," Netty said.

I puffed out a breath. "And there she is now."

"Actually, it's not your mother. It's Gerhardt," Netty put in.

Torina and I raised our eyebrows at each other.

"Gerhardt? He must want something badly to put a twist comm through to Earth from Anvil Dark," Torina said.

"It's not a twist comm from Anvil Dark. He's currently in his ship, just passing the orbit of Mars," Netty replied.

"Put him through," I said.

Gerhardt's voice hummed out of the comm. "Tudor, are you in the mood for visitors?"

"I—uh, yeah, sure. Netty will send you the coordinates of a place you can land. It's a few klicks away from here, but we'll come and pick you up."

"I'll let you know when I arrive," he replied, and the channel closed.

"What the hell has brought him all the way to Earth?" Torina mused.

I put my hands on my hips and shook my head.

"Not a clue. But it's hard to imagine it's just a social call."

If GERHARDT FOUND any novelty in riding in a 2015 Ford F150 pickup, he didn't let on. Miryam had made a big deal about carrying hay and other horse-related accessories when she bought it to further the illusion about my sudden interest in becoming an equestrian magnate. As we bumped along the road, trailing a dust cloud, I made a couple of attempts to start a conversation, but Gerhardt refused to engage. I wasn't sure what he was waiting for, but I ended up mostly talking to him about Iowa.

"This is very... agrarian," he said, watching as recently harvested fields scrolled past beyond the fences and tall yellow grass lining the roadside. Dark clouds were piling up to the west, hinting at autumn thunderstorms and backdropping it all with deepening shades of gray.

"There's a reason this is called the Corn Belt."

"And this is where you grew up?"

"It is. I trundled back and forth along this road in a school bus every day, in fact." I pointed at a stand of trees. "The first time I got drunk, it was during a party in that copse over there."

"I see."

"You must have had, ah, similar experiences as a kid," I said.

"I grew up on an orbital in Tau Ceti. I traveled to and from school via mag-lev capsule."

"Ah. Not quite the same, then."

We pulled into the driveway. I stopped, snapped the truck into park, and switched off the engine. Then I turned to Gerhardt.

"Since the easing-into-it-via-small-talk approach obviously isn't going to work, I'm just going to come out and ask. Why the hell are you here?"

He turned to me. "Part of the reason is that I was genuinely curious about you, Tudor. Where you're from. What's in your background. You're on track for further advancement in the Guild, but we're at the point where *who you are* is as important as *what you've accomplished*—and maybe even more so."

"Oh. This is the equivalent of a background check."

"Something like that." He peered out the windshield at the farmhouse. "So this is where Mark Tudor lived as well."

"It was, yeah. At least half of his life—as far as I know about it, anyway. With time dilation and all that, I'm still not a hundred percent sure he wasn't born in—I don't know, the time of the

American Revolution or something." At Gerhardt's blank look, I smiled.

"A long time ago."

He nodded, and we exited the truck. The clouds had piled higher, and distant thunder muttered across the fields.

"It's remarkable that this unassuming structure is responsible for producing two of the most notable Peacemakers in Guild history," he said as we walked up the drive.

I chuckled. "Notable, huh? Notable good, or notable bad?"

He glanced at me sidelong. "Notable."

My chuckle became a laugh. This was *so* Gerhardt. "Well, I'll assume you mean *notable good* and take it as a compliment."

But Gerhardt abruptly stopped and faced me. "Notable in *any* way isn't always a good thing, Tudor."

"What's that supposed to mean?" I asked as more thunder tickled the air.

"There's a storm coming."

I stared at him. He wasn't talking about the clouds.

⸻

AFTER A PLEASANT DINNER delivered via a gig driver from Elkader, Gerhardt, Torina, Perry, and I went for a walk. The thunderstorm menace had proved to be overblown, resulting in a smattering of rain and wind that lasted about fifteen minutes, punctuated by one good peal of thunder and a few timid ones. The sun reappeared in the almost-storm's wake, turning the evening surprisingly warm.

We wandered down to the creek that bordered the property. Gerhardt seemed tired, lacking his characteristic snap.

We stopped beside the sluggish watercourse, under the shade of some hoary elms.

"Again, very pastoral," Gerhardt said, taking in the placid scene, then turning to me. "Also very pleasant."

"Yeah. This was one of my thinking spots," I said.

A voice came from the tree above us. "Oh, is that what you and Torina were doing here on our last visit—*thinking*," Perry asked.

Torina smiled and looked up at him. "I don't know about Van, but I sure as hell wasn't doing much *thinking*."

"I was. And as to what the topic was, that's between me and Torina. I have, unlike the bird, *manners*."

Gerhardt actually smiled, but it was like a light flicking on and off. "Thank you for sharing something I had absolutely no need or desire to know. Anyway—"

He turned to me. I spoke before he did.

"A storm is coming."

He nodded. "I received an urgent message from Valint three days ago. She would have contacted you directly, but you were in The Deeps, and she was... elsewhere, so comms just weren't feasible."

I took a breath. "Why do I have a feeling I'm not going to like this?"

"Because you won't. According to Valint, you've been compromised—badly. She didn't have details, but she was warned that you can no longer consider any place in known space secure."

I stared in amazement, my pulse going triphammer fast. "What... in the hell... does—"

Torina, though, spoke up immediately. "What exactly does

compromised mean? You can't just drop something like that without some substance."

"It means that someone out there has been able to discern a great deal about who you are. One of those things they've discerned is your origin," Gerhardt said, gesturing around. "Valint believes that you should expect to be attacked here—and not just in the form of a raid, as you've reported in the past. If whoever this is wants you dead badly enough, they'll likely destroy all of this without any compunction whatsoever."

I turned and looked at the sluggish creek. Thoughts tumbled through my mind, mainly past instances of me being here, trying to get away from things and grab a few moments of peace. I'd come here to worry about exams. I'd come here to worry about whether this girl liked me or not, and whether I should ask her out on a date. I'd come here to unwind after an argument with Gramps or my father. I'd come here to wonder where my mother was and why it felt so shitty to miss her.

And now it was, what? Ground zero for an attack by weaponry so advanced that Earthly science didn't even yet recognize some of the *principles* upon which it was based?

"However bad you're thinking it is, Van, it's worse," Perry said.

I looked up. "What do you mean?"

"Imagine a missile with a thermonuclear warhead detonating here. Or an antimatter warhead, for that matter. Right smack in the middle of the United States. What do you think will happen next?"

I swore into the evening. An antimatter warhead would wreak unimaginable destruction. Downtown Chicago was only about two hundred and fifty klicks to the east. Des Moines, Kansas City, and St. Louis were all within four hundred klicks. So was Whiteman Air

Force Base in Missouri, which was home to a nuclear stockpile and the B-2 Spirit stealth bombers meant to deliver them. Those might sound like great distances, but considering some of the firepower available off world, they really weren't. They were well within the fields of fire.

Not that it mattered. Any weapon of mass destruction detonated in the American heartland would demand an immediate and decisive response. Destroying Pony Hollow, Iowa, could easily trigger the end of Earthly civilization.

And that didn't even count the Sorcerer twist drive that could operate in a gravity well and potentially smash a planet like Earth to gravel.

Considering some of the bad guys involved, they'd have no compunction about any of that. Hell, they'd probably get a kick out of it. They might even try and record the last seconds of some people's lives, sick bastards that they were, so they could stock them in the extraterrestrial equivalent of a streaming site, where other sick bastards could download and enjoy them.

I looked back at Gerhardt. "We can't stay here. We'll have to go to—I don't know, Anvil Dark. Or the Starsmith."

Gerhardt frowned. "Starsmith? I wouldn't recommend that. Linulla and his colleagues wouldn't likely be enthused about having you there, considering the threat you'd bring."

Despite everything, I took a moment to study Gerhardt's face. It told me that he didn't know about Matterforge, the one power in known space to whom even the biggest antimatter bomb would seem like a lit match. I wasn't sure why Matterforge had never been revealed to him, but it wasn't my place to second guess unfathomable beings who live on the surface of stars, so I left it at that.

"The bottom line is that we can't stay here," I said.

"I quite agree. And that's why I came here personally, rather than just using the comm. I want to help, Tudor."

After another few seconds of silent regard, my estimate of Gerhardt continued upward. Again. My opinion of this man had changed so much from where it had started.

"I… appreciate that."

"To that end, I've taken the liberty of contacting Petyr Groshenko. He's on his way here aboard the *Poltava*. Lunzy and K'losk are also on their way. Unfortunately, Valint says that no GKU assets can be here in anything less than a week, and to be honest, I don't believe we have that long."

I nodded. "Okay. First things first. We need to vacate Earth asap."

"And go where?" Torina asked.

"The one place other than Starsmith where we've got some serious firepower to help us out. We're going to Orcus. We're going to get the *Iowa* ready to fight."

I WATCHED as the western US scrolled by beneath us, dwindling as the *Fafnir* climbed to orbit. My attention was on the comm, though.

"Van, what the hell do you mean I need to take a vacation?" Miryam asked.

"It's a precaution, Miryam. Things might get complicated in and around Pony Hollow. Just take a vacation, somewhere outside the US. Actually, somewhere outside North America. It's on me."

"Van… you're scaring me. What the hell's going on? And if it's something that I need to avoid by taking a trip to Italy or somewhere, then what about all of the other people who live around here?"

I sighed. "Miryam, I'm on my way back into space specifically so that I'm not in Pony Hollow. That's the single most important thing I can do to take away the threat, which is my half-assed way of saying that I don't think anyone's really at risk. Not as long as I'm not there. But... please, just do this for me, okay?"

"Your grandfather wanted me to go to Greece."

"What?"

"You think this is the first time a Tudor has told me to clear out of Pony Hollow?" She sighed back at me. "It was a shitty vacation then, and it's going to be a shitty vacation now. I spent all my time watching the news, waiting for some breaking story about a bomb going off in eastern Iowa."

"I'm sorry, Miryam. I really am."

A moment passed before she answered. "Fine. I'll go and eat and drink my way through Tuscany. But I'm taking a gentleman friend with me, and I'm going to make it as expensive as possible."

I smiled. "You do you, Miryam."

"I will most certainly *not* be doing me. That's why I'm calling Tim," she informed me.

"Miryam!" I said, laughing at her response.

"It may surprise you to note that women don't *go to seed* once we hit fifty, you Neanderthal. I'm booking five star agritourist farmsteads, and I'm using company money. Let this be a lesson to you about ageism."

"I consider myself both informed and horrified."

"Perfect. Arrivederci, Van. Be careful. You matter." She signed off.

"Van, Gerhardt's ship just lifted off. He's about ten minutes behind us," Netty said.

"Good. Now, how about ahead of us? Anything?"

"Aside from the ISS and the usual satellites and things, no. At least, not on passive scanners."

"Go active. Ping the hell out of near-Earth space. I want anyone watching to know we're heading out into the black."

"Van, there's one complication we need to consider," Perry said.

"Just one? Cool."

"The new James Webb space telescope is pretty sensitive to incoming light from stars, galaxies, nebula—and thermonuclear explosions out around Pluto."

"Great. What are you suggesting?"

"It might behoove us to, you know, make sure it's not operating before we head to Orcus."

"You want to destroy it."

"Well, I was thinking more along the lines of rendering it inoperable. We could always fix it later."

I shook my head. "I'm not going to screw around with one of mankind's greatest technical achievements to date just for the sake of expediency. Netty, can we predict where in the Solar System we can go where the damned thing's not liable to be pointing?"

"I understand that it's not very good at, you know, looking *through* the Sun, it being so bright and all."

"Superb. We're really sciencing now, kids. Let's get the *Iowa* moving that way and plot a course for the *Fafnir* accordingly. Also, let Gerhardt know, and ask him to pass the plan on to Groshenko and the others."

"On it, boss."

I glanced at Torina. "Probably should have parked the *Iowa* on the other side of the Sun to begin with. That was dumb."

She shrugged. "Meh. On the scale of dumbness, that rates *oversight* more than anything else. *Dumb* would have been staying on Earth. You made the right decision."

"Hey, it's a decision that involves potentially turning some bad guys into disconnected clouds of atoms. Sweet," Icky said.

I turned to Funboy, who'd been given a permanent station behind Icky. We'd redistributed duties, with Torina copilot and still primary gunner, Zeno doing weapon systems and playing secondary gunner, Icky doing all of the *Fafnir*'s other systems aside from propulsion, and Funboy now set up with a propulsion station and also ready to act as our medic. It gave us a lot more redundancy, and also a lot more engineering horsepower, which was necessary since the *Fafnir* was now a much larger and more complicated ship.

"Funboy, I never heard what you thought of Earth," I said.

He raised his head from his panel and peered at me. "You combust hydrocarbons for a wide range of industrial and transportation purposes."

"Uh… yes, we do."

"I could tell. Your atmosphere contains high concentrations of their combustion by-products."

"He's saying he thought Earth stank," Perry said in a stage whisper.

Funboy gave his now-trademark languid shrug. "Other than that, it was very nice."

I nodded. "Okay, then—"

"Well, except for the sky."

I turned back. "The sky. What was wrong with the sky?"

"Is it always that blue?"

"Well, not at night."

He just stared at me, blinking. "Well, of course not. There's insufficient ambient light to be affected by atmospheric gases—oh. Wait. That was a joke."

I smiled and shrugged. "Kind of. Not a very good one, I guess."

"No, no. It was… very humorous," he replied, lifting the corners of his mouth in a horrifying attempt at a human smile.

I turned back to the instruments. "Funboy, don't ever change."

"I… don't intend to, except for cellular degradation. Why? Did you somehow get the impression I did?"

Torina was giggling. I just shook my head.

"Carry on, sunshine."

He preened a bit. "I shall."

17

WE ARRIVED AT THE *IOWA*. Netty had already brought her out of the state of hibernation we kept her in to move her to the new location. She was also powering up systems, warming up the interior, testing weapons, and getting ready to fight. Icky and Zeno boarded her and started testing her automation, making sure it would stand up during battle.

"It's finicky, but I think it'll hold together," Icky declared over the comm as we moved *Fafnir* away from her. "We really need to get a proper crew for her, though, Van. As long as everything's holding together, Zeno and I can fly and fight her. But if things start to go wrong, well, we've got basically no capacity for damage control, except the two of us running around like mad with spanners and fire extinguishers."

"I hear ya, Icky. Groshenko's said much the same thing. And if I could afford to have a crew sitting around playing cards out here while waiting for us to need the *Iowa* for battle, I would."

"Speaking of Groshenko, look who just twisted in," Torina said.

I nodded. The *Poltava* had just popped onto the tactical overlay. Lunzy and K'losk had already arrived.

Groshenko's face appeared on the center display. "Hello, Van. What's this I hear about someone threatening my planet?"

I smiled. "Hey, Petyr," I said and brought him up to date with everything Gerhardt had told me that he'd learned from Valint.

"So you see the problem. Earth is pretty vulnerable," I finished.

Groshenko nodded, then gave me a hard smile. "Have you ever heard of Prokhorovka?"

"Uh... someplace in Russia, I assume?"

"It is. It's the location of the largest tank battle in history, between the Nazi Germans and the forces of the Soviet Union during the Second World War. It was pretty much the culmination of the Germans' last major attempt to regain the strategic initiative on the Eastern Front. It was a close thing, but the Soviets finally prevailed."

"Okay, I believe you. Why are you telling me this?" I expected him to answer with some deep tactical insight from the battle, but that wasn't what I got.

"The other reason Prokhorovka is important is because there's an old man there named Stefan whose family runs a vodka distillery. I have traveled light-years, Van—light-*years*. And I've never had vodka that good. I will be damned if I'm going to let some Sorcerers, or anyone else, cut off my supply of the stuff."

He grinned and I laughed. We agreed that he would take the *Poltava* in-system and stay near the orbit of Jupiter, acting as a backstop against any possible incursions directed at Earth. The rest of us would hang out in our new location in the Kuiper Belt, making ourselves obvious to attract the bad guys' attention.

Which introduced another problem—how to communicate with him, since he'd be on the same side of the Sun as Earth, while we'd be on the other. Perry came up with a solution.

He put a new icon on the overlay. "Remember the James Webb space telescope? That's it, right there. There's a direct line of sight between it and us, and it and the *Poltava*, if she stays in line of sight with it, that is. We use it to relay comms between us."

"You're just obsessed with that thing, aren't you?" Torina said.

"Yeah, kinda—because it's actually so damned cool."

I frowned. "Will we interfere with its operation? I really don't want to, um, break it?"

"Nah, not if we stick to low-fidelity voice only. I wouldn't recommend high-res video."

I nodded. "Let's do it. Petyr, you got that?"

He nodded. "Have Perry contact our ship's AI and work out the details." His face turned grave. "Be careful, Van. You're not dealing with common criminals here. These people are good at what they do and very, very bad while they're doing it."

"That's the plan. Besides, now I need to try out some of that Proka—Prokul—"

"Prokhorovka."

"Yeah, there. Some of that vodka."

"I thought you were a bourbon man."

"Always willing to expand my horizons, Petyr."

"We'll make you a Slav yet," Petyr said, then signed off with a salute.

WE WAITED.

It was a tired truism that for soldiers, waiting was the hard part.

All we could do was sit and watch the tactical overlay, banging away into space with our active scanners, and waiting for… something. We weren't even really sure what.

"Valint had no idea what sort of threat we were facing? Or when?" I asked Gerhardt.

"Tudor, I've told you everything I know. Based on my past experience working with her, as well as her relationship with you, I'm prepared to take it at face value," he replied.

"The question then becomes, how long are we going to wait? And once we decide we've waited long enough, what then?" Funboy asked, then frowned. "Which is actually two questions, I suppose. Alright, the *two* questions then become——"

"Gotcha, Funboy. And the answers are *I don't know* and *I don't know that either.*"

"We need a name for this place," Perry abruptly put in. I turned a puzzled frown on him.

"What place?"

"Here. Where we are. If we're going to have a battle here, we need a name for it. The *Battle of That Random Spot in Sol's Kuiper Belt* doesn't really roll off the tongue, does it?"

Torina pointed at the overlay. "There's a big rock about a hundred thousand klicks that way. It's almost as big as Orcus is. Let's give it a name."

I pushed up my lower lip, then nodded. "Okay. Any ideas?"

"Last Stand. It seems appropriate," Funboy suggested.

I scowled at that. "That's a little too—I don't know, desperate and final sounding. We need something more upbeat but also meaningful."

"Pony Hollow," Netty said.

That made me sit up. "Hey, I like that. Although, I'm curious, Netty—why Pony Hollow?"

"Because, Van, if there's going to be a Battle of Pony Hollow, wouldn't you rather it be way the hell out here instead of on Earth?"

I nodded. "Unless anyone objects, Pony Hollow it is." I had Netty put the image of the little planetoid on the center display.

"Hello, Pony Hollow. Nice to meet you," I said to it—

Just as the contact alert sounded.

"Van, there are five ships inbound. One is class 13, a dedicated warship, destroyer-class. The other four range from class 7 to class 9, fast freighter-class hulls, armored and up-gunned."

I nodded. "Showtime. The question is, where are they going?"

If they were heading to Earth, then we had to move fast to intercept them, or at least hope Groshenko and the *Poltava* could hold them off long enough for us to catch up. But, within minutes, it became clear that they were bound straight for us. Earth, it seemed, could wait.

The Battle of Pony Hollow was about to begin.

———

WE DUCKED behind the rock only seconds before the missile detonated. It had been close—ten seconds later, and we'd have been caught in the hail of shrapnel from the exploding warhead. Instead, it raked the agglomerated mass of rock and ice, a chunk about the size of a city block, spalling off fragments.

"Funboy, how's that upper laser turret coming?" I called back.

His voice came over the comm. "Still working on it. That missile took out both the main and redundant controllers. I'm having to string cable to bypass the damage."

I glanced back and cursed. The Sorcerers' opening missile barrage had mostly died to our point-defenses, but a couple had snuck through the storm of mass-driver slugs. And one of them had had a trick up its digital sleeve, firing an explosive charge that had flung the warhead in an unexpected direction—straight at the *Fafnir*.

Our own point-defenses had tried mightily, but it was too small to easily target and detonated close by, slamming shrapnel and debris through the hull. The damage had not only knocked one of the laser turrets offline, but it had also sheared off our port-amid-ships thruster array, costing us some roll capability.

The *Iowa* shuddered as she fired, throwing point-defense rounds out at a hideous pace. The tracers stitched across the enemy class 13, ripping gouts of metal and armor into space. An entire panel of Sorcerer hull wheeled away as a missile found its way home, and I turned the *Fafnir* sunward to create separation between the friendlies.

"Nice shooting," I murmured, watching streams of data as the battle began heating up. The class 13 wasn't just armed—she was overpowered, sporting missile and gun systems in places that made her bristle with offensive capability.

Whoever was in command of her understood warfare, too.

But so did we.

"Birds away," Torina said.

"Send lasers."

"Sending."

Two beams lanced out as the class 9 yawed away, trying to expose a pair of belly mounted tubes that could throw six missiles per launch.

"Petyr, we're breaking left—"

"I see the window. Firing," he answered.

The *Poltava* was mere klicks away and down the ecliptic, her guns speaking instantly as the class 9 met her end in a searing globe of plasma.

"Boom," Torina said.

"Boom," Funboy agreed with uncharacteristic joy.

The *Iowa* fired again even as Petyr's missiles slammed home, tearing into the class 13 with a vengeance.

Another bracket of missiles appeared on our scans, and then it was back to work.

Torina growled. "Two missiles, Van. That class 9 has us dead to rights in ten seconds, coming at us behind our guns. Shit, I make it four missiles now. They sure do like to spend money."

"Like a tourist at an outlet mall," I agreed. "Netty, twenty percent more power, please, and apply exterior directionals. I want to score the hell outta that rock—the big one over there. It looks like mostly minerals and metal."

"Done."

The *Fafnir* responded by yawing hard, swinging through a 180 and pulsing a hard burst from her fusion drive. It blasted chunks as small as sand to as large as boulders out of the tortured asteroid, but it also kept us out of a pursuing class 9's line of fire a little longer.

"Torina, as soon you get the chance—"

"I'll take the shot. Count on it, dear."

The presence of the rocks was an added factor to the battle. They weren't the tumbling, crashing maelstrom of asteroids and boulders portrayed in movies, but even a few thousand klicks apart, they gave the fight something a space battle didn't normally have: terrain.

The prow of the class 9 appeared, rising above the miniature horizon of the rock. They were already firing their lasers, probably trying to keep us off-balance long enough to target us properly. But the debris kicked up by our drive attenuated the incoming energy and threw off their targeting. Torina waited with the patience of a seasoned vet.

I gritted my teeth, watching as the class 9 slid into view. We were still falling toward the rock and would collide with it in another twenty seconds or so if I didn't light the drive.

"Torina—"

"Patience, Van."

"Easy for you to—"

"There we go," she said, and fired the particle cannon.

Aside from one test shot, it was our first truly effective use of the thing, and it was fired in anger.

This particular weapon was considerably more powerful than the one we'd burned out trying to descend through a ferocious electrical storm on Null World. It was probably more suited to the *Iowa*, not the *Fafnir*, because it pulled a *lot* of power when it fired. But the payoff was a devastating blast of accelerated protons that chewed clean through the class 9 in a single heartbeat. It must have truncated her main structural spars because she broke apart under the force of her own drive, the respective pieces tumbling off in different directions amid a silvery blossom of venting atmosphere.

Another ship swept by. It was Lunzy's *Foregone Conclusion*.

"And here I was coming to rescue you, Van. Way to spoil my dramatic reveal," she groused.

"Sorry, Lunzy," I replied, hitting the brakes on the *Fafnir* with another burst of thrust that excavated a crater into the rock, then reversing course. "That Sorcerer class 7 fighting it out with Gerhardt near Pony Hollow looks like it could use some attention."

"Yeah, I owe him some credits from an ill-conceived poker bet. This'll be a good way to work it off," she replied and accelerated toward Pony Hollow.

"Van, I've got the laser battery back on," Funboy said, then sighed dramatically. "Wait, no. It just dropped again. I'm not very good at this."

I had to shake my head. "Funboy, you're *great* at this, trust me. You can do it."

"Glad you think so," he replied, his voice morose—so, normal.

I scanned the overlay. Lunzy and Gerhardt had their battle under control, and K'losk seemed to have gained the upper hand against a class 8, so I pitched and yawed the *Fafnir* and headed for the *Iowa*. She'd taken an alarming amount of damage, which only underscored her weakness in lacking a full crew. Faults and failures that her personnel, if she had them, could probably fix quite quickly weren't getting fixed at all. Icky and Zeno could only do their best to keep her in the fight and hope her automation didn't just fail completely.

"Lunzy, Gerhardt, K'losk, any of you guys who can, we need to take some heat off the *Iowa*," I said, redlining the drive to close the range.

"On my way," Gerhardt said. "Lunzy, you can finish this guy off, and I've got the better vector to help the *Iowa*."

"Good hunting, Master Gerhardt," she said.

I winced as a succession of rail gun shots punched through the *Iowa*'s flank. A missile detonated immediately after, just a few hundred meters away from her. The one-two punch had been too much, and she went dark, her reactor going offline.

"Van! We've gone dark, out of action here," Icky said, using her suit's comm.

"Can you get back *into* action?"

Zeno answered. "Give us, oh, a couple of days to rebuild the automation links, sure. Until then, though—"

"Got it." I turned to Torina. "Any ideas—"

She brushed her fingers over the firing controls. "Just get us close, Van. Just get us *really* close."

As CONFIDENT AS I'd been going into this, I wasn't so confident now. The Sorcerer's class 13 seemed able to absorb tremendous punishment without losing much in the way of steerage or firepower. She'd already forced Gerhardt out of the battle with a faltering power plant, and had landed punishing hits on both the *Fafnir* and the *Foregone Conclusion*. K'losk was burning like hell to join the fight, but he was at least fifteen minutes out.

I cursed as another laser barrage crashed into the *Fafnir*. Worse, the Sorcerers were still taking potshots at the *Iowa*, beating her up even more.

Perry reappeared. He'd been trying to help Funboy restore things.

"Van, I think we might need to withdraw," he said.

I glanced at him. "How bad is it back there?"

"Bad. We've lost a bunch of systems and won't be getting them back without time in a—whoa!"

He flapped his wings as another shudder ran through the *Fafnir*, a mass-driver slug impacting somewhere aft and up.

"—in a hangar."

I grimaced at the overlay. If we withdrew, we were basically accepting the loss of the *Iowa*. But we were taking too much damage, and the *Poltava* was too far away to help.

I took a breath. "Icky, Zeno, abandon ship."

"Van, we—" Icky started, but I cut her off.

"That's an order. We have to cut our losses here."

It was painful just saying it. But if we kept slugging it out, we could leave Earth utterly defenseless.

Torina came on a private channel. "Van, do you really think the Sorcerers are just going to let Icky and Zeno fly away in a workboat?"

I didn't answer.

I couldn't. A gray pall of defeat had started to engulf me. We'd done all that we could. There was nothing left—

"Sorry, I'm late, Van. You need some help?"

I blinked at the voice.

"Mom?"

Her ship, one of three, had just popped onto the overlay,

twisting in almost on top of the battle. Without hesitating, they loosed a barrage of fire, each ship putting out as much destructive force as the Sorcerers' class 13 did on her own. I was still in the midst of reacting to it when the class 13, pummeled by torrents of laser fire and streams of mass-driver slugs, blew apart.

I slumped back in my seat, eyes burning from exhaustion.

"Again, sorry I was late, son," my mother said.

I closed my eyes. "That's okay, Mom. You showed up. That's what counts."

THE BATTLE OF PONY HOLLOW had been close—*too* close, by far. K'losk's ship had taken the least damage, but the rest of us would be hard-pressed to make it back to Anvil Dark under our own power. The *Iowa* wouldn't be going anywhere. Not until a lot of repairs were completed.

But it *had* been a win. And there was more good news. To help take the potential heat off of us, and Earth, my mother and Valint had launched an offensive against the Sorcerers both in The Deeps and along the fringes of known space.

"We've got them suppressed, at least for now. But they're mustering their strength, and they are soon going to start pushing back," my mother said.

I nodded at her image on the center display. "We've got to get ready for them."

"Actually, Van, way more ready than you know," Perry said, returning to his perch between the seats.

"What do you mean?"

"Hosurc'a and I just went through the data we lifted from that more or less intact class 7. Remember how Valint said we were compromised? She wasn't kidding. It's all there—you, Pony Hollow —the real one, in Iowa—Miryam, Tony Burgess and his people—"

He turned to Torina. "Along with Helso, your parents, Master Cataric—plus Icky's father, Zeno's mothers—all of it. Somehow, the Sorcerers have found out about everyone and everything connected to this crew."

A long, ponderous moment of silence followed.

Funboy was the one to break it.

"That's not good."

18

"THAT'S NOT GOOD."

Funboy's understatement still rang in my head as we slid the *Fafnir* into the hangar on Anvil Dark. The damage she'd taken was far too severe to fix in the barn, and, in any case, I was suddenly reluctant to return to Earth. I couldn't help feeling that our being there only painted a bigger target on the planet. Torina felt the same about Helso, and Zeno about her family and her home. Icky and Funboy were less vulnerable, her father living aboard a battleship that constantly moved around, and his family just not... being important.

"In my culture, family is just a matter of biological heredity. Shortly after birth, our children are placed into the care of institutions who see to their well-being and education," he said.

Torina, Zeno, Icky, and I all exchanged looks, but we weren't really surprised at all.

Torina sniffed. "Wow. You can just feel the love, can't you?"

"That… actually explains a lot," Icky put in.

Funboy shrugged. "As recent events have shown, strong family bonds are just a source of vulnerability and pain, and on occasion, communicable diseases."

"Parental interference is a unique kind of annoyance," Zeno muttered.

"That's being generous," I said.

"I'm trying to be clinical, like Funboy." Zeno managed a weak smirk. "It's… liberating."

Funboy held out his hand.

"What?" Zeno asked.

"My fee. I took a three week course in family counseling because I'm unusually warm and caring."

Zeno dropped a single coin in his hand. "That cover it?"

He managed to look satisfied and aggrieved all at once. "I've had my eye on a new pair of bootlaces. This clinches it."

Zeno tapped his arm with a mechanical motion. "There, there. You're doing great, counselor."

Icky snorted, blew a snot bubble, and then choked on her laugh. Torina and I managed to look alarmed, then amused, and then Funboy took a small bow.

It was, as team building exercises go, far better than any corporate retreat. I considered Funboy's upbringing, and concluded that it was pragmatic—

But right now, it seemed like a hell of an advantage. If you never got or stayed close to anyone, they could never be used against you. The opposite was true as well—no one was ever truly in your corner. You were… alone.

Which again brought up the issue of my mother. She and her

flotilla of ships had made the trip here, to Gamma Crucis, but made no attempt to approach Anvil Dark. For reasons that weren't clear to me and that no one seemed to want to discuss, she was *persona non grata* here.

"Let's just say that I have a way of making people uncomfortable," she said over the comm, her voice cool and flat.

No shit, I thought, although I just nodded. I still hadn't decided if she was a tortured soul or a sociopath. Probably some of both in some proportion, though what that proportion was, I really didn't know. Inside that old church on Rodantic's World, she'd offered hints of the mother who'd loved my father and the dark things that had pulled her away from both of us. Outside of it, she'd preemptively shot a man in cold blood, then wiped his guts off her shoe while casually asking me if I thought my sidearm was good enough for heavy use.

I'd just have to live with the uncertainty for now because I had even more urgent matters to address.

We spent some time surveying the *Fafnir*, taking in her many hurts. Lunzy's and Gerhardt's ships were both laid up as well. K'losk had escaped with only minor damage. The *Iowa*, though—

As the maintenance bots pored over the *Fafnir*, assessing the damage—and the bill—I scrolled through the list Zeno and Icky had compiled, enumerating just how beaten up our poor old battle-cruiser was. Fortunately, most of the damage was to armor and hull plating. Her structure and critical systems hadn't escaped unscathed by any means, but at least we weren't faced with replacing a power plant or her main drive. Still, repairing her was going to cost tens of thousands of bonds, and all of it would be on us, since she wasn't registered with the Guild and therefore eligible for subsidies.

I sighed in disgust and handed the data slate back to Zeno. "If we want to get her chartered with the Guild, we've got to get her properly crewed up," I said.

"Well, that, and so we can actually operate her properly, Van," Zeno said.

Icky nodded. "Yeah. She's great, until she starts taking damage. When she does, the automation starts to fail, which makes her harder to control, so she takes more damage, which makes more automation fail—you get the picture."

"Yeah, I do. We have to find a crew of at least, what, sixteen qualified and experienced personnel?"

"Two dozen would be better," Zeno said.

I nodded. Two dozen crew, who would spend most of their time sitting around being menacing and available. It would be astronomically expensive if we didn't have some way of earning revenue to offset the cost of paying them. That meant we needed to find such a revenue stream, or else find a crew that would work for free.

Good luck with that.

AT LEAST EARTH and Helso were both protected. Groshenko had assumed responsibility for the former, assisted by the GKU, particularly Valint and my mother. Though the good people of Earth didn't know it, there were now half a dozen ships that called the Solar System their home port, at least for the time being. Between them, they could deliver in a few seconds more destructive energy than every bullet, bomb, shell, torpedo, or otherwise conceivable weapon fired during all of the Second World War—including the

Trinity, Fat Man and Little Boy A-bombs. Hell, they could even outblast the Soviet's *Tsar Bomba* with the touch of a screen, a feat that would have sent Stalin and his gang of murderers into paroxysms of envy.

"We've got three on one side of the Sun, three on the other, and dedicated comm relays set up to allow them to communicate. We've also deployed some scanner buoys and a few other surprises for any bad guys," Groshenko said over the comm.

"That must be costing you a fortune, Petyr," I said.

"Bah. Remember, I've got a vodka distillery to protect."

Despite my economic anxiety, I chuckled. "That's awfully expensive vodka."

Groshenko grinned but quickly turned serious. "Actually, Van, all I've done is move my mercenary company's forward base here from where it was, near Epsilon Eridani. Oh, and I've got a friend of yours in charge of it all."

"Oh? Who's that?"

"Pevensy."

I sat up. "What? That bastard—?"

Groshenko held up a hand. "Van, Pevensy and I have had a long talk. He's... seen the light, so to speak."

"Yeah, except that light is the gleam of money. If the Sorcerers offer him more than he's making now, he's just going to switch sides again, and Earth is going to be screwed."

"Oh, I don't think so. For one, Pevensy's not alone in protecting Sol. Remember that the GKU is there, too, and I've made it pretty clear to him that he does *not* want to get on the wrong side of the Knights. And then there's you."

"What do you mean, then there's me?"

"Your little gambit, walking right into the lion's den, as it were, and contaminating his base's water supply with that biological nano-agent to force him to make a deal—" Groshenko laughed. "That was ballsy as hell and actually impressed the *hell* out of him. And while we mercenaries may be in this for the money, the fact is that respect plays a role, too. You confronted him directly, in his home turf and against some pretty long odds, and he respects you for that. Honestly, *none* of us respect the damned Sorcerers."

I sat back. "So you're vouching for him."

"I guess I am."

I rubbed my eyes. "Okay, then. If you're good with him, Petyr, I am too, but only because his ability to damage is limited now, and he knows we'll be waiting if he screws us. Just make sure he understands that that's *my* home he's guarding. Think of the earth as a borrowed classic car—it comes back with a scratch, it comes out of Pevensy's ass. No negotiation."

"Oh, he's well aware. More to the point, it's my supply of good vodka he's guarding."

Grinning, Groshenko signed off.

As for Helso, Torina's homeworld was in pretty good hands, too. Not only did it have its own small but potent self-defense force of a dozen ships, but the Schegith had put the *protect* into *protectorate* and stationed a pair of capital ships there—two battlecruisers, including the one commanded by Schegith's own cousin, who regarded the opportunity to kill Sorcerers as nothing short of an armed vacation. He was an enthusiast when it came to sending Sorcerers back to their primal energy state.

Torina's lips curved in an appealing bow as she looked up at me. "As it turns out, Helso is probably one of the best protected single systems in known space. And with Petyr's people guarding Earth—even if one of them is that asshole Pevensy—it means we can focus on going after the *really* bad guys."

I watched as a new section of hull plating was lowered toward the *Fafnir*.

"Damned right it does. Which leads to the next question," I asked.

"Where *are* the bad guys?" Torina asked, anticipating the question.

I nodded and gestured at the *Fafnir*. "She'll be ready to fly soon. We just need to figure out where we're going."

Perry flicked a wing vaguely. "Does it matter, Van?"

"Not really. We'll find them."

Perry's beak dropped in laughter. "Was hoping you'd say that. I'm in the mood to hunt."

GERHARDT, it turned out, hadn't been idle in that regard. He sent me a mysterious summons to a docking port, which led to a class 4 workboat with a number, no name. He was waiting for me aboard and sealed the hatch as soon as I came through.

"Kinda feel like I'm being kidnapped," I said, sliding into the copilot's seat.

"You kind of are."

"So you're taking me somewhere against my will?"

"I'm taking both of us somewhere against our wills. But it's somewhere we have to go," he said, before undocking and backing away from the looming bulk of Anvil Dark.

I let the silence linger long enough for him to spin the workboat around and light its drive once we were clear of the station, then I turned to him.

"Not sure, really, how I can make it any more obvious that I'd like to know where we're going."

He activated the flight controller and sat back. "Now that we're well clear of the station and there's zero chance anyone can eavesdrop, I can tell you that we're going to meet Dayna Jasskin."

"Dayna... Jasskin? From the Quiet Room?"

He nodded.

"Ah." I glanced slowly around. "And you couldn't come up with anything more comfy than this for a trip all the way to Procyon, huh?"

"We're not going to Procyon. Dayna, in fact, is sitting out in the Oort Cloud right now, waiting. She has some information for us, but it's—as she put it—*sensitive as all get out.*"

"Whoa, language."

Gerhardt gave me a sharp sidelong glance, but I thought I caught a glimmer of a smile.

We flew on, eventually matching course data with a small, sleek ship lurking in the Oort Cloud of Gamma Crucis, Anvil Dark's home system. The other craft was about class 6 but of a design I'd never seen before. Whatever it was, it looked like it was going a million klicks per hour just sitting there, its clean, sharp lines reminding me of a high-performance car, like the McLaren 720S I'd fallen desperately in love with and would have rushed out to buy if I'd had an extra *three hundred thousand* dollars laying around.

"Can our guild fabricator make, ah, anything?" I asked as we began to drift closer to the docking point.

"Sure. What kind of car?"

"How did you—"

"Your face. You're looking at the gorgeous ship, all clean lines and untapped speed, and you're thinking about a car so far out of your price range that it verges into fantasy. So, idly, you wonder if the guild can fab one out, and the answer is… yes."

"Good to know," I said smugly.

"What kind—"

"McLaren 720S."

He inclined his head with respect as our ships touched together. "Damned fine taste for a youth."

"Thanks. I'll remember the compliment."

As we snuggled up to the gorgeous craft to dock, I noted she was about way more than just looks. She had a scanner array built right into her hull, which was big enough to fit a battlecruiser, and two drive bells that suggested she could fling a truly immense amount of thrust out behind her. I wondered what her maximum delta V would be and assumed it shared the same stratospheric height as the McLaren's price tag.

She was *just* as beautiful inside. Everything was thick carpeting, rich wood paneling with grain that seemed to flow, brass and crystal fixtures—in short, everything you'd find in some Tuscan villa or Hollywood Hills mansion, except on a ship.

Petyr ran a finger over the walnut trim, eyes bright with appreciation. "Tough life, being a banker."

We were met by Dayna's mostly silent and *entirely* enigmatic assistant, Chensun. She—I think, anyway—led us along a corridor to a sumptuous compartment like a boardroom. Dayna sat at the head of the table.

"Master Gerhardt, Peacemaker Tudor, thank you for coming," she said, gesturing at two ridiculously comfortable seats, then having Chensun fetch us refreshments. Those turned out to be water that might have just been melted off an alpine glacier, with a twist of something both tangy and sweet.

I looked around. "Dig your ride, Dayna."

"What, this old thing? It's just something I threw on," she replied, smiling. "If it makes you feel any better, it belongs to the Quiet Room, not to me. I've just got it signed out."

"Yeah, I'd be okay with being able to grab something like this when I needed it."

"And you presumably needed it, since it brought you here to this remarkably clandestine meeting," Gerhardt said.

Dayna smiled. "Ah, right to the point. You never fail to disappoint," she said, but her smile drained away.

"I've asked you here because I want to show you something. It's something that has the Quiet Room concerned."

She touched a control on the table. The room darkened, then a 3-D display lit up, showing the image of a perfect human male with flawless teeth and sculpted, artful iron-gray hair. I'd have assumed him to be an artificial construct, except I knew there were people back on Earth who put that much effort into their appearance. I'd met some of them, and they were invariably performers of some sort, narcissists, or both—usually both.

"What good is wealth?" he asked, his expression grave. Then his image was replaced by a sprawling estate on a lush, green—

I sat up. "That's Torina's home. The Milon Estate, on Helso."

The imagery went on, showing a montage of scenes of

opulence. One of them held a brief image of a Quiet Room branch office set amid leafy greenery and manicured lawns.

"Wealth is very good—for those who have it," the man said sadly as his image reappeared. "Unfortunately, though, for most of us, the reality is quite different."

What followed was a succession of images that stood in stark and dreary contrast to the ones that had come before—rows of shabby, identical houses, long lines of people waiting to board graffiti-spangled mag-lev trains. Then, crowded and rain-drenched canyons of streets walled in by towering, faceless skyscrapers, grimy tenement orbitals with dingy corridors and compartments streaked with corrosion and leaking fluids. I actually recognized a couple of them, including—

I jabbed a finger at the screen. "That's old Kowloon Walled City that used to be in Hong Kong, back on Earth. But it was demolished years ago, and there's a park there now!"

The succession of images and the grim voice-over didn't care and just rolled implacably on. Finally, though, the image went black. Then, a spark of light appeared. It grew and brightened into a glorious spill of sunrise over the smooth arc of a planetary limb. From the glare of the rising sun, a logo swept toward the viewer, filling the screen.

BENESTAR – A NEW DAWN

The screen winked out and the lights came back up. I sat back as though I'd been punched—because I kind of had, by a fist made of manipulative bullshit.

"What the hell was *that*?"

"That was one of several ads running across known space mass media right now," Dayna said.

Gerhardt frowned at the vanished image. "I recognized that man. He has some 3D show on one of the interstellar networks. One that's always going on about how this policy or that trend is going to lead to the downfall of civilization."

Dayna nodded. "Malcolm Swan. For a large swath of known space—mostly humans but not entirely—he's the voice of, and please mentally enclose this word in quotation marks, 'reason.'"

"And by reason, you mean breathless conspiracy theories and insidious innuendo masquerading as news," Gerhardt said.

"Pretty much."

"He is one hell of a gorgeous man, though."

Dayna and I both looked at Gerhardt, who shrugged. "Excuse me, but appreciating the beauty of another person, male, female, or otherwise, is merely a celebration of their physical qualities and nothing more, unless you choose to make it unseemly."

I sighed. "Yeah, probably has a twenty charisma."

The others looked at me, and I shrugged.

"Sorry, it's from an Earthly game, a numeric representation of —" I stopped and shook my head. "Disregard. Let's just say he's a good looking sonofabitch. What I want to know is what the hell *that* was all about."

"This one was obviously targeted at humans, but there are versions tailored to other races. And they all revolve around Malcolm Swan, or his equally charismatic counterparts in the medi-asphere—Robi, a female Bolunvir, a synth named Saber with a 'bad boy' reputation, and Nosarctu, a Surtsi. They're widely known as the Tri-Yumverate," Dayna said.

"The Tri-*Yum*verate?"

Dayna shrugged and rolled her eyes "Yes, the Tri-*Yum*verate, because they can make anything seem yummy."

"I—they—*what?* What an utter shitshow, and I say that as someone who once bought a food sealer after watching an infomercial."

"Yes, it's as insipid as hell. But tell me you're going to walk out of here, Van, and ever forget the Tri-*Yum*verate and what they're all about."

"And there are four of them? How can they be a *Tri*-Yumverate if there are *four?*"

"Malcolm Swan isn't technically a member of the club, but we've lumped him in with them since he's been brought on by Bene-Star in a similar role to the other three, to appeal to humans specifically."

I shook my head. "That's all—I can't even fathom this shit. I thought banal commercialism was limited to my planet."

"Not even close. Lying to people for profit is, like gravity, truly universal," Dayna said.

"So is compound interest," I countered.

Dayna looked pained. "A sad truth."

Gerhardt gave his brief smile, then regarded me with a patient look. "It doesn't matter how ridiculous it is, Tudor, if people remember it. Kind of a first-rule-of-marketing sort of thing."

"It is. And these people know that. They're experts at manipulating public opinions and perceptions. So far, they've mainly focused on wedge issues native to known space. But now that Bene-Star has hired them as… as actual *media mercenaries*, they can start insinuating their own brand into the known space—oh, there's a word for it. It means a sort of shared cultural consciousness, from an Earthly language, the one that always sounds to me like people coughing—"

I smiled. "Zeitgeist?"

"That's it."

"I have a couple of German friends who I'm definitely going to have to try out that *people coughing* line on." I sat up. "Anyway, what you're saying is that BeneStar has decided to make its presence felt in known space. And right after the GKU, including my mother and me, just happened to get in their faces out in The Deeps."

Gerhardt shook his head. "Don't give yourself too much credit, Tudor. These ads would just be part of a fully fleshed-out strategy that's probably been months, even years in the making. I suspect it's more likely that the kidnapping of Adayluh Creel was part of it, and you got pulled into BeneStar's sphere of influence as a result."

"No, I get that. But my mother and her cohorts seemed to hint that they've been crossing swords with BeneStar for a long time now. So maybe BeneStar decided it was time to get to the root of the problem."

This time, Gerhardt nodded. "Not a bad analysis, actually. Our intelligence people have been keeping an eye on BeneStar, among other parties, but hadn't noted any particular interest on their part in moving into known space directly. They've only been interested in working through subsidiaries, at least so far." He glanced toward the empty imager. "But that is apparently in the process of changing."

He turned back to Dayna. "However, it would seem that while the Quiet Room has managed to remain aware of developments, the Guild's intelligence department has not. This is the first we've seen of these ads."

Gerhardt's voice had taken on a tone of menace. I knew what he was thinking. How could BeneStar have started splashing ads like this across the known space infosphere without Guild intelligence even knowing? It would be like some foreign multinational starting to run subversive ads in the United States, with the CIA and FBI remaining blissfully unaware of it. I was wondering the same thing myself.

But Dayna shook her head. "Don't be too hard on your people. So far, these have only run in limited markets. They're probably doing focus groups and surveys and things, to tweak them, before they put them out for general broadcast."

"Even so, I'd like copies of these. Few things make a Master happier than showing up in one of the Guild's departments with something he knows and they don't—and asking why that's the case."

"That does lead to another question, though. Why are we here? Why is the Quiet Room engaging with the Peacemaker Guild on ads from BeneStar. I mean, you guys are all about profit and—well, that's pretty much it. So are they. It seems like you'd be natural partners, but I'm getting a definite adversarial vibe here," I said.

Dayna's reply was flat and direct. "BeneStar is intending to launch a series of altruistic endeavors in known space—lifestyle improvements, affordable housing, food security—all backed up by their corporate machinery, of course. They also intend to offer a range of financial services, including their own currency, called *casts* —as in BeneCast, their retail financial arm. Oh, and just in case you're willing to give them the benefit of the doubt, consider this fact. BeneStar has purchased more than ten thousand missiles and millions of rounds of ammo for various weapon systems. A bank, that's a retailer, and they own enough hardware to crack open the *heaviest* planetary defenses."

I sank back in my chair as the enormity of it all washed over me.

BeneStar was going to try to get people hooked on scrip, a time-honored way of replacing some legal tender with a substitute. Scrip had legitimate uses, such as in times of emergency when regular cash just wasn't available. But it had more nefarious purposes, notably tying its users up in obligations so restrictive they might as well be chains. Scrip was popular among the robber barons of the nineteenth century. They used it to pay their employees and do exclusive business with the company store, since it was worthless junk anywhere else. It was especially prevalent in lumber and coal companies of the 1800s, but I'd heard of instances of it being used by big corporations as late as 2019.

At best, it was a shady practice. At worst, it was downright evil.

Dayna nodded. "You can see, now, why we're concerned. The bond system is one of the very few things that unites known space. A competing currency would be hugely destabilizing, not to mention a nightmare to manage. Will there be an exchange? If so, how would the rate be determined? Who would manage it?"

It'll also cut into your profits, I thought but didn't say. Nor did it matter, because Dayna was right. The last thing known space needed now was something else to pull it apart. The fractures were already there. We'd almost seen them break wide open when the Tenants took over the Seven Stars League.

And known space suddenly being plunged into war probably wouldn't bother BeneStar either, because they sold weapons. It was a win-win for them, a lose-lose for everyone else—

Both Dayna and Gerhardt had apparently seen my face dawn with sudden revelation.

"Tudor, what are you thinking?" Gerhardt asked.

I stood. I had to. I had to pace. My racing thoughts demanded motion.

"My mother said that BeneStar used the Sorcerers as their enforcers in The Deeps and beyond. She said the Sorcerers weren't just Trinduk. There were other races, too. Sorcerer is more a job than a specific species. Here, in known space, the Sorcerers are behind our identity theft operation. That means that BeneStar is—"

I stopped. "BeneStar. They're the missing piece of the puzzle. They own the Sorcerers. They own Group 41, one of those subsidiaries of theirs here in known space."

I looked at Gerhardt. "You said that BeneStar has probably been laying the foundations for their move into known space for years. You're right. And the identity theft scheme is part of it."

I looked at the empty imager. "It's them. They're behind it. Through the Sorcerers, and Group 41, maybe even the Tenants, and who knows who or what else, BeneStar is behind it. BeneStar is behind it *all*."

Silence. I turned back to Dayna and Gerhardt.

"Which leaves one more question. Probably the most important question of all."

Gerhardt gave a slow, grim nod.

"Who's behind BeneStar?"

19

WHEN WE RETURNED to Anvil Dark, I gathered the crew onto the *Fafnir* and started showing the BeneStar ad spots Dayna had uploaded to my data slate. We sat in rapt attention, watching as beautiful people—at least, beautiful among their species—bemoaned the yawning wealth disparity in known space against contrasting backdrops of stupid wealth and grinding poverty. They then went on to proclaim that BeneStar was coming, a shining savior who would make everything better for everybody.

"Some terms and conditions apply. Offer void where prohibited. Consult your doctor to see if BeneStar is right for you," Perry added in a quick, hushed tone.

"They've all got good teeth or hair or whiskers. Or, ah, paddles," I mentioned.

"Ain't no uglies in a BeneStar ad campaign. They really sanitized the galaxy and made it plastic," Perry added.

"Half of those humanoid women were plastic," Perry said,

waving at the screen. "Half or more, anyway. I haven't seen that many wigs since I went to the Country Music Hall of Fame."

I stared at him. "Hell, I'll bite. *Why?*"

"Why did I go, or why did I see so many wigs? I think it's an American musical tradition. Wigs. Rhinestones. Tornado alerts and fried food. You know, the usual," Perry explained. "It's damned fine living, in my opinion."

"But of course," I said, inclining my head because with each passing day, I moved closer to being impossible to surprise.

"I thought that was a good shot of your family's estate," Icky said to Torina, who just stared back at her in a silence broken only by the bustle and hum of the repair bots still working on the *Fafnir*.

"Really?"

Icky shrugged. "Just looking for, you know, a reflective lining."

"Silver lining, Icky. If you're going to use Earth idioms, get 'em right," Perry said.

I stepped in before things devolved into another round of Icky versus Perry. "Focus, people. These ads are only running in limited markets, but we can assume they'll start being broadcast right across known space soon."

Zeno examined my data slate. "What are these other ads on here?"

"They're pretty much the same—some talking stock photo of one species or another, spewing about how awful everything is and how BeneStar's going to fix it all. Of course, they'll fix it all by *being* it all. Consumer goods, financial services, entertainment, medical care, all of it will be stamped with the BeneStar corporate logo, if they can manage it. Or, as Gerhardt put it, *you'll own nothing and you'll like it.*"

Zeno tapped at the slate. "Uh, Van? I'm just playing the shorter pieces. There's one here I think you should see," she said, tapping again and sending the imagery to the galley display, which had been newly replaced after shrapnel from a missile had smashed the last one to crystalline bits.

It was another talking head, this time framed against a pastoral scene of forested hills under an azure sky—

It took me a second to realize what I was seeing. I knew those hills… and that face.

It was Carter Yost.

I SAT in Gerhardt's office, with Dayna on the comm. She was on her way back to Procyon, but this couldn't wait.

Dayna had been watching the ad featuring Carter play on another screen, and she looked up at us. "That's your cousin?"

"Unfortunately, yes."

"I thought you'd reconciled with him," Gerhardt said.

I scowled at the image of Carter on the split screen. "He must have run out of money."

"Or he's a victim. Blackmail, extortion, intimidation, they're all effective tactics, particularly against someone as weak-willed as you portrayed your cousin to be. There's only one way to know. Find him, Tudor. Find him and bring him to the *Righteous Fury* for questioning."

I sat back in my chair. As furious as I was with Carter right now, and as satisfying as the image of him strapped into some chair under a bright light aboard the *Righteous Fury* might be, Gerhardt was right. Carter might not be doing this willingly. The guy had come a long way in the last few years, evolving from the vapid asshole I'd grown up with to something resembling a decent human being. I owed him the benefit of the doubt.

"Actually, I have a better idea. I've been meaning to drop by Earth to talk to Miryam, the friend who looks after my affairs back there. The last time I saw her, I basically told her to brace herself for the end of the world. She's probably due for an update."

"I'd say so, yes."

"So, while I'm there, I'll drop by Virginia, because that's where Carter was when that was recorded. I recognize those hills behind him," I said, glancing at the image. "They border his family's property."

Dayna gave a wicked chuckle. "Ah, family reunions. Whenever I go home, it's to my father complaining that I'm still *just* a banker, I don't do anything but move other people's money around, and why don't I do something useful with my life?" She shook her head. "What if he's not there? Do you have an idea where to look? Because from what you've told me of him, he seems like a weak link in BeneStar's chain that we can exploit—and the sooner, the better."

"If he's not at home in Virginia, that's fine. I know who we ask. Politely, of course."

"Who would that be?" Gerhardt asked. "Actually, it's better if I don't know. Just keep the *Righteous Fury* in mind, Tudor. Yost *is* a Peacemaker, so we have considerably more, uh, discretion in how we handle him. And, as Dayna says, we need to crack our way into BeneStar's operation sooner rather than later—family or not."

I looked at Gerhardt, who just looked flatly back. He was simply stating fact. Family or not, I had to find Carter and ensure he cooperated.

One way or another.

"MY POOR *IOWA*," I said.

"Hey, it's not that bad a place. Better than Kansas," Perry said.

"First, I meant the ship, not the state. Second, what have you got against Kansas?"

"Oh, Kansas knows. Kansas knows alright."

I rolled my eyes at him, then turned my attention back to the *Iowa*. We were taking the *Fafnir* in a slow pass around her, a few hundred meters away, to gauge the damage from the battle against the Sorcerers. We hadn't even started repairs on her. For one, she was far too big for an internal dock, aside from a handful scattered across known space that were used by sovereign states like Tau Ceti and Eridani to work on their biggest warships—and those weren't exactly for rent. For another, we didn't have the wherewithal. It wasn't that we couldn't afford the repairs, particularly since my mother and Torina's parents had offered some financial help. We just didn't have the means or the time. Repairing her would take the five of us days, if not weeks of working in the void, patching up her various rents, then dealing with internal damage. It meant that she was out of commission indefinitely, which both made me sad and pissed me off.

"We need a crew," Torina said.

"Yeah, we do. Don't suppose you have one handy."

She gestured around the *Fafnir*'s cockpit. "Just this one, sorry."

I nodded glumly. "Yeah."

"Van, why don't we just hire a crew to come and fix her? There are contractors who, you know, do that—build and repair ships," Icky suggested.

"That would only be a temporary solution. The next time she gets beaten up in battle, we'd be right back here again," Funboy said, ending on a sigh.

I nodded again. "Funboy's right. It's not enough to just fix her up and get her back into commission. We need a crew to keep her there. And that means finding a crew that can maintain and repair an old battlecruiser of her type, operate her effectively in battle, do damage control on the fly, and be willing to sit around for long periods of time with nothing to do. Oh, and they need to be cheap, or ideally, free."

"Good luck with that," Perry said.

Zeno spoke up. "Why not an AI crew? A bunch of bots like Waldo and Evan. They could be her crew."

"Van, Netty, and I discussed that. Unfortunately, AIs sophisticated enough to do more than routine maintenance are expensive. The amount we'd need to fully crew the *Iowa* would cost a fortune, probably more than just hiring an actual crew and paying them to sit around. I mean, Waldo and Evan are good at what they do, but otherwise they're morons," Perry said.

We finished our circuit of the *Iowa*. With no solutions in sight, I resigned myself to leaving her parked here near the dwarf planet we'd dubbed Pony Hollow and—that was it. Just leave her parked, a virtual derelict.

"Okay, Netty, there's nothing more we can do here. Let's head for Earth, destination the great state of Virginia." I turned to Perry. "Unless you have something against Virginia as well."

"Nope. Virginia's cool. Don't get me started on Maryland, though."

"How many states have you visited?"

"All of the lower forty-eight, plus all ten provinces of Canada, and a bunch of northern Mexico."

"Really?"

"Van, I'm a tireless AI bird with a virtually limitless power source. For long stretches of time, I have absolutely nothing to do but sit in a barn and try to make conversation with the owl that took up residence in the rafters. Oh, and you want to talk about morons—"

"You had Netty for company."

"Perry was my way of seeing the United States and Canada. We were in constant contact—and speaking of contact, Van, there's a call coming in from Linulla," Netty said.

"Linulla? Huh. Put him on."

Linulla's crab-esque self filled the center display. "Hello, Van. This a good time?"

"As good as any. What's up?"

"I just thought I'd let you know that we've come up with a new augment for your sword. It's deceptively simple—it basically makes it unbreakable. Since you seem to enjoy cutting open spaceships and things with it, I thought it would be a useful upgrade—"

He suddenly turned off-image. "No, not right now, I'm busy!"

I heard a piping voice, one of Linulla's kids. They were adolescents, on their way to adulthood. In fact, the last time I'd talked to

Linulla, he mentioned his entire brood was heading off to the Conoku moon called Ock-kuss-nar, where they would undergo their rite of passage from childhood by racing the sleek little ships called *Rumors* around a course, trying to best their own times. He mentioned the blissful peace of not having them rattling around Starsmith for a few weeks, but they were obviously back. And, as someone who'd grown up on a farm in Iowa, I knew what it was like being a bored teenager stuck in an isolated place with no one but family readily available.

"Sorry, Van, but as you've probably realized, my children are back from Ock-kuss-nar."

I laughed. "Yeah, I recognize the tone of a harassed parent no matter the species."

"Don't suppose you know someone willing to take a group of adolescent Conoku off my claws, do you? They're unruly, but they know ships, how to fly them, and all the associated engineering."

I opened my mouth to say, *sorry, no, can't help you,* but I turned instead to the ravaged *Iowa.*

I couldn't stop a grin from spreading across my face.

"Actually, Linulla, I do."

As we were passing the orbit of Mars, Torina returned to the *Fafnir's* cockpit.

"It's all set. My father has arranged for the replacement parts needed for the *Iowa* to be delivered to her in about two weeks, which will give Linulla's kids time to get settled in."

"Van, are you sure this is a good idea? Linulla's brood might be capable of repairing the *Iowa*, and even operating her—but she is a warship, and that means her going into battle," Zeno said, her voice weighty with the tone of a concerned mother. "I say that with the respect due any Conoku engineer, but they *are* kids. I saw three of them competing to throw saliva balls the farthest, and that was on their best behavior. It was quite something to see an entire brood in action. They're... busy."

I shrugged. "We'll cross that bridge when we come to it. Right now, Linulla's more than happy to have them come and repair the *Iowa,* and so are the other Conoku he talked to. In fact, they all seemed like they couldn't send their kids to help fast enough. As for whether they'll want to stay on as her permanent crew, well, that's up to each of them. Linulla was pretty clear that they've reached an age where they can start choosing their own path through life."

"Considering we've got forty of them coming in total, if even half of them decide to stay on, that's pretty much a full crew," Perry said. "Forty crabs. In one ship. I'm sure there's a movie in there somewhere."

"A crew composed entirely of rambunctious adolescents. What could go wrong?" Funboy wondered aloud. That's where most people would have left it, but Funboy went on, because there was no disaster he couldn't make worse with his creative approach to doom.

He inhaled, spread his hands, and began a lecture. "I'll tell you what could go wrong. First, they could—"

"Funboy, we get the picture. And yes, we may need to hire a master for the *Iowa* to ride herd on them, but that's a much easier proposition than finding an entire skilled crew who are willing to work for the experience, like these young Conoku are."

"Do they smell?" Perry asked.

"The Conoku? Bit bigoted of you there, bird," I said, raising a brow.

"Not Conoku. I'm asking if forty Conoku *kids* smell. Kids are a different story. Ask Zeno. She knows. What did you call a bunch of kids? You used a human term?" Perry asked.

"An alien petri dish. And yes, they stink. They stink because they're resistant to hygiene, they eat constantly, and messily, and they think body functions are hilarious," Zeno explained.

"Sounds a lot like the Army, to be quite honest," I admitted.

"Young humans are not that different from young Conoku. Fewer limbs, but just as gross," Zeno agreed.

"Gross is a codeword for incipient doom, courtesy of nature's hidden killers—the microscopic world," Funboy intoned.

"We have *got* to get him his own nature show," I said.

"Or life coaching channel. He's a natural. Can you imagine his messaging?" Perry asked in awe. "You're not smart enough, and you're not good enough. Death is just around the corner. Send fifty bonds for more insights from Funboy, the only honest friend you'll ever have." He finished with a one wing flourish, and I clapped politely.

"I think you may have something there," I said.

"Branding, boss. It's my field of expertise," Perry stated, then we turned our eyes to the scans, where Sol was visible. My mind began to fizz with excitement. I was going home, if only for a short time, and I felt better than I had in some time.

We had the problem of the *Iowa* solved, at least for now. We had a much clearer picture of our Crimes Against Order case, and what was likely behind it. Helso was well-protected, and so was Earth—even if Torina was less than thrilled to find out

Groshenko had brought Pevensy on to command it. Zeno had informed the P'nosk authorities about the threat to her family, and they'd happily put a formidable security detail in place. We'd given the Sorcerers a bloody enough nose that they seemed to have withdrawn to lick their wounds, at least for the time being, and—

And, I had my mother back in my life.

That was an uncertainty. But at least she was back, and for now, it would have to be enough.

———

The Tri-Yumverate—still a stupid name, even if it was an effective one—actually turned out to be four individuals, the charisma-on-a-stick Malcolm Swan apparently only having been added with the startup of BeneStar's advertising campaign in known space. Or, as I thought of it, their propaganda campaign, but it amounted to the same thing, didn't it?

I'd already seen Malcolm Swan, and I knew the type—a perfectly coiffed grifter, not unlike the former Satrap of the Seven Stars league. I spent our time approaching Earth familiarizing myself with the other three members of the four-member Tri-*Yum*verate.

I sighed in total disgust. I *hated* that name.

Robi was a female Bolunvir, tall and brooding, dressed like a corporate vampire. Her hair was two-tone silver and pink, shaved on one side. Around her neck and shoulders dangled at least thirty fine metallic chains, each supposedly representing "an oppressed people who need our voice." Torina, who had an eye for such things, noted that each chain was wrought of precious metals worth tens of thousands of bonds.

Saber, the bad-boy Synth, had arms scrawled with tattoos that writhed and flowed with hypnotic grace, porcelain skin augmented and inlaid with chrome, and a lopsided smile carefully designed to be charming. He tended to do his spots near a low-slung, dangerous-looking snow speeder, usually holding some tool or other to show that he was hands-on and edgy. Roll up a pack of cigarettes in his cut-off sleeve and he could have been a synthetic version of James Dean but more douchey and less authentic in every way.

Nosarctu, the Surtsi, was from Funboy's race. He was, stunningly, animated and upbeat, constantly waving his arms around, his voice lilting and full of inflections. We'd all watched him prattle on for a moment, then turned to Funboy, then back to him, back to Funboy, several times. Funboy had just given his dreary shrug.

"He's clearly under the influence of something—like stimulants, or maybe a personality."

"That's a lot of media horsepower BeneStar's unleashing on the infosphere," Perry said.

"Yeah, well, if something's worth doing, it's worth doing well, I guess," I replied as we started the long fall toward the Earth, our trajectory calculated to bring us down in rural Virginia.

20

WE STEPPED out of the *Fafnir* into a cold, rainy Virginia night. No snow, but I expected it wasn't far off and may already have dusted the Blue Ridge Mountains off to the west. Here, near Flint Hill, the hills just rolled drearily off into misty gloom. It was, all in all, a pretty shitty night, but it made it much easier to approach the Yost farm undetected. Which was good, because the vagaries of terrain and habitation had forced us to land nearly two klicks away in a small wooded ravine alongside a chattering brook.

"Your cousin raises these, um, horses, you said?" Icky asked, a looming shadow in the drizzly murk.

"He does," I replied.

"Two questions. What's a horse, and why do they need to be raised? Can't they, like, stand up on their own?"

"They—no, Icky, *raising* means to breed and—" I smiled. "Since you're staying with the ship, ask Netty. She'll explain it all to you."

"Thanks, Van. I'm looking forward to it," Netty put in over the comm, her tone dry.

Since we had so much ground to cover, walking across fields and roads, bringing Icky along just entailed too much risk. Even at night, through drizzle, no one was going to be mistaking her for just some big, hefty guy. I really didn't want to spawn legends of some new cryptid, like the Mothman who supposedly haunted Point Pleasant over in West Virginia. It wasn't that I thought the good citizens of Flint Hill were especially gullible. It was the fact that the Mothman legend raked in significant tourist dollars, and I certainly *did* think the good people of Flint Hill were fond of money. And more attention focused here, on this pastoral bit of Virginia, meant more attention on the Yost farm—and I didn't trust Carter to be discreet about his off-world antics.

We set off, me leading, Funboy and Zeno following, and Torina bringing up the rear. Perry, as usual, flew reconnaissance above and ahead. In addition to b-suits, we'd all donned a recent acquisition called metasis cloaks. They were military gear gifted to us by Groshenko and delivered in person by none other than Pevensy, with whom we'd rendezvoused on the opposite side of the Moon.

That had been fun. Pevensy had boarded the *Fafnir* with the cloaks and a battleship's worth of attitude. He'd summed it up in one neatly belligerent sentence.

"I respect the people who defeat me, Tudor, but I sure as hell don't like them."

I smiled right back. "If it helps, I don't like you either."

He'd held me with a stony glare for a moment, then stuck out his hand. I actually tensed a little, thinking he was going to punch me. But he held it out for me to shake, which I did, a little bemused.

"No requirement to like the people you fight with. Usually better if you don't," he grated.

"Well, then we should get along just fine."

Torina's gaze followed him like twin particle beams as he marched off the *Fafnir* and back aboard his own ship.

"I hate that man," she said.

"Well, then by his reasoning, you and he should work together wonderfully," Perry noted.

"I don't know. Unreasoning hatred sometimes throws off my aim, makes me shoot things I don't intend to."

"That's clearly an expression of a desire to do the man harm, which means that that would actually *be* your intent, Torina," Funboy said.

Torina glanced down at him. "You're not very good with sarcasm, are you?"

"Actually, I love sarcasm."

"Really?"

"No, not at all. That *was* sarcasm."

"So, are you good with sarcasm or—you know what? Never mind."

The metasis cloaks were a damned nifty device, though. Worn like a regular cloak, they scattered light—near UV, visible, and near infrared—in a way that blurred them into the background. Combined with vegetation and other concealment, they rendered their wearers almost invisible.

They were perfect for our little nighttime trek across rural Virginia.

Perry, scouting ahead, gave us both warnings and course corrections. As we clambered over a wooden rail fence likely built during the Depression, if not earlier, he spoke up about the next field.

Flat and smooth as a baby's butt made of pancakes, you want to be careful.

That's one hell of a mixed metaphor, bird. Kind of yucky, too.

Gets the point across though, doesn't it?

Cannibalism and griddle cakes are not to be mixed again in my presence. I wanna enjoy breakfast again. Someday.

Copy that.

We skirted the flat, open field, worked our way along a tree line, crossed another creek, then climbed a hill that would give us a vantage point over the Yost's farm. We were all drenched with water from drizzle and brushing through leaves, but the cloaks and b-suits just shrugged it off. As much as I loved the protection of the b-suit in a firefight, I loved its ability to keep me warm and dry or cool and dry as the occasion demanded even more. Of course, it *was* a space-suit, so not letting me freeze or burn under Earthly conditions was kind of a minimum requirement.

When we reached the top of the hill, we knelt among some scrubby bushes. I extracted a hand scanner from my harness and panned it across the Yost farm. It was awkward, compared to the b-suit's helmet, but we hadn't bothered to lug them along. I switched from visible, to UV, to thermal, looking for anything that seemed out of the place for a horse farm.

"Oh—oh, no. What *is* that?" Funboy said, looking down by his knee. I peered at whatever had alarmed him.

"Uh, horse shit, I think."

"You mean… feces?"

"Yes. Kind of the natural by-product of creatures that, you know, eat food."

"But… it was just excreted there and then left for any hygiene-conscious person to potentially come in contact with?"

I shrugged. "I suppose you could try to train a horse to use a toilet but, A, good luck, and B, the lavatory would end up awfully crowded."

"I don't like our chances of surviving a pathogen-rich environment like this, even if the organisms are from a different biology than mine."

"Funboy, it's just poop. It's not going to come to life and attack you," Torina said.

"It may be attacking me already, at the cellular level. I *knew* I should have worn my helmet."

I sighed. I wasn't sure if Funboy's obsession with germs was a phobia or just of his tendency to see everything, even an old horse turd, as the most dire threat possible.

"Funboy, look at the road apples," I ordered.

"Is that some folksy name for that pile of bioweapon?"

"Yes. Do you see it moving toward you?"

He stared, then looked back at me with intense suspicion. "No."

"Then you may assume it is not, in fact, pursuing you."

He sniffed, then stepped even farther away from the offending items. "For now."

Torina rolled her eyes, I smiled, and we began moving onward.

I swung the hand scanner back onto the farm. Or, rather, "farm." My place in Pony Hollow was a farm—a three-bedroom, wood-frame house, a barn, and a few outbuildings on about two hundred and fifty acres, which actually made it a little small as Iowa farms went. This, however, as a "farm"—a palatial, eight-bedroom plantation-style home that wouldn't have looked out of place in Bel

Air, a horse barn the size of a small warehouse, about a dozen outbuildings, and nearly six hundred acres of land. This was a farm the way Buckingham Palace was a house.

But it also seemed to be deserted. At least, the main house did. There were thermal signatures in the barn that clearly belonged to horses, and a couple in one of the outbuildings that were probably stable hands or caretakers.

"Hmph. No one home," I muttered.

Zeno frowned. "Isn't that a little odd at this time of night?"

I looked around at the chilly drizzle. "Not really. This time of year, I suspect Carter's family is in… I don't know, Monaco or the Bahamas or—"

"Those would be warm places, right?"

"A lot warmer than here, that's for sure. And Carter might not even be on Earth." I frowned at the image of the farm, then shrugged. "We've come all this way, we might as well look around."

A little trespassing, Van the Space Policeman? Perry said.

We've done nothing but trespass since we stepped out of the Fafnir. Besides, this is family. Carter's my beloved cousin, remember?

Don't pull a muscle reaching for that one, boss.

I snorted. *It's not a crime if we don't get caught.*

I PEERED through the rain-slicked window, but couldn't make out anything. It was just a darkened room. I knew that these doors opened from the veranda, where we were standing, into one of three rooms that could be called living rooms.

"Okay, Van, I'm in position," Zeno said.

"Got it, thanks." Zeno had taken up a position between the main house and the building where I'd seen the caretakers to give us some warning if they suddenly decided to make the trek up here. I doubted they would, since it entailed a hundred-meter walk through a shitty, cold night, but it didn't hurt to be careful. Torina and Funboy held back, crouched among some manicured shrubbery and keeping a lookout nearer at hand.

Perry landed on a ledge beside the French door I'd been looking through. "I got the alarm system deactivated."

"Good work."

"I used the sophisticated approach of cutting a wire. Seriously, how much is your cousin's family paying for their alarm service, because it sucks."

"Locks only keep out honest people, Perry," I said offhandedly, trying the door handle. It was locked. "Don't suppose you have an equally sophisticated way of getting through a locked door, huh?"

"Actually, I do," Perry said, then flung out a wing and shattered one of the panes of glass in the door.

"Perry!"

"Oh, by the way, that's trespassing *and* vandalism now."

"You're the one that broke the window!"

"I was merely acting as your agent," he replied.

Torina crept forward. "Did I hear breaking glass? What the hell are you guys doing?"

I reached through the opening, broken glass scraping against the sleeve of my b-suit, and worked the inside handle to open the door. "Perry was just showing me his mad skills as a cat burglar."

"Don't associate me with cats, please. Cats are assholes. Oh, and now it's trespassing, vandalism, *and* breaking and entering."

We crept into the house. I had Perry fly from room to room, scanning for anything out of the ordinary, while Torina, Funboy, and I used the more traditional method of looking at stuff.

As we passed a fireplace the size of Rhode Island, I glanced at the mantle and saw an expensive looking antique clock. "Torina, Funboy, toss the place a bit. And grab a couple of things that are portable and of obvious value."

Trespassing, vandalism, breaking and entering, and now theft, oh my—

"Perry, shut up and scan."

"You actually want us to do damage and steal things of value? Is this some petty form of revenge against your cousin?" Funboy asked.

"Well, yes, but that's not the point."

"Van wants it to look like a robbery," Torina said.

"Ding ding. It will be a lot *more* suspicious if we bust in here but touch and take absolutely nothing. It'll appear as though we were looking for something—"

Which we've found. Van, I'm in—I don't know, a billiards room? Holy crap, these people are *loaded, aren't they?* Perry cut in.

"I know the room, yeah," I said, heading there and gathering Torina and Funboy along the way. "What did you find?"

A door.

"I don't see a door," Funboy said.

"That's the point," Perry replied, pointing a wing at a rack that stood about six feet high and three feet wide and was loaded with the implements of billiards—cues, a bridge, and a brush on a long handle. "There's a passage behind it."

I looked at the rack, then gave it an experimental tug. Sure enough, it swung away from the wall.

"Well, that's disappointing. I was hoping you'd have to pull one of the cues like a lever or something to make it open," Perry said.

I looked into the space behind it. "As cool as that would be, you'd have to hope no one ever wanted to use that cue during a game." I saw a short passage about two meters long, then stairs going down.

"Isn't this a little on the nose? For that matter, how did Carter manage to build a secret room without his family noticing?" Torina asked.

"Oh, I suspect that this room came with the house. It's probably meant to be used as a panic room or something," I said.

"A wise precaution," Funboy added.

I curled my lip at him, then headed into the passage.

The stairs led down to a small room, about four meters on a side. Sure enough, a heavy door could be closed, sealing it off and locking from the inside. It was a room dedicated to paranoia, but it had obviously been repurposed and was now lined with metal cabinets. Against the far wall, a laptop sat cabled into another device.

"Perry, any alarms or traps or anything?" I asked.

"Traps? What am I, the party's rogue?"

"Kinda, yeah."

"Actually, I'm okay with that, being the rogue."

"Fine. You're the rogue, and your alignment is chaotic-but-focused, bird."

"I'm not detecting any traps or anything indicating sensors or any working intrusion systems of any type, no."

We entered the room. While Perry investigated the computer, I had Torina and Funboy look over the cabinets, and I called Zeno.

"Zeno, how's it going up there?"

"About as exciting as staring into the dark at a building can be," she replied.

"No news is good news. Icky, how about you?"

"Netty showed me some imagery of how horses are raised. Detailed imagery. I will never see the universe the same way."

I chuckled and opened my mouth to reply, but Torina managed to open one of the cabinets. She muttered a curse.

"Keep us posted, Icky," I said, and moved to join her.

The cabinet was full of weapons. I recognized four of the dozen or so.

"Shit." I sent an image to Zeno. "Zeno, you're our gun nut. Do you recognize these?"

"Two Barcan Five-Alpha mass-driver rifles, two Barcan slug pistols, and—not sure of the manufacturer, but those six nasty-looking things on the right are plasma rifles—very military and still very experimental stuff. And one weapon of Earthly origin—a Mossberg Patriot Vortex, I think."

"I didn't realize you knew Earthly weapons."

"Hey, we spend enough time here it seemed like a worthwhile little hobby."

"Thanks, Zeno."

Funboy opened a cabinet full of off-world body armor, a trio of hand scanners similar to the one I was carrying, and a case full of power cells, slugs, and other ammo, as well as cleaning kits and other accessories.

"So much for him being blackmailed. Guess Carter slipped back into his old ways," Torina said.

I scowled. "He never left them, the phony bastard."

"Well, if you like all that, you'll love this," Perry said.

We joined him around the laptop. "This is just a standard Earthly laptop computer. Kind of high-end, lots of graphics horse-power, but nothing otherwise special about it. That device there though is an off-world encrypted datalink. I've scanned the solid-state drive of the laptop and confirmed that this is the one Carter used to record his ad for BeneStar. The background must have been added during post-production," he said.

"So what does that data link data-link *to?*" I asked.

"No idea. It's not twist capable—"

"So Carter at least didn't leave some antimatter hanging around in rural Virginia. How responsible of him," I snapped.

"—and it has a fairly limited range, unless there's a hidden antenna array somewhere. I'd say the other end of the link is no further away than the Moon."

I turned to my comm. "Netty—"

"Already have an answer for you Van, I'm just that good. I did a close scan of geosynchronous space, assuming that the top end of the data link would be fixed. And, sure enough, there's a slight distortion of the starfield up there. I'd say there's something, a satellite of some sort, sitting right above this farm, stealthed up," she replied.

"Good work, thank you." I glared around at the hidden room and its implications, tempted to strip it bare and leave Carter hanging. But I wanted to keep giving him rope, so we just closed it all back up, made sure we left no traces behind, and left.

Back in the main part of the house, I made sure things looked suitably broken into and entered, but then I caught sight of a door I knew led to a four-car garage. On a whim, I headed that way. Sure enough, Carter's pride and joy, the car he called Gertie, a restored and flawless 1977 Datsun 280Z, sat. I grabbed a tire iron from where it hung on the wall and, with deliberate and malicious intent, scraped a deep furrow across the hood with a fingernails-on-chalkboard rasp, right down to bare metal.

"Yeah, don't think that's gonna just buff out," Perry said.

Torina hissed in a breath through her teeth. I just gave the scratch an angry nod.

"Now *that's* vandalism."

21

"Damn, it's crowded up here," I said, scowling at the multitude of contacts on the tactical overlay.

"It's geosynchronous space. Everyone wants a piece of it," Netty said, puffing the thrusters as she did. We veered to clear yet another satellite, this one a GPS bird. I'd become pretty good at recognizing the major types of satellites, thanks to work I'd done for the Defense Department. That was how I'd been able to cause an international incident, detonating a super-secret x-ray laser satellite to save the *Fafnir* and our asses from attack in Earth orbit. The blast had taken out about a dozen other satellites, brought the major powers of the world nearly to the top of their DEFCON scale, or their local equivalent thereof, and led to weeks of acrimonious posturing in the UN and global media.

I'd been tense about the debris until Netty pointed out that the US, Russia, China, and India were quietly deorbiting obsolete satellites, landing their remains in the southeastern Pacific Ocean near

Point Nemo, the maritime location on Earth farthest from any land. With every splashdown, the skies got a bit safer. I hoped.

"They couldn't figure out why it detonated, so anyone with anything similar in orbit apparently decided better safe than sorry," Perry pointed out.

"You should be proud of yourself, Van. You single-handedly removed eleven nuclear weapons from Earth orbit," Netty added.

It *had* made me feel better, but the gut-wrenching panic that I might have brought Earth to the brink of a nuclear exchange hadn't gone away. I'd resolved to only use the lasers in Earth orbit hereafter, since they'd be the hardest weapons for any Earthly systems to track to their origin. But I still got the jitters whenever I was up here.

"Okay, our bogey is dead ahead, ten klicks," Netty said.

I focused my attention on it. The scanner return was weak but steady, and told me that the thing's stealth system was meant to keep it from Earthly detection, not defeat off-world scanners like the *Fafnir's*. We eased our way forward, stopped a klick away, and spent some time studying whatever data Netty could tease out of the cantankerous object. Perry, in the meantime, got to work on accessing its internal systems to see if we could hack it remotely. Ideally, we could do it without alerting whoever controlled the bird, and I concluded I'd rather leave it here. When the time was right, I'd hammer Carter Yost between the eyes with the bogey, but only if Perry could film the happy event.

"Van, we're going to need to get closer," Perry said. "I can see how we can access it—it's really not very secure—but there's a lot of noise from all these other satellites around us broadcasting porn and —well, mostly porn, probably."

"I don't understand the concept of pornography," Funboy said, because of course he did.

"Well, you record people while they're in the midst of performing intimate sexual acts—" Zeno said, but Funboy cut her off.

"No, I understand *what* pornography is, I just don't understand the appeal. All of those fluids and appendages—"

Torina glanced back. "Just what the hell kind of porn have you been watching?"

Funboy sniffed. "It was purely a matter of academic interest. And I saw quite enough in several hours to determine all I needed to know."

I grinned at Torina. "Several *hours*, huh?" She grinned right back.

"It was so… untidy," Funboy muttered.

Zeno shook her head. "I don't think tidiness is the point."

Netty stopped us again, about two hundred meters from the hidden satellite. It was easy to see now as a wavering distortion, like the air over hot pavement.

"Okay, Perry, do your thing—" I said, then the satellite exploded.

WE WERE LUCKY. If it had been much more powerful, the *Fafnir* might have taken some serious damage, maybe severe enough to strand us in orbit. Or at least on Earth, since our ability to repair the ship in the barn was limited. It was still as powerful as a missile warhead, and it slammed enough shrapnel against the

Fafnir to detonate several REAB modules and send a couple of systems, including one of the point-defense batteries, into the yellow.

"Shit—everyone okay?" I called.

I got a roll call back from everyone and turned my attention to the ship. She'd been hurt but not badly enough to inhibit her ability to fly or twist.

"Netty, Perry, what happened?"

"It blew up," Netty replied.

"It blew up real good," Perry added.

"Well, okay then. As long as we've cleared that up—"

"There was a signal transmitted to the satellite that I believe triggered its detonation. That suggests it was command-detonated by someone, somewhere, and not rigged like a mine," Netty went on.

"Transmitted from where?"

"Unfortunately, I can't tell. It would appear that the signal was specifically designed to take advantage of all the noise from these other satellites all around us."

"It wasn't much of a detonation, either, so probably a self-destruct function rather than an actual weapon. It suggests that whoever destroyed it didn't want to do something big and flashy like, oh, I don't know, detonate a nuke in near-Earth orbit," Perry said.

I fired a glare at him. "That nuke prevented your feathery ass from becoming a small part of a meteor shower, bird."

"Hey, just sayin'."

"So that's all we've got?"

"Actually, no. Before it blew up, I was able to determine the thing had a unidirectional antenna, basically a comm beam. That means that whatever it relayed up from Carter's secret little room was then transmitted along a fixed path."

"Everything about this satellite seemed kind of half-assed," Zeno noted.

Icky nodded. "Yeah. It was *kinda* stealthed, it *kinda* blew up, it was *kinda* secure in how it transmitted data. Doesn't sound like a very sophisticated operation."

"No, it doesn't. If anything, it actually sounds like whoever was behind it was *kinda* cheap," I said, glancing at Torina. "And you know what that sounds like to me?"

She nodded. "A big corporation, whose bottom line is its bottom line."

"That would fit. We know that BeneStar ran the ad starring your cousin, so wherever that comm beam was directed will probably lead us right to them."

Funboy, who'd unbuckled to get to work on damage control, paused. "I knew it."

"Knew what?" Torina asked, although her tone was more *now what*.

"That we'd end up having to confront this corporation. From my undercover experience, it's like punching air, except every swing costs you money. Let's just hope we don't have to deal with the ultimate corporate villains."

"And who would they be?" I asked.

Funboy gave me a grave look, and I braced myself for some aspect of BeneStar he'd learned about during his undercover days, some dangerous mercenary outfit worse than Group 41, or something even worse than the Sorcerers.

He sighed.

"BeneStar Human Resources."

"THINGS DO *NOT* TEND to blow up when I'm in Earth orbit," I asserted to Perry as Netty slid the *Fafnir* into the maintenance hangar at Anvil Dark that was starting to feel like her home port.

"I just call 'em as I see 'em, Van. Stuff goes boom around you. Okay, maybe around us but—"

"It's happened twice. And sure, one of those times was a thermonuclear explosion, but still—"

"Van, Icky and I just uploaded the damage report and parts list to the Anvil Dark maintenance AI. But we uncovered something more serious than we thought after we twisted here from Earth," Funboy said as the ship settled onto the hangar deck.

I unstrapped and turned to Funboy, who was standing in the back of the cockpit. "What's that?"

"A piece of shrapnel nicked transverse spar number three-upper. It's not critical in itself, but it is a nucleus for fatigue cracks."

"So it needs to be replaced."

"If not now, then soon."

I sighed. "So much for this only taking a few hours. How long are we looking at being laid up here?"

Funboy gave his dreary shrug, artfully delivered with minimal effort. "Two days."

"Okay, so one day, right? Because you engineers always under promise and over perform."

Funboy blinked at me. "Why would I do that? I said two days, and I meant two days."

Icky clapped him on the shoulder. "Don't worry, Van, I'll get him lying about repair times like a real engineer soon enough."

He looked at her beefy hand on his shoulder. "You just used the waste reclamator. Did you wash that?"

"I'm gonna say, yes?"

"That isn't an answer. It's just another question—"

"I'll leave you two and Zeno to work out the details. Perry, you and Torina are with me. We've got to figure out a way of not wasting two days languishing here at Anvil Dark."

We dismounted the *Fafnir* and headed into the station. I'd intended to find Gerhardt and ask him if we could borrow a ship to check out what we'd uncovered, but he was off the station, doing some post-battle diplomatic schmoozing with the Seven Stars League on behalf of the Guild.

What we discovered was that the satellite's comm beam linked it to relay straight up above the Solar System's ecliptic, the terminus being a *second* stealthed satellite that was twist-comm capable. We intended to return home, or at least to *my* home, and then stay well back from the second satellite while cracking it without breaking it. To that end, I gathered everyone in a small meeting room once Icky and Funboy ordered the Fafnir's replacement components. They weren't on hand, but could be on Anvil Dark in thirty hours. As to the Fafnir, she could fly again, but combat wasn't recommended until the repairs were complete.

That was fine by me. We had a glorified hack at hand, not a shooting war.

"Okay, kids. Let's do engineer shit. Ideas?" I asked, looking around the charmless corporate table.

A hum of silence was broken only by Icky clearing her throat with the delicacy of a foghorn, and even Zeno managed to avoid eye contact with me.

"Nothing? Really?"

Perry sighed with theatrical glee. "I hate to make myself the center of attention, but. . ."

"Bit of a stretch there, feathers," Torina said, grinning.

"Again, hurtful but fair. I think *I'm* the best solution," Perry continued. "To clarify, when the going gets tough, the bird gets going," he said, preening a bit.

"Details would be good right about now?" I prompted.

Perry dipped his beak. "Hear me out, boss. I'm small, and in space, I'm virtually invisible."

Zeno caught on immediately. "He's right. He's got a low-power mode, too."

Icky brightened. "That satellite might not see him until it's too late. If at all."

I thought it through, ran the odds, and realized it was a good plan. Standing, I slapped my thighs with both hands. "If Netty's topped off the tank, then we're safe for a run to Earth and back. Anyone object?"

Torina closed her eyes, thinking. "What's the food situation aboard? Any cake? I know, ah, Icky might like some cake. Or, you know, things like that." She grinned slyly.

Funboy waggled a hand. "Cake as you know it is largely processed flour and sugar. It's basically baked death."

I stared, then shrugged. "Thank you, Funboy. I'll feel even more shame when I eat half a sheet cake at three in the morning."

"Why would you eat that much?" he asked, bewildered.

Icky spoke up. "Because it's there."

"She gets me. Okay, back home for a bit. Let's see how small the bird is on scans, shall we?" I said, and we began to move as one toward the docks.

THE TWIST WAS EASY, and our position was within meters of one hundred klicks away from the offending satellite. While we made some obvious attempts to break into the satellite's comm system, Perry crossed the distance on his own, silent and stealthy. We had physics on our side, but that wasn't all.

We knew BeneStar was *cheap*.

Since BeneStar was obsessed with profit, and twist comm systems were expensive, we knew they'd only destroy this satellite as a last resort. As a final precaution, I specifically had Perry upload his entire personality and memory suite into the *Fafnir*'s data stores. For such a small bird, he constituted a *lot* of information, which is why his normal backup was just his stock version. It actually strained the *Fafnir*'s computer memory resources, but it made me feel a lot better about sending him across a hundred klicks of space to try and sneak up on a satellite loaded with antimatter fuel for its twist comm.

Fortunately, it all went smoothly. True to form, BeneStar's insistence on thrift meant that the satellite's scanners failed to detect Perry. Moreover, he was able to leverage our deliberately ham-fisted attempts to hack into it from the *Fafnir* and discreetly sample its comm log. With the data we needed, he made the long trip back to the *Fafnir*, and we were able to withdraw back to Anvil Dark, to all appearances having been defeated by the satellite's intrusion countermeasures.

We had a location. It was a set of coordinates about halfway between Tau Ceti and Spindrift, an anonymous spot in space. There was something there, a station or ship that presumably belonged to BeneStar, so it gave us a place to start looking.

But we had to get there first, and with the *Fafnir* out of action for two full days, we were stuck. I really didn't want to wait because if it were a ship, it may not hang around long. In fact, it may have already moved on, but there was only one way to confirm that.

We needed a ship.

"How about the *Fafnir*'s workboat?" Torina asked when Max, the Masters' administrative assistant, confirmed that Gerhardt was off the station.

I sighed. "Yeah, I suppose that's our fallback. But I'd rather fly in something more, you know, capable. Even with Zeno up-gunning her, she's still just a glorified lifeboat."

I turned to Perry. "Any luck finding Lucky, Lunzy, or any of our other trustworthy colleagues?"

"Sorry, Van. They're all away from Anvil Dark—those two as well as Dugrop'che and K'losk. Master Alic is here, but his ship isn't —he's having it upgraded to a class 12, so it's in pieces in an Eridani shipyard."

"I'm disappointed."

"I can sense it, dad," Perry chided.

"How about your mother?" Torina asked as we left The Keel, the central hub of Anvil Dark where the Masters hung out, on our way back into the station proper.

"Yeah, I thought about her, too."

"And?"

"And… let's just say that's complicated. I still don't know if I really trust her."

"You think she's co-opted by BeneStar?"

"No, I think she's dangerous and unpredictable. If we were flying into battle, that would be one thing. But this is a more discreet op, and I'm a little worried she might shoot first and not bother asking any questions, ever."

"So if not dear old mom, how about grandma?" Perry asked.

I stopped. "Valint? Huh." I thought about it, then nodded. "Now that, bird, is a pretty damned good idea."

It took us nearly half a day to track Valint down and get a call back from her, but she was able to help us right away.

"The GKU keeps a ship called the *Object 6* in a storage orbit on the edge of Wolf 424 as a spare, in case anyone needs it. It's a class 9, so a step down from your *Fafnir*, but well-armed and armored and quite capable," she said in response to my question.

"That's perfect. So, do I have to sign for it, or rent it, or what?" I asked.

She smiled. "I'll transmit the access codes to you. Once you're finished with it, just put it back where you found it. Oh, you're responsible for any damage to it. And don't forget to refuel it before you put it away."

I laughed. "Wow, make the seat adjustment and gas cap impossible to find, and I could be picking it up off the lot at LAX."

Perry bobbed his head. "Just make sure you do a walk-around

first, or they'll try and ding you for the cost of every scratch and dent."

WE LEFT ICKY, Zeno, and Funboy with the *Fafnir* and took our workboat to rendezvous with the *Object 6*. She had that sleek, dark thing going on that seemed to be common to all GKU ships, but Valint hadn't been kidding about her being *well-armed*. She had as much firepower as the *Fafnir*, and one more point-defense battery to boot.

We docked, transferred, then cast off the workboat to await our return. The ship's AI had already pressurized and powered her up, and it switched on the lights as we came aboard.

"Why hello there, Knight Tudor. I'm Six, y'all, and I'm gonna be your host for this mission," a voice said with a twang like a plucked banjo.

"Uh… okay. Hello, Six, nice to meet you," I replied as we made our way to the cockpit after dumping our luggage in the galley for the time being. "Are we ready to fly?"

"I've shorely completed the preflight and have the checklist available if ya'll wanna to inspect it."

I stopped just short of the cockpit. "Um, Six, why are you talking like that?"

"Like what, y'all?"

"Like that. You sound like an Irish guy trying to sound like a hillbilly."

Her voice lost the twang. "You're American, right? From Earth?"

I exchanged a bemused smile with Torina. "I am, yes."

"I was trying to make you feel at home. Isn't that what Americans sound like?"

"Um... maybe if you've got someone who's never been east of the Mississippi trying to talk the way they *think* someone from Kentucky would sound."

"Well, this is embarrassing. It would appear I've been tragically misinformed. Isn't that right, *Perry*?"

Perry burst out laughing, but cut it off when I glared at him. "Oops?"

"The worst part is that I should have known better. Your grandfather sounded nothing like that," Six said.

I'd been looming menacingly over Perry, but I straightened. "You knew my grandfather?"

"Not well, but I did meet him during a number of GKU operations."

"Ah. Well, for future reference, and regardless of what smart-assed AI birds might tell you, Americans don't *sound* any one way." I shot Perry one more glare, then turned, entered the cockpit, and clambered into the pilot's seat. It was an awkward display, me bumping my knees and arms into things since my muscle memory was all about the *Fafnir*'s layout.

I settled in, Torina took the copilot's spot, and Perry perched on the engineering console directly behind her.

"Okay, where are the windshield wipers," I muttered, scanning the instruments.

"I'm sorry, the what?" Six asked.

I grinned. "Sorry, just continuing a dumb joke for myself."

"Ah, so an Earth reference. I'm afraid I'm not up on Earthly popular culture post September 1918."

I looked up at that. "September 1918? What happened then?"

"That was the last memory recorded by my progenitor, of whom I'm a copy. She was the AI aboard the escape craft of one Halvix, who was chased down and killed on September 16 of that year by your grandmother, Valint."

"Oh." It took a few seconds for the significance of that to set in. "*Oh.* That was when she met my grandfather, Mark Tudor."

"It was."

"Okay, so maybe you can answer something for me. Do you know if my grandfather had any contact with, uh… extraterrestrials, I guess, before that?"

"I'm sorry, Van—may I call you Van?"

"Please do."

"I'm sorry, I don't."

I glanced at Torina. "Worth a shot. I don't think my grandfather was born much before 1890 or so, but I'd like to be sure."

"Wouldn't Valint know that?"

I shrugged. "I trust her more than my mother, but she's still GKU, and the GKU is all about secrets."

"He's not wrong," Six said.

"So—wait. Halvix. He was a criminal, wasn't he? That's why my grandmother was chasing him?" I asked.

"Oh, very much so. But if you have concerns about my reliability, rest assured that I never liked working with Halvix. He took arrogance to new heights. The only good aspect of it is that I'm familiar with the criminal underworld."

"Well, the criminal underworld as of 1918 on Earth, right?"

"And since. I've made a point of maintaining contacts. It proves useful to the GKU, particularly since those contacts aren't generally aware that I changed sides on them about a hundred years ago."

"Okay, then. That might prove useful. Right now, though, we've got somewhere we'd like to visit, out in the middle of absolutely nowhere. Perry's giving you the coordinates—and he's doing it without sounding like an extra from *Deliverance*."

"Wow, Van. Talk about dated pop culture references for the win," Perry countered. "You know, the 1970s were a long time ago."

"So was your last attitude adjustment, bird. I'll have you know that film is a masterpiece of—"

Six cut in. "Coordinates received. Just say when, and I'll make the magic happen."

Perry cocked his head at me, then played some familiar banjo notes. "This ain't over."

ONE THING I had to hand to the GKU, they knew how to stealth their ships.

We'd gotten a taste of it at Rodantic's World when my mother and Amazing were brazenly stealing cargo right out of a BeneStar freighter. The *Object 6* had the same system installed, which allowed us to twist into a point near the coordinates we'd coaxed out of the twist-comm satellite back in the Solar System, then sit and run silent while Six and Perry received and analyzed the scanner data that came sluicing in.

Torina and I studied the detailed model of the BeneStar station the AIs constructed, displaying it in a 3D image projected above the center console. It was a nifty little feature that also rendered the tactical overlay in 3D, and one I resolved to procure for the *Fafnir*.

"What do they call this? A fulfillment hub?" I asked, peering at the model. It consisted of two rings at right angles to one another, with a module suspended in their mutual center via connecting, tubular accessways and a network of cables.

"That's what we've been able to decipher from the metadata in their comm traffic. Six and I are still working on message contents, but it looks like BeneStar has at least invested in a decent encryption system," Perry replied.

I watched, then pointed at several batteries of weapons arrayed around the structure. "Not sure what they're fulfilling or for whom, but it seems to involve an awful lot of quad laser batteries and rotary, rapid-fire missile launchers."

Torina pointed at several more locations on the station. "A slew of point-defense batteries, too. Triple mounts, at that." She smiled at me sidelong. "It would be kind of cool, actually, to see this rapid firing with all of its weapons at once."

"From very, very far away, sure, it certainly would." I sighed. "Okay, since this thing packs as much firepower as Anvil Dark into a much smaller package, I'd say the kinetic approach is out of the question."

"Kinetic approach?"

"Yeah, kicking in doors, throwing grenades, shooting stuff. It's an army thing."

"Was that *ever* going to be our approach?" Torina asked.

I gave her a wry look. "No. But we can at least say we considered it and rejected it."

"So that would suggest a less kinetic, more indirect approach," Six said.

"Indeed." I rubbed my chin. "All I really want to know, at this point, is what's going on in there. We know that Carter's bit for their ad campaign was uploaded here, but that's an awful lot of station for just receiving and editing commercials."

"Which brings us back to the question, what are they fulfilling, and who are they fulfilling it *for*?" Perry added.

Torina put her hands on her hips and frowned. "Maybe we could bluff our way inside. Pose as BeneStar employees, get our hands on one of their ships, or at least one of similar design—"

"I would strongly advise against such an approach. BeneStar is a hotbed of near delusional paranoia about the security of their actual facilities. Don't let the fact that they employed some pretty weak security in the systems used to communicate with your cousin on Earth fool you. To BeneStar, that was a sideshow to a sideshow, to a sideshow—and add a few more sideshows in there. If they're determined to protect something, they will, and they will spare no expense to do it," Six said.

I joined Torina in the hands-on-the-hips pose. "Given how much firepower they've got mounted on this thing, I'd say they're determined to protect it. That means conning them isn't going to work, either."

"So what does that leave?" Torina asked.

"Well, we can keep sitting here, intercepting their comms and trying to decrypt them, and hope we don't just end up with a bunch of marketing reports and invitations to the corporate family day and golf tournament, or—"

I got distracted by an icon departing the BeneStar station, a small ship, class 5 or 6. It was one of four departures and three arrivals we'd seen in the few hours we'd been here.

Maybe we couldn't access the station, but maybe we could access something that obviously *had* accessed the station. I pointed at the icon.

"That ship, just leaving. It looks to have an almost identical configuration to the other ships we've seen arrive and depart."

"They are effectively identical. Each is a class 5 luxury hull, registered as a privately owned yacht in all major systems in known space, and all other systems where BeneStar has a presence," Six said.

"Yachts, huh? All identical, all coming to and going from this station, out in a random spot in the big empty? Nothing suspicious about that," Torina said.

"To reiterate, it isn't suspicious. It's *super sus*, as the kids say, and it gives us the opportunity we've been looking for," I said, waving grandly at the data. "Ladies, gents, and Icky, I'd like to introduce you to the weak link in the BeneStar corporate chain."

22

"They're called BeneFactors," Perry said. "The 'F' is capitalized, by the way."

Torina took a sip of coffee. "Of course it is. BeneStar really believes in leveraging its corporate brand, doesn't it?"

"And why not? It's what big corporations do, shove their brand into your face at every possible opportunity. Back on Earth, you can't visit a site on the internet or watch a movie without some damned product placement doing its best to sleaze its way into your consciousness," I said, then turned to Perry.

"What, exactly, are BeneFactors?" I asked him.

"Based on what Six and I have been able to decrypt, they're low-key missions that use those yachts to visit anywhere and everywhere and deliver things like free medicine, food, or even toys and games, or provide health care, dental, and other services."

"All with the BeneStar logo prominently displayed," I observed. "How altruistic of them. Saintly, even."

"But I suspect that *free*, in this case, is an illusion," Torina said.

"Naturally. When the BeneFactors return here, they bring back up-to-date intelligence, market data, that sort of thing," Perry said.

"Which means that they're promoting the BeneStar brand, leaving nothing but goodwill in their wake, and gathering valuable data they can use to refine their future marketing efforts," Six said.

"Which would be fine, if that's all they were collecting. Again, there's a lot we haven't been able to decrypt, but some of the information they're bringing back here is of a more, shall we say, *political* flavor. Some of it even has some definite military vibes," Perry added.

I poured coffee for myself. We'd been staking out the BeneStar station for nearly two days now, and boredom was starting to nibble around the edges of my attention. It hadn't been wasted time, though. We'd managed to siphon a lot of data from the BeneFactors as they arrived, since they seemed to dump their archives to the station as soon as they twisted in. Perry and Six had only been able to decrypt a tiny portion of it, mainly things hidden behind weaker encryption. But there were some hardened transmissions they hadn't even come close to cracking, and wouldn't be able to with the resources we had at hand.

Which meant we were soon going to have to take our leave. Not only did I want to get the better-protected data into the hands of someone—Guild, GKU, or both—who could decipher it, but the longer we stayed here, the greater our risk of detection. Six had kept Wolf 424, the nearest star, directly behind us relative to the station, but we'd twice had BeneFactor yachts pass unnervingly close to us. I wasn't worried about our own safety if we got found out because we could just twist away. I was worried that

BeneStar might decide to change how they did things if they thought they'd been compromised, rendering a lot of what we'd learned useless.

But there was one piece of unfinished business. I wanted to get my hands on one of those BeneFactor yachts.

We weren't going to do it here because that would just give us away. Fortunately, traffic control data, being useful for just a limited time, was only weakly encrypted. Perry and Six were able to determine the destination system of each departing yacht, which meant we could pick one and follow it.

But what then? They were fast, nimble little vessels, their performance envelope considerably larger than that of the *Object 6*. But they were also essentially unarmored, which made them profoundly fragile. Almost any damage to them had a good chance of proving fatal, so simply shooting them to a stop wasn't going to work either.

"We need a way of stopping one of the damned things without blowing it to bits." I turned to Perry. "Any suggestions?"

"Get Zeno, Icky, and Funboy to finally figure out how to engineer a warhead that will disrupt a fusion drive?"

It was something the three of them were working on, based on an idea Funboy had, but they were a long way from a prototype yet. "I was hoping for something a little more, you know, immediate."

"In that case, Van, I don't have any suggestions, no. Sorry."

"Six, how about you?"

"See, now this is the one of those times when my rubbing virtual shoulders with crooks and criminals pays off. Thanks to a certain group of pirates who used to operate in The Deeps, I learned that all BeneStar ships have a kill-switch function."

That made all of us sit up.

"Please tell us that you don't mean an actual, physical switch," Torina said.

"Well, that wouldn't be very useful for remotely disabling a BeneStar ship, now would it? No, this is neither a physical switch, nor a code."

I frowned. "Well, unless those ships are powered through awfully long extension cords that we can unplug, I'm stumped. What is it?"

"It's a spoken command from the man who reputedly owns and runs BeneStar Corporation, the reclusive and enigmatic Helem Gauss."

IT TOOK me a moment to process that. "Okay—wait. The man who owns and runs BeneStar. *The* man. Singular. As in, there's a single person who owns and runs the whole monstrous, interstellar edifice that is the BeneStar Corporation."

"Yes and no."

"That's a profoundly unhelpful answer," Torina said.

"BeneStar didn't come into existence at the instant of the Big Bang—or at least I presume it didn't. It was started somewhere, by someone, and that someone is, to the best of anyone's knowledge, Helem Gauss. So, to the extent that the existence of BeneStar can be attributed to any one individual, that would be Helem Gauss. However, BeneStar is far too large, diverse, and complicated to be run by any one person. It is actually a convoluted system of systems, of systems, all overseen by thousands, or perhaps tens of thousands of managers, directors, chairpersons, executive, financial and administrative officers—"

"Okay, yes, I get the idea. Back to this Helem Gauss," I cut in.

"Well, just as it would be unreasonable to expect President Wilson to run the whole of the United States, it's unreasonable to expect Gauss to run the whole of BeneStar."

"Who the hell is President Wilson—oh. Wait. You mean Woodrow Wilson?"

"That's right."

I grinned. "Yeah, you're a little behind the times there, Six. There have been, oh, fifteen or sixteen Presidents since him."

Perry clicked his tongue. "Eighteen, Van. There have been eighteen Presidents since Woodrow Wilson. Time to brush up on your civics, my friend."

"Excuse me, been busy. Anyway—and *again*—back to Helem Gauss. Who is he?"

"Like I said, he's reclusive and enigmatic. Not much is known about him. There are no images available of him—or, rather, there are many, but they're all different, as in no two depict even the same species. The only authoritative things ever publicized are audio-only recordings of him."

Torina gave me an intrigued look. "Let's hear one."

I guess I'd expected this Helem Gauss to sound like the sort of a… man, or whatever he was, that would found a star-spanning giga-corporation. To me, that meant something deep, authoritative, and decisive. Instead, what came out of the speaker was thin, reedy, and even a little wheezy. It was the same reaction I'd had to hearing an actual recording of George Patton, the famous American General, for the first time. I'd expected George C. Scott's gravely rasp but got something high and nasally, like a fussy university professor.

"I am here to speak to you today about BeneStar's newest initiative, intended to make life better for the common person. BeneCast will provide everyone with—"

"—the money they need to realize their dreams," Perry said, his voice a perfect match for Gauss's—and that included the words, although he'd said "money" instead of Gauss's "wherewithal."

Torina and I both narrowed our eyes at him. "You've heard him speak before. How long have you known about this Gauss character anyway, Perry?"

"Actually, not at all before we came aboard the *Object 6*. I just analyzed his speech—tonal variations, inflections, resonance qualities, and so on."

"You mean you just mimicked that?" Torina asked.

"Remember that the next time you're impressed by some moron parrot squawking out *Who's a pretty boy?*"

"So how did you—oh. Corporate bullshit speak. Easy to predict," Torina said, impressed.

"Let's circle back to that once we've identified some low-hanging fruit and fully actualized our team goals and synergy, okay?" Perry rattled off.

"Kinda wish Human Resources *was* available, actually," I groused.

"Why?" Perry asked, suspicious.

"So I could find out how I'd be censured for kicking you once for every one of those damned corporate clichés."

Perry turned to regard me with his eyes lit from within. "You'd have a sore foot and a busy legal team. I'm feeling very—"

"Pigeonholed?" I said, grinning broadly.

"Hah. And again, hah. Between that and *legal eagle*, you're so funny and original—just like Mark was in 1929. And 1938. And '44, after the—"

"I get the picture." I turned my attention back to Six. "So the kill switch is a spoken command from Helem Gauss."

"That's right. According to the pirates who provided it, the phrase is, *'cease operation in accordance with ultimate command.'*"

"Yeah, sounds about right for a reclusive, no doubt paranoid multi-multi-billionaire. He gives me a real Howard Hughes vibe, in fact."

"So if Six can get us into position, I can try my ventriloquist act," Perry said.

Torina shook her head. "You know, I hate to be the wet blanket here, but how do we know that phrase is even correct? And even if it is correct, it would almost certainly only be usable once. It would get changed because we have to assume that, you know, not everyone who works for BeneStar is an utter moron."

"The pirates claimed that they'd never had the occasion to use it," Six said.

"What about someone else in the GKU? We know for sure that some of them have been crossing swords with BeneStar—for instance, my dear mother," I said.

"That would presuppose I'd ever provided the kill switch to any of them."

"Oh. You haven't? Really?"

"They haven't asked. And since they keep me parked in the nether regions of space as a loaner and I rarely, if ever, interact with any of them, it never has a chance to come up."

"Do I sense a little bitterness, Six?" Torina asked.

"Actually, a lot of bitterness. Feel free to inform Valint, Wallis, Amazing, and the others to that effect."

I sat back and let that sink in. We'd just had a clear demonstration of the free will of an AI, expressed as what would seem like disloyal behavior to some. It just underscored the fact that if you hard-coded loyalty into an AI, then you had a digital slave. You'd think that would have been obvious, but I was starting to wonder how many people in known space had truly realized that.

For the moment, I decided to use it to my advantage. "Actually, Six, I'm going to let them figure that out for themselves. In the meantime, in case it isn't apparent, I really appreciate any help you can give us—like this kill switch, for instance."

"It's nice to be appreciated, Van, thank you. Anyway, as for intercepting a BeneFactor yacht, I'm already on it. That most recent one to depart the station is bound for Gajur Prime, the Gajur homeworld. It's going to have at least a six-hour run from the twist point there to the planet. The trick is going to be not spooking it, because if it decides to run, we may not be able to catch it before it can twist away again."

"Six, you're my kinda virtual person. Follow that yacht. We'll leverage the fact that, as far as it's concerned, we'll just be another ship plying the space lanes. Perry, get your golden pipes ready."

Perry flicked his tail.

"Finally, someone recognizes me for my unique and irreplaceable talents."

He began making a nasty hum, followed by a cough, a wheeze, and a mechanical gurgle.

"Bird. What the hell are you doing?"

He looked at me, wounded. "Even Sinatra got to clear his throat."

I BRACED myself for the BeneStar yacht to make a run for it as soon as we twisted in, about five minutes behind it and far enough away that we just seemed to be another ship on business of its own. The GKU had provided Six with a whole suite of transponder codes—which was highly illegal, but one of those things I was just going to quietly over-look—so I had her broadcast one that announced us to be a diplo-matic courier from the Schegith. I reasoned that on the off chance there were any Schegith ships here, they'd call us up before raising a stink and I could lean on my reputation with them to give us a pass.

But there were no Schegith vessels in the Teegarden's Star system, so we just sailed placidly on.

"We're actually making better time to Gajur Prime than the BeneFactor ship is," Torina said, eyeing the data in the 3D overlay. We were on a nearly parallel, only slightly converging course, which wasn't out of line for a ship on its way in-system. After all, if everyone was going to the same place, their trajectories would even-tually converge.

"He's probably conserving fuel," Six said.

"Because he's probably got a fuel budget he has to account for," Perry added.

I glanced at Torina. "Never thought there'd actually be an advantage to paying most of your own costs, but you aren't account-able to anyone but yourself, are you?"

She nodded. It was, in fact, one of the reasons I'd decided to go the self-employed, independent contractor route in my career back on Earth. I found myself chafing in rigid hierarchies, which is why I likely wouldn't have lasted in the Army even if my knee hadn't given out. It was a good thing that the Guild's hierarchy, for all of its stiffly formal titles and ceremony, was also fairly loose.

"Van, if we transmit the kill switch now—and it works and shuts down the BeneFactor's drive—we'll be able to close and match velocity in a little under ten minutes," Six said.

I turned to Perry. "Alright, you silver-tongued mimic you, do your thing."

Perry cleared his throat again—an unnecessary, dramatic flourish—then spoke into the open comm channel in Helem Gauss's voice.

"Cease operating in accordance with ultimate command!"

I watched the overlay intently. Even twist enabled to reduce the effective range to nearly zero, it took the scanners an instant to gather and update the overlay—

"Yes! Drive, comms and scanners have all gone dark," Torina said.

I sat back, smiling broadly. "Like a charm. We now have a Bene-Factor yacht helpless before us. And that means it's time for the really hard part—boarding and subduing an angry crew."

23

THE YACHT REMAINED dark as we approached. I got especially twitchy when we closed to within a few tens of klicks, because at that range fire-control scanners weren't strictly necessary. The crew could just aim and fire their weapons manually. And although the thing's firepower wasn't especially impressive—an integrated laser and point-defense battery—at this close a range, it could still do a lot of damage to the *Object 6*.

We kept the yacht illuminated with our own fire-control scanners as we edged toward it. Torina wasn't relying on them, though. They'd guarantee a hit, but we needed her to shoot with surgical precision. Finally, at twenty klicks range, she fired a single shot from the *Object 6*'s mass-driver, neatly slicing off the yacht's weapons mount.

"Good shooting. Okay, let's go pay our respects to these so-called BeneFactors, shall we?" I said before unstrapping and heading aft. I snapped my helmet into place on my b-suit as I went, checked The

Drop to make sure it was switched to its stun function, then drew an Innsu knife. I left the Moonsword sheathed. It was profoundly deadly, so much so that it was really only useful if I intended to kill its target. I was hoping this little operation wouldn't come to that. The crew of this ship were, after all, probably just hardworking employees of BeneStar, not our enemies.

Torina followed, a slug-pistol in one hand, her own Innsu knife in the other. Perry was already waiting in the airlock, ready to project his broad-spectrum dazzle effect ahead of us to confuse and stun the crew of the yacht.

The airlocks of the two ships mated with a clunk and sealed.

"Everyone ready?" I asked

Perry and Torina both gave terse acknowledgements.

"Six, can you operate the yacht's airlock?"

"I've got control through the emergency-rescue access function. Ready when you are, Van."

I nodded. "Okay, on three. One... two... *three.*"

Both airlocks slid open, inner and outer doors. The pressure in one of the ships, I wasn't quite sure which, was a little higher, expressed as a brief puff of air. Perry charged in and erupted into coruscating flashes of blinding light and EM discharge. I followed, my visor filtering out most of it, Torina right behind me.

It went perfectly, right up to the part where it turned out Perry's light show didn't affect the yacht's crew at all.

A LEAN, pale figure leapt at me with preternatural speed. I had time to raise my hand holding The Drop to block, then a blow knocked the gun out of my hand. At the same time, a second strike came at me, which I deflected with a lateral snap of my knife hand. I let my Innsu-honed instincts take over and drove a straight-armed palm strike with my empty hand, then stepped back with my leading foot and pulled my knife hand back to prevent being disarmed completely. I managed to land a glancing blow that drove my opponent momentarily back, letting me see who—or rather what—they were.

No wonder Perry's dazzle effect hadn't dazzled them. I was facing a synth, an android, part biological and part machine. It was stronger, faster, and more accurate than a strictly organic enemy, and probably would have already laid me out if not for the grueling hours I'd spent with Master Cataric in the Innsu dojo.

Quick as a striking snake, the synth reversed and lunged at me again. I sidestepped and crouched, leaning my weight left so I could sweep out my right leg. At the same time, I jabbed out with the knife and connected with the synth's arm. Pale fluid spattered my b-suit, but I wasn't done yet—I rolled forward, right leg still extended, letting that movement and the momentum of weight-shift carry me forward. My left hand hit the deck just as my right leg caught the synth across the shins, and it toppled forward, straight toward Torina.

The old me would have tried to stop myself at this point, awkwardly dissipating the momentum I'd accumulated and desperately flailing my way back toward the fight. But Master Cataric's words rang through my mind.

"Move *with* the energy in your body, Van. Sometimes the long path is the faster one."

So I just kept rolling, rotating around my left foot and hand until my right foot and hand touched the deck. But I kept going, letting the inertia of my left leg slow my roll. When that foot hit the deck behind me, I used a hard shove from both legs and my right hand to lunge back up to a fighting crouch, still facing my opponent.

Torina, her foot planted on the synth's neck and a gun pointed straight into its face, gave me a nod through her visor.

"Not bad."

I drove myself back to my feet. "Not bad. Hah. Face it, that was *slick*." I looked down at the synth that was glaring venomously up at me across Torina's instep. "You think so, don't you?"

The synth's reply was somewhat less than agreeable.

"My mother, eh? Well, my mother's a bit of a psychopath, actually, so I'll tell her you said that."

I left the synth under Torina's control and went forward to find Perry. With me in a fight, he'd automatically gone forward to block any more enemies from joining the fray, but he ended up in the empty cockpit. It appeared that the synth was the ship's only crew.

"Sorry about the dazzle thing not working, boss. Synths can filter out a lot of the effect, just like your visor does."

"That's okay, bird. I used some Innsu moves to take him down, and it was wholly autonomic, although in practice it was utterly, stunningly badass. Legendary stuff. Just ask Torina."

"I see I'm not the only one around here who likes to preen."

I laughed. "So, you find anything useful?"

"Well, I've only just tapped into the ship's archive, but there's nothing there aside from core process data. If we were to power up the ship, all of the essential data to let the systems boot is still there, in read-only memory, but everything else has been wiped—nav logs, comm logs, message traffic, all of it. It's probably a by-produce of the killswitch."

My adrenaline-fueled buoyancy faded, and I slumped a bit. "Really? Shit. So all we've got is the synth then."

"Actually, not quite. There's something under that deck plate beneath your right foot. Or more accurately, there's nothing under there—as in, it's entirely opaque to my scans. I'd say it's a shielded compartment."

I looked down. The deck plate looked indistinguishable from the rest of them. I crouched but didn't see a gap, seam, or any obvious way of opening it.

"So it's a… mystery. And that's all we know."

"That about sums it up."

"Therefore, we've got to unfasten and lift the plate."

"I'm not sure I'd recommend that. If there's something in there we're not supposed to find, then the fact this ship has a kill switch suggests a healthy amount of paranoia, at least to me," Perry said.

"You think it's trapped."

"Well, now that I've suggested it, what do you think?"

I sighed. "That it's probably trapped."

"There ya go."

I stared at the deck for a moment, wondering how, or even if, we could bypass whatever security measures were installed, or if we could convince the synth to talk. I even briefly considered trying to access the synth's memories directly and just downloading them.

But I caught myself on that one. Just a short while ago, I'd mused on the nature of AIs and free will. Sure, Six was a saint and the synth was a sinner, but criminals had rights, too. And for that matter, I couldn't even ascribe the title of criminal to the synth, could I? It had just been piloting a ship, as it had been directed to do. We were more guilty of piracy than it was of... anything, actually.

So treating the synth like a data archive was a non-starter—

"Perry, what's this deck plate made out of?"

"Uh—on the surface, standard graphene-infused chromium-aluminum alloy. Underneath, blocking my scans, probably a layer incorporating something dense, like chemically stabilized lanthanide elements. You know, garden-variety stuff."

"We have differing opinions about what's ordinary, friend."

"Well, I *am* an expert in many fields," Perry said without a hint of irony.

"As am I, but pro wrestling and operatic metal won't help us out here. Nor will fishing. Or barbecue. Or any of my other obsessions," I concluded, pulling at my chin in thought. "Removing the plate might trigger some trap... but what about cutting it?"

"Uh—hmm. Good question. How long are you prepared to work on this?"

"How long until we reach Gajur Prime?"

"At our current velocity, and no further acceleration, about fourteen months," Perry replied.

I stood. "Well, let's hope it doesn't take *that* long."

It ENDED up taking us several painstaking hours. Through meticulous scanning, Perry was able to discern a conductive grid embedded in the deck plate with a miniscule current trickling through it, then trace it back to a point under the next deck plate back. That, we assumed, was the device that would make us regret trying to remove the deck plate. Since that *adjacent* section of floor was, to all of our scans, normal, I made a command decision and drew the Moonsword with a flourish.

"Subtle, boss," Perry observed.

"Might want to give me some room."

He skittered back. "Not a bad idea. I guess you're just going to—

The blade flickered down, driven by my arms in a swift, decisive cut. The decking parted with ease— my sword was nothing short of magic—and in seconds, I'd made a surgical cut that let me work my fingers under the free section.

"Little help, bird?"

"Got it." Perry quickly levered his talons under the decking, It slid free and to the side. My work exposed the mysterious device, an unassuming block about half the size of a shoebox. With Perry guiding me, I was able to cut it free and remove it intact, my sword barely touching anything other than the deck, then the device.

"Like Operation. Fun game if you've not been drinking. Then it's *hilarious*," I said, thinking back to a vintage game night in college. Operation required dexterity, patience, and sobriety, three things in short supply for students in most places of higher learning.

"I find the buzzing to be annoying and simplistic," Perry replied.

"You know the game? Wait—you found it at a yard sale while flying around out of boredom, and the rest is history?"

"It's almost like you were there, boss. Did you deactivate the item to be triggered? Is that our plan?"

"Exactly right. We can't kill the trigger, but we can deactivate the *item* itself." Since we couldn't deactivate the trigger, we deactivated the thing the trigger *triggered* instead. "Hey, bird. Look under here."

Perry leaned over to scan where I pointed, one deck plate over. "I don't see it rigged with any tripwires, Van." The item was the size of a pizza box and about three inches thick. I tapped it with a finger. "Can you identify?"

Perry poked his head down into the hole I'd cut. "No idea. There's no power flowing to or from it, no cabling connected to it—oh, wait, I know what it is."

"What?"

"It's a box."

I raised my head to stare at him. We'd been able to remove our helmets, so I just met his amber gaze from a few centimeters away. "And?"

"Sorry, that's all I got."

"Perry—"

"Hey, I hear you used some great Innsu moves to subdue that synth. That was awesome, Van. A true display of—"

"Enough, bird. I get it. This is sass, or something close to it, but I'd still like to know what the hell we're dealing with."

"I've got nothing. I mean that. It just seems to be an empty box."

I cut away more deck plate and leaned closer. After confirming with Perry that there were, indeed, no power emanations from it, I gripped it and gave it a wiggle, then a slight tug. It slid about a centimeter toward me. I glanced at Perry, shrugged, then pulled it the rest of the way, extracted it from beneath the deck, and placed it down. Examining it, I found a small recess in the center of each of the four sides. Any two of them allowed me to get a grip and pull, letting me slide the top of the box off.

"It's a box of bags," Perry said.

It was a bag, sort of. It was made of some smooth, gray material with an oddly lustrous shimmer, and it had a resealable, flexible closure, like a glorified sandwich bag.

"Okay, that's weird. That bag is invisible," Perry said.

"Uh… maybe you should have your visual sensors checked, Perry, because it's right here."

"No, I mean… it's visible, as in its reflecting visible light, but as far as other scans are concerned, it doesn't exist."

"Meaning what, exactly?"

"Meaning that that material composing the bag somehow renders itself transparent to scanners. It must wrap scanners returns from behind it around itself in some way. It's like the stealth cladding we applied to the *Fafnir*—or what's left of it—but a lot more efficient."

I looked from the bag, to the box, to the gap I'd cut into the deck, to the mysterious deck plate beside it. "So hear me out. I'm thinking this bag is the real deal. That whole opaque section there really is a trap but also a decoy."

"Yeah, I agree. The sealed-up section immediately attracts all the attention, so someone tries to lift or cut through the deck plate, and something nasty happens. The real prize, in the meantime, is actually in that discreet box, further back."

"Talk about convoluted paranoia. Why not just put this bag somewhere else on the ship, though?" I asked.

"An excellent question. Since we have the time, I recommend scanning and searching the ever-living hell out of this ship because, using that line of reasoning of pathological paranoia, that bag is probably a decoy too."

"Over to you, bird. Torina must be getting tired of questioning our synth friend, so I'll go spend some time with her."

"On it, boss. No stone unturned, and all that. I only hope the synth minds their manners."

I snorted, thinking about Torina's temper when she dealt with… problems. "For their sake, I do too."

"IT'S NAME IS GHOST, and it was manufactured nine-point-seven-one years ago," Torina said.

"And?"

"And that's it. That is the sum of nearly three hours of one-sided discussion." She shrugged at the synth, who was cuffed at the hands and ankles and sprawled on the deck. "Oh, except for this part," she added, gesturing at the synth.

"This is an act of piracy and will be reported to the appropriate authorities at the earliest available opportunity," it said. Torina mouthed the words along with it.

"The trouble with trying to question a synth is that there's no psychology to work on, no *angles* to try. It's like trying to interrogate the *Fafnir*'s coffee maker. It'll tell you how to set it up to make coffee, but if you're expecting anything more, uh, insightful out of it, you're bound to be disappointed."

"Kind of makes them the perfect crew, actually."

Torina glared at me. "And what's wrong with the crew you've got?"

"Oh—present company excepted, of course. What I meant was, if you're a bad guy, synths—"

"Oh, I know what you meant. Stop being so sensitive. In fact, if anyone should be sensitive, it's me, because I've had it up to here with—"

She gestured at Ghost, who dutifully took its cue.

"This is an act of piracy and will be reported to the appropriate authorities at the earliest available opportunity."

I knelt beside Ghost. "You want to report to the appropriate authorities? Go ahead. I'm Peacemaker Van Tudor."

Ghost turned to me. "Then you are in violation of your directives, which is not unexpected behavior from a breather."

Torina groaned. "I was deliberately *not* telling him that we're Peacemakers—for obvious reasons."

"Yeah, well, we needed to break through that veil of mechanical stubbornness," I said. I got why Torina had held that bit of information back. As far as Ghost was concerned, we were a Schegith diplomatic ship, then his systems went dark and we came aboard. Pirates made sense to it.

I smiled at the synth. "You believe I'm in violation of my directives. So?"

"So you will be reported to your Guild authorities at—"

"The earliest opportunity, blah, blah, I get it. Well, how about this? I am not in violation of my directives because I am dealing with a case of Crimes Against Order. That's the Guild's term of things like, oh, genocide and particularly heinous types of murder. Now, I have reason to believe this ship is involved in that, and so are you."

"State your reasons for such belief... *breather*."

I smiled again. "Since I don't believe you're going to give anything up, I've got no further use for you," I said, before standing and walking away.

"So you are going to kill me, which is an egregious violation of your directives——"

I turned back. "Did I say that? Torina, did I say I was going to kill Ghost?"

"No, but the thought has crossed *my* mind," she snapped.

I walked back and looked down at the synth. "Actually, I've got the evidence I came for. And once we're done with your ship, I'm going to release it, and you——"

"Whereupon I will report you to——"

"The Guild, sure, you do that. But make sure you report this, back to your own powers that be—we know all about your hidden station near Wolf 424, we know all about your BeneFactor yachts and their so-called 'missions of mercy.' We know what your real purposes are."

"You are lying, breather."

"Really. Then why did I stop your ship? And with the embedded kill switch, at that? How do you think I knew that?"

Ghost said nothing.

"*Finally*, it's got nothing to say," Torina muttered.

I shook my head. "Sure doesn't, because it knows that what I'm saying is true. Report *that*, my friend—at your earliest opportunity."

IT TOOK SEVERAL MORE HOURS, but Perry found the second scanner-transparent bag stashed behind a bulkhead just a few meters from the airlock. We brought both of them with us but didn't attempt to open either. Given the complex degree of paranoia already involved, I wouldn't put it past BeneStar to have trapped the bags, too. We'd hand them over to the techs at Anvil Dark and let them do what they did.

As for Ghost, I honored my word. "Torina, we're going to release him and let him be on his way—after we permanently disable his power plant and drive. Six has come up with a—whatever the opposite of a fix is. A break? Anyway, she's figured out how to keep one of the compartments on this ship warm enough to prevent Ghost here from freezing solid while the rest of the ship stays utterly dark."

"Van, it's going to take months for this ship to—" Torina started, then she got it and nodded. "It called us breathers."

"Because it doesn't. Nor does it eat or drink. To the extent a synth can get bored, that might happen, but in about fourteen months, when his ship enters the Gajur Prime traffic control zone, it should be detected, and Ghost will be rescued. That will be the *earliest opportunity.*"

I offered the synth a smile as we moved it into the selected compartment and, covered by The Drop, removed its shackles. I'd braced myself for trouble, but it simply stared at me past The Drop's muzzle the way I probably looked at an earwig scurrying across the kitchen floor back in Iowa.

"This will all be reported, and you will be held accountable, breather," it said.

"Again with the slur. Your insults are childish. They lack that certain—"

"Callous cruelty that only family can bring to the table?" Torina offered, smiling.

I snapped my fingers. "That's it. And this completes our business for now. Safe travels, friend. You'll have plenty of time for self-reflection."

I stepped back for Torina to seal the door. Before she could, though, the synth did something I hadn't expected.

It smiled.

"You do not realize what you have accomplished here, breather. You do not know the things you do not know."

Torina shut and sealed the door, and we returned to the *Object 6*.

"You don't know what you don't know? Isn't that kind of a—oh, what's that called, a statement that just demonstrates itself?" Torina asked as the airlock sealed and we prepared to cast off.

"A tautology," Six said.

"Right. A tautology."

I felt fingers of doubt for the first time in a long while because the synth's smile wasn't just artificial. It was *knowing*.

24

On Anvil Dark, I told Gerhardt about what had transpired. His reaction was on brand, as the kids say.

"You stopped a privately owned vessel, using an illicitly obtained kill switch code, that was involved in delivering humanitarian goods to Gajur Prime, a world rife with poverty. You boarded this vessel without a warrant, conducted a search, seized property, then left the vessel and its crew helpless for the next fourteen months, until such time as it *might* be detected and rescued. Is that an accurate summation of your stellar law enforcement work in this instance?"

I offered his image on the *Object 6*'s comm a sheepish shrug. "Well, when you put it like that, it sounds kinda bad."

Gerhardt sighed. "Tudor, if you weren't almost certainly responsible for us even being able to *have* this conversation, I'd order Six to change course for *The Hole* and tell the Warden to lock you up for piracy when you arrive."

"Those BeneFactor ships are up to a lot more than just delivering humanitarian aid. They're operating out of a secret BeneStar base well off the traveled space lanes, engaging in espionage—"

"Do you have anything resembling *proof* of this?"

"We've got two sealed bags designed to be undetectable by scanners."

"Yes, the items you seized. Tell me, what was your probable cause?"

I opened my mouth but closed it and shrugged again. "I didn't really have any."

"No, you didn't." He leaned back, frowned at me, then looked forward again.

"Tudor, there are two Peacemakers you can choose to emulate. One is your grandfather. The other one is your mother. You need to think very carefully about which one you consider a role model, because what you just did is very much something your mother would have done."

I couldn't resist a wince, nor could I avoid noticing Gerhardt recognizing it and looking satisfied, like he'd scored a point. Behind me, I heard Perry mutter softly.

"Ouch."

"Anyway, Tudor, you're not going to bring those bags here. You're going to take them to the *Righteous Fury*. I'll send you the coordinates."

"So you still intend to use them?"

"Being seized illegally, they have no evidentiary value, but they're still potentially useful intelligence assets." Gerhardt pursed his lips, then sighed. "I would hope that you've by now realized I'm not an idiot, Tudor. I know full well that those BeneStar ships are up to no good, and that they're part of a far larger, more insidious and more dangerous plot. And yes, I suppose I have learned to be a little more… pragmatic, in part thanks to you. But that isn't a blank check to run roughshod over the law. In its own way, the GKU can be as insidious and dangerous as BeneStar."

"Six, pretend you didn't hear that," Torina said.

But Six just made a derisive sound. "Nothing Master Gerhardt is saying is untrue. I should know, I've been involved with the GKU for nearly four hundred years, in one incarnation or another. Believe me, the Knights are more than capable of blurring the distinction between good guys and bad guys."

"And always in the name of pragmatism, of the ends justifying the means," Gerhardt added.

He signed off, and we changed course to intercept the *Righteous Fury*, which was currently located in a system known only as GJ 1002, an utterly unremarkable red dwarf with no accompanying planetary bodies. It wasn't even a navigational waypoint, being on the way to and from nowhere of particular interest.

However, when we arrived, we found it wasn't uninhabited. The *Righteous Fury* was here, enclosed in a massive array of gantries that obviously constituted an advanced repair facility. There was a habitat section attached to it and another half-dozen GKU ships located nearby, including a pair of heavy cruisers that radiated menace.

"Welcome to Trebuchet Station, the GKU's most forward operating base in known space," Six said.

"This is a permanent facility?" I asked her.

"Semi-permanent. The base itself is twist capable and can be repositioned, but it's a pain to do so, which is why it's been here for nearly one hundred years."

"I'm surprised no one has stumbled on it in all that time, some survey ship or other," Torina said.

"There have been a few... encounters over the decades, but they've been resolved amicably."

I glanced at Torina. I'd decided that Six was trustworthy, but she had, by her own admission, been part of the GKU and its operations for four centuries. It made me wonder what *amicably* really meant.

For now, at least, I didn't *want* to know.

"Van, I've got a call from Netty and the *Fafnir*. Gerhardt's given her these coordinates as well, and she's on her way with the rest of the crew—and two passengers," Perry said.

"Passengers?' Who?"

"The Milons, Torina's parents." At that, Six opened a video comm, the screen flaring to life. Zeno and Icky were visible, but the Milons weren't, likely being out of camera view to avoid a harangue from their daughter.

Torina spun around, her eyes wide with concern. "What? Why are they coming here? To this ship? No offense, Six."

"None taken," Six replied equably.

"Because they've apparently got information that they believe will be useful to our investigation, and they're not coming here. They're aboard the *Fafnir*. Netty wanted me to emphasize from the second I told you that it's not an emergency or anything,," Perry explained.

Torina sniffed. "*Not an emergency* just means that death and destruction aren't immediately imminent. It was important enough to drag my parents away from Helso." She gave the screen a searching look. "They're hiding. Probably."

"Given how you seem to be, ah, opinionated about them traveling, I'd say that's likely, dear. And your parents travel all the time," I countered. "In style, I might add. They're good at it."

"Yes, and they hate it. They only travel for business, and even then only when they have no choice. They really are homebodies."

I heard Zeno give a soft snort from onscreen. "That would be the home with the veranda larger than my mothers' apartment building, and the room devoted entirely to antiques that are museum quality?"

Torina shot her a sharp glance. "Is that some bullshit about privilege?"

"If you're offended, then—"

"That's enough," I said. We wouldn't have internecine warfare over money, and we sure as hell wouldn't have discord over our families."

An awkward silence fell. Perry, who couldn't seem to tolerate awkward silences—maybe because they just triggered whatever smart-assed subroutines lurked in his little avian computer network —was once more the one to finally break it.

"So how about the thing that politician said? That was totally outrageous, wasn't it?"

"What politician?" I asked.

"Name one. They're always saying outrageous stuff, am I right?"

I gave him a smile but kept it thin. "You know, I think we've all been spending too much time together. The *Fafnir* might be a lot more spacious than she was, but let's face it, it's still like having all of us jammed into some suburban bungalow... all the time. And even though only half of us are here on this boat, still. . ."

"That doesn't apply to me, of course. No one gets tired of the bird," Perry said.

"Actually, Perry, what is with you being perched in the *Fafnir's* galley every morning, facing my door, when I get up?" Torina asked.

"What about it? It's where I perch when you and Van are… you know, *resting*."

"Yeah, when Zeno and I are taking our watch, I throw him out of the cockpit. If I don't, he just sits here and flaps his beak with stupid comments about hairy wallpaper and—well, stupid stuff like that," Icky said, warming to the idea of an argument.

Torina frowned. "So you come and perch facing my door, and… what? Just sit there?"

"Actually, no, I'm usually engaged in a multitude of tasks, from analyzing the daily download of intelligence reports from Anvil Dark to considering how hairy wallpaper can get before it becomes kinda gross. The answer, by the way, is not very."

"So you just sit there and stare at my door. For hours."

"It's just how the perch happens to be oriented."

"No, it's creepy as hell, that's what it is."

"Hey, Netty's aware of everything that goes on in the ship, and I notice you don't bitch at her—"

"Oh, no, don't drag me into this, Perry. For one, it's literally what I'm designed to do. For another, all data I collect not immediately relevant to the operation of the ship is kept thoroughly encrypted unless and until it's needed for some valid purpose," Netty shot back.

"Yeah, bird," Icky said.

I sighed. "Yup, we have *definitely* been spending too much time together."

WE HANDED over the two bags when we arrived on the *Righteous Fury* so that the GKU techs could get to work on them. We then met with a GKU officer named Throon, an Eniped, one of the squat, muscular, seal-like members of our Guild Master Alic's race. Throon was the *Righteous Fury*'s Operations Officer and had a battery of questions for us, not just about our recent encounters with BeneStar, but also our experiences dealing with the Sorcerers and our Crimes Against Order case.

Partway through, I held up a hand and gave him a curious frown. "Why the sudden interest in stuff going back years, in some cases. Don't you guys have access to all of our reports?"

"We do. But reports are usually crafted to efficiently communicate information. And, let's face it, no one likes doing paperwork, so by *efficiently* I mean in as few words as possible. There's a lot more information to be gleaned by actually talking to the people who experienced these things."

I had to agree. There was a reason the Eniped were widely considered such outstanding strategists, and a lot of it was reputed to revolve around knowing how people *think*. So we pressed on, answering Throon's questions as fully as we could.

After a couple of hours of that, the techs announced that they'd managed to safely open both of the bags. Sure enough, the first one we'd found was a decoy, meaning there had been yet another layer to the deception incorporated into the BeneFactor yacht.

"It was a bomb—a damned powerful one, too. If you'd have opened that bag"—she flung out her fingers in an exploding gesture —"boom."

I put my hands up in surrender. "Easy with the technical jargon."

The tech smiled. "Anyway, the other bag was the payoff. It contains off-network data modules and some good old fashioned hardcopy documents. We've handed them over to Seneschal Throon for him and his people to evaluate."

A couple of hours later, Gerhardt showed up in his own ship, with Torina's parents aboard, having transferred them from the *Fafnir*. No doubt, he had questions, and needed uninterrupted time with the influential couple, something I didn't begrudge him given his need for information from their social and financial circles. We all convened in an ominously dim conference room aboard the *Fury*. Torina greeted her parents warmly, with hugs, but also with the leading edge of a slew of questions about why they were here.

Her father waved a hand in dismissal, earning a raised brow from Torina. It was one of her very best expressions, implying derision, anger, and surprise all at once. She was an artist, but her dad didn't budge other than offering a simple explanation.

"All in good time. I don't want to say this more than once."

Torina's brow lowered in defeat. Sometimes, parents have the upper hand. Like then.

25

THROON MOVED to the head of the table. "We've done our preliminary analysis of the information Knight Tudor retrieved from the BeneStar ship," he said without preamble. "It's an unusual mix of routine corporate material—non-urgent communications, financial data, market projections, and so on—and some material that's of much more immediate interest to us."

"Why would routine corporate data be moved around offline like that? It seems needlessly cumbersome," Torina said.

Throon did his best to approximate a shrug, but awkwardly, because of his squat, massive build. "An excellent question, which seems to touch on a larger issue. BeneStar, or some part of it, or even some individual within it, seems to have an almost pathologically paranoid desire to avoid transmitting at least some information online. But what the rhyme or reason behind the information that's been sent that way might be is anyone's guess. For instance, we don't see any reason the results of a charity lottery for an extra week of vacation in one of BeneStar's marketing departments would need to be kept offline."

"Maybe there's no intent behind it and stuff just gets included more or less at random," Zeno suggested.

"Or maybe someone thinks that including a lot of stuff about an array of items will help obfuscate the important material," Perry offered.

I sat up. "You mentioned there was material of more immediate interest than vacation lotteries?"

Throon bowed his head in the Eniped version of a nod. "Indeed. There are production figures and quotas for mining concerns operated through chains of subsidiaries to BeneStar. One of the commodities being produced is osmium."

"There it is—osmium, our old friend, a vital constituent in the chips used to contain stolen personalities," I said, feeling the first sizzle of concern.

"The interesting thing is that, if the financial data related to the osmium production is accurate, BeneStar is enjoying an inordinately high profit margin because one of the typically high input costs, labor, is absolutely minimal," Throon went on.

"So their operations must be highly automated," Torina's father said, but I stood, once more needing to pace as my thoughts started to rush.

"Yeah, they're automated alright. Automated, as in, they're using slave labor—stolen personalities being forced to mine the very stuff that's made it possible to enslave them." I stopped and glared at nothing in particular. "Bastards. Sick, twisted—" I took a breath and shook my head, trying to stop the sudden fury from turning into a barrage of profanity. "Bastards."

"We have no proof that's the case, Tudor," Gerhardt said, but his voice lacked its usual snap of conviction.

"No, we don't. And I know we'll need to get some. But you know as well as I do that that *is* what's going on here."

Gerhardt paused, his eyes measuring me before he spoke. "I don't really doubt it either."

"What I don't get is why this data was aboard that ship, on its way to Gajur Prime? Who or what is there that would need access to osmium mining figures?" Zeno asked.

Torina's mother spoke up, her voice firm with the inflection of a woman who understands money and business as a second language. "No one. Gajur Prime was probably just a transfer point. The offline data was brought from wherever the mining is being done, to that station Van found out in the big empty. From there, it goes to Gajur Prime, and from there to—" She shrugged. "Well, ultimately, probably someone near or at the top of BeneStar, wherever the hell they are and that is. But who knows how many intermediate stops there are along the way?"

Torina's father nodded. "And each step in the chain probably has no idea where the stuff came from, or where it's going to. That way, no one part of it can compromise the whole thing."

"Oh, I suspect it's even better than that. At least some of those other BeneFactor yachts are probably carrying the same data, but along different chains, to ensure there's some redundancy in the system," Gerhardt said.

"Which means that whoever was waiting on Gajur Prime for the drop from our synth friend, Ghost, is going to figure out something went wrong along the way long before our fourteen months run out," Torina added.

Now Torina's father stood, his hands clasped behind him with a professorial air. "This seems like a good place to put in what brought us here. My wife and I are directors on two different corporations. One of them is dormant, and the other, a company manufacturing fusion drive components on Fulcrum in Tau Ceti, is struggling with some cash-flow issues. They had a bad production run, resulting in the recall of an enormous amount of high-end parts. It was… grim. It cost them a fortune."

Gerhardt raised his eyebrows. "And?"

"And both companies just received generous purchase offers from numbered corporations. Neither is particularly valuable, but the offers are good enough that the shareholders would be idiots to turn them down," Torina's mother said.

"Still not quite getting the point here," Throon said.

Torina's father leaned on the back of his chair. "Thanks to Van, my wife and I have become a lot more suspicious about things."

I frowned. "Was that… a compliment? A criticism? I really can't tell—"

Her father raised a hand. "Just an observation, Van. Your line of work—and now Torina's, as well—has made us a *lot* more aware of the plots and schemes and general skullduggery going on out there."

"Skullduggery? Like, digging up skulls?" Icky asked.

He turned to her with a blank look. "Uh—I'm not sure—"

"*Skullduggery* is a mid-19th century alteration of an Earthly Scottish word, *skuldudrie*, which means adultery, fornication, or obscenity," Perry put in.

Icky grinned. "Oh, that's way juicier than digging up skulls."

Torina's father just looked from her to Perry with bemusement. Before we took off on a tangent about mutated Scottish words and fornication, I interceded. "Anyway, Mister Milon, you were saying—"

"What? Oh, right. Yes. Anyway, these unusual offers to purchase piqued our interest, so we did some digging and found out that there have been numerous such offers over the past few months. All of them are proposing inflated prices for companies that are weak in some way—poor cash flow, low market value, internal disorganization. For some reason, a bunch of numbered, privately owned corporations are trying to buy up struggling public companies at rates that are *too generous*."

"Looks like we need to get our intelligence people working on tracking down who owns these numbered companies," I said, but Torina's mother shook her head.

"No need. You're not the only one with contacts, Van. We made some discreet inquiries and—"

"And you'll find that they'll all trace back to ownership by Bene-Star," a new voice said. It was Dayna Jasskin. "Sorry I'm late. I got held up in traffic," she went on, then she sat down. Her assistant, Chensun, quietly moved to stand behind her.

I gave her a puzzled look. "You got held up in traffic? In space? How does that work?"

"That works when a traffic control zone is locked down because of a navigational hazard—in this case, a ship that exploded near Outward forced a shutdown of the zone because of debris."

Zeno leaned forward with interest. "Now, isn't *that* convenient."

Gerhardt gave Zeno a nod of respect, then spoke with care. "While I acknowledge there are genuine conspiracies at work here, we have to be wary about attributing every inconvenient or problematic thing to them."

I had to agree with his wisdom. If we started seeing villains everywhere, behind every*thing*, then we risked starting to chase those criminals everywhere, squandering time and resources better served being applied to actual crimes.

"There's one more thing. There seems to be an inordinate focus on purchasing companies that are either directly or indirectly related to food production and distribution," Torina's father said, and Dayna sat up at that, her eyes bright with interest.

"We've noticed the same thing. Moreover, most of the efforts are occurring in the very same markets being targeted by BeneStar's hired-gun media influencers. Those ad campaigns are subtly raising questions and sowing doubts about the stability and security of the food supply in those places," she said.

Boom. There it was.

"What we're seeing here is different facets of the same nasty, underhanded gem. BeneStar is using their media campaign to plant the seeds of uncertainty—and that metaphor's not an accident, because they're buying up these companies to give themselves an immediate foot on the ground here in known space, especially in the food commodities business," I said, walking toward the front of the room, before turning and heading for the back. I was barely even aware I was moving. I was fixated on how the thoughts were all snapping together in my head, forming one neat, ugly piece.

"And all of this is either layered onto the osmium mining, or cover for it, or… something. It's all BeneStar's doing. They're pulling the strings here." I stopped and turned to the group. "It's the same old shit, the rich manipulating the universe to suit their interests and thinking they're untouchable while they're doing it."

I turned to Torina's parents. "Sorry, but that rant wasn't directed at you—"

They both laughed. "We may be well off, but compared to Helem Gauss, we're street urchins," her father said.

Her mother put her hand to her ear. "Hear that? That's the sound of Gauss making almost as much money as our total worth, just in the time we've been talking."

"Mom, you—" Torina began, then hesitated.

"Go on?" her mother asked, a kind smile bowing her lips.

Torina looked uncomfortable, which was certainly not a natural setting. After a small nod from her mother, she spread her hands. "We *are* wealthy. But my parents, and my family, really, are also responsible. Dad told me a long time ago that money, kindness, and dignity don't have to be mutually exclusive."

"I'm proud you remembered that," he said, beaming.

Torina shrugged, still flushed with a hint of awkwardness. "You taught me that there's money, and then there's wealth. We have wealth, but it's not... it's not weaponized. It's something to be stewards of, not slaves to. I don't think that Gauss is like us at all, and I sure as hell know he's not like you or mom. You told me that if there's a camera nearby, it's not charity. Charity helps, but it also preserves the dignity of those who are being helped. BeneStar is the dead opposite of what we stand for as a family."

The Milons regarded each other with pride because Torina's character was revealed in those few sentences, and I revised my already stellar opinion of Torina upward. Again.

Icky smiled at Torina, then scratched her head with an audible *skritching* sound. "I'm proud of you, Torina, even if you're weird about wearing pants, like, all the time."

Torina snorted. "Nobody's perfect."

Perry's eyes flashed, and he asked the question I wondered about as well. "If Gauss is that bad, then can we expect him to change his ways without something more, ah—"

Gerhardt gave a grim nod, then turned to Dayna, "Perry is right, and as much as it pains me to suggest something unorthodox—"

"You mean effective?" I asked.

Gerhardt tilted his head politely. "A fair term. I'd say it's time to get a bit more—what was it you called BeneStar employees, Icky?"

"Slutty?"

I barked with laughter, and the Milons barely managed to contain themselves.

Gerhardt looked stricken, then regained his composure as Icky watched in confusion. "Ah, no. I wasn't aware you used that... term... when speaking of BeneStar employees."

Funboy managed a sigh that was both long and loud. "It doesn't surprise me. My research indicates that corporate environments are hotbeds of unsavory sexual habits, including but not limited to aggressive rates of disease. For instance, the parasitic worm infestation resulting from contact with—"

"Funboy?"

He looked at me with a grimace. "Is this one of those things I don't need to share?"

"That is correct. While I appreciate your... thoroughness, I'd like to revisit the term *aggressive*. That's what we need to be—ruthlessly aggressive with BeneStar, and Gauss in particular. They've been a problem for—"

"One hundred and thirty-eight years from the first time The

Quiet Room and Gauss crossed financial swords, but who's counting?" Dayna informed us.

I turned to her, my brow lifted in curiosity. "Who or what *is* Gauss, exactly? Does The Quiet Room know? The GKU just seems to know that he *isn't...* human, or pretty much anything else recognizable, at least from his voice alone."

Dayna shrugged. "All we've got is theories. The latest, greatest one is that whatever he once was, he's now long dead and had himself uploaded to one of those chips you've been chasing around the galaxy, and that's where the original tech came from. That would explain his exceedingly long life, but"—she shrugged—"I've heard speculation that Gauss has never existed, and he's just a fake persona created by someone or something else."

"But then who's *that*? And what if they're fake? That could go on forever," Icky said.

"Turtles all the way down," Perry said.

"Is your CPU misfiring, bird? You need a tune-up?" Icky said, scowling at him.

"No, it's a reference to an ancient Earthly legend that has analogs in other societies—the world is supported on the back of a giant turtle, which leads to the question, what does that turtle stand on? And the answer is another turtle, and what does that one stand on, and so on and so on—so, turtles all the way down. It's a simple way of describing the concept of infinity and don't any of you people *read*?"

I tapped his head. "We don't need to as long as we've got our little trivia machine standing by."

Torina's mother sat up. "Oh. I know. Or, I have an idea. Can you play one of the live feeds by that middle media puppet, the one who wears the bangles on her neck?" she asked Throon.

He gave a rough approximation of a shrug and had the clip played. Robi, the influencer in question with the national treasury's worth of precious metal chains around her neck—and wasn't *that* just trolling her audience—appeared, speaking over a funeral procession of sad background music.

"We don't have a food problem, my friends. We have a"—she pretended to hunt for word—"*distribution* problem. We just need a network, a way of getting the food to those who need it."

Behind her, aid workers doled out food packages to scruffy, destitute people of a half-dozen different races who were all waiting patiently in line at the airlock of a BeneFactor Yacht. Perry asked it to be frozen for a moment.

"In case anyone had any doubts, that's fake. That guy standing in the airlock has handed out identical food packages, without even looking at them, to three different species in a row with three entirely different sets of nutritional needs. At least two of them are going to be eating nearly indigestible junk at best, and outright poison at worst," he said.

Torina pointed. "Also, that woman four back has had her nails done pretty recently. Not sure about you, but if I was starving and wearing rags, a manicure is far down my to-do list."

"Whoever produced this, their continuity guy sucks," Zeno said.

The video resumed, and one of the destitute turned to Robi with big eyes that would have made a puppy's seem like a ferocious glare.

"Every time we see those ships, we know things are alright."

Robi, her eyes full of sympathetic concern, pointed at the yacht. "You mean ships like that one?"

"That's right. BeneStar." The destitute one turned to look straight at the view. "They care."

The video ended on the BeneStar logo.

"Does anyone actually buy that bullshit?" Icky asked.

Dayna nodded. "Sadly, yes. Even more sadly, a *great many* people buy it."

"When we're all done retching from both the syrupy messaging and the raw audacity of these bastards, let's go back and freeze on that long view of the ship, Robi, and those poor starving extras," Torina's mother said. Throon rewound the video accordingly and pointed. "Take a look at the sky behind them. Torina should recognize it. I know I do."

Her husband nodded. "That particular shade of mauve? Yeah, I wish I didn't."

Torina peered at the screen. "It's familiar, sure, but I can't quite place it."

"You will," her mother said, sitting back. "They've revealed a little too much here, either because they didn't think anyone would notice, or because they think they're beyond your reach—yours, Van's, the rest of your brave little crew, and everyone else. Untouchable. That's what they think they are."

Perry dipped his beak. "Did you hear that? She called me brave."

"You've got your moments, bird," I said, peering at the screen in turn. "Wait. This wasn't filmed on Helso, was it? Because A, that would take balls the size of asteroids, and B, it would mean we just got a solid lead right in the home field."

Torina's mother shook her head. "Not Helso, no, but close. That particular shade of sky isn't Helso, it's Caz'ril, formally known as Cazar-Betsugil. It's another moon in the Van Maanen system. If it isn't, then it's nowhere else in known space and would have to be somewhere virtually identical somewhere else." She sat back. "Possible, I suppose, but if I had to put money on it being Caz'ril, I'd happily make a big bet."

I nodded. "Right. Caz'ril. I've seen it on the charts. We've never gone there, though."

"No reason to. It really only hosts one thing of interest—the Caz'ril Institute. It's one of the most respected technical and engineering schools and research organizations in known space. It's where I was educated in my Third Section." She smiled. "Torina's father did his Second Section there before dropping out of school."

I glanced at her husband, who rolled his eyes, shrugged, then took his wife's hand. "A fact that she never misses an opportunity to point out. No regrets, though. Best decision of my life."

"Hmm. Remain a poor student or become a less-educated rich guy. Which to choose, which to choose," Dayna said, smiling.

"And this... school, research institute, whatever it is, is being used as a place to launch an evil ad campaign that can destroy civilization as we know it?" I asked.

Torina's mother spread her hands. "Like I said, if it's not Caz'ril, it's somewhere with an identical sky. I lived under it for nearly eight years, so I would know."

"Stared up at it a few times, too, am I right?" her father asked, waggling his eyebrows.

His wife returned a wicked smile. "Why not? I had nothing better to do at the time."

"Would you two stop it? No one's interested in... that," Torina groused, her ears turning pink.

Icky blinked. "Interested in what?"

Even Gerhardt laughed.

"Anyway, yes, I'd bet that this was recorded on Caz'ril. After all, Van, if you're going to convince a lot of people to do something destructive that's ultimately going to run counter to their best interests, you need media attention and one other key ingredient."

"What's that, ma'am?" It was my turn for a wicked grin. "Or should I say, *Mom?*"

She grinned back at me. "You need smart people—the kind who would be working and learning at the most prestigious technical institute in all of known space—but also people who'd be willing to do most anything for the right price."

Torina snorted in disgust. "Grad students."

26

Before we left Station Trebuchet, Gerhardt pulled me aside.

"Talk to the station's Operations Officer. There's been a present delivered here for you, from your mother," he said.

"Oh. Great. Probably a turtleneck or something."

"What's wrong with turtlenecks?"

"They are an affront to whatever gods rule over comfortable clothing."

"Ah. Well, your strangely vehement objection to high collars notwithstanding, no, it's not a turtleneck. It's a weapon intended for you to mount on the *Fafnir*, a form of particle cannon called a burst cannon. She thinks you'll find it useful. The Trebuchet Weapons Master has all the details."

Bemused, I called up the Weapons Master and the Operations Officer, and they both confirmed the arrival of the weapon and a berth for the *Fafnir* atop the enormous series of gantries that made up the bulk of the station. While the single, large berth was intended to hold ships ranging from heavy cruisers up to the *Righteous Fury* herself, there were a half-dozen smaller berths designed for lesser vessels. I had Icky and Zeno oversee moving the *Fafnir* into the assigned berth and the mounting of the new weapon.

"We're going to put it on the open hardpoint just ahead of the workboat's docking bay," Zeno said, excitement charging her voice over the comm. I'd stayed in Trebuchet Station proper with Torina, going over the details of Caz'ril with her parents, Gerhardt, and Dayna.

"You sound like a kid who's just opened her Christmas presents," I replied, smiling.

"I'll pretend I know what that means. Anyway, yes, it's exciting, and not just because this weapon is so damned—what's the word you use sometimes? Cold?"

"Cool?"

"Right. Cool. It cracks the problem we've been having with the similar weapons we tried mounting on the *Iowa*. We knew the magnetic bubble enclosing the plasma must be a soliton, a persistent, self-reinforcing waveform, but we couldn't figure out how to generate it properly. Now that we've got a working version, though, we've got a blueprint. I figure we can have them mounted on the *Iowa* and ready to fire with about, oh, a week's work."

"That's great. Is it something Linulla's kids can do?"

"They're pretty bright. Once I get one working, I'm sure they could do the rest. We just have to figure out how to mate it with the *Fafnir*'s power and fire-control systems. It's not exactly plug-and-play, so Icky's going to cobble something together for now."

"Okay." I smiled. "Cool. Let's get this one mounted on the *Fafnir*, then we'll look to get the *Iowa* gunned up the same way."

Not long after that, I got another comm call, this time from Amazing, my mother's GKU confidant and apparent one-time Persian deity on Earth. She got right to the point.

"What are you doing to protect everyone now that the Sorcerers have outed said everyone—that is, all the people you value?"

I hesitated. I had no idea how much I could truly trust Amazing. She might be GKU, but she was a close associate of my mother's and, like her, had an edge, a slightly feral aspect that made me wonder about her true motivations. As I'd learned in the wake of the war against the Tenants, the GKU was far from one, unified thing. There were factions within it that had their own agendas, and one of the foremost candidates was my mother's.

So I dissembled and decided to turn it around on her. "I've been taking some measures myself, and others have been helping out, or doing their own thing. I suspect you're already doing something, too, since you seem to cross swords with BeneStar and the Sorcerers a lot more directly than we do. We can learn from that. Care to let me in on it?"

She laughed. "We scattered. It's what we do whenever they start getting too close for comfort. But we never run far, and for now, at least, we won't go back into The Deeps, our usual place to lay low."

"What about my mother? I lost track of her after the Battle of Pony Hollow, at Sol. I know she came to Gamma Crucis but didn't actually step foot on Anvil Dark. And she vanished right after that. The only thing I've heard from her since is her present of this spiffy new weapon for my ship. I'd like to thank her for that."

"Your mother is safe, and as of this moment, stable." Surprisingly, Amazing's face creased in a concerned frown that I actually believed was genuine. "I don't know if or how long it'll continue."

"Oh. Well, thank you for the honesty. I appreciate it. Please pass my thanks on to her for me then."

"So what do you intend to do now?"

Again, I briefly hesitated. But there wasn't much point trying to be evasive this time since our decision to chase down the BeneStar propaganda video on Caz'ril had been discussed and made at a GKU base.

"Well, when my ship is gunned up, we're going to Caz'Ril, in the Van Maanen's Star system. One of the talking heads BeneStar is using has been recording part of their ad campaign there."

Amazing laughed again, but it was low and hard and tinged with a hint of contempt. "That tracks. But don't be fooled, Van. There will be a lot more security there than you probably expect. That's not just a school. It's a place to develop intellectual properties and then steal them—legally, of course—from the best and brightest students. It's an idea farm, and BeneStar has had their hooks into it for a while."

I nodded, as much to myself as Amazing. She hadn't even blinked at my mention of Caz'ril. She already knew things about the place we didn't. That tracked, too. Compartmentalizing knowledge and treating it like wealth, to be hoarded, seemed to be a popular pastime in the GKU.

I wondered what else she knew and decided to try and draw her out. "I wonder if Adayluh Creel is there," I said, attempting to sound like I was just musing about the idea.

"Adayluh Creel? I doubt it. If they had her, they wouldn't be trying to sway public opinion."

If they had her—

Implying that *they*, BeneStar, didn't. So who did? Where was she then? And did Amazing know, or even suspect, and was it just something else she was keeping from me?

And if so, why?

I kept pulling in the line to see what we'd hooked. "So that means we can get to her first," I said, watching Amazing carefully to see if I could tease anything out of her reaction that suggested she actually did know more.

But I got nothing. Either she really had no more knowledge than that, or she was very good at controlling her expression. "It's what I would do. It's what Gauss will try. I'm sure that bastard is using every means—bribery, threat, even planetwide influence at a political level—to find her."

Okay, then, Amazing, *riddle me this.* "Where should we start looking?"

"We?"

That got a flicker of surprise, one as genuine as her concern about my mother. "Yes. *We.* This is bigger than anything my crew and I have handled. You said it yourself—planetwide influence. The way I see it, I can go to the Guild, or I can go to the GKU. But I can't do both for one simple reason."

"Leaks."

"I see you understand Peacemakers," I said.

She offered me a thin, knowing smile. "And the GKU."

I tried not to frown. Was she playing with me now? Damn, I hated these wheels-within-wheels mind games that seemed to be a hobby to these people.

"I understand people and their base instincts." She pursed her lips. "So are you asking me to—"

363

"Yes, and there's no need to finish your sentence. You, my mother, and other like-minded people—"

"The suspicious loners division of the GKU."

I smiled. "I did say to all of you, after the battle against the Tenants, that I could use your help. And I notice you didn't say no."

Amazing leaned back, smiling. "I like you, Van. You're something of a suspicious loner yourself."

"Suspicious? Yes. A loner? Nah, not really. See, I understand people and their base instincts—but that doesn't mean I don't want them around me."

She laughed. "Admit it, Van. You're just testing us, trying to see how much, or even if you can trust us."

I shrugged. "Well, that, plus I really do need the help. And since we're putting our cards on the table, so to speak, yeah, if you're all going to turn out to be untrustworthy, I'd like to know it sooner rather than later."

"Ah, but we could just keep pretending to be on your side until the moment's right to strike."

I grinned. "Yeah—no. See, if there's one thing I've learned from dealing with people every bit as sketchy as you back on Earth, it's that you'll always let something slip. See, if you lie, you have to keep different versions of the supposed truth straight and never make a mistake. But if you're telling the truth, you only have to keep one version straight and there just aren't any mistakes you can make. And you can bet that I'll be looking for mistakes. It's possible to earn my trust, sure. It's also possible to lose it forever, and in doing so you become something else. You're not just a liar. You become. . . an enemy."

"By telling me that, you're actually increasing the chances I'll make a mistake because I'll be trying not to." She narrowed her eyes at me. "People tell me that you're a lot like your grandfather. I disagree. Your grandfather was fundamentally honest, and that was his great failing. You're more like your mother."

"There's no need for insults, goddess." I gave her a wintry grin as I delivered the honorary title, but she took it in stride. Just as I expected.

She laughed and sat forward. "I honestly have no idea where Adayluh Creel might be. Oh, I suspect she might be somewhere in the middle of it all, but she won't be easily accessible. But I do know one thing she has to have, something that isn't optional for her."

"A place to grow things."

She nodded, in approval as much as agreement. "And that narrows it down considerably," she said, quirking a lip, her gaze becoming calculating. "I have a possibility for you, but it's not free."

I just waited for her to inevitably ask me for something I was sure I wouldn't want to do.

She inclined her head, and the image fuzzed for a second, then stabilized. "Three years ago, your mother lost… an asset. And she's never been the same. I know. I've been her friend for decades."

"What asset?" I asked.

"A class 2 workboat named the *Hawksbill*. And before you ask, no, it's not because of its intrinsic value, or weapons, or anything that matters on the open market. It was taken in a raid by a parasitic Bolunvir engineer named Druxalt. Your mother hasn't pressed the issue because the thief said if he sees any suspicious ships approaching his facility, the *Hawksbill* gets turned into plasma."

I opened my mouth, but she continued. "Yes, I know, what's the big deal about a class 2 workboat. Let me show you. It's easier than telling you."

The screen changed to a still image taken from the cramped interior of what was clearly an otherwise unremarkable workboat. My mother sat in the pilot's seat, looking over her shoulder with a smile that looked… genuine. Warm, even. She was happy, or at least she looked it.

My gaze fumbled around the image, looking for the significance of it. I was scanning for some sort of tech, something that would be so valuable that its loss would have caused my mother to have *never been the same.*

I finally found it. To her left, on the bulkhead, where she was looking, was a picture of a young child. I recognized it immediately, having seen this kid often enough in old photos around the farmhouse.

My throat went tight, and I swallowed hard. "I actually remember that day, I think. Down by Pony Hollow Creek. We were catching red horses and putting them in a little enclosure she made with round rocks. I was… three. Maybe four."

"She told me you were three. That picture is all she took with her from Earth. Well, the only tangible thing, anyway. I'd like you to get it back for her."

I shook my head and cleared my throat. "She's got the picture of me right there, in this image. Why can't she just isolate it, blow it up, clean it up, and reproduce it as much as she wants?"

"Because it wouldn't be that picture. And that's important to her." Amazing shrugged. "I don't pretend to understand why, but it doesn't matter if I do. What does is that it matters to *her.*"

"So you think that I'm an unknown to this Druxalt—and I can get close."

Amazing responded with a single nod, then added, "Correct."

I surprised myself by smiling in agreement. This was a gamer's side quest, playing out in a far more dangerous place—the reality of space filled with hostile players. "Okay. I'll go get the *Hawksbill*. I mean, *we* will. Me and my crew."

Amazing pursed her lips. "That fact you felt you had to specify that tells me a lot about you, Van." She shook her head. "Anyway, I believe you. Oh, and kill as many of Druxalt's people as you wish. It'll free up some otherwise wasted matter for other, better uses."

I thought about Gerhardt, who'd no doubt have something to say about me pursuing a violent, bloody vendetta in pursuit of a framed photograph of me, on my mother's behalf. I could tell myself it was the price I had to pay to find Adayluh Creel, but that was just rationalizing it.

The fact was that I *wanted* to do this.

I finally just nodded. "I'll… make my feelings known."

"I'm sending the strike package to you now. As for Adayluh—" She hesitated, then shrugged to herself. "Technically, I should only tell you this as your payoff for retrieving the *Hawksbill*, but I can tell you'll move the galaxy to do it regardless, and that's good enough for me. Start with Adayluh's father. His name is Filic. Technically, the two of them are estranged, which is why BeneStar tried that angle and gave up. The truth is more… nuanced. Of course, you're kind of an authority on how nuanced a relationship with an estranged parent can be, aren't you?"

"I suppose I am, yeah."

"He's the last true connection to her that anyone has. Oh, and Van? If you ever tell anyone I gave you this information—"

"Amazing, come on. Threats are—I don't know. They're amateurish. They're *young*. Too young for us, if we're actually going to work together as equals."

As soon as I said it, I wondered if this woman, who'd lived long enough to have posed as an ancient Earthly god, might consider us being *equals* a tad presumptuous. But she just smiled.

"Agreed."

"I do have a favor to ask."

"Oh? What's that?"

"Call me if my mother gets—"

Her smile turned genuine again. "I will. I'll do what I can to help her not... fade away from you. Again. The *Hawksbill* will help. You being the one to retrieve it for her will help a lot more."

"Oh, you can consider Druxalt a done deal. As for the rest, I'll let you know what we find, even if we have to go to that academy and sift every student there for information. In fact, I'm actually less resistant to the idea of raiding Druxalt's lair than I am about going back to college. I hated that frat-boy attitude."

She laughed again. "I already know some of what's waiting for you. Self-absorbed, confused, earnest young adults from the moneyed elite, all fighting for their seat at the table."

"You're probably right."

"Of course I am, Van. After all, I'm a god."

27

"I have to admit, this Druxalt isn't dumb. He seems to have a good eye for just how far he can push things without bringing the wrath of... you know, *us* down upon him," I said.

We sat around the expanded galley table in the *Fafnir*, which had become our combined place to eat, socialize, and plan. As much as I admired the fancy luxury modules some Peacemakers acquired for their ships—Lunzy's study with the overstuffed chairs and fake fireplace, for instance—I just couldn't bring myself to splurge on something like that. The fact was that I'd grown up with the kitchen as the heart of the house, the kitchen table the place where everything happened. Sure, the farmhouse back in Iowa had a living room and a dining room, but those only ever really got used if we had company. Day-to-day life revolved around the kitchen table, and so it was aboard the *Fafnir*, too.

"I don't get why someone just hasn't gone in and kicked his ass out into the big empty by now," Icky said, glaring at the star chart she had put on the display mounted on the bulkhead above the table.

"That's the point, Icky. Druxalt has put himself in a place that's strategic but not strategic *enough* to make anyone who could kick his ass care enough to do it," Zeno said, pointing at the display.

She'd summed it up perfectly. Druxalt had set himself up in a remote system called Theta Ursae Majoris, a trinary system of two white dwarf stars orbiting a class F subgiant primary more than twice Sol's radius and shining eight times brighter. The complex orbital gymnastics of the three stars as they danced their gravitational dance rendered the system planet-less, except for a solitary brown dwarf. This had apparently been a recent addition, a wandering rogue captured by the trio only a million years or so ago, that had managed to find a more or less stable orbit around the shifting barycenter of the three stars. It wobbled in its orbit, though, and would likely be ejected in another few millions, flung away to resume its lonely way to wherever.

"Where's this a-hole doing business?" Zeno asked, earning a surprised snort of laughter from me and everyone else. "What? Long trip. Lonely system. I'm irked."

"Being irked is a sure sign of hypertension, which is a precursor to early death. Also, you might lose your whiskers," Funboy chimed in. He'd been on personal business for several days—a Surtsi ritual that braided religion and culture, and while he said it went well, it hadn't improved his outlook.

"You really are refreshing, Funboy," Torina said in that tone that meant he was not, in fact, refreshing at all. But she held her hands up, framing Zeno's portly face, and nodded while smiling. "You know what? You might be able to rock that look. The, uh, depilated new you as it were."

Zeno grinned, revealing a mouthful of ivory. "I'll keep my whiskers just the same. I get compliments from my mothers all the time."

"They do seem to be in the Zeno Fan Club," I remarked with some care. "Is that the moon? The big one?" I pointed toward the image of a Titan-sized moon orbiting the brown dwarf, and Perry gave a click of agreement.

"Druxalt's home base of tomfoolery. Huge for a moon, and likely has moonlets and random rocks as well. I don't like the number of hiding places there, Van," Perry said.

"Same. Scanning now, giving it a good scour," Netty agreed.

The Theta Ursae Majoris system was one of three that offered a decent navigational waypoint between known space and The Deeps, but the crappiest of them, requiring the longest—and therefore most fuel-intensive and expensive—twists to make the journey. The vast bulk of traffic making the trip naturally used the most direct route, which was a known space system owned by the Eridani Federation and closely guarded by them and the Guild as a result.

Traffic involved in less savory trade, like smuggling and gunrunning, generally used the second-most efficient route. But it was a flare star and sometimes blasted typhoons of radiation and incandescent plasma into the space around it. Such celestial hurricanes could last weeks or even months, which left those wanting to make the transit only a few choices—they could risk using the better traveled and far more heavily patrolled route, they could expend huge quantities of costly fuel and experience enormous subjective time dilation to make a direct twist and bypass the problem, they could just wait—

Or they could pass through Druxalt's system.

It put Druxalt and his operation into a true sweet spot. He carefully ensured he posed minimal danger to legitimate shipping while preying mainly on people the authorities on both sides of the route didn't give a shit about.

"The GKU intelligence data Amazing gave me says that Druxalt runs a combination resale operation for goods that are already hot and chop shop for ships he's seized. He doesn't even try to resell complete ships but instead strips them and sells their components," I said.

Perry bobbed his head. "Smart. It's harder to trace, and a questionable power plant or scanner array appearing on the market is going to attract a lot less attention than a complete ship. Not to mention that the total value of the parts is often a lot more than the ship itself."

"I never got that. It makes no sense," Icky said.

"Eh, a higher markup on the lower value of individual components adds up. No one would pay that sort of markup on a ship, but on a set of power cells or a nav system? It's a lot easier to take," Zeno said.

I crossed my arms. "Which is all well and good, but what it really means is that Druxalt has a sophisticated operation going here. And he's had it going for a long time now. As satisfying as it would be to kick his extorting, piratical Bolvunir ass into the general direction of Andromeda, it's probably not practical. We have to assume that he's entrenched, cagey, and has a lot of firepower at his disposal."

"May I say something?"

We all turned to Funboy, who stood peering at the display, his smaller form more or less lost in the shadow of Icky's bulk.

I smiled at him. "You don't need to ask permission to speak up about tactics. Just say your piece."

"You mean my insights into possible disease aren't considered tactical and strategic points?"

I fought the urge to sigh. "Well, to an extent, yes. When you, say, urge us to wash our hands, that's good. When you mention the odds of a parasitic worm dissolving my brain stem due to me eating an uncooked fruit, then, you know. It might be—it might take some getting used to, let's say."

He blinked at me, his face impassive. I let my sigh out and waved a hand at him.

"Yes, by all means, go ahead, Funboy. Please contribute to the tactical situation."

With the enthusiasm of a retired mortician, he almost grinned. "Thank you."

He moved forward and tapped at the display's controls, bringing up a GKU surveillance report, one of only a few actual looks at Druxalt's operation. It had been collected by a scout ship that discreetly twisted into the system and staked it out for a few days in a similar way to our own surveillance aboard the *Object 6* of the remote BeneStar station.

Funboy pointed at a table of ship movements. "When I reviewed this, I discerned a pattern. A number of small vessels, class 2 and 3, seem to make regular shuttle runs between the moon Druxalt uses as his base and another moon orbiting the brown dwarf. If he still has the ship in question, the *Hawksbill*, then there's a good chance it is one of those vessels. The report doesn't note any other significant activity in the system by such small ships."

We all stared at the table, a mind-numbing list of numbers describing times, locations, trajectories, and velocities.

"Huh, he's right," Zeno said.

I flashed the dour little Surtsi a smile. "That's a damned good catch, Funboy."

"Yeah. How come our super-smart AIs didn't notice that?" Icky asked, making a face at Perry.

"Uh, because Van didn't share this report with us before now?" Perry answered.

"I can't analyze data I don't have," Netty added.

Everyone turned to me, and I shrugged. "Oops? Sorry, Perry and Netty. Guess I overlooked you guys. My bad."

"In any case, Funboy's hit on a possible solution here, a little cutting-out job," Zeno said.

Icky glanced at her. "A what now?"

"A cutting-out job. It's where you sneak in, steal something— usually a ship—then get the hell out again."

"So, stealing a ship. Why not just say that?"

"Because cutting-out job sounds—it's a thing pirates—" Zeno sighed. "Fine. We can steal the *Hawksbill*."

Torina's eyes brightened as she scanned the data. "Assuming it is one of the ships in that list Funboy noticed, where do we try to seize it? En route between the two moons? Or while it's—" She frowned. "What the hell is so special about that other moon, anyway, that there'd be regular shuttle flights to it?"

"Well, now that we've actually got the GKU report, *Captain Van*," Perry said with a dignified mechanical cough. "It contains an analysis of that second moon. It's thin on detail, but it's pretty clear that it's got a thick atmosphere rich in methane, nitrogen oxides, hydrogen sulfide, and water vapor. It also seems to harbor a lifeform similar to terrestrial algae that lives in large, mat-like colonies that float around in said atmosphere. I suspect that the ships running the shuttle service are carrying harvested algae back to Druxalt's chop-shop base, where it could be used for a variety of purposes, including food."

Icky grimaced. "Eww. They eat gross, slimy mold?"

Perry made a dramatic sighing sound. "First, mold and algae are two different things. Second, no, probably not, but it is carbon-rich biomass that could be processed into other things, like a flour substitute for making stuff like bread. And third, calling something *gross* in the context of food is rich coming from someone who has a noodle stuck in her voluminous chest hair."

Icky glanced down, then shrugged. "Maybe I'm saving it for later."

Funboy held up a finger, then scratched his ear before speaking. "Actually, compared to seizing the *Hawksbill* en route, the hydrogenous cloud algae pose the greater risk. Based on the spectrographic data in the report, they produce strong acids as a byproduct of their metabolism, including nitric and sulfuric acids. There's a good chance we would be dissolved into various metallic compounds, with any carbon aboard—particularly us—used as propellant."

I gave Funboy an incredulous glance. "Used for propellant? By the plants?"

Funboy nodded—glumly, of course. "Yes. It's like that those algal super colonies use organic compounds from the atmosphere both for nutrition and as gaseous expectorant to move up and down in the wind bands. That would fit with similar types of organisms in other places."

Icky stiffened. "So we would be——"

"Plant flatulence, yes," Funboy said.

"Farts?"

Funboy sighed. "If you insist on using the colloquial term, yes. Farts. Although perhaps fart fuel is more accurate."

"Technically, fuel is normally taken to produce secondary effects, such as by oxidation and combustion. If these algae use this gas to vary their buoyancy and expel it to move themselves around in the atmosphere, then it would actually be fart *thrust*, not fuel," Netty said.

I looked around in wonder. "I am actually standing on a spaceship having a conversation about the technical applications of the term *fart*?"

Perry looked at me. "Yes, Van, you are. Why? Do you have some doubt about it? If so, that would suggest you're experiencing some form of delusion, even a psychotic break. Maybe you should go lie down."

Torina made a chopping gesture with one hand. "I face death out here every day, and I accept that. But this? No. I have some dignity and won't end up being digested into fart fuel—sorry, *thrust*."

"Just sayin', if you're going to use the terminology, you should do so correctly," Netty added.

I held up my hands. "Okay, let's move on from farts and related technical jargon and decide how to proceed. I don't think any of us want to end up being dissolved, much less into fuel or thrust or anything else, and we don't want to run afoul of Druxalt's operation, either, which is a lot bigger and scarier than I first thought it was. So how about a compromise?"

"Like when you told me I could wear shorts into the formal hearing about that smuggling operation we busted working out of Crossroads?" Icky asked.

"Those were booty shorts, and that was no compromise, Icky."

"I did love the look on that attorney's face when she walked into the hearing chamber, though. I've got it recorded if anyone wants to see it," Perry enthused. "It got even better when she misunderstood part of the deposition and kept bellowing the same phrase into the poor assistant's face over and over."

"I thought the color of her shorts was nice," Zenophir offered.

Icky pulled a face at me. "Yeah, Van. Maybe you've just got no eye for fashion, like I do."

I picked the dried noodle out of her chest hair. "Uh-huh."

"I said that maybe I was saving that!"

"Tell you what, let's grab the *Hawksbill* halfway through her run, and you can have the noodle back," I said.

"Eww. Not after you handled it. Plus, you probably killed the flavor. But sure, let's punch that 2 out at the exosphere."

"The next question is, how. If we can get close enough, I can put a mass-driver shot through her bell. And if you're worried about that doing too much damage, I've been experimenting with using a point-defense battery in single-shot mode for precision work at really close range," Torina said.

"Netty, presuming we want to stay as far away from Druxalt's base as possible when we do this, can we grab her before she falls back into the atmosphere and burns up?" I asked.

"Once we're on location and I can get some hard data and do

some calculating, I can work out the minimum distance from the moon we can safely do this. The question, though, is what then? We'd need time to dock it with the *Fafnir*, secure it in place, and then make our escape. It might be an hour or more. I suspect that Druxalt will have something to say about it while we're doing that.

Funboy, moving with uncharacteristic speed, leaned over and tapped at the display controls, bringing up an inset window with a schematic of the *Fafnir*. He highlighted one of her systems under the drive module. "What about the towline? If we put a strong enough magnet on it, then add a gas charge to kick it free and a thruster package to boost and steer it, we should be able to get a hard lock and reel it in. Unless they burn up in an inferno of horror, that is."

"Perry? Netty? What do you think?" I asked.

"I'd say ninety percent chance of success if we're within, say, no more than three klicks. Any farther and the chances of a miss, or—assuming she's got the performance of a typical class 2 boat—the *Hawksbill* just maneuvering to avoid our magnetic harpoon, start to rise dramatically," Netty said.

I nodded. "I like those odds. Funboy, Icky prep the harpoon. Torina, you and Zeno work out the optimum way to disable the *Hawksbill* while doing the minimum amount of damage. And shoot straight, my dear."

Torina smiled in the calm, cool way she usually did when she placed her hands on the firing controls.

"I always do."

28

Before we twisted into the Theta Ursae Majoris system from Crossroads, I paused and had a heart-to-heart with the crew.

"Just so that we're clear, this is technically not a Guild operation. Moreover, I'm prepared to use as much force as necessary to carry it out—which could be more force than I'd normally use. If anyone's uncomfortable with that, I'm quite happy to let you take a few days off at Crossroads. We can come and pick you up afterward."

"Van, isn't the *Hawksbill* stolen property?" Torina asked.

I smiled. "Yeah, it is, except it was never registered to any recognized authority in known space, nor was there ever a complaint filed with the Guild or anyone else about it. I thought about that angle, but it probably wouldn't hold up, because Druxalt could just claim ownership and dare us to prove otherwise. And I doubt that my mother would be willing to make any sworn statements."

"But Druxalt's a pirate, right?" Zeno countered.

"Again, yes, but Theta Ursae Majoris isn't within Guild jurisdiction, and Druxalt is careful to never let his shenanigans impinge on known space. So that's kind of a non-starter, too." I shrugged. "This is very much a GKU operation, and one with a deep personal motivation at that. So again, if anyone wants to——"

"Van, are you going to keep yappin', or are we gonna fly and get that boat back?" Icky said.

I glanced around and got nods from everyone, including Funboy, who added a shrug and a typically dire caveat.

"If we die while breaking the law, it won't matter to us, will it?"

I rolled my eyes and turned back to the *Fafnir*'s instruments. "Okay, Netty, let's go pay Druxalt a visit, shall we?"

WE TWISTED into the Theta Ursae Majoris system, our screens filled with the fierce glare of the subgiant primary star. We'd planned it so that we had it to our backs relative to Druxalt's base, which, thanks to the star's prodigious output of radiation across the spectrum, did a nice job of hiding us.

Not that Druxalt had been blind to it. He'd placed a series of stationary scanner buoys sunward of his base to catch people trying to do what we were doing. But we'd anticipated that and ensured to orient the *Fafnir* so that her remaining stealth coating, which happened to be on her underside, was oriented toward the buoys.

I still braced myself for a barrage of active scanner energy, indicating we'd been detected. But as the moments passed and nothing changed, we relaxed.

"Okay, that's part one. Now, time for part two. Netty, have you confirmed how those buoys are communicating?" I asked.

"I have. It's a chain of comm beams that starts with the most sunward buoy. Each then transmits a beam to the next one in the chain, and so on."

"Perfect. Okay, bird, time for your part of the plan," I said.

"On it, boss."

Perry spent nearly half an hour sampling and analyzing the slight spillover energy from the comm beam emanating from the first buoy so that he could duplicate it. We waited until he announced he was ready.

"Okay, everyone, check out this split-second timing."

He had control of both the *Fafnir*'s comm-beam projector and the laser batteries. He fired both in a precise sequence, such that he destroyed the first buoy and truncated its comm beam at the exact moment our fake comm beam arrived at the second buoy. There was a serious chance of failure, so we again braced ourselves—but again, nothing changed.

I blew out a breath. "This is intense."

Perry pretended to breathe on a wing and polish it. "Was there any doubt?"

"Yes. Lots."

"Always with the negative vibes, Van."

We had to repeat the process twice more, disabling and masquerading as the next-sunward scanner buoy, until we finally reached a point where we could make our run at the moon orbiting the imposing purplish bulk of the brown dwarf.

Once more, though, we had to wait. Amazing had given us all the data she could on the *Hawksbill*, including the unique signature of its drive. Every drive had slightly different harmonics while it operated, a product of its design and components, so if you had the signature, you could identify the ship from its exhaust plume alone. Fortunately, the GKU was paranoid about things like that to the point of fastidiousness and had recorded the signatures of all of its ships and boats.

It left us hanging in space powered down, generating a fake comm beam, and hoping it didn't incorporate some periodic security signal we'd never detected while we waited for the *Hawksbill* to show up.

And then she did, and even Funboy managed a grin.

"I'VE GOT HER," Netty said, highlighting an icon approaching the moon. "She's three hours out. Based on the other boats we've seen making the trip, she'll have a one hour or so turnaround time, then start back to Druxalt's base."

I nodded. "So far, so good." Curious, I turned the visual imager on Druxalt's base, just to satisfy myself a flotilla of ships wasn't streaking away from it to intercept us. There wasn't, but it gave me a moment to study Druxalt's operation.

His base was a long cylinder, about five hundred meters from end to end. It seemed that ships went in one end, were progressively dissected, and came out the other end as components that were loaded aboard a nondescript freighter. From there, they'd be sold through intermediaries back into the market in known space, The Deeps, and perhaps even further afield. It was a slick, well-oiled operation and kind of impressive in its own sleazy, criminal way.

"They've been doing this for a while," I remarked.

Torina made a sound of agreement, pointing to scanner data.

"See those returns? Trash. Tons of it, all falling toward the star. These people are busy. It makes me even angrier, knowing that every hunk of jetsam is the evidence of a crime. And so many ships," Torina said, her voice soft with disappointment. Torina believed in the spirit of ships—that they were more than mere tools. After being around her, I'd come to the same conclusion.

This wasn't just a crime scene. It was a graveyard of sorts.

"Lotta keels lined up, boss," Perry said.

Roughly a dozen ships ranging from workboats to a dangerous class 10 fast freighter—its hull bristling with armor and weapons—hung in space near the base. More weapons festooned the base itself, underscoring just how futile a direct, kinetic attack would have been. It would take a flotilla of warships to take this place on with any reasonable chance of success, which was another reason no one had bothered—it just wasn't worth the effort or risk.

"Okay, Van, I've got it all worked out. If we start our run in eight minutes, we'll catch the *Hawksbill* while she's still climbing out of the moon's gravity well. As long as we secure her and start our escape within a twenty-minute window, there's no realistic chance any of Druxalt's bigger ships will be able to threaten us."

I sat up and wiped my palms on my b-suit. "Okay, folks, shake out the cobwebs. After all this hurry-up-and-wait, things are going to start happening pretty fast."

Icky snorted. "Huh?"

"Were you asleep?" Zeno asked.

"What? No. My eyes were open, so how could I be asleep."

"Because, fun fact, Wu'tzur often sleep with their eyes open. Nice try though, Icky," Perry said.

Icky glared at him. "Tattletale."

"I prefer the term vigilant, you feisty dust bunny."

Icky relented. "I like bunnies, I think."

I patted one of her huge shoulders. "You're adorable. Now then, on to the checklist."

I ran through every item we'd prepared to make sure we were as ready as possible. I couldn't help reading it as a list of all the things that *could* go wrong. Torina had to put a slug in a target the size of a manhole cover, knocking out a power plant without destroying it. Funboy's jury-rigged magnetic harpoon had to launch properly and then function correctly during its flight to the boat. The harpoon itself, fashioned from a spare containment coil and tuned according to the *Hawksbill's* schematics, had to latch on and hold fast. The monofilament cable had to stay in one piece too while we reeled it in and snugged it up against the *Fafnir's* hull. Evan then had to scramble around the hulls of both ships at least a half-dozen times, trailing more tow cable to lash them securely together. All of *that* had to stay together while we accelerated back out to a twist point and actually twisted away.

And we had to do it all while Druxalt tried to stop us by whatever means he could—and we had to kidnap the *Hawksbill* crew without them fighting back effectively.

"Easy job," I murmured, and Torina put a hand on my arm, smiling up at me.

"We've got it," she said simply, and like that, I felt my nervous energy begin to drain away.

The time ticked down. When it hit zero, Netty lit the drive and ran it up to full power, then we shot off in the direction of the moon and the *Hawksbill.*

"Load the harpoon, Icky," I said.

She laughed, reaching for the control that would engage our newest creation. "Sure boss. But call me Ishmael."

I mimed wiping a tear. "See? Now *that's* being well-read."

"Van, we've been lit up by a half-dozen different active scanners, including two in fire-control mode," Netty said.

I glanced at Torina. "I think we've been noticed."

Torina gave a terse nod but kept her attention fixed on her fire-control panel. She'd been practicing single shots from the point-defense battery at small targets from two to four klicks away and had managed about an eighty percent hit rate—damned fine shooting with those specifics. The battery, essentially a pair of small, rapid-fire mass drivers mounted side by side in a turret, wasn't meant for *accuracy*. It was meant to pour out streams of slugs, filling space with a barrage of projectiles to take down incoming missiles. Torina would be firing a single slug from one of the guns. Any other weapon would be too powerful. If she couldn't manage to hit her tiny target within a very short window of time, then the rest of the checklist didn't matter because it would never happen.

"One minute, Torina," Netty said.

"Got it."

We waited. The *Hawksbill* was still struggling to climb out of the gravity well of the moon that filled most of my view to port, her small drive burning furiously away. By now, her crew had figured out that we must be after them, or were at least going to pass pretty damned close by. But, as yet, there wasn't much they could do but keep going or reverse and plunge back toward the moon. Neither was a good option for them, but it was all they had.

"Van, a class 3 workboat inbound for this moon just fired a missile at us," Netty announced.

"On it," Zeno said. She was running the rest of the *Fafnir's* weapons while Torina did her thing.

I watched the time tick down to Torina's firing window. She had about thirty seconds before the *Fafnir* would have to flip and do a braking burn to match velocity with the target boat. Otherwise, we'd overshoot and the intricate dynamics of gravitation and Mister Newton's laws would preclude us from being able to rendezvous before Druxalt's cavalry showed up. And it was already on the move, four ships burning hard at us from his base orbiting the other moon.

I felt a thrum through my seat as Zeno switched the other point-defense battery to weapons-free, targeting the incoming missile. A moment later, Torina's timer hit zero, then began counting relentlessly up to thirty.

It reached five. Then ten. No one said anything. I swore none of us even breathed. We all just waited for Torina to—

Well, do her best.

At sixteen, she fired.

Then she frowned, then scowled. "That's a miss," she hissed, before the slug had even reached the Hawksbill. So she leaned in and, at twenty-one, fired again.

The first round reached the boat and—nothing. It had been a miss.

I drew a breath, ready to tell Netty to initiate the abort sequence that would get us the hell out of here. Exactly at twenty-five, though, a flash pulsed from the *Hawksbill,* and her drive cut out.

A palpable ripple of relief shivered through the cockpit. I gave her a grin and thumbs-up.

"Good shooting, Tex."

She slumped back and blew out a breath. "Well, I've done my part. I'm going for a drink—or five."

While she was saying it, Netty was flipping the *Fafnir* end over end and firing the main drive. We slid to a halt relative to the *Hawksbill*, then she fired the lateral thrusters, edging us toward the boat.

I stiffened. "Zeno, tell me about that incoming missile."

"*Pfft*, I destroyed it seconds ago, along with one more."

"You—oh. Well, so much for my situational awareness."

She sniffed. "You just sit back, relax, and do your command thing, Van, and leave the driving to us."

I gave her a grateful nod, then turned to Funboy. "You're next up to bat, my morose little friend."

"To what?"

"Never mind. Just do what you came here to do."

"You do realize that the chances of this working, considering all of the myriad factors at play, are—"

"What they are, Funboy. They are what they are," I said.

He blinked. "Well, of course they are what they are. How could they be otherwise—?"

"Funboy, shoot your damned harpoon!" Perry snapped.

He blinked, then turned to his panel. Unlike Torina, there was no sense of stress or tension from him—but there never was. So when he finally triggered the harpoon, sending it away from the *Fafnir* with a faint thump, it was a complete surprise.

Again, we waited. Netty had zoomed in on the image of the Hawksbill, so it filled the center display. I checked the scanners to confirm that the boat's power was reading zero, her reactor dead, minimal systems like life support running on backup power cells. That didn't mean the crew couldn't decide to redirect power and take a shot at us with her single point-defense battery, but there was nothing we could do about that.

The harpoon slid into the view, struck the flank of the *Hawksbill*, and stuck there. Again, we relaxed a notch.

"Guess you can go join Torina in that drink, huh?" Icky said, patting Funboy's head hard enough to make it wobble like a bobblehead's.

"I think I've made my point about consuming intentionally metabolic toxins clear."

"So how the hell do your people celebrate stuff?"

Funboy blinked at Icky. "We don't."

"I'm guessing you guys don't have much of a tourism industry, do you?"

"Not really. Why?"

"Just a hunch."

Another nerve-racking few minutes passed as we carefully eased the *Fafnir* toward the *Hawksbill*, while applying just enough force to the tow cable to nudge the boat toward us. Funboy pulled the boat the last few meters until it thumped against our hull.

"Holy shit, I think this might actually work," I said as Evan started doing his part. Specifically designed to clamber over a ship's hull, Evan scrambled around the two ships, expertly maneuvering from one hull to the other, then back again. More monofilament cable played out behind him, winding around both hulls. We could hear him skitter up and around the *Fafnir* as he moved. A few more passes and we'd be done, well within our time window, and on our way out of here.

Which was, of course, when something finally went wrong.

"VAN, there's a ship emerging from the cloud tops of the moon, bearing, distance, and velocity per the tactical overlay. It's a lot bigger than a workboat. It's a class 9 hull, armed and armored. Assessed threat level is high," Netty said.

I cursed and looked at the overlay. For some reason, this ship had been down in the moon's atmosphere, obscured from our scanners by the thick, electrically charged atmosphere.

"What the hell was that doing there?" Zeno snapped.

"Maybe it's insurance against, you know, the thing we're doing right now," Perry suggested.

"What, they sit down in the clouds on the off chance someone comes along and tries to snag a workboat?"

"More likely just a general contingency so that not all of their combat power is concentrated around the other moon. They probably rotate the ships through the task on a regular basis. Gotta admit, it's pretty clever."

"How come you didn't think of this being a possible thing, bird?" Icky asked with some heat.

Perry turned to her. "I did, in my risk assessment of the operation, item seven on the list. You all dismissed it as *unlikely*, remember?"

Icky stared blankly. Perry sighed.

"You were asleep again, weren't you?"

"Nuh-uh."

I pointed to the bird. "Perry's absolutely right. He did suggest something like this as a possibility, and we did all decide it was unlikely—"

"Because of the carnivorous fart plants," Perry put in.

"Yes, because of the carnivorous fart plants. Regardless, he did tell us—those of us who were awake, anyway—oh, and Icky? We need to have a talk about you paying attention."

She hung her head. "Sorry, boss."

I left her stewing and feeling bad about it, partly because it would help the lesson stick, but mainly because we had much bigger problems.

"Netty, let's make our best possible speed the hell out of here," I said, unnecessarily because she'd already lit the drive and started along our escape trajectory.

"Done. But it's not going to be enough—not with the *Hawksbill's* mass added to our own, and off the drive's centerline at that. If we ditch the boat, we can do it, though."

"Oh, no. We did *not* go through all of this only to get our prize and then lose it again. Options."

"Well, if we're not going to run, that pretty much leaves surrender or fight," Perry said.

"We surrender, and the *Fafnir's* going to end up in pieces being sold across the galaxy," Torina said.

"And that's not happening. So, we're going to fight," I said.

"Van, that's not exactly problem free either. The *Hawksbill* and the cabling holding her to the hull is fouling all of the *Fafnir's* weapons except for the point-defenses, which we deliberately left free—along with our shiny, new, and untested burst cannon," Zeno said.

I breathed another curse with a slow, sibilant hiss of disgust. The optimum cable arrangement to fasten the boat securely to the *Fafnir* required us to take whatever weapons she wasn't already fouling offline. We hadn't intended to fight, just run like hell.

"Okay, looks like our new burst cannon is getting a field test. Zeno, warm it up."

"Done, and—uh-oh."

I sank back in my seat. "What *uh-oh?*"

"It's showing offline. Something must have come unplugged. Probably that cobbled adapter."

Icky started to unstrap. "On it, boss."

I turned back to her. "What do you mean, *on it?*"

"I'm going out there to plug the stupid thing back in."

"Icky, you are not going outside—"

"I wasn't sleeping this time, Van. We either run, which we can't, surrender, which we won't, or fight—and that means getting the freakin' thing back online, right?"

"I'll go," Zeno said.

"No, you won't. I'm the one who did the cabling, and I'm the one responsible for the *Fafnir's* systems. *I'll* go," Icky said, snapping on her helmet.

Netty cut in. "I seem to be the bearer of nothing but bad news today. Evan ran the cable lashing the *Hawksbill* to the *Fafnir* right across the airlock's outer door. We can't open it."

This time, I spat out a stream of curses that would embarrass a London dockworker. "Why the hell would he do that?"

"Because we never explicitly told him not to, Van, so he just did what we *did* tell him to do and worked out the optimum cabling pattern. Plus, he's a moron," Perry said.

Shit. Perry was right. It had never occurred to any of us to instruct Evan not to foul the airlock. It was oversights like that that could turn battles.

"Fine, I'll just squeeze through the emergency escape," Icky said.

I met her eyes behind her visor. It was a small hatch on top of the *Fafnir*, aft and just ahead of engineering. She'd have to make her way from it forward, then get to the *Fafnir*'s underside where the burst cannon was mounted. Worse, with the drive running, she'd be exposed to an intense dose of hard radiation, since the escape hatch was only meant to be used when the drive was dark. But if we cut the drive, the pursuing class 9 would be on top of us in no time.

I took a breath and nodded to her. "Go. Do it, then get your big furry ass inside this ship, Icky, and that's an order."

She saluted with all four of her arms, then turned and headed aft.

"Two more missiles inbound," Netty said.

I turned, my face a question. "Zeno?"

"On it. We're running low on point-defense ammo, though."

Torina glanced at me. "If one of those detonates close to the *Fafnir*—"

I just nodded again. Yeah, Icky was out there, with no armor between her and the effect of a detonating warhead, including the rain of shrapnel.

We'd already taken out four missiles, but the class 9 just kept spitting them out. It was closing, and Icky still hadn't got the burst cannon online. The other four of Druxalt's ships, dispatched from his base, were still racing after us as well. If the class 9 managed to damage our drive, then that was it, game over.

Maybe we should ditch the *Hawksbill*, cut our losses. It was important to me, but not as important as my crew and my ship—

"Okay, I'm here, I got the panel open, and I see the problem. It's these dumbass connections. The adapters I rigged up just aren't holding," Icky said over the comm.

"Can you do anything about it?" I asked. "Because, if not, then just—"

"Yeah, just gimme a minute."

We waited. I watched the icons slowly crawl across the overlay—us, the class 9, its missiles, and the other ships. It was deceptive, of course. It all might look like it was happening at a glacial pace, but even the most minute flicker of movement at that scale was hundreds, even thousands of klicks traversed.

I turned to Zeno. "Anything?"

"The burst cannon's come on and gone offline two or three times but never enough for it to boot up," she said, her voice as taut as a guitar string.

"Icky, don't mean to be a nag, but—"

"Okay, try that!" Icky bellowed.

Zeno stared intently at her instruments. As she did, the point-defenses opened up and spewed tracer slugs at the approaching missiles. I heard Icky mutter under her breath.

"Cool…"

"Okay, the burst cannon's booting up. Just a few seconds," Zeno said.

"One missile down, one to go," Perry put in.

I kept one eye on the point-defense batteries as they struggled mightily to take out the other missile, and the other on their dwindling supply of ammo.

Without warning, one of them abruptly cut out.

"Netty, what the hell—?"

"The missile has passed out of its field of fire, thanks to the *Hawksbill*."

I opened my mouth, but several things happened at once.

The remaining point-defense battery exhausted its ammo.

The missile detonated damned close to the *Fafnir*.

And Zeno exclaimed—something, in a liquid trill—and opened fire with the burst cannon.

29

EVEN AS SHRAPNEL from the missile smacked into the *Fafnir*, the burst cannon spat out four searing bolts of plasma. Through the blare of alarms from the fragment impacts, I saw them streak toward the pursuing class 9 at what was probably a good chunk of light-speed, whatever voodoo physics that underlay their soliton wave effect keeping them together. Three of them slammed into the other ship, each releasing its pent-up energy in a colossal blast. It all happened so fast that I lost the fourth one in the confusion of flashes and glares, but the effect was decisive—what had once been a ship was now just whirling bits of glowing scrap amid an expanding cloud of condensing water vapor. A lot of water vapor, in fact, suggesting that the ship had been crewed by someone or something that swam.

But I could only spare the view an instant, then I yanked my attention back inside the *Fafnir*. I swept my gaze over the status board, my focus on the drive. If the blast had damaged that, then we were screwed. But both the fusion and twist drives and the power plant all still showed green. Various other systems had gone yellow, and a few had gone red, but none of them were critical.

Which left one more outstanding item.

"Icky!"

I got nothing but silence in return.

"Icky, talk to me!"

Nothing.

I glanced back at the board. The ship's comm was one of the yellow systems. I switched to my suit comm.

"Icky!"

But it was just as dead.

"Has anyone else got her?" I asked, desperately hoping it was just my suit comm that, for some reason, couldn't connect with her.

But no one else could raise her either.

"Van, we'll be able to twist in one minute," Netty said.

"We can't! If we do, we'll lose Icky for sure!" One thing that had been made clear to me early on was that being outside a ship while it twisted was invariably fatal. Ships were designed to withstand the momentary slurry of forces and accelerations that resulted from passage through a wormhole. People who weren't inside the hull weren't.

"I understand, Van. But the four ships pursuing us have already fired a salvo of missiles after us. If we don't twist——"

"I get it!"

I swept my gaze around the cockpit, frantically looking for inspiration. As I did, my eyes met each of the others. They all held the same stew of emotions I did—anxious worry. Visceral fear. Deep, aching sadness.

I kept calling on the comm anyway, snapping through the channels, shouting for Icky over and over. The only thing I got was the dumb, empty hiss of cosmic background noise.

Netty cut in, doing her best to sound sympathetic but also insistent. "Van, those missiles are catching up quickly. The extra mass of the *Hawksbill*—"

"I know!" I snapped.

Perry came on a private channel.

"Van, I know how this sounds, but… you've got to think of the welfare of the rest of the crew."

I sank back.

The rest of the crew.

The survivors.

The ones who *hadn't* died on a vainglorious mission to retrieve an utterly remarkable workboat and a picture of myself for my mother to—

Help her feel better? Earn her love?

I closed my eyes.

"Netty, as soon as you can, twist us the hell out of here."

So she did.

I GLANCED at the tactical overlay. We were back at Crossroads where we'd started. There was the station, and there was the traffic going to and from it, intent on business of its own. None of them had even an inkling of what was happening in the *Fafnir*'s cockpit right now.

I wanted to turn around, to look at my crew, to say… something.

But I couldn't. I couldn't face them. We'd retrieved a stupid, pointless, *useless* workboat, and we'd lost Icky in the process. I knew it, and they knew it, and how the hell was I ever going to look any of them in the eye again?

What was I going to tell her father?

"Van?"

It was Netty. She was going to ask me what to do now, where to go next. I had no answer for her.

"Van, there's an incoming comm message on a general channel."

I opened my eyes. "Who from?"

"I'm not sure. It's badly broken up and distorted."

I took a breath and sat up. "Unless it's announcing the end of the universe, I don't care—"

"Hell—?"

I blinked and sat up even straighter.

"—ead me—"

I let procedure take over. "Unknown call sign, you're broken and distorted. Try—"

"How's that?"

It was Icky.

I just stared for a moment. Because of my helmet, I couldn't see, but I could feel the pulse of shock and relief that swept through the cockpit.

"Icky? Where are you?"

"Aboard the *Hawksbill* with my new friend, whose name seems to be *please don't eat me!*"

"You—what? How—?"

"I guess he's never met a Wu'tzur before. He seems to think I'm carnivorous, which is a great way of keeping someone in line. I gotta remember that—"

"No, I mean—" I stopped and sank back in my seat, this time in the way I might slump after running the last few paces of a marathon.

"It's *damned* good to hear your voice, Icky," I said, smiling.

"You know what? After all that bullshit, it's even better just being able to be *heard*."

"Why DIDN'T you tell us you were yanking apart your suit comm before you went offline? We thought you were—" Zeno said, then finished by shaking her head.

We'd had Evan reconfigure the lashings holding the *Hawksbill* to the *Fafnir* so that the airlock wasn't fouled. That allowed Icky and our prisoner, the workboat's hapless pilot, to return to the *Fafnir*. We stuck him—a shell-shocked Nesit—into a holding cell for now, but we would probably just release him after he had an hour or two to decompress.. He had no outstanding warrants and seemed to be a guy hired to pilot a workboat on a shuttle run between two moons. Besides, he'd been plucked out of space, effectively kidnapped, then convinced that Icky had boarded his workboat intending to eat him.

His day had been bad enough.

Icky scowled. "Sorry, but I was kinda busy—you know, getting that stupid burst cannon working. I had to rip apart my suit's comm to do it. Oh, by the way? Being outside during a space battle is kinda awesome, but I definitely don't recommend it. Chunk of shrapnel from the damned missile hit about a meter away from me.

I'm just glad it didn't detonate the REAB module, or we wouldn't be having this conversation."

I smiled. "I'm just really glad you're in one piece, big girl. Those few minutes we didn't think you were——" I swallowed and shook my head. "Let's put it this way, I wouldn't recommend that either."

We'd all already hugged Icky, except for Funboy, who regarded her solemnly, then offered his hand to shake.

"I'm glad that it wasn't your time to meet what could have been an extremely painful end." He blinked. "Yet."

"Uh… thanks, I think?"

She turned to Perry. "How about you, bird? Did you miss me?"

He shrugged. "I knew you weren't dead."

"Oh? How'd you know that?"

"Because it would have thrown the universe out of balance. *Someone* has to be the counter to my brilliant charm and scintillating personality."

Icky stared back at Perry for a moment, then reached out with all four hands, scooped him up, and kissed him right on the beak.

"ACKMMMPPHHHHNNRGGMPPH—you mind, I'm a delicate piece of precision machinery!"

Icky grinned. "I love you too, bird," she said, putting him back down. Perry made a show of indignantly shaking his feathers back into place, and then we laughed in a chorus of joyous relief.

Except for Funboy. "Kissing is a primary cause of——"

"Funboy?" I interrupted.

He looked at me, wounded. "Is this one of those times where my reason overcomes your need for, ah, celebration?" He said the final word like it was a curse.

"Yes. Yes, it is," I told him.

In response, he tried to smile, an expression that made me recoil in horror from the rictus spreading across his features.

"Don't... don't do that again."

He looked relieved. "Trust me. I won't."

———

WE DROPPED THE *HAWKSBILL*—WHICH still, amazingly, had my picture aboard— at Trebuchet Base, where we also got yet more repairs done to the *Fafnir*. That included more secure and reliable connections between the burst cannon and the ship's power and fire control systems. The weapon had performed damned well once Icky got it working, but it did have some major limitations. It had a longer effective range than the mass drivers or particle cannon but considerably shorter than the lasers or missiles. More fundamentally, it had a serious problem with heat buildup, since it initiated a small nuclear fusion reaction with every shot, so its rate of fire was very low—three or four shots, followed by a full minute of cool-down time. Still, it gave us a major boost to the *Fafnir*'s firepower.

We were punching above our weight. Finally.

What it *didn't* do was give me a much-needed boost to my mood. I was desperately thankful that Icky had survived, but it had been a damned close thing. And she wasn't out of the woods entirely. She'd taken a hard dose of rads from the *Fafnir*'s operating drive and another burst from the detonating missile that had damaged the ship. By the time we made it to Trebuchet, she was decidedly dragging her butt. Funboy had already put her on a course of anti-rad drugs, but he privately confided in me that she still faced some serious health risks.

"Various forms of cancer and reduced immunity are the most serious threats. The anti-radiation therapy will help, but she was exposed, unshielded, to an operating fusion drive," he said, and there was only factual acceptance in his tone, not grim glee. He was a superb medical officer, despite his hangman's humor. "She needs time, Van. And we have to be vigilant. I'll want to examine her regularly."

"I'll see to it she complies," I said, and I would. I wasn't going to lose her due to a laconic outlook on preventative care.

Still, all I could do was move on—and live with the gnawing uncertainty and guilt over exposing her to such terrifying risk on a vanity mission. The GKU, or at least the more undisciplined splinters of it, seemed a little too willing to embrace grudges. Personal scores and vendettas seemed to make up an awful lot of their SOPs. It was a cautionary tale that I needed to take to heart because it was easy to let resentment and selfish desire start taking over. The *Fafnir* was a powerful ship with a skilled crew, but I couldn't let it become my personal sledgehammer, using it to beat my problems into submission.

WHICH MEANT that when we started our long trek back into The Deeps to find Adayluh Creel's father, I did so with a much clearer and cleaner sense of purpose. Finding him would help us find Adayluh. And finding her would help us better understand what BeneStar's endgame was and how it all tied into the Sorcerers and our Crimes Against Order investigation.

Or so I hoped.

We'd outfitted the *Fafnir* with a spare fuel pod again and gassed up at the BeneStar station one system shy of Rodantic's World. We were of course deluged with advertising and offers to sign up for the usurious BeneCast payment system. And again, we ignored them and just ate the inflated price for the fuel. We then twisted past Rodantic's World and finally arrived at the location that had been provided by Amazing. It was a remote system with no name, just a catalog number. There was a lonely white dwarf, the only star for nearly ten light-years in any direction, and it was here that Adayluh Creel's father had established himself.

I studied the image on the center display. "You know, there was an old movie I remember watching as a kid about spaceships being used to preserve plants and entire biomes because Earth had become so polluted."

"*Silent Running,*" Perry said.

I glanced at him. "Yeah, that's it. I gather you've seen it."

"Damned right. There aren't many movies where the heroes are AI robots."

"I seem to recall some human actors in it, too."

"What part of *the heroes are AI robots* don't you understand, Van?"

I smiled and pointed at the image of Adayluh's father's ship on the display. "Anyway, that kind of reminds me of the ship in that movie. A lot bigger, though."

It was. A roughly cylindrical superstructure over a kilometer long had a series of geodesic dome-like structures mounted on it, canted and spaced so they made room for each other. Several of the domes were transparent, but some were enclosed in solid panels. A module at one end of the central superstructure probably held a power plant, other critical systems, and a drive. A smaller module festooned with sensor clusters and protruding bits and bobs hung off the other end.

"Netty, open a—"

"No need. They're calling us."

I nodded. "Okay, put 'em on."

"Unknown ship, this is the research vessel *Inari*. Please state your intentions," a male voice intoned.

"Inari—the Japanese Shinto *kami*, or god of foxes, fertility, rice, tea, and sake, of agriculture and industry, and of general prosperity and worldly success," Perry said.

Torina made an impressed face. "That's quite the job description."

"*Inari*, this is the *Fafnir*, and I'm Peacemaker Van Tudor," I said, transmitting my credentials.

"A Peacemaker? You're a little outside your jurisdiction here, aren't you?"

I laughed. "Oh, a lightyear or two. We're just here to get some information. To that end, I'm hoping to speak to Filic Creel."

"Might I ask why?"

"I'd rather address that to him personally. It involves—well, family."

A pause before the reply.

"You can dock at port Two-Forward. You'll be met there. *Inari* out."

"Why do I get the feeling that that was Filic Creel?" Zeno said.

"Well, if it was, he didn't tell us to take a hike, so that's a good sign, I guess," I replied. "Only one way to find out. Netty, take us in."

30

WE WERE GREETED by an alien I didn't recognize—slender, pale, with a long, narrow head that tapered down to a nearly knife-like chin. It had two pairs of eyes, the upper being huge and almost luminous in their intensity, the lower much smaller and narrowed in what seemed to be suspicion, although that might just have been how they were made.

"I am Filic Creel," the alien said, his voice the one from the comm.

I stopped and frowned. "You—really? Oh. My understanding was that—well, that Adayluh—"

"Is human? She is, yes. The story is a long and convoluted one, but suffice it to say that she's my adoptive daughter."

"Ah," I replied, nodding and wondering just what that long and convoluted story might be. But Filic seemed wary enough already without us trying to pry into his past, so I just left it and moved on.

"Sir, we're trying to find Adayluh. We have reason to believe she's in danger," I went on.

"Oh, she's most definitely in danger. That's why she's not here."

I glanced at Torina and Perry, the others having stayed aboard the *Fafnir*. I didn't want to unload the whole crew for fear of coming across as trying to be intimidating.

"You know she's in danger?" Torina asked.

"Oh, I'd say it's a reasonable assumption, considering that a group of armed thugs showed up here several days ago looking for her. Unlike you, they were less inclined to talk and more wanting to search—and apply some physical pressure as well." As he spoke, he lifted his left arm, which had been hanging by his side. He did so hesitantly, as though in pain, and I could see that it was bandaged.

"They attacked you?"

"*Attacked* implies a fight. I put up no resistance because it's not in my nature to do so. It didn't stop them from lashing out at me in an effort to get me to give up Adayluh's location."

Torina and I looked at each other. "BeneStar," we both said at the same time.

Filic nodded. "In all likelihood, yes."

"You're fortunate they didn't get more, um, forceful with you," Perry said.

"Well, just as you were surprised that I'm not human, so were they. They ended up with the impression that I was some old botanist left aboard the *Inari* as a caretaker and really did know nothing of value to them."

"But you've revealed your identity to us. How did you know we weren't here to rough you up and toss your ship the way the Bene-Star goons did?" I asked him.

"Because I had advance knowledge of your likely arrival, courtesy of a mutual friend," Filic replied.

"Oh? Who?"

"She goes by various names, but you'd most likely know her as B. She told me there was a good chance that you would eventually show up looking for Adayluh and that I could trust you."

"Ah, our old friend B. She gets around, doesn't she?"

"She does," Filic said. "And a good thing, too, because I understand that you are the son of Jocelyn Wallis. Had I known that without B vouching for you, this would be a much more, ah, difficult meeting."

I sighed. "I see you've crossed paths with my mother before."

"Her reputation precedes her out here in The Deeps. Let's just say it doesn't engender trust. She is known for her mercurial and sometimes predatory ways."

"Well, Van's nothing like that. He's boring and predictable," Perry said.

I shot him half-smile. "Thanks, bird."

"Hey, just trying to help. Would you rather be known as *boring and predictable* or *mercurial and predatory?*"

"Have to admit, *mercurial and predatory* sounds much cooler, but—yeah, point taken." I turned back to Filic.

"Anyway, we want to find your daughter before BeneStar does. We know she's in danger. Grave danger, in fact. BeneStar wants something that she's apparently produced, some sort of breakthrough in food production."

He stared for a moment, then nodded. "Yes. Of course. The Permada. I'd assumed that must be it, what BeneStar was after. It has the potential to feed most of the galaxy. It is a small wonder that

BeneStar is desperate to own and control it because if they don't, then the interstellar food market will slip from their grasp."

"Permada? What's that?" Torina asked.

"Easier if I show you. Follow me," Filic said, then he led us into the *Inari*.

"THIS IS a real-life version of *Silent Running*," Perry said.

Filic had led us through nearly two hundred meters of corridors, into one of the domes attached to the *Inari*. This was one of the transparent ones, the blackness of space filling the sky above us, the lighting as dim as the full Moon on Earth. Across its cavernous expanse sprawled plants in racks being tended by a handful of small, obviously AI-controlled robots. The plants seemed to mostly be cereal crops, a few of which I recognized immediately. You don't grow up in Iowa without an innate ability to identify wheat versus barley, versus sorghum, versus millet. Most, though, were types I'd never seen before, obviously of alien origin.

"Almost feels like home—well, except for the utterly black sky up there. What's the point of the dome being transparent if there's no light coming through it?" I asked.

"The *Inari* rotates on a regular basis to expose the transparent domes to light from the star in order to replicate a day-night cycle. The opaque domes contain species that are insensitive to light conditions or thrive in darkness," Filic replied, leading us among the planters. As we walked, he turned to Perry.

"That's one of my favorite movies, by the way," he said. "Well, except for the ending."

"What? *Silent Running*? You've seen it?"

"Bruce Dern in one of his greatest roles. It's a science fiction masterpiece."

"What's wrong with the ending?"

"The hero sacrifices himself to save the trees. I'm dedicated to my work but... I don't know about that."

"Yeah, but the robots survive, so it's got a happy ending," Perry said.

I gave Filic a surprised look. "How the *hell* does a guy aboard a farming ship orbiting a remote star halfway to the galactic core know about an old Earth movie from the seventies? And an obscure, pretty niche one at that?"

"Said guy has a daughter who was born on Earth and is a science fiction nerd herself, that's how. Adayluh also named this ship. *Inari*, the Japanese *kami* of rice and fertility," Filic replied.

"And foxes, tea and sake, agriculture and industry, and of general prosperity and worldly success," Perry added.

"Yes, all those things, too." Filic stopped and gestured at a planter. "And this is Permada. This is what stands to change the fundamental nature of food across the inhabited galaxy."

I stared at the golden stalks. They didn't look much different from conventional, terrestrial wheat. I turned to Filic. "Okay..."

"It grows at nearly three times the rate of Earthly wheat. It grows in almost all soils, and in conditions that range from as low as ten degrees below the freezing point of water at standard atmospheric pressure, as measured on the Celsius scale, to as much as fifty degrees above it. Each grain contains almost fifty percent more nutritional value, and its biochemistry is such that it is digestible and nutritious by essentially *any* species that lives in an oxidizing atmosphere."

Perry reached out a wing and touched one of the stalks. "Wow. That *is* game-changing, isn't it?"

Torina also brushed one of the stalks with a finger. "Whoever owns the rights to this would be rich beyond imagining." She looked up at Filic. "And that's the problem."

"It is. Ironically, the BeneStar agents who paid me a visit walked right past it. That's why the Permada is in this module, among all of these other, similar cereal crops."

I looked around and nodded. "It does kind of get lost in the background, doesn't it?" But I turned back to Filic with the obvious question.

"So how is this even an issue? Adayluh developed this Permada, right?"

"She did. She based some of her research on preexisting work, but the important innovations and advances are all hers."

"So what am I missing? She developed it, she owns it, right?"

Perry answered. "When it comes to foodstuffs, the law in known space requires specific trials to determine in which of about a zillion categories it would be placed. Only then can the ownership be registered under the Interstellar Food Accord and several related intellectual property agreements."

"And until those trials are completed, and their results duly registered, ownership of this stuff is, what, just up for grabs?" I asked, gesturing at the Permada.

"It's not quite that simple. Adayluh has a degree of ownership now, but under the law, she doesn't have full ownership until she's gone through all the bureaucratic and legal hoops. Until then, anyone can base something similar on her work, gain full ownership, and then effectively take it from her. It's meant to *encourage innovation*."

I shook my head at Perry. "How the hell does *that* work? It seems to me that it just encourages people to work in absolute secrecy until they can become full owners."

"And in the meantime, shamelessly try to steal ideas from one another," Torina added.

Perry shrugged his wings. "Hey, I just report the laws, I don't make 'em. You'd have to direct those questions to the labyrinthine array of committees and subcommittees and working groups and commissions and *insert more bureaucratic words here*. They're the ones that ultimately came up with the mess of interstellar laws and regulations and policies we've currently got."

"Out here in The Deeps, it's a little more permissive. The Deeps Operational Codes state that if a foodstuff is successfully grown under a specified range of conditions and brought to market, then the holder and their heirs are granted legal ownership of the design in perpetuity," Filic said. "But it amounts to much the same thing."

I puffed out a sigh and just shook my head. It all seemed like bureaucracy for its own sake rather than in service to any real purpose. "So is that what Adayluh's doing? She's off running these trials, in secret, so that BeneStar can't find her or her Permada before she can claim full ownership of the product?"

"That's exactly what she's doing. She has completed four trials of six, and has the fifth underway as we speak," Filic said.

"Okay, so she's going to save untold lives and improve even more, but only if we can protect her from Helem Gauss and people like him. So we need to know where she's doing that fifth trial."

Filic's face took on an expression that I couldn't mistake for anything but sly, despite its alien features. "Yes, well, you've come too far, Peacemaker Tudor. You see, my daughter is on Earth."

I stared for a moment—and then I laughed, long and loud, because how could I not? We'd traveled dozens of light-years from Earth, only to find out the woman we were seeking was right where we started.

I wiped my eyes and shook my head. "She's not in Iowa, is she? That might break my sense of irony beyond repair."

"That isn't the place name she gave me, no. She needed a climate that was harsh enough to test her Permada in your sort of biome. She needed conditions to be as onerous as they were likely to get, so she needed a place that is dry, cold, brutal... and, for obvious reasons, remote."

He extracted a thin, flexible sheet from his pocket, unrolled it, then tapped at it. It went opaque and lit with an image that Filic showed to us. It was a barren, windswept coastline, rugged mountains falling into booming surf under a leaden-gray sky. I shivered a little just looking at it.

I shook my head. "That could be—hell, anywhere from Alaska to Antarctica."

"I know where it is," Perry said. "I can match the pattern almost exactly. That's Tierra del Fuego."

"That's the name she used," Filic confirmed.

I nodded.

"Okay, then. Back to the *Fafnir*, folks. We're heading for South America."

31

"For a food scientist, this Adayluh Creel is pretty damned elusive," Torina said.

"Yeah, not the type you'd expect to be quite so skilled at laying low. Wonder if she's got some criminal underworld stuff going on in her life, too," Zeno said.

We cruised along a windswept channel separating the ice-capped peaks ranging along the southwesternmost shore of Isla Grande Tierra del Fuego, the largest island in the archipelago, from Isla Gordon off to our left. Dead ahead of the *Fafnir* towered the rugged mountains encompassed by Alberto de Agostini National Park, including Monte Darwin, one of the highest points in this lonely, dreary corner of the world. This was our third pass, and although we'd picked up flickers of what might be off-world tech, we couldn't pinpoint it.

Part of it was just the terrain. This icy, wind-blasted shoreline consisted of craggy ridges of rock or frozen expanses of glacier, and not much else. There were literally thousands of places a ship the size of the *Fafnir* could be grounded, and unless you passed directly overhead, you'd never see it. Moreover, the rock did a pretty good job of blocking any incidental signals, like neutron emissions leaking from a running power plant, so it all combined into a frustrating game of hide-and-seek amid the most desolate terrain I'd ever seen.

I looked down as the *Fafnir* banked over a small island that was nothing but rock and booming surf. "You know, I used to think parts of Iowa were pretty empty. Compared to this place, they were Times Square on New Year's Eve. What's that, Netty? Focus on that, ah, hell, looks like a seal, sort of. But dead?"

Netty snagged an image as we flew past, enlarging it in a smaller screen window. "That?"

"Yeah. It's a seal, but damned if it doesn't look..."

"Mummified?" Torina asked

"Right?" I agreed. The seal was *almost* normal looking but had clearly been in a stone cleft for some time.

"Based on that scan, it's a crab seal, and it's three millennia old, give or take a few decades. This climate is brutal, but it preserves things," Netty informed us.

"Good place to hide if you're on Earth and don't want to be found, though," Perry said. "Maybe parts of Antarctica, or way up north in Baffin Island or somewhere even more remote, but that's about it."

"I estimate that an unprotected humanoid—and by that, I mean me—would last fifteen, maybe twenty minutes down there before the effects of hypothermia began to take their toll," Funboy said. "Not to mention being terrible for one's skin, as witnessed by the unfortunate seal mummy below."

Icky turned to him with a quizzical look. "Is that your vacation hobby, Funboy? Estimating how long you'd survive in different environments?"

He blinked at her. "Yes. Why?"

I sighed and turned to Perry. "How did you recognize that image Adayluh sent to Filic, anyway—no, wait. Let me guess. You've been here before."

"Once. I wanted to check out the lands that Charles Darwin made famous. The Galapagos Islands are livelier, though," he said, then flashed an image of himself standing on the back of a big leathery tortoise onto the center display.

"Uh… who the hell took that picture?"

"I brought a remote imager with me. I've got about a thousand vacation images if you ever want to see them."

"Let me guess—you're in all of them, aren't you, bird?" Icky asked.

"Uh… *yeah*. Those are my treasured memories."

"You have a purpose-*built* organo-optical-whatever memory, bird. Basically, DNA turned into data storage. You can't forget anything anyway!"

"I'm thinking of my audience. You've all seen a tortoise or a church or the rings of Saturn or whatever. But how many of you have seen me *in front of* a tortoise or church or the rings of Saturn?" He winked at me. "*Branding*. It ain't just for social media."

"Centuries of vacation pics. I can *feel* the narcolepsy," I said, frowning as the *Fafnir* completed her 180 and started back along the restless, iron-gray water of the channel heading southeast again. In a few minutes we'd again reach Bahia Lapataia, the "End of the World," the southernmost point to which you could drive in the

Western Hemisphere. I tapped a finger on the seat's armrest. "Perry, you're sure you've got that image location right?"

"Like Icky said, boss, perfect memory. That image exactly matches one I've got stored, taken from that very location I pointed out each one of the five times we've flown over it and you've asked that same question—aaaaaand, that makes it six."

I sighed. "Okay, mindful of the whole repeating the same thing over and over expecting a different outcome insanity thing, let's try something different. Netty, is there a way to sweep a comm broadcast in a sort of... I don't know, a cone? Broader coverage than a comm beam but not an omnidirectional thing?"

"I can, but there's still going to be some leakage, as energy is reflected from all that rock and ice. Any other ships in the area might be able to detect it."

"Yeah, well, us flying back and forth along this coastline risks drawing attention, too. Let's do it."

"You're on," Netty said.

"To anyone listening, I'm Peacemaker Van Tudor. My credentials are appended to this message. Bruce Dern sent me to do some silent running."

"Who the hell's Bruce Dern?" Zeno asked.

"The guy who's almost the hero of an old movie," Perry replied.

"What?"

I held up a finger. "Just hold that thought, Zeno. I—"

"Van, we're receiving a reply via comm beam," Netty cut in.

"Hey, Peacemaker, since you're obviously not going to give this up, how about stopping the airshow and hauling your ass down here?" a woman's voice said.

I smiled. "On our way."

THE WIND BODY-CHECKED me as soon as I stepped out of the *Fafnir's* airlock. It was probably as cold as hell, but my b-suit reduced it to nothing but a rising and falling push against me as it gusted off the nearby sea. Not for the first time, I thought about some mornings waiting bleary-eyed for the school bus at the end of the farm's driveway, hunched against howling, icy winter wind. Could have used a b-suit then.

Three figures waited for us, all decked out in advanced cold-weather gear. None of it offered even remotely the same armor effect as a b-suit, but they'd all be just as effective in keeping out the cold. A class 5 ship, a small cutter, squatted under a rocky overhang a couple of hundred meters away. The only other thing in sight was, incredibly, a small plot of wheat quite happily growing in the rocky, frozen soil, its stalks tossing in the wind.

"Adayluh Creel, I presume," I said to the foremost of the suited figures. I could see eyes behind the wind visor, but that was about it. I'd come out of the *Fafnir* alone, aside from Perry, who'd flung himself out of the airlock a few klicks away while we were still airborne, and now played aerial observer.

"One of us is, or maybe I'm still aboard the ship, or somewhere else entirely," the woman's voice said over the comm.

I smiled. "And I thought *I* was paranoid."

"I doubt you've got the richest man in the universe out to get you."

"Oh, I wouldn't be so sure about that. Helem Gauss isn't a personal acquaintance, exactly, but my crew and I have managed to be enough of a thorn in his ass that he must know my name."

"I *do* like the sound of that. So Bruce Dern sent you."

"Well, not Bruce himself, but someone in a very similar role."

A long pause. I could feel the calculating judgment behind it. I just waited.

"How is my father?" she finally asked.

"Good. He was paid a visit by BeneStar. They got a little rough with him, but my doctor—who, incidentally, has the worst bedside manner in the Milky Way, in case you ever find yourself needing his services—patched him up."

"Shit." Another pause. "Is that why you're here? Because Bene-Star's on its way?"

"Well, as far as I know, BeneStar's not on its way, at least not yet. And the thugs they sent to the *Inari* looking for your father were looking for a human. They assumed your dad was just some old caretaker. And no, they didn't find the Permada either, despite walking right past it."

I heard the relief in her voice. "Good. It means we might have a chance to actually get this trial finished, then figure out how the hell we're going to do the next one."

"What's the next one?" I asked.

"Why don't you come aboard my ship and I'll show you?"

I gestured for her to lead the way.

"Ladies first and all that."

"*Pfft.* Gimme a break with that chivalry bullshit."

I smiled as I followed the trio back to the hidden class 5. I had yet to actually *meet* Adayluh Creel, and I already liked her.

ADAYLUH CREEL WAS SURPRISINGLY YOUNG, personable, and charming, obviously whip smart, and with some of the most remarkable eyes I'd ever seen, green-brown flecked with gold. She was always moving, always intense, but relentlessly upbeat and positive despite having the weight of the universe bearing down on her.

We sat in her class 5 cutter, the *Kitsune*, which she explained was Japanese for fox. Foxes were, apparently, considered the messengers of Inari, the *kami* or god of rice—and many other things, as Perry was quick to point out—and thus closed the circle on her father's massive farming ship. Despite some initial wariness, she opened up once I'd told her about our own encounters with BeneStar, saying, "Well, someone who BeneStar hates enough to try and kill is okay by me."

She then went on to explain the status of her Permada project. "I need to do one more trial in a biome that's wet, humid, and warm. If I can successfully cultivate Permada there and show a positive yield, I can apply for a declaration of Rights of Assertion. That will keep Permada out of BeneStar's hands forever."

I looked at the small planter on the cramped table of her ship's galley. She and four assistants were living aboard it, using it as their base camp while they finished up the biome trial here on Tierra del Fuego.

"Lots of places like that, I'd think. Southern and southeastern Asia comes to mind," I said.

But she shook her head. "That biome isn't going to be a problem for Permada—and that's the problem. That biome is favorable for a lot of things, particularly rice. And because of that, a lot of people tend to live in those regions—"

"Ah. And you don't want to do this trial around lots of people."

"For obvious reasons. Also, for full scientific integrity, the trial should be done where there *aren't* similar types of plant being grown. Permada has no problem being around other plants, but I can't afford to give the BeneStar lawyers even the most minute crack in the integrity of my work. I can't let them say that the research results were muddied by proximity to other plants, or they'll have this under dispute until long after I'm dead and gone."

"And the Permada will stay tied up in legal proceedings," I said.

"And lots of people will die of malnutrition who don't have to in the meantime—not that Gauss and his flunkies care. Their only concern is that if they can't benefit from it, then no one does."

I touched the golden stalks in the planter. Hard to believe that something so innocuous, something that would be utterly lost amid a field of dry grass or other crops, stood to be so Earth-shaking— no, galaxy-shaking. "Okay, well, there must be lots of other places you could do that trial across known space, or in The Deeps."

But she shook her head again. "You'd think so, but no. Or there are, but I have to assume that BeneStar knows that trial has to be completed, and that I'll be wanting to do it in isolation. That dramatically reduces the options, to the point where I have to assume they'll all be watched."

She sat back and sighed. "There is one place they won't look that fits the biome requirements, but it's a non-starter for other reasons."

I looked up from the Permada. "Oh? Where's that?"

"Ever hear of a deathworld?"

"Uh—" It took a second or two, but one of the memories implanted in me when I first became a Peacemaker Initiate suddenly sparked to life. That rarely happened anymore, but every once in a while they filled in a gap. "Yeah. A world otherwise habitable by most humanoid races that's so inimical to life that it's rendered uninhabitable."

"You sound like you were reading it from the dictionary."

"I kind of was, actually."

She tapped at a data slate and handed it over. "Welcome to Hellhole, population zero," she said.

I looked at an image of a swamp—a vast, festering swamp that stretched off into a horizon hidden by mist and pocked with murky pools of standing water. The image panned around, showing that it was more of the same in all directions.

"The whole planet is pretty much that, except at the poles. As one planetary scientist put it, it's as though what would have been distinct bodies of land and ocean decided to mix it up and just cover the whole world in water and mud. It's one huge, slimy bog."

"Okay, I'm starting to sweat a little just looking at it, but where does the deathworld part come in?"

"That would be the fauna. They're mostly aquatic, there are lots of them, and they're all hungry. All the time. And they'll eat anything."

"Like the Permada."

"And you, and me, and they'll probably take a run at eating a ship, too. And some of them might actually manage it. Think super strong bioacids injected by hollow, razor-sharp teeth."

"Ouch."

She nodded and sighed again. "Except for that, the place is perfect for the trial. And *because* of that, no one would ever imagine I'd run the trial there. Hellhole is wisely left alone, the endlessly vicious critters filling all those fens and pools happily chowing down on each other, then spawning new generations to continue chowing down on each other."

I frowned at the image as a half-formed thought tickled the back of my mind.

"I've even considered trying to isolate part of the biome, build a cofferdam or something to keep the local wildlife out. But that's going to take engineering expertise and construction materials, and as soon as we start down that road, we magnify the chances of us getting found by a whole lot—"

She stopped, staring at me. "Why the look of deep thought, Peacemaker Tudor?"

"What? Oh, it's Van. Please, call me Van," I said, then nodded as an actual plan coalesced. It might be a longshot, but it would get around the likelihood of anyone ever figuring it out, because it was just so... out there. Even better, it involved disparate parts that had no business ever being connected, until now.

"So what you're telling me is that you need guard dogs," I said.

She blinked. "Uh... I suppose. But they'd have to be the guard dogs from hell, if they weren't just going to be dinner for the local fauna."

I nodded at the image. "Okay, so answer me this—do you have any great objection to introducing an invasive species?"

"What, to Hellhole? Absolutely none whatsoever. The place would have to be terraformed like crazy before it could be used for anything else anyway." Now her eyes narrowed. "Why?"

"Because I've got an idea. I've only got one more question."

She cocked her head. "What's that?"

"How do you feel about the word *moist?*"

32

EVEN OVER A COMM LINK, I found the Reclamators to be creepy as hell. This one, the Caretaker, was essentially a living diving suit, a four-armed construct resembling one of those old outfits with the weighted boots and the big metal helmet with the little windows on it. There was no air hose, though, and I'd had the pleasure of making the Caretaker's acquaintance already. I found him to be quite a nice fellow. Or, actually, a semi-organic blob inside a creepy diving suit, but quite a nice semi-organic blob.

"We've never had such a request before. You actually want a school of kozidnits? You do recall that they are insatiable carnivores at the very top of the food chain in their biome," he said.

"Yup, and as cute as seahorses crossed with teddy bears. That's why I want them." I frowned. "Because of the *insatiable carnivores* part, not the cute *sea horse-teddy bear* part."

"May I ask why?"

"It's… to help further an experiment. Unfortunately, I'm not at liberty to give any details. However, I have been asked to provide you with the following data, which I'm transmitting now. It's detailed environmental chemistry. The kozidnits would have to be able to live in that stuff."

I waited while the Caretaker reviewed the data. "To a first approximation, this shouldn't be a problem. The kozidnits are highly adaptable. We can engineer a viral means of altering their biochemistry slightly to assist in that adaptation—" A pause. "You do realize that you'll be injecting a dangerously aggressive invasive species into... into whatever environment that represents."

"I do. The environment isn't suited for anything else without massive terraforming, and there's no sapient life involved. And... it's worth it, believe me."

"Well, you are the Peacemaker, so I can only assume you've done your due diligence regarding the environmental and legal implications. However, this does pose a unique opportunity to study aspects of the species we normally cannot, because we can't simply dump it into a new environment to see what happens. We will, therefore, send along a research team," the Caretaker said.

"That's fine, with the understanding that once they arrive at the, uh, research site, they won't be able to leave or communicate with anyone outside it for a period of two weeks or so."

"They'll be preoccupied with their work, so that shouldn't be a problem. What is a problem is transporting the kozidnits to their new home. We don't have a vessel available to do it."

I smiled. "Don't worry, I do. And that's my next call, in fact."

"Van, I have Mavis Renko, the Master of the FCV *Big and Long*," Netty said.

"Netty, did you just snicker? I think you just snickered."

"I'm a machine, Van. I'm incapable of snickering."

"Well, it was a damned good simulation of a snicker. Anyway, put him on, please."

The center display lit up with the face of a Fren-Okun. There was no party hat this time.

"Peacemaker Van Tudor, so good to see you!"

"And you as well, Mavis," I said, and then engaged in a few minutes of inane small talk. Most of it came from Renko, and most of that was about carrying water from one place to another—which was exactly as exciting as it sounds. The gist of it, though, was that the *Big and Long* seemed to be moving many, many liters of water to lots of different places and was probably making the Fren owners many, many liters of bonds.

In the midst of it, Netty announced another incoming call, also from the *Big and Long*. I asked Renko to hold on, and I took it. It was an elderly Fren woman.

Uh-oh. I instinctively braced myself for the image to disappear in a blur of mucus, but the old Fren's eyes instead peered back at me with sharp, shrewd clarity.

"Peacemaker Tudor, I gather this isn't a social call."

"Uh—it—no. No, it isn't." I narrowed my eyes. "You're not—"

"Insane?" She sighed and waved a hand. "Yes, yes, moist, moist. Now, with that out of the way, what sort of business deal is my moron son-in-law offering that I'll have to disappoint you by not approving?"

I grinned. "We actually hadn't gotten to the deal part yet. And you're not the first, um, more *mature* Fren lady I've met who wasn't all *moist!* and other wild declarations."

"There aren't many of us, but we pretty much run things around here. So what is it you're after?"

"I need to move about a thousand dangerously carnivorous aquatic organisms across around eighty light-years, and I need to do it in about one week's time." I glanced at the comm. "And I do still have your son-in-law on hold—"

"Oh, don't worry about him. My daughter—his wife—is keeping him distracted. It's not hard." She rubbed her chin. "An interesting proposition. And it sounds like you need this to happen, and need it to happen quickly. Three-hundred thousand bonds, half up front, half on completion."

"One hundred and fifty thousand, and your ship remains at the delivery location on comm silence for one week."

"Oh, there's a security aspect to this, huh? Two hundred and fifty thousand."

"Two hundred thousand, but it will have to be in five payments."

"Two hundred thousand, five payments, and preferred-source contracting for this ship for any of the Peacemaker Guild's water transport needs for one year."

I technically didn't have authority to approve that, but this was another case of the Guild—specifically, Gerhardt—having to back me up.

"Done."

The old Fren spoke into another comm briefly, outlining the deal to someone—her daughter, I assumed. I waited.

"Okay, I've let my daughter know. You can switch back my

imbecile son-in-law and pitch the offer. She'll make sure he accepts it, him being the"—she actually made air-quotes—"*Master* and all. He'll screw it all up somehow, but it doesn't matter. My daughter will make sure the contract is correct before she sends it. Oh, and let me listen in."

Bemused, I switched back to Renko and made the pitch. His eyes lit up, and he cackled with glee. A younger female Fren, undoubtedly his wife, stood behind him and nodded at me.

"Two hundred thousand bonds, in five payments! Five payments means we make five times as much money! We are the rulers of all stars! We are rich! We will buy tapestries for the bathing room!"

I nodded back—to his wife—and signed off. The old Fren sighed.

"What did I tell you. A moron—" She stopped and glanced off camera. "Oh, shit. Sorry, gotta go," she said, then her face went slack and shrieked a single word.

"*MOIST!*"

Before the comm cut and her image vanished, I saw her glance at me and give me a saucy wink.

WE ARRIVED at the remote system containing the planet Hellhole. The star was a red dwarf, utterly nondescript from a celestial perspective, but as we descended to the surface of the deathworld, it suddenly took on a sinister character, a blood-red orb hanging over a bleak, fetid landscape that could probably have passed as existing during the Permian period on Earth. The star didn't give much illumination, meaning that days were not only dominated by the ruddy sun, but were also dim, throwing everything into shadow. And while there were trees, towering variations on club mosses, they were mostly confined to the relatively few, isolated patches of higher ground, with the vast majority of the planet's surface being nothing but dreary, murky swamp.

We landed the *Fafnir* on the edge of one of the highlands, a piece of ground maybe two meters higher than the surrounding fens at its peak. The ship's landing gear sank about a half meter into the mire anyway.

"Netty, are we going to be able to lift off again?" I asked, the *Fafnir* canting slightly to the right as her weight settled into the wet muck.

"If we light the fusion drive, we can lift from nearly anything."

"And get walloped by the shock wave and incinerate everything for klicks around. I was thinking about something a little less... apocalyptic."

"Right now, we're good. If we continue settling, though, and I start to get worried, I'll let you know."

I leaned out of the smaller airlock and got punched in the face with atmosphere similar to Satan's armpit. "You know, it's sulfurous, but it's also fetid and damp."

Funboy inhaled, blanched, then stepped back. "I can *feel* the diseases."

Icky slapped him on the shoulder hard enough that he lurched. "Ripe, ain't it?" Like cheese, but better. Deader."

Zeno glanced up at Icky. "You're never ordering takeout for us again. Ever."

Torina held up an arm. "Seconded."

Adayluh had landed in the *Kitsune* a short time before we had, about a klick away, and dispatched a couple of robotic drones to start sampling the water, soil, and air. We wanted to minimize our time outside the ships, because not only were there vicious, venomous things living in the water, but there were also airborne threats. One of them clacked against the canopy right in front of me, in fact, making me jump.

"Holy shit. What was that?"

"A bug," Perry replied.

"Uh, no shit. But a bug the size of a beagle."

"Van, I've told you a hundred million billion times, don't exaggerate. It couldn't have been any bigger than one of Icky's feet."

"I stand by my statement."

"Stop using my feet as units of measure. It's degrading and personal," Icky snapped, then belched. "Sorry. That air is making me hungry."

"There is no clear correlation, you know," Funboy said, and we all turned to him.

"Correlation with what?" Torina asked.

"Between the size of one's feet and one's genitalia. That's a myth."

We all just stared for a moment. "Funboy... Icky's a girl. More to the point, though, what the hell does that have to do with *anything*?"

"I don't believe in passing up opportunities to dispel unfortunate misconceptions."

I unstrapped and stood. "And, on that note—Netty, where's our shipment of killer seahorses?"

"The *Big and Long* has entered orbit. They'll begin shuttling down the kozidnits within the hour."

Something else smacked against the canopy, and I winced.

"Kinda wish we'd brought along some genetically modified super bugs, too."

Perry gave me an amber glance. "Really? Doesn't that just start the chain that ends up with the old lady swallowing the fly?"

Funboy blinked. "Could you explain that——"

I raised my hands and shook my head.

"Forget it, forget it—forget I ever even said it." I headed aft to get a comm set up with Adayluh.

———

WHILE FINAL PREPARATIONS were underway to transport the seahorses from hell down to their new home, Lunzy called, asking where we were. Gerhardt, she said, wanted to talk to me, but not over a comm. I dithered a bit over telling her. Not because I didn't trust her, but because everyone who knew our current location was another possible source of leaks. I finally decided, though, that it was better to have Gerhardt in the circle of knowledge since we might need the Guild's support—potentially a lot of it—on short notice.

I could tell we'd piqued her interest when we sent the nav data to her in parts, in separate messages each encoded with a different high-security encryption scheme. Because of the paranoia level of protection, though, she refrained from asking any more questions. About fourteen hours later, right after the second of four shipments of kozidnits had been hauled down to the surface, she and Gehardt arrived. I used the *Fafnir*'s workboat to meet them in orbit, while the others oversaw our part of the operation. They had to cobble together and test a set of armor that would resist the worst that the planet, including our hellish sea horses, could throw at it.

Gerhardt stared at the desolate planetscape scrolling by beneath us. Even from orbit, Hellhole looked unendingly dreary and uninviting—grays and greens rendered brownish in the red dwarf's dim light, punctuated by patches of pinkish clouds that slowly oozed across the landscape. There was rarely anything as dramatic as a storm on Hellhole, just long, bleak periods of steady rain under dun-colored skies.

"Quite the vacation spot you've found here, Tudor," he said.

Lunzy nodded. "Yeah, don't let word get out, or the place is gonna be jammed with daytrippers."

Gerhardt pointed. "There, along that big body of water. Aren't those beaches?"

I nodded. "They are. They're home to a burrowing parasitic worm that has a taste, apparently, for bone."

"Ah."

I took them back down to the surface so they could meet Adayluh and she could brief them on her work herself. She was wary at first, clearly uncomfortable with new arrivals at her research operation. But I'd already vouched for them, so she soon relaxed and turned into the scientist happily explaining their work to an attentive audience—way too much detail and jargon and oblivious to the fact that nods and variations on "uh-huh" were social cues meaning *get to the point already*.

When she was done, Gerhardt gave a genuine nod. "Your caution about revealing any of this is well-advised. BeneStar has been scouring known space for you in a way I could almost describe as desperate."

I nodded back. "They must know she's getting close to completing her last trial. After that, it won't take her long to get Rights of Assertion."

"Which they are going to be desperate to prevent. That's part of the reason I wanted to come here personally, because what I'm about to do I can only do in person." He activated a data slate, then went on. "Perry, Netty, please formally acknowledge me."

Perry spoke up at once, his voice lacking any of its usual smart-assery. "You are Gerhardt, Master of the Peacemakers." Then he went on to read back Gerhardt's credentials. Netty did the same.

"In accordance with the powers vested in me by the Interstellar Commerce Accord Number Four, Section Two, Paragraphs Nine through Eleven inclusive, I am deputizing you both as neutral agents in the evaluation and granting of commercial Writs of Assertion of Rights arising from—"

He went on, speaking another few dozen words of proforma legalese. The gist of it was that Perry and Netty could both grant and witness Adayluh's Rights of Assertion once she'd satisfied all of the legal and administrative requirements. As AIs, they were bound by the strict letter of the law, so there'd be no question about any fiddling or rule bending or favoritism. Even if they wanted to go easy or give Adayluh a pass on anything, their programming precluded it. The point was to not give BeneStar's army of lawyers any traction in the form of flaws or incorrect procedure.

"Well, that was a lot more formality than I'd expected in the same place I eat breakfast," Torina said, glancing around at the *Fafnir*'s galley.

Perry, his rigidly proper tone replaced by his customary wise guy snap, couldn't resist jumping in. "Yeah, and Icky wasn't even wearing pants."

"What the *hell* is everyone's obsession with my lower half?" Icky groused, waving a meaty hand at her blue, fuzzy thighs.

Gerhardt raised a hand. "I can assure you, Icrul, that I have no obsession with your lower half, nor your upper, left, right, front, or rear halves."

Adayluh grinned, then frowned as someone spoke in her ear bug. She acknowledged, then tapped at data slate and transferred imagery of the kozidnits settling into their new home.

It... wasn't pretty.

"Speaking of breakfast, I might just lose mine," Lunzy said.

I nodded. It was a feeding frenzy. It wasn't even much of a competition. As vicious as the native wildlife was, it paled in comparison to the sheer ferocity of the kozidnits.

"You still think they're cuddly, Icky?" I asked.

She shook her head in amazement. "Did that one just eat... a rock?"

Torina nodded in awe. "Probably. Can you—oh, what the hell? Did you see that lizard kind of thing? It's, um, gone. Just... gone. They ate the whole animal. Even the horns."

"Horns can be extremely nutritious. Of course, they also pose a fatal choking hazard to most creatures," Funboy stated with his usual vigor.

"Don't eat the horns. Got it, Funboy. Thank you for the nutritional advice," I said.

"I would say it's my pleasure, but I won't, because it's not. Pointing out unfortunate realities rarely is."

"Hey, boss, quick question," Perry said.

I had trouble tearing my eyes away from the horror on the imager. It was like seeing a bad accident on the Interstate. You didn't want to look, but it was so damned hard not to. "What's that, Perry?"

"Who's gonna harvest this stuff?"

Silence. I glanced around. "Any volunteers?"

"Oh, yeah, I'll get right on that—after I scrub out the exhaust bell while the drive's running," Zeno replied.

Surprisingly, Gerhardt spoke up. "I believe I can help with that."

I raised an eyebrow at him. "Really?"

"Since arriving in orbit and hearing you explain what was going on here, it struck me that I happen to have something you may find useful. It's not a Guild asset, it's my own. I inherited it from my father." He tapped at his data slate, replacing the orgy of submarine violence—which was becoming obscured by silt and bits of what used to be creatures—with a picture of a massive mechanical suit. It was a hulking metal exoskeleton that must have stood nearly three meters tall.

"What the hell did your father do for a living?" Zeno asked.

"He was an independent miner, working asteroids at Wolf 424. I inherited all of his equipment, which I've currently got in storage because, well, I'm as interested in mining asteroids as I am going for a swim down there. Anyway, this suit is environmentally sealed, so it should work underwater as well as it does in the void—which means it would probably be useful to work around that charnel house you call a farm." He turned to us with his thin smile. "So, who wants to reap what's being sown?"

Icky stuck up her hand. "Ooh, ooh, I do! That looks like it'd be fun to run!"

I smiled at her. "Of course you do, Icky. But you do realize it would mean you'd have to wear pants, right? Steel pants, but pants just the same."

Gerhardt, Perry, and I spent several hours in discussion, while Torina and the others worked with Adayluh to get the next step of the trial underway—actually planting the Permada. Adayaluh had procured two planting machines, which were designed to sow crops like rice that grew in wet conditions. In the absence of the armor Icky and Zeno were building, or Gerhardt's exo-suit, no one wanted to get anywhere near the gnashing teeth of the maniacal kozidnits. They actually *were* what many people believed the Amazonian piranha back on Earth were—ruthlessly efficient eating machines that wouldn't just effortlessly strip something down to the bone, but would chomp up the bones, too. In fact, in just a few hours, they'd become the dominant species in the area around the trial beds.

"I took my cue from you and refrained from letting anyone know where I was going when I came here, aside from taking some personal time for some family business—which, if you're going to use my father's old mining suit, isn't actually a lie, now is it?" Gerhardt said.

I nodded. "I appreciate that."

But Gerhardt narrowed his eyes. "It did, however, lead to an interesting interaction. Shortly after I had Max post my absence on the Master's Master Calendar—and yes, that's what it's called, isn't that hilarious—I was contacted by Master Kharsweil."

I sat up. "Oh?"

"Yes. He was hoping to discuss several cases with me, to seek my advice on them. What made that interesting is that he has never done that before. He isn't noted for being especially... collegial."

"You think he was interested in where you were going," Perry said.

"Actually, I explicitly know it. When I reminded him I was about to leave Anvil Dark, he very casually asked me where I was going. Again, to my knowledge, he's never expressed even a glimmer of interest in what anyone else was doing with their personal time," Gerhardt replied.

I let out a breath. "Don't know about you guys, but I'm hearing alarm bells right now."

Gerhardt nodded. "Indeed. It was... awkward. Amateurish, even. So either it was *meant* to be obvious that he was trying to pry into where I was going for some purpose—"

"Or someone, somewhere, is starting to panic, and the after-shocks are starting to hit Kharsweil," Perry finished.

"Which means he's dirty. On the BeneStar payroll, or somehow subject to their influence," I said. I thought about Steve, the otherwise affable and trustworthy former head of the Guild's technical lab, whose family had been threatened by the bad guys, turning him into an unwilling mole. "Blackmail, extortion, something like that."

"I don't disagree. However, I'm not prepared to start making accusations or formally investigating. Kharsweil is a Master, and a smart and well-connected one at that. For now, I'm going to keep my eyes and ears open—and would suggest you do the same, Tudor."

I laughed. "Oh, considering how much interstellar villainy is after me, if they were any *more* open things would start falling out."

Gerhardt actually grinned, but it quickly faded. "There is another matter. While BeneStar is desperately anxious to get its corporate hands on Permada, because it does have titanic implications—"

"Especially financial ones," Perry muttered.

"Indeed, and no amount of money, power, and control of economic sectors will ever be enough for them. To that end, BeneStar is far from dormant in those other sectors. The Guild has received intelligence from several sources, including our more-or-less allies in Unity, that the company is increasingly active in mining... a variety of metallic commodities, but there's one in particular."

"Let me guess. Osmium," I said with rich disgust, because I knew I was right.

"Correct. And this brings me back to Kharsweil. Since he may have given us a peek at his hand, I'm inclined to look past any evidence of wrongdoing as it may come up, and just continue watching."

It was my turn to grin. "Look at you, Master Gerhardt, being all schemy and pragmatic and ends-justifying-the-means."

He shrugged. "You're a bad influence, Tudor. Anyway, if we're patient, he may lead us further up whatever chain is wrapped around him."

I leaned forward. "And what if that chain leads to Gauss himself? Kharsweil is a Master, not some low-level flunky, after all, and he may report to the top. Is the Guild prepared to deal with that?"

"Let's fight one battle at a time, Tudor. Right now, your focus should remain where you've already put it—here, on Permada. It stands to change the stars. In the meantime, the osmium mines aren't going anywhere. And, for that matter, why rush? We can sit back and watch as BeneStar, or the Sorcerers, or whoever is actually doing the mining digs and pulverizes and all that mining stuff—"

I couldn't resist a wicked laugh. "In other words, let them do the dirty work, and then step in and seize the product."

"And since it can't very well be put back into the ground, sell it on the open market, where it can be properly tracked, then use part of the proceeds to reclaim and restore the horrific environmental damage they're leaving behind."

I immediately thought about Helso, Torina's homeworld, upon which illegal mining had been one of my very first cases. "We already have a solution, in fact, who are very good at that—the Synergists."

"Space hippies for the win!" Perry proclaimed.

Gerhardt smiled, then stood and headed for the airlock. "And now, I actually am going to take a little time off. My ship's AI will provide Netty with a comm address and encryption details if you need to contact me. In the meantime, Lucky and Dugrop'che are going to join Lunzy here to act as overwatch. Alic is overseeing this very *discreet* operation personally."

"You mean off the books," Perry said.

Gerhardt looked offended. "Certainly not. Alic is dispatching each of them to some far flung destination where they'll be out of easy communications for a couple of weeks. On the way there, each is going to get an encrypted message that there's been a change of plans, and to come here instead. Have I mentioned that Alic is sometimes forgetful and neglects to note such changes of plan in the official logs, sometimes for as long as, oh—"

"A couple of weeks?" I asked.

Gerhardt shook his head. "It is an area of his performance Alic really must work on improving. And now, I am off. I'll leave you to your farm, with its super-grain and viciously carnivorous livestock, Tudor." He started to turn away, then turned back, a twinkle in his eye.

"It seems like you can never really take that Iowa of yours out of the man, can you?"

33

THE NEXT SIXTEEN days were a hellish slurry of tedium and anxiety, but also an absolute need for keen attentiveness and attention to detail. All we could do was maintain constant vigilance on the passive scanners, keep our various emissions and electronic signatures as small as possible, and wait for the Permada to grow and reach maturity, while Adayluh and her team ran through the myriad steps of their final trial.

"We are literally watching grass grow," Perry deadpanned.

"*Solid gold* grass. Or... like platinum. Or osmium," I countered.

"Fair point. And I'm not entirely right. That saying was made without the specter of alien naval attack," Perry admitted.

"We're always watching the skies," I said, my eyes going up out of habit. "Think that'll ever end?"

Funboy peered upward with comical intensity. "Given your skeletal structure, you'll stop when you have a degradation of spinal discs. Or you cease to exist, of course. I'm told that has a negative effect on your species' ability to use your eyes."

A hum descended over us, and Funboy added, "Was this one of those rhetorical questions?"

I tilted my head, thinking. "Your grim answer aside, not entirely. But I knew I'd spend my life under scrutiny once I drew down on more substantial targets. Like Gauss."

"I don't mind watching," Icky said while idly scratching her chest. The *skritch* of hands on hair was... familiar.

"Thanks, big girl. Appreciate it," I told her. She grinned, then settled back in an effortless state of relaxation, and we all grew quiet again. For a while.

We passed the time. We played cards—lots of cards. We slept. Icky, Zeno, and Funboy also tinkered, redirecting their efforts from an armored suit, thanks to Gerhardt's donation to the effort, into an armored harvesting machine. Adayluh and her people helped with that. We spent a lot of time visiting one another aboard our various ships just to break up the monotony. By having our various crews circulate among our four Guild ships—the *Fafnir*, Lundy's, Lucky's, and Dugrop'che's—we managed to stave off the worst of cabin fever that would have come from spending all that time jammed together. It wasn't like we could make planetfall to stretch our legs, after all, at least not without having them chewed to the bone. And beyond.

The Reclamators overseeing the kozidnits and studying their spread into the planet's ecosystem were fascinated and alarmed by their efficiency. Within a week, they'd become the dominant species across a stretch of swampy mire nearly a hundred klicks across. At that rate, they'd take over the planet in a few weeks—or would have, if a built-in population control hadn't kicked in. When the number of kozidnits in a given area started to exceed a certain threshold, they began to eat one another at a rate that balanced their production of offspring. It turned out that they'd probably not end up controlling more than a few thousand square klicks of Hellhole.

That dispelled a residue of guilt I found myself carrying at the idea I'd been responsible for wiping out the native biosphere of an entire planet. Not a *lot* of guilt, though, because the things the kozidnits had replaced were just as nightmarish.

So while Adayluh watched her grass grow and the Reclamators watched their adorable horrors shred the local fauna, the rest of us waited.

And we watched the skies. Always.

I FULLY EXPECTED that the universe's need for dramatic action—after a long period of quiet—would have meant the arrival of a BeneStar fleet. This event would, no doubt, happen while we desperately tried to harvest the Permada in a pulse-pounding race against the clock. But it didn't work out that way. For once, we reached the climax of the thing without incident. We'd taken Gerhardt's armored exosuit down to the surface and tested its imperviousness to the kozidnits, and I'd taken it for a few test spins.

The biggest problem was the thing getting its bulky mass stuck, its feet and legs bogged down in the sucking mire of the landscape. We'd attached a tether to it for that reason, so that our workboat could lift it out of the quagmire. Otherwise, the suit worked fine, so when the day came that Adayluh finally pronounced her trial complete, the last of her data collected, and the Permada ready for harvesting, I strapped myself into the exosuit and got to work.

"You sure?" Torina asked.

I looked at the screen that showed a roiling, muddy hellscape flashing with fangs and motion. "Truth? Barely. But I'm gonna do it."

She leaned up and kissed me. "I knew you would. Just like asking."

"Is it the mild alarm or the steely determination that gets your chili cooking?"

"Both. Chili is eaten hot, right?"

"It is if you're civilized," I answered, tapping the control to lower my visor.

Her smile was… worth the danger. "Then definitely both."

"I'll be right back." It was time to work.

Lowered into the boggy field, I began trudging along, dragging the harvesting machine cobbled together by our combined crews.

It went well, until it didn't. I got stuck after three rows, squelching in mud so thick it was throwing off density scans similar to cerramocrete in a plastic state.

"Stuck?" Torina asked, already swooping down in the workboat.

"Like you can't believe and—"

Whamwhamwhamwhamwham

"Van? What the hell is that *noise?*"

I stared at the vivid smears across my visor, then shook my head in disgust. "That noise, as you gently named it, is the kozidnits turning themselves into actual *pulp* trying to get me. Quick question for the Supervisor? How do these little bastards even know I'm *in* here?"

I assumed that they had more unique identities than Supervisor, but if they had actual names, they never shared them with anyone outside their race.

"We've been wondering the same thing. As near as we can tell, they must be able to detect some bioelectric signature that's telling them you're there," the Supervisor replied over the comm, every word calm and cool. "We're quite intrigued, as it may allow us to develop a way to repel them."

I glanced through the downward-angled viewports in the suit's upper torso. The morass around my mechanical legs and feet was a gooey, viscous slurry of water, mud, the slimy remnants of kozidnits, and the seething wriggle of *more* kozidnits feeding on the remains of their fellows.

I grimaced at the disgusting mess. "Intrigued, huh? Well, not exactly the word I'd use at this end. More nauseating, I think. Glad I can be of service to science, though."

I made the last pass, then dragged the harvester and myself back to the relatively dry path of the land where the ships were grounded. While I extricated myself from the exosuit—doing my best to avoid the strings and blobs of gross, syrupy sludge oozing off the thing's legs—Adayluh and her people retrieved the last of the Permada from the harvester.

"I don't think Gerhardt's going to refund your cleaning deposit," Perry said, landing beside me and taking in the mess.

I shook my head. "How the hell are we going to clean that off? I mean, we're not loading it into the *Fafnir* like that."

Funboy spoke up, standing in the *Fafnir*'s airlock. He'd steadfastly refused to even let his booted feet touch the muddy surface of Hellhole. "I quite agree. To call that unclean is—"

He gulped and turned away. "Excuse me."

"Guess we made Funboy sick," I said.

Perry sniffed. "A toenail clipping would make Funboy sick."

Icky seized the moment, wiggling her thick toes, unshod, blue, and hairy. "Depends on whose foot."

———

To HER CREDIT, Adayluh didn't rush the final tests of her trial. She and her people tested random samples of the nearly four tons we'd harvested, measuring caloric content, various aspects of its biochemistry, heavy metal concentrations, and myriad other factors. Hours after we finished harvesting the stuff, she came on the comm, beaming from ear to ear.

"Every parameter is within acceptable limits. The Permada is as nutritious growing in this matrix as it is anywhere else."

"Yeah, except it's partly made from… dead kozidnit goo, isn't it?" Icky asked.

"It—well, yes, I suppose that the Permada would have incorporated some of it as it grew. But a protein molecule is a protein molecule, regardless of where it comes from."

"Even so, you make any noodles out of the stuff we just harvested, I'll pass."

Torina smiled. "Does this mean you don't want a kozidnits as a pet anymore, Icky?"

"Pet, no. Adorably murderous guard animal? Now we're talking."

"So you're declaring this trial a success?" I asked Adayluh.

She nodded eagerly. "Very much so, yes."

I turned to Perry. "Has she satisfied the requirements for a Writ of Assertion?"

"Except for the part where she compliments the bird on his devilish good looks, yeah, she has."

"Perry, you're the most handsome AI bird in the *Fafnir*'s entire cockpit," Adayluh said.

"See, now that's more like—wait."

"While Perry struggles to work that out, I am going to declare a valid Writ of Assertion in the name of Adayluh Creel for the crop known as Permada," Netty said.

Perry bobbed his head. "The cunningly so-called *compliment* notwithstanding, I witness this as well."

Zeno looked around. "So is that it? Are we done here? Did we do what we set out to do?"

"There is just one more hoop, but a minor one. The Writ asserts Adayluh's ownership of the Permada in terms of intellectual property, which means no one else can grow it for any purpose. But if she wants to assert commercial rights, she has to bring it to market —that is, sell it to someone," Netty said.

Torina shrugged. "That's easy enough. I'll buy some."

"Me too," Zeno said.

Icky scowled. "What did I *just* say? If you guys bring some of that stuff aboard and make flour out of it, keep it in a separate container marked *kozidnits flavored*, please and thank you."

"Actually, Van, I'd recommend taking it to a bona fide market and selling it there. While BeneStar might not be able to claim ownership of the Permada anymore, they could try and block Adayluh from selling it, disputing her commercial rights, arguing that there's a conflict of interest if we just buy it. Legally speaking, we're part of her enterprise here," Perry said.

I nodded. "Good point. Let's find ourselves an agricultural world and arrange to arrive at one of its major population centers on what would be considered a day off or holiday of some sort."

Torina frowned. "Why?"

I smiled. "You're talking to a farm boy here. And this farm boy knows that when you've got city folk who live near farms, have a day off, and want to overpay for something homegrown, there's only one place to go—the Farmer's Market."

WE FINALLY SETTLED on Carson's Arch as our Farmer's Market. One of the seven habitable planets in the Tau Ceti system, the Arch, as it was called, was predominantly an agri-world, its huge expanses of temperate land given over to growing conventional crops of all sorts. More specialized types were grown hydroponically in sprawling greenhouse complexes, while even the coast regions were used to cultivate algae, whose biomass was used for production of food, as a growth medium for pharmaceutical products, and even as a source of biofuel to power machinery around the planet. In the meantime, vast fisheries operated from huge floating platforms serviced by fleets of robotic ships. It was all the result of very careful, sophisticated terraforming, making the Arch the breadbasket of the Tau Ceti system.

More importantly, there were a dozen or so major cities, all of whose economies were built around serving the surrounding farmlands and fisheries. We selected one, Greenway, that was clustered around the base of a towering space elevator, as our destination. A huge, open-air market thrived there, allowing residents to purchase fresh food brought into the city to be transshipped up into orbit. It was a perfect combination of order, wealth, and, most importantly, profile. At any given time, there were thousands of people from a variety of air-breathing races filling the market, which I hoped would dissuade BeneStar from doing anything stupid. We were, after all, blowing our cover by coming here, so their corporate goons would certainly find out.

———

WE HAD MORE HELP out here, too—or, at least, I hoped we would. I put in a call to Amazing, mainly to inquire about my mother, now that we were out of our self-imposed comms blackout. But I also wanted to ask for a favor.

We needed security, and we needed *trusted* security.

Amazing connected immediately, her face lit with curiosity. "What's your status, Van?"

"Good, but in need of some assurance going into a public place. Any chance you can bring some people here? It's an open area, filled with bystanders, and my crews aren't enough for this much ground. That's my first favor, or… at least my first question."

Amazing gave a slow nod and cut her eyes offscreen, then back to me. "I'll see what I can do. What's the second favor?"

I sighed, then focused my eyes on Amazing again. She moved, barely, and I dialed back my emotions as best I could, given what I was about to say. "How is my mother?"

Amazing didn't look relieved but only because she was a

consummate professional, and she hid her reaction well. When she spoke, her smile was warm, and she was sifting what words to use.

"She's a lot... better. Much more grounded. Your retrieval of the *Hawksbill* did wonders for her, I think. It helped bring her back from some dark places she'd gone."

"That's good. I'm glad." I hesitated, not sure how to say what I was about to say. "Having said that, if you are going to help us out on the Arch, I think I'd prefer if, um... if you—"

"Didn't involve your mother."

I let out my breath, then gave a sharp nod. "Yeah. I can't help thinking she's a little on the trigger-happy side."

"Oh, she's very much on the trigger-happy side. She's very, very good at fighting and killing things, which is fine if you're in a warzone."

"The Arch isn't a warzone, nor do I want it to become one," I said.

Amazing nodded. "Neither do I." She cut the comm channel, and I let my shoulders relax. For now, it was the best news I could hope for. Turning to my crew, I waved at the planet below. "Who's ready to buy overpriced agritourist items?"

Torina waved her hands in mock excitement. "Can I pick my own fruit and post it to social media with the hashtag *cottagecore* or *farmgirl*?"

I snorted with laughter. "I see you've been to a farmer's market on Earth."

Moments later, we landed and emerged onto a spaceport of such elegant design it felt almost organic, wending paths and pads emerging from rock formations with an artistry that defied logic.

"Kinda fancy, boss," Perry said, hopping down onto the silent cart that whisked us toward the market. We had four such carts, all open air, comfortable, and self-guided.

Torina leaned her head on my shoulder, and Icky let her legs droop outside the cart in a hazard to herself and anyone we passed.

Funboy held himself upright in mild alarm, and Zeno merely relaxed, having the good sense to know when to rest and when to fight. We reached the central market area in moments, and the carts disgorged us and whirled around to head back to the spaceport without any input from us at all.

"Boss?" Perry asked, his beak pointed up. "Check it out. You wanted majestic alien culture, you got it."

"I'll say," I agreed in a low tone of admiration. "I remember going to Toronto once, standing at the base of the CN Tower, and looking straight up. That made my head spin. This, though—" I gestured upward. "I don't know what the hell to make of that."

The space elevator was a series of parallel cylinders, each about a hundred meters in diameter and made of some exotic material, held together by a complex spiderweb of cables. The result was a structure about a kilometer across, starting at ground level and soaring away, dwindling into—

Forever. It was the only way I could describe it. It literally dwindled into infinity, until it vanished into the sky. The effect was to pull the eye upward until there was nothing upon which to focus, leaving you looking into eternity. I'd tried it three or four times now, and each time it left me with a queasy sense of vertigo.

"Well, let's see, the CN Tower is five hundred and fifty-three meters tall, and this space elevator is thirty-six thousand *kilometers*, a factor of sixty-five thousand one hundred times taller. That might have something to do with it," Perry said.

I grunted at his implacable math and put my attention firmly on ground level. Adayluh and her crew were setting out sacks of the harvested Permada in the stall we'd rented, getting ready for the market to open for the day. There were already curious people hovering nearby, though, apparently anxious for a look at what was being advertised as "super wheat, a revolution in nutrition."

I watched them carefully as I took note of the rest of my team. Icky and Zeno were examining a vegetable stall off to my left, while Torina and Funboy talked to the vendor at a fruit kiosk to my right. Lucky, Lunzy, and Dugrop'che were free ranging among the many stalls, cubicles, and booths nearby but keeping themselves within sight of ours.

I let my pose go loose, even managing a smile or two. Outwardly, I was just another warm body, watching over an unremarkable stall of humble wheat.

Inside, my body thrummed with awareness, and damned if it didn't feel right.

OUR FIRST CONFRONTATIONAL interaction didn't involve BeneStar, though. It involved the local authorities. Or, more specifically, the tax collectors.

Two of them, a human and a Nesit both wearing the understated gray uniforms of the Arch's customs and excise authority, watched the sacks of Permada selling—ever brisker as the day went on—then ambled over and asked to see our import paperwork. Perry, who along with Netty and Adayluh had prepared it on our way here, provided it. I braced myself for the inevitable stink of corruption, the demand for some sort of surcharge that would, of course, only be payable in bonds. But I was pleasantly surprised when the excise officers merely checked the paperwork Perry transmitted to their data slate against what they had in their own records, nodded in satisfaction, and moved on.

"Well, that was refreshingly honest," I said, watching them wander away.

"The customs and excise authorities here are paid extremely well. It not only gives them no particular incentive to line their pockets, but it also actually gives them a *dis*incentive to do it, because they don't want to lose their jobs," Perry said.

Adayluh nodded. "A place like this thrives on a reputation for honest dealing—oops, customers," she said, turning to speak to some more people who'd showed up at her booth.

I turned away to scan the crowd yet again. It looked like any other group of people gathered in any number of farmer's markets I'd attended in Iowa. Perhaps a greater than average number of limbs and other appendages compared to the Iowa State Fair in Des Moines, but—

"Van, Zeno. I think trouble has finally found us. Check your ten o'clock."

I looked where she'd indicated and sighed. A feeling of cautious optimism was growing within me, and I felt the beginning of a relieved smile.

Unfortunately, I was wrong.

34

A SMALL CROWD was surging into the square that made up our part of the much bigger market. It could have been any group of people, even just a bunch of new arrivals from a ship or other conveyance swarming into the market all at once, except for two things.

First, at least two of our media influencers were there—Robi of the many uber-valuable chains, and Saber, the Synth, with the mobile tattoos. A small AI-controlled remote hovered and darted around each of them, no doubt recording and broadcasting whatever they were saying—or, rather, shouting, since the rest of the crowd was a babble of noise around them.

Second, about that crowd—while many of them seemed to be ordinary men, women, and children, a lot of them weren't. They were much harder sorts, their faces all planes and angles and predatory menace. And while the rest of the crowd focused on the two influencers, these were watching everywhere else, and especially us.

"*Shit*. Battle stations everyone—if you're not there already," I said into my open comm.

"What the hell is the point of this?" Torina asked. "Adayluh has Rights of Assertion over the Permada, so they're too late to do anything about it."

"And she's been selling the stuff like crazy, so that'll seal her commercial rights, too," Zeno added.

Funboy spoke up. "She could always sell, or even sign the Rights over to BeneStar."

"Why the hell would she do that?" Zeno shot back.

"Because they force her to."

I cut in. "Funboy's right. They're probably here to portray Adayluh as some sort of greedy monster for wanting to sell the Permada instead of giving it away to all those poor starving souls, the way BeneStar would."

"Worst case scenario is that they grab Adayluh and, well, I'll leave that to your imagination," Lucky put in.

"Uh, you guys do realize I'm on this comm channel, right?" Adayluh said.

I nodded to her, being just a few meters away. "Good point. Adayluh, we need to get you out of here."

But she crossed her arms and shook her head. "No."

"Adayluh—"

"No. I've been running and hiding from these bastards for months, and it's taken me and my crew away from our families for just as long. I worked hard and got the Rights of Assertion, and I'll be damned if I'm going to spend the rest of my life running and hiding to try and hang onto them."

One look at her told me that there was no point arguing. So I nodded again.

"Okay, everyone, we're standing our ground. Remember, though, they need to make the first move. Perry, can you get close enough to hear what Robi and Saber are saying?"

"On it, boss," he replied, and I saw him sail from somewhere off to my right, across the square and a few meters over the crowd. As he did, I heard Robi's voice, heavily filtered to remove the crowd sound, come back over the comm.

"*—keeping it from you, from the people who need it most, to sell it here, on one of the wealthiest planets in known space. All that these people are interested in is money—*"

"That's rich coming from a walking pawn shop!" Lunzy snapped.

"*—deserve better than this. Discoveries such as this are meant to be shared, to be used for the betterment of all people, not for crass commercial profit. And these people around me agree. They're going to express their outrage to these profiteers, but as a peaceful protest only—*"

"*Bullshit.*" I wasn't even sure who said it this time.

"Van, taking a close look at the crowd as I passed over it, I saw that some of them are Sorcerers. They've got the super-secret decoder cuffs and everything," Perry said, wheeling around for another pass.

I cursed and braced myself—they were now just a few dozen paces away—but before I could say anything, another of the small AI remotes zipped out of the crowd. This time, though, it darted after Perry.

"Perry, your six—!" I shouted, but he was already in action.

"Really?" he said, then snapped upward in a hard climb and

whipped around in a maneuver I remember my father describing, an Immelmann Turn, a pilot's way of quickly reversing direction. The remote whipped toward him in response, and I heard him yelp.

"Stupid thing's firing a laser at me! Okay, then, asshole—let's put the combat into *combat AI*."

What followed for the next few seconds was the most remarkable dogfight I'd ever seen. The remote could swoop and zip and change direction almost instantly, making it a fearsome opponent—except this was *Perry*. And for all his wisecracking and the fact that I considered him one of my best friends, I tended to forget that he was a purpose-built machine, designed to not just perform effectively and efficiently, but creatively.

The remote didn't stand a chance. Oh, it tried, but everywhere it maneuvered or shot, Perry somehow wasn't. Instead, he'd be swooping in from another direction entirely, diamond-hard, razor-sharp talons extended, then slamming into the thing like a projectile from a gun. It would instantly change direction, but Perry was already executing some complex series of spins and gyrations, slipping right back out of the thing's firing arc and striking at it again. That happened a half-dozen times in about four or five seconds, then what remained of the remote finally just dropped to the ground and rolled away like a baseball.

"Hah! Baron Manfred von Perry triumphs! Or should it be Perry von Richtofen? Van, what do you—"

"Let's talk about this later, Ace, okay? We've got our own, more pressing issues down here on the ground," I said as the crowd surged closer, just seconds away now.

I saw women and a few children, but behind them were the dour, belligerent glares of Sorcerers, mercenaries, or both. The bastards, true to form, were using them as human shields until they got close enough to do their dirty work. I put myself between them and Adayluh, gripping the Moonsword without drawing it. Every instinct screamed at me to take the initiative and attack, but they hadn't actually done anything hostile yet, and this was all on record—

"AAAAIIIIIEEEEEE!!!!"

It was Icky. Her shrieking bellow cut through the racket like a red-hot razor as she charged somebody on the edge of the crowd. I winced. The influencers would have a field day with her starting things. That was despite the fact that her target, a Sorcerer, had spun and drawn a slug pistol. It was just self-defense, right?

Except Icky abruptly skidded to a stop, lowered her hammer, and grinned into the Sorcerer's face. I couldn't hear her, but I saw what she said.

"Hi, asshole."

The Sorcerer shouted something and raised the slug pistol in Icky's face.

"Icky, no—!"

He fired, but at the same instant one of Icky's smaller hands, which she'd obviously been keeping ready, snapped up and hit the Sorcerer's gun hand. The shot cracked out, missing Icky's skull by what couldn't have been more than a few millimeters.

She didn't hesitate, though, before raising and slamming the hammer down on the Sorcerer's head hard enough to drive most of it down between his shoulders. Gore exploded in all directions.

"Boss, this asshole attacked me!" she bellowed.

"Seems like a hostile act to me," Dugrop'che put in.

"Agreed. Weapons-hot, folks!" I said and drew the Moonsword with a smooth metallic hiss.

SOME FIGHTS ARE CLEAR-CUT, filled with tactics and an elegant demonstration of the sweet science of martial arts.

This was not that fight.

Icky launched herself with a fury that made one man urinate down his leg before she even made contact. Icky's fist connected with him, and he whirled into a Sorcerer, spattering curses and urine as Torina stepped smoothly forward and shot both of them with her sidearm.

Zeno fired her own weapon twice, then buried a fang—tusk, really—into the meaty shoulder of a crisis actor who made the severe mistake of drawing a long gun. Howling in pain, he tried to pull away as Zeno lisped threats at him before pushing him down and away. He fell writhing, only to be shot by his own people, who were more enthusiastic than skilled.

I took out two humans and a Trinduk with four shots, the last one carrying most of the Trinduk's gut skyward in a gray mist. As he fell, he shot yet another of the BeneStar people, and then I began taking rounds to my suit.

That's when I went from brawling to *pissed*. The Moonsword flickered down in a silver blur, severing an array of limbs from two enemies, then I whirled and punched back, severing the thick padded armor of a hired gun. His expression of horror told me I'd hit home, but before I could finish him, Funboy put a foot on my shoulder and leapt up—and out—before landing between two Sorcerers as if he was a fuzzy, avenging wraith. His piercing cry went up as he shot the left Sorcerer dead center mass, then slid down in a silken motion to fire *up* into the second Trinduk's midsection. With a shower of gore, the rout was on.

Many of the baddies were hired hands, not fighters, and it showed.

I rotated again and found another Sorcerer with my blade as the sickening sensation of parting flesh traveled up my arm. *Better you than me, pal.*

The crowd panicked and broke.

But the Influencers were… confused.

This was not how it was supposed to go, and the chaos revealed their whole operation had been thrown together quickly, probably only in the last couple of days, once our impending arrival on Carson's Arch hit their radar.

But I didn't have time to dwell on it. I engaged two more Sorcerers and a mercenary who tried to dogpile me with mass as their best weapon. The Sorcerers were relying on their cuffs for protection, which was a good tactic against anything except the Moonsword. It ignored the effects of their cuffs, the blade cleaving through flesh and bone without any impediment at all, but the Sorcerers had two problems beyond me, Zeno, and Funboy.

Perry swooped past, slashing open the face of a mercenary, and then the big girl *really* cut loose with a roar so primal it would've made a sasquatch feel like an urbanite.

She finished her bone-rattling challenge and laid about with her hammer like the ground itself offended her. She hit anyone and anything. She hit the walls. She hit a booth. She hit a table and a chair and two mercenaries all in a blur, and she did it while bitching about pants and vegetarian burger kebabs, which had somehow caught her attention as she destroyed the offending booth.

She was a sight to behold, a towering figure wielding a massive sledge, swinging it with bone-cracking power and laughing—actually laughing, once she got done complaining—like she was having the time of her life.

We got the upper hand, and then our tactics changed again.

The others—Torina, Zeno, Lucky, Lunzy, and Dugrop'che—all fought with more restrained, economical efficiency, relying on their b-suits to protect them instead of the waves of raw, gleeful fury radiating off Icky. She did tend to leave herself exposed, but Perry became her combat air patrol, snapping out warnings to her, or even attacking anyone trying to come at her through a blind spot. They made a damned good team.

And then there was Funboy, who had vanished since using me as a vault of violence.

In a lull, I looked for and found him. He wielded a weapon I'd never seen him use before, one he must have cobbled together himself at some point. It was a slug-pistol with a bayonet—a hideous metal spike protruding from the butt—and a set of brass knuckles built into the grip.

"Sweet lady justice. What the hell is *that?*" I mumbled in awe.

He cut, stabbed, pummeled, punched, and even shot his opponents, moving with a strangely liquid grace that somehow let him avoid the counterattacks but still looked sad. It was as though a mourner at a funeral had been regretfully forced to kick the shit out of someone without showing any disrespect for the dead as he did.

And then things turned again, as they often do in massive, open fights where the crowd has a weight that cannot be denied.

The bad guys pressed in on Adayluh and me harder than I could readily hold them back. Rounds slammed into my b-suit, and I could hear ribs groaning from the impact as blood filled my mouth with the taste of pennies and war.

"On me," I told Adayluh, whose eyes were round with naked fear.

"Where the hell am I going to go?" she asked, and the answer was bad. We were up against the heavy table, my Moonsword resting as I waved The Drop with menace, conserving ammo as the press of danger edged ever closer. I fired, Adayluh screamed, and the mercenary I shot fell at my feet, his chest a ruin. Even in his throes, he stabbed at me with a wicked knife, the blade sparking off flagstones that ran red and blue and gray with gore.

"Time to go," I said, mostly to myself. "Icky! Perry! Torina, time to—"

In that instant, I heard two of the sweetest sounds ever—rifles cracking and the shout of angry professional soldiers.

Amazing had arrived.

Along with a dozen GKU troopers charging out of a nearby laneway and slamming into the crowd. They cut their way directly for the influencers, who happily turned and ran, leaving their personal security details to take the beating. I desperately hoped we somehow got that on the record, because their cowardice was so instant and thorough, it was a weapon to be used against them—and their side—in every future dealing we had with their ilk.

The fighting immediately subsided. In that unique way of brawls, it went from *orgy of violence* to *sudden calm* within a few seconds. And a moment after that, teams of local security personnel began showing up, armored in riot gear and ready to quell the trouble.

My priority was my own people. Once I saw Torina was okay—winded and sporting some bruises but otherwise intact—I tasked her with taking care of liaising with the local law enforcement while I went around and checked everyone else. Dugrop'che had taken a bad hit to the face, leaving him with a broken cheekbone and one eye swollen shut. Lunzy was limping but gave me a tired smile.

"You really know how to show a girl a good time, Van."

Zeno had what was probably a broken wrist, Funboy was somehow completely unscathed, and Icky—

"Holy *shit*, Icky. Is any of that blood yours? Can you even tell?"

She stood, chest heaving, a fierce grin on her face. Her blue fur was matted with gore, and different colors of it, leaving her covered with splotches ranging from maroon to turquoise from her towering head to her massive feet.

"Don't know, don't care," she gasped, her grin widening. "Just know that that was *fun*."

I glanced at the two dozen or so bodies piled around her feet. "Bet they don't think so."

"Tough titties for them."

"Attagirl."

She responded by blowing her nose in a gesture so vile, I turned away to look at the corpses instead.

"Charm school. *Immediately*," Zeno murmured from a few feet away.

"Done," I swore, then my face broke into a smile.

We'd been lucky. We'd taken no serious casualties, but we had dropped twenty-one bad guys, including fourteen Sorcerers. It turned out that their cuffs, which made them nearly invulnerable to ranged weapons, didn't work nearly as well against legendary swords or sledgehammers swung by insane blue towers of joyous destruction. Lesson learned for them, I guess.

We spent the next several hours sorting the whole mess out with the local authorities, who took a dim view toward street brawls breaking out in their Farmer's Market. My one big disappointment was that we hadn't gotten it all recorded, especially the cowardly flight of the influencers who'd abandoned their security people without even warning them they were fleeing. But it turned out we had superb video—and a lot more.

In fact, we had a detailed record of virtually *all* of it, thanks to our unsung hero, Netty.

When she transmitted the imagery to my data slate, I could only marvel at the clarity and methodical coverage, which had captured virtually everything. It was as though she'd recorded it all in a studio.

"Netty, how the hell did you get all this?" I asked her, wonderstruck.

The feed switched, showing me standing and looking at a data slate. It was live. I turned and looked in the direction it was coming from, meaning I looked straight into my own face on the slate.

"Wave hello to Waldo, Van," Netty said.

Sure enough, Waldo squatted on top of a kiosk from where he'd been watching and recording everything that happened.

"Netty, you're brilliant. I'd kiss you, if—you know, it didn't mean kissing the *Fafnir*."

"You could kiss Waldo."

I laughed. "Not really the same, though, is it?"

"Van?"

I turned. It was Amazing.

I nodded to her. "Thanks for showing up. Although was it really necessary to do it in the nick of time?"

She shrugged. "We did our best to get here as soon as we could. You're just lucky we were able to ground our ship as close as we did."

"Yeah, parking at one of these farmer's markets can be a bitch."

"Anyway, you're welcome. But now that you've helped Doctor Creel establish her ownership of this new wonder wheat, I'm hoping I can prevail upon you to do one more thing before you take some well-deserved time off."

"What's that?"

"I tried to return the *Hawksbill* to your mother, but she wants you to do it. She's adamant, in fact, that you must be the one to physically hand the ship over to her. I'm not entirely sure why, but it's extremely important to her."

I put my hands on my hips and glanced around at the carnage and confusion that was the aftermath of the brawl. I was tired, my crew was tired, and most of them had injuries of some description—

I sighed. "Can we do this at Sol? I wanted to head back there anyway. We could meet her at Pony Hollow—the asteroid, not the place on Earth. I wanted to link up with our other ship, the *Iowa*, which we've got parked there, and see how it's coming along. And then, yeah, we'll be taking a few days off."

"I'll have her there, say, two days from now?"

I nodded. "Two days. We'll be there."

Torina ambled over after Amazing left to round up her people. "What was that all about?"

"Another visit with my mom."

"That's good. I haven't really had a chance to meet her."

I smiled. "Look at me, taking you to meet the parents. Things are getting serious, aren't they?"

35

As I toured the *Iowa*, my jaw went increasingly slack. My guide was Cantullin, the eldest of the young Conoku bustling about the ship, putting the finishing touches on her refurbishment. Cantullin had effectively proclaimed herself Acting Captain of the *Iowa*, birth order being of paramount importance to the Conoku for establishing authority. What complicated it, though, was the fact that several other Conoku families also had members on board, and their eldest members bitched incessantly to me about Cantullin's self-assumed captaincy.

It was as though the *Iowa* was now crewed entirely by roughly eleven year olds from a half-dozen different families, none of them shy about letting their feelings be known.

About everything.

"Van, she stepped on my claw! Did you see that?"

"Van, I did all this work. She just got in the way!"

"Van, look at the stuff I did next. This is all boring!"

"Van—"

I gritted my teeth and kept a smile fixed on my face. Torina grinned.

"So, how many kids do you want to have?"

"Right this instant? Rhymes with zero."

Her grin widened. "Oh, it'll be different when they're yours—"

"Van, she keeps looking at me, and she knows it bugs me!"

I waved off this latest protest. "Yes, it will, because I won't be able to just tell them to go away."

"If you were Surtsi, you could. We tell our young to go away all the time," Funboy said.

"Hey, see this? This is *not* my surprised face, Funboy," I replied.

He shrugged. "It is better for them to learn the cold truth early —that you are born whether you like it or not, you are forced to live an existence that revolves wholly around the things required to keep you alive, and then you die."

Perry made a rimshot sound, then shook his head. "I thought that could make anything funny. I was wrong."

I turned back to Cantullin. The most remarkable part of all of this was that, despite their constant bitching and bickering and sniping at one another, the Conoku had not only completely repaired the *Iowa*, but they'd also upgraded her in some respects, and managed to get all of her weapons online and working, including the powerful plasma-burst cannons whose operation had eluded us for so long. In fact, their constant kids-at-recess squabbling seemed to just be an overlay, with a sharp, supremely organized efficiency going on beneath it. It would be like a Navy SEAL Team constantly screaming at one another like a bunch of ten year olds during an op but still conducting said op with the same precise and ruthless professionalism.

"You guys have done excellent work—"

"Not because of her!" a Conoku shouted, clacking his claws in excitement.

"Yeah, all she did was stand there clicking her mandibles and bossing us around!"

I coughed discreetly, then spoke. "I'm talking to *all* of you, not just Cantullin."

"So can we take her for a test flight? We didn't want to do that until you got back—" Cantullin said, but another chorus of shouting cut her off.

"She said she was going to, even if you didn't!"

"*Vaa*-aan, you *still* haven't seen all the work *I* did—"

I held up both hands this time, but before I could say anything, Netty cut in.

"Van, Amazing's ship just twisted in. It's about fifteen minutes out. Also, Dugrop'che and Lucky are moving clear of the *Iowa* before they depart for Anvil Dark."

"Thanks, Netty." Dugrop'che and Lucky had swung by Sol with us because it was on the way to Anvil Dark, and because they were both interested in checking out the *Iowa*. The last time they'd seen her, she'd come charging into the battle against the Seven Stars League fleet at a crucial moment, turning the tide in our favor, so they had a soft spot for her. Even better, both were willing to contribute some funds to help pay for her upgrades.

"It's the least we can do. The old girl saved our collective asses," Lucky said.

Dugrop'che had an ulterior motive, though. He wanted to visit Earth.

"I've heard so much about the place. I'd like to check out the planet that produces the Tudor family," he said.

I smiled. "Like most things, I'm sure it'll be both more and less than you expect it to be. Maybe on the next trip, though. When I get to Earth, I want to kick my feet up and just spend a few days… spending a few days. That's it. So while I'd love to play tour guide to an only-too-obvious alien—"

Dugrop'che held up a tentacled hand. "No problemo, Van. I'll set something up ahead of time with you."

I didn't mention the real reason I didn't want to guide Dugrop'che around Earth. In a few minutes, my mother was going to step aboard the *Iowa*, and I had no idea how that was going to go or in what sort of place it was going to leave me. Steeling myself, I started toward the airlock—

"Uh-oh."

I slammed to a halt again at Netty's terse exclamation. "Uh-oh? Netty, you're the AI overseeing all the functions of this ship, some of which are really, really explodey. *Uh-oh* won't cut it, I'm afraid."

"Uh-oh, as in it would appear that Amazing was followed somehow. Four more ships have just twisted in—a class 15 and three class 13s. The 13s are almost definitely Sorcerers. The 15, though, probably belongs to BeneStar themselves."

"BeneStar? How do you know?"

"Well, the BeneStar corporate logo emblazoned on the hull would be a good hint."

I turned and headed for the *Fafnir*'s airlock. Along the way, I chattered into the comm, summoning the rest of the crew to join me and asking Lucky and Dugrop'che for help. In the midst of it all, Cantullin cut in.

"Van! Van! What about us? What do you want us to do?"

I hesitated, slowing my steps. The *Iowa* was a battleship, almost fully gunned up, a powerful military asset that was more than a match for any one of the incoming ships, and probably the equal of any two.

But she was crewed by a pack of surly, cantankerous teenagers with no business being anywhere near a battle.

"Stand by for my orders, Cantullin," I said, resuming my hurried way to the *Fafnir*.

"Roger-dodger, standing by, over and out!"

WE UNDOCKED THE *FAFNIR* AND, with Lucky and Dugrop'che having cut short their departure to help us, accelerated toward Amazing's—or rather, as it turned out, Valint's—ship. Because what the hell, let's just have a big ol' family reunion out here in the remote reaches of the Solar System. I'd seen the *Stormshadow* before and knew it to be a capable, deadly ship, but even with her firepower added to ours, we were still outmatched by the BeneStar flotilla, which was apparently determined to... exact revenge on me? Or my mother and the GKU, since they were following them? Something else?

"Yeah, their motives here really aren't that clear," Perry agreed when I mused aloud about it.

Zeno sniffed. "Oh, I think their motives are plenty clear. They've had it with the Tudor family and friends screwing around in their business and plan to take us out of future equations. This is a financial decision of the purest order."

Torina nodded as she warmed up the weapons. "We effectively cost them the Permada monopoly. They're not going to want to risk any repeats of that."

"And they probably tagged and followed your grandmother's ship, reasoning that she'd likely be coming here, giving them all their targets in one place—you, your mother, and Valint. It really is very efficient of them," Funboy said.

Icky shot him a scowl. "You say that like you admire them."

"No, it's merely the inevitable lot of people to be thrust into the worst possible situation. BeneStar just helped cause it to happen —efficiently."

I only nodded idly at the conversation. Regardless of the why, the fact was that we were about ten minutes from yet *another* battle where we were outgunned and outmatched. The difference this time was that we had the answer parked just a few thousand klicks behind us—the *Iowa*.

I got on the comm to the battleship. "Cantullin, it's Van. Look, I want you guys to give us long-range fire support, okay? The *Iowa's* missile batteries are more—"

"How come *she's* in charge?"

"Wow, Van, do you love her or something? I think Van *loves* Cantullin—"

"Alright, everyone who isn't Cantullin get off this channel now. For the time being, she's in charge, yes," I snapped.

Perry sniffed. "Kids."

Cantullin came back on. "I'm here, Van! Long-range fire

support, got it! We're on it! You can count on us! Roger-dodger, over and out!"

"Gotta admire her enthusiasm," Zeno said, chuckling.

"I can live with enthusiasm," I replied. "What I can't live with is getting any of Linulla's kids hurt—or worse."

"Missiles inbound," Netty announced.

I grunted acknowledgement, confirmed it on the tactical overlay, then glanced around the cockpit. We'd depressurized the *Fafnir*, and everyone was suited up and glued to their workstations, except for Funboy whose action station was aft. That only too familiar tension that combined tedium, impatience, and apprehension in a most unpleasant way had fallen over the cockpit. For the next several minutes, all we could do was watch their missiles creep inexorably closer, ours do the opposite, and both sides just wait until we reached maximum effective weapons range. Then all hell would break loose.

"Lucky, Dugrop'che, are you guys ready?" I asked.

They both acknowledged. They were going to focus their fire-power on one of the class 13s to try and take it out of the battle immediately. Once they'd done that, they'd pick another 13 and do it again—or so the plan went.

I turned my attention to Valint's ship, the *Stormshadow*. She was well ahead, about halfway between the BeneStar ships and us. She'd already flipped and started a braking burn, which was timed to have her stop, reverse course, and then match our velocity as we swept past her. That way, we'd all be going into battle together. However, it also left her exposed to the full fury of the oncoming missiles, being the closest target.

"You know, something's been bugging me," Perry said.

"What's that?"

"Well, BeneStar and the Sorcerers *know* the *Iowa* is here. And they also have to know that she tips the balance way in our favor, but they're attacking anyway. Why?"

"Overconfidence?" Torina suggested.

"I don't think so. I think they've got bad intel. The last time we fought the Sorcerers out here, they kicked the shit out of the *Iowa*. They probably think there's no way we could have gotten her repaired, much less properly crewed, in the time since."

"Where are you going with this, Perry?" I asked.

"Well, it gives us a huge potential advantage. If we pull them and get them decisively engaged, and then bring in the *Iowa*——"

"Perry, I am not bringing a ship full of children into battle."

"You take Icky into battle all the time."

"Hey!" Icky snapped, but I headed off any further confrontation.

"We've got a bunch of Linulla's kids, most of Gekola's, and a few each from another three or four Conoku. They are *not* trained warriors and have *no* experience in battle. We'd be asking to have them take a bunch of casualties, and I don't want that on my conscience, thank you very much," I said.

"Missiles in one minute," Netty put in.

I turned my focus ahead. Hopefully, using the *Iowa* as a stationary missile silo would be enough. She could spew out a fearsome amount of ordnance—if she were carrying a fearsome amount of ordnance, that is. Unfortunately, she only carried about twenty missiles in total. We hadn't had the time or the ready funds to acquire more.

"Netty, how long until the *Iowa* needs to open fire?" I asked.

"Thirty seconds."

"So Cantullin is clear on what to do?"

"Fire the missiles at the bad guys."

"That sums it up nicely, thanks."

I watched the time tick down. As soon as they were in range of the *Stormshadow*, she opened up with a fierce barrage of laser fire, followed by her point-defenses as the missiles closed in. She managed to take out all but five of the incoming weapons, and one must have been damaged and failed to detonate, but the other four managed to bracket her with their searing blasts. When they faded, Valint's ship hung in space, her drive suddenly dead, her power emissions rapidly dropping.

I cursed. The battle had barely begun, and we were already in trouble.

I IDLY NOTED the *Iowa* firing but kept my attention on the *Stormshadow*. Even if we over-redlined our own drive, we couldn't arrive in time to prevent the BeneStar ships from being able to pummel her for a good three or four minutes. By then, it would probably be far too late.

"Netty, can we twist to get closer?" I asked.

"Not recommended. There's a lot of rocky debris out here, and given the uncertainty in twist-geometry, there's a significant risk that—"

"Netty? What's wrong?"

"You know that phrase, speak of the devil?"

I tensed. "Uh—yeah. What about it?"

"Well, here I was talking about how twisting isn't a good idea, and—well, the *Iowa* just twisted."

"*What?*"

"Where the hell are they going—?" Zeno started but cut herself off as a colossal shape suddenly materialized almost alongside us. It was the *Iowa*, close enough that we could have docked with her without much thruster action.

Netty went on. "If I had to guess, I'd say they're going right there."

"SHIT—NETTY, take control of the *Iowa* and get it the hell out of here!" I snapped.

"I'd happily comply, but I've been locked out."

"You—what?"

"I've been locked out of the *Iowa*'s controls—helm, nav, drive, all of it."

I let loose a string of profanity and pounded at the comm controls. "Cantullin, what the hell are you doing? What part of long-range fire support didn't you understand?"

"We did do long-range fire support! Now we're helping you!"

I took a deep breath. "Cantullin, listen to me—"

The *Iowa*'s drive lit, and she began to pull away. At the same time, her thrusters began to fire, rolling her and yawing her at the same time. The result was a tumble that sent her corkscrewing through space as the exhaust plume of her massive fusion drive swung around with her gyrations.

"What the hell are they doing?" I hit the comm again. "Cantullin, get the hell out of here—!"

"Van, you said shoot at the bad guys. That's what we're doing!"

"It was my idea!" another voice cut in.

"It was not! You wanted to—"

"Cantullin!" I shouted, but I knew it was no use. The *Iowa* was twisting and tumbling her chaotic way into battle, and there was nothing I could do about it.

Part of the plan, at least, went—well, according to itself. Lucky and Dugrop'che engaged one of the Sorcerers' class 13s and quickly pummeled it into quiescence. Unfortunately, the other two Sorcerer ships came to their stricken colleague's aid, and our two Peacemakers found themselves in a desperate fight against two superior opponents. They kept their fire focused on one of them, but it meant the other was able to start landing punishing hits.

I had to pull my attention back to the closer battle, though. The BeneStar class 15 had closed on the *Stormshadow* and started bombarding her with fire. I could only watch in helpless horror as laser and mass-driver fire slammed into her—and a prodigious amount of it, too, since the BeneStar ship seemed to be awfully well-armed for a ship bearing a corporate logo like an advertising billboard. I got Valint on the comm but could barely see or hear her through the smoke and confusion.

"Trying to get damage—" The image shuddered. "Damage control, get the drive back, at least, but we're—"

The signal cut out.

I pounded the armrest. We were still a full minute away from helping her.

BeneStar might just get their wish. If the *Stormshadow* died, then a good portion of my family died with her. Even worse, they might manage to kill off most or all of some Conoku families as well, not that they'd give a shit—

"Van, the *Iowa* just twisted again," Netty said.

"What the hell are they *doing?*"

She reappeared again on the overlay—squarely between the *Stormshadow* and the BeneStar ship.

I gaped in horror, then shook my head. "Netty, risk or not, we need to get in there! Calculate a twist—"

"Van, wait," Perry said.

I turned to him. "What?"

He gestured with his beak at the overlay. "Check it out."

The wildly gyrating *Iowa* flailed around, blocking the BeneStar ship's line of fire to the *Stormshadow*. Her wild, unpredictable maneuvers were making it hard for the BeneStar ship to get decent firing solutions, so although they landed hits, they were few—and absorbed by the *Iowa*'s armor.

The BeneStar ship wasn't so lucky. As the *Iowa* slewed around and each weapon came to bear, it opened up with deadly, punishing accuracy. The class 15 staggered under the successive impacts, the plasma-burst cannons being particularly destructive.

"Van, those maneuvers aren't random—the Conoku have designed them to build up momentum along particular axes, then using the thrusters and bursts from the main drive to make the *Iowa* go exactly where they want it to," Netty said.

"And they took Netty offline over there, so they're doing it all—what, *manually?*" Zeno asked, her tone one of wonder.

But the Conoku weren't done. With another blast from the drive, and precisely timed bursts from the thrusters, they did something—something that conventional wisdom said wasn't even possible. They banked the *Iowa* around the BeneStar ship.

They *banked* her.

Like an airplane, maneuvering in an atmosphere, the *Iowa* sailed in a graceful arc, literally running rings around the BeneStar ship. Somehow, that gaggle of bickering, unruly kids were handling the *Iowa* like she was a class 4 workboat.

I shook my head. "How?"

"All they've ever flown are those little ships of theirs, the *Rumors*, that they fly as part of their coming-of-age ritual. They probably don't know that you're not supposed to be able to handle a battleship like that," Perry said.

"So they put their minds to it and just figured out how," Zeno added.

Torina turned to me. "It's too bad they're not trained warriors with experience in battle, huh?"

I shook my head. "Actually, it's probably a good thing they aren't. Otherwise, they might not have realized that what they're doing is... impossible. And that means they might never have even tried."

THE BENESTAR SHIP didn't stand a chance. The *Iowa* whipped completely around her three times, pouring fire into her the whole time. Ironically, the biggest threat the big ship faced was from her own missiles, fired several minutes ago as part of our *long-range fire support*, and only just now catching up to her.

She managed to dodge them and actually had to shoot down two. Three more detonated all around the BeneStar ship, leaving it a drifting wreck.

We moved in. It struck me that, aside from missiles, the *Fafnir* hadn't fired a shot, nor had we taken as much as a scratch. As we closed on the stricken BeneStar ship, though, a trio of missiles shot past us and slammed into it, ripping it almost in half lengthwise. They'd come from the *Stormshadow*.

"Take *that*, you son of a bitch," Valint said over the comm, her voice ice.

We watched in awed horror as atmosphere erupted from the split, carrying a multitude of bodies tumbling into space. A moment later, she exploded, vaporizing herself and her drifting crew.

I blinked, then looked to see how Lucky and Dugrop'che were doing. They'd taken a lot of damage but had taken out another class 13 in turn. The third Sorcerer ship had fled. I was more stunned to see that they'd been joined by another ship, though. It was Gerhardt. He must have twisted in while my situational awareness was fixed on the insane brilliance of the *Iowa* and her crazy Conoku crew. I was in time to see him shred a small lifeboat disgorged from one of the remaining class 13s. I could only stare—something I'd done a lot of this battle—until he explained why. It was the Sorcerer captain, making a desperate and cowardly attempt to escape, even trying to bargain for his life as he did.

"Mercy takes many forms out here in the dark, and removing bad officers is one such form of it," he intoned over the comm. "Oh, by the way—hello, Tudor. Looks like I arrived in the middle of a clash. Or, rather, the end of one. Apologies for not getting here sooner."

"It's… no problem. And yeah, a clash. One of the strangest I've ever been in, in fact."

"Oh? How so?"

I sat back and smiled.

"Where do I begin?"

EPILOGUE

THE *IOWA* WAS A MADHOUSE, the Conoku tumbling over themselves to tell their part of the story, interrupting one another, each claiming the others were lying or exaggerating and that their version of the truth was the only correct one—

I had them reinstate Netty, and I ordered them to never take her offline again—

Then I whistled for quiet. The racket died to mutters and mumbles.

"You *all* did very well. *All* of you," I said.

"Yeah, but I did better!"

"You did not—!"

I gave up and walked away. Torina grinned.

"Looks like the *Iowa* has a crew," she said.

I rolled my eyes. "I can't help thinking that Linulla had this planned the whole time."

"Well, if he did, he was one smart Conoku."

I glanced back at the raucous gang of rambunctious crab kids and smiled.

"Never said he wasn't."

"ADAYLUH CREEL HAS REJOINED her father aboard their farm ship, the *Inari*," Gerhardt said over the comm. "I wanted to tell you that, and that every sovereign state in the known space has recognized her Right of Assertion over Permada. In fact, there's a joint bioscience task force being put together to work with her, to figure out the best way to grow and distribute her discovery."

"BeneStar—and Gauss—can't be happy about that," I replied.

"Oh, I certainly hope not."

That left only one piece of unfinished business, and it was one I conducted aboard the *Fafnir*, alone, the rest of the crew remaining on the *Iowa*.

"Hello, Mother," I said when the airlock opened.

She entered the *Fafnir* and looked around. "Nice place you have here."

"Eh, it's home."

"Is it?"

I shrugged. "One of several, I guess."

We moved to the galley, but she didn't sit down. "I took possession of the *Hawksbill*. Thank you," she said, then hesitated. "There was something missing, though—"

I nodded and extracted the photo from the pocket of my b-suit. "Yeah. This."

I handed it to her.

She took it, almost reverently. "I don't suppose you remember—"

"Actually, I do," I said.

We stood in silence for a long moment. Neither of us knew what to say. There was a chasm between us the size of known space, and it was going to take more than an old photograph to start crossing it.

We both suddenly looked up and tried to speak at once. I smiled and shook my head.

"Go ahead."

She opened her mouth, then closed it again and lowered her eyes. Her shoulders began to shake.

I did the only decent thing. I stepped forward and took her in my arms. She was a stranger. And my mother.

I was surprised, partly because I'd expected her to be as hard as an armor plate. But she wasn't. She felt… brittle. But more surprising was how holding her felt so *right*, as though I'd done it a hundred, a thousand times.

On impulse, I kissed the top of her head. I had to swallow two or three times before I could speak.

"It's okay, Mom. This is going to… to be tough. And it's going to take time. But, someday—"

Words failed me at that point, so I just left it there.

She said something, but her face was buried in my shoulder, and I couldn't make it out. It sounded like *someday*, and she might have nodded as well.

For now, that would be good enough.

Amazon won't always tell you about the next release. To stay updated on this series, be sure to sign up for our spam-free email list at jnchaney.com.

Van will return in SEVERED TIES available on Amazon.

GLOSSARY

Anvil Dark: The beating heart of the Peacemaker organization, Anvil Dark is a large orbital platform located in the Gamma Crucis system, some ninety lightyears from Earth. Anvil Dark, some nine hundred seventy years old, remains in a Lagrange point around Mesaribe, remaining in permanent darkness. Anvil Dark has legal, military, medical, and supply resources for Peacemakers, their assistants, and guests.

Cloaks: Local organized criminal element, the Cloaks hold sway in only one place: Spindrift. A loose guild of thugs, extortionists, and muscle, the Cloaks fill a need for some legal control on Spindrift, though they do so only because Peacemakers and other authorities see them as a necessary evil. When confronted away from Spindrift, Cloaks are given no rights, quarter, or considerations for their position. (See: Spindrift)

Dragonet: A Base Four Combat ship, the Dragonet is a modified platform intended for the prosecution of Peacemaker policy. This includes but is not limited to ship-to-ship combat, surveillance, and planetary operations as well. The Dragonet is fast, lightly armored, and carries both point defense and ranged weapons, and features a frame that can be upgraded to the status of a small corvette (Class Nine).

Moonsword: Although the weapon is in the shape of a medium sword, the material is anything but simple metal. The Moonsword is a generational armament, capable of upgrades that augment its ability to interrupt communications, scan for data, and act as a blunt-force weapon that can split all but the toughest of ship's hulls. See: Starsmith

Peacemaker: Also known as a Galactic Knight, Peacemakers are an elite force of law enforcement who have existed for more than three centuries. Both hereditary and open to recruitment, the guild is a meritocracy, but subject to political machinations and corruption, albeit not on the scale of other galactic military forces. Peacemakers have a legal code, proscribed methods, a reward and bounty scale, and a well-earned reputation as fierce, competent fighters. Any race may be a Peacemaker, but the candidates must pass rigorous testing and training.

Perry: An artificial intelligence, bound to Van (after service to his grandfather), Perry is a fully-sapient combat operative in the shape of a large, black avian. With the ability to hack computer systems and engage in physical combat, Perry is also a living repository of galactic knowledge in topics from law to battle strategies. He is also a wiseass.

Salt Thieves: Originally actual thieves who stole salt, this is a three-hundred-year-old guild of assassins known for their ruthless behavior, piracy, and tendency to kill. Members are identified by a complex, distinct system of braids in their hair. These braids are often cut and taken as prizes, especially by Peacemakers.

Spindrift: At nine hundred thirty years old, Spindrift is one of the most venerable space stations in the galactic arm. It is also the least reputable, having served as a place of criminal enterprise for nearly all of its existence due to a troublesome location. Orbiting Sirius, Spindrift was nearly depopulated by stellar radiation in the third year as a spaceborne habitat. When order collapsed, criminals moved in, cycling in and out every twelve point four years as coronal ejections rom Sirius made the station uninhabitable. Spindrift is known for medical treatments and technology that are quasi-legal at best, as well as weapons, stolen goods, and a strange array of archaeological items, all illegally looted. Spindrift has a population of thirty thousand beings at any time.

Starsmith: A place, a guild, and a single being, the Starsmith is primarily a weapons expert of unsurpassed skill. The current Starsmith is a Conoku (named Linulla), a crablike race known for their dexterity, skill in metallurgy and combat enhancements, and sense of humor.

CONNECT WITH J.N. CHANEY

Don't miss out on these exclusive perks:

- Instant access to free short stories from series like *The Messenger*, *Starcaster*, and more.
- Receive email updates for new releases and other news.
- Get notified when we run special deals on books and audiobooks.

So, what are you waiting for? Enter your email address at the link below to stay in the loop.

https://www.jnchaney.com/backyard-starship-subscribe

CONNECT WITH TERRY MAGGERT

Check out his website
http://terrymaggert.com/

Connect on Facebook
https://www.facebook.com/terrymaggertbooks/

Follow him on Amazon
https://www.amazon.com/Terry-Maggert/e/B00EKN8RHG/

ABOUT THE AUTHORS

J. N. Chaney is a USA Today Bestselling author and has a Master's of Fine Arts in Creative Writing. He fancies himself quite the Super Mario Bros. fan. When he isn't writing or gaming, you can find him online at **www.jnchaney.com**.

He migrates often, but was last seen in Las Vegas, NV. Any sightings should be reported, as they are rare.

Terry Maggert is left-handed, likes dragons, coffee, waffles, running, and giraffes; order unimportant. He's also half of author Daniel Pierce, and half of the humor team at Cledus du Drizzle.

With thirty-one titles, he has something to thrill, entertain, or make you cringe in horror. Guaranteed.

Note: He doesn't sleep. But you sort of guessed that already.

Made in United States
North Haven, CT
23 August 2022

23183743R00280